131078

A Garland Series
Foundations of the Novel

Representative Early

Eighteenth-Century Fiction

A collection of 100 rare titles
reprinted in photo-facsimile in 71 volumes

Foundations of the Novel

compiled and edited by
Michael F. Shugrue
Secretary for English for the M.L.A.

with New Introductions for each volume by

Michael Shugrue, *City College of C.U.N.Y.*
Malcolm J. Bosse, *City College of C.U.N.Y.*
William Graves, *N.Y. Institute of Technology*
Josephine Grieder, *Rutgers University, Newark*

Memoirs Concerning the Life and Manners of Captain Mackheath

Anonymous

A Trip to the Moon

Anonymous

The Adventures of Abdalla

by

Jean-Paul Bignon

with a new introduction
for the Garland Edition by
Josephine Grieder
UNIVERSITY LIBRARY
GOVERNORS STATE UNIVERSITY
PARK FOREST SOUTH, ILL
Garland Publishing, Inc., New York & London

1973

The new introduction for the

Garland *Foundations of the Novel* Edition

is Copyright © 1973, by

Garland Publishing, Inc., New York & London

All Rights Reserved

Library of Congress Cataloging in Publication Data
Main entry under title:

Memoirs concerning the life and manners of Captain
  Mackheath (anonymous).

  (Foundations of the novel)
  Reprint of 3 works, the 1st originally printed in
1728 for A. Moore, London; the 2d printed in Dublin
and reprinted in 1728 for J. Roberts, London; and the
3d printed in 1729 for T. Worrall, London.
  1. English fiction--18th century. I. McDermot,
Murtagh. A trip to the moon. 1973. II. Bignon,
Jean Paul, 1662-1743. Les avantures d'Abdalla fils
d'Hanif. English. 1973. III. Title: A trip to the
moon. IV. Title: The adventures of Abdalla.
V. Series.
PZ1.M4774 1973 [PR1297]   823'.5   79-170573
ISBN 0-8240-0564-3

Printed in the United States of America

Introduction

The three works contained in the present volume, though very diverse in nature, have one point in common: each is typical of a particular literary genre popular at the time. The Adventures of Abdalla *is a collection of oriental tales.* A Trip to the Moon *is a Swiftian imaginary voyage.* The Memoirs Concerning the Life and Manners of Captain Mackheath, *masquerading as an attempt to set Gay's version straight, is a political satire. A brief word about each will show how it fits into the literary fare of the period.*

The English had already become thoroughly familiar with the oriental tale through translations from the French, like Petis de la Croix' The Persian and the Turkish Tales *(1714),* Gueulette's Tartarian Tales *(1716),* Moncrif's Indian Tales *(1718), and* Armeno's The Travels and Adventures of Three Princes of Sarendip *(1722), to mention only a few.* The Adventures of Abdalla *is another such translation. Its author, Jean-Paul Bignon (1622-1745), was a man of considerable note in France, librarian to the king and member of innumerable academies, including the Académie Française; but he found time to amuse himself by composing (though never completing) the story of Abdalla who, seeking the elixir of youth for his shah, encounters an extravagant variety of adventures and personages. The stories vary*

INTRODUCTION

from brief fables told by eight-year-old Loulou to the longer stories of Rouschen and her lover in Topsy-Turvy island. They are playfully imaginative, and their exotic decors please as the magic delights.

A Trip to the Moon *by "Murtagh McDermot" is avowedly dedicated to the "Worthy, Daring, Adventurous, Thrice-renown'd, and Victorious Captain Lemuel Gulliver," and as such it joins the company of similar Swiftian imitations like the anonymous* Memoirs of the Court of Lilliput *(1727) and* An Account of the State of Learning in the Empire of Lilliput *(1728). The author, showing perhaps an equal familiarity with the fiction of Cyrano de Bergerac, transports his hero to the moon rather than to Lilliput; but he adopts a great number of Swiftian elements, reminiscent in general of the Laputa section — absurd scientific experiments, peculiarly ridiculous inhabitants, scatalogical descriptions.*

Unlike Swift, however, the author has only a narrow satirical talent. As he himself admits at the end of his work, very likely the only people his satire might vex are tea-drinking ladies, beaux, and critics. Nevertheless, he makes some swipes at contemporary notions of virtue in society, and his moonpeople, whose bodies become more bestial as they lose their human feelings (the king, though elected because he was the most virtuous man on the planet, has already grown a lion's paw), are not unamusing satires of human vice.

The British Museum catalog records that the Memoirs Concerning the Life and Manners of Captain

INTRODUCTION

Mackheath is a "political satire," without indicating the basis for that judgment; but it is not improbable that underneath the guise of setting straight John Gay's presentation of his rogue hero, the anonymous author is aiming in fact at Sir Robert Walpole. Various details support this view. Mackheath is stigmatized as being "the Bubble of every Projector, Painter, Toyman, Architect, and Virtuoso in Europe" (p. 21) (Walpole was much criticized for spending extravagantly to redecorate Houghton, his home); his mistress Betty Flareit finds him an innocent lover (Walpole was always faithful to Molly Skerritt); the author concedes Mackheath's extraordinary skill in managing people of diverse views (one of Walpole's chief talents). Mackheath, made cashier of the gang, is accused of having robbed the thieves' strongbox and successfully defends himself to his colleagues. Early in 1728, Walpole, then first lord of the treasury and chancellor of the exchequer, was indeed harassed by charges that he had misappropriated money from the sinking fund and in March eloquently convinced Parliament that the state of the national debt warranted his behavior. The author describes Mackheath's dealings with the clever old Frenchman Trapanté, a receiver of stolen goods; this is perhaps a reference to Walpole's relations with the Cardinal de Fleury, prime minister of France, whose aid he was anxious to secure in order to maintain the balance of power in Europe. No doubt a political historian could identify further similarities between the two men's careers, but the Memoirs takes its place in the literary

INTRODUCTION

history of the time as a minor political scandal chronicle for the initiated.

Josephine Grieder

Memoirs Concerning the Life and Manners of Captain Mackheath

Anonymous

Bibliographical note:
*This facsimile has been made from a copy in the
Beinecke Library of Yale University
(IK G252 T728m)*

MEMOIRS

Concerning the

LIFE and MANNERS

OF

Captain *Mackheath*.

MEMOIRS

Concerning the

Life and Manners

OF

Captain MACKHEATH.

Ὅυτος ἐκεῖνος.

ANON.

LONDON:

Printed for *A. Moore* near *St. Paul's*.
M.DCC.XXVIII.

PROEM.

IT is apparently the Duty of every Man, who takes upon him to deliver down to Posterity, any Part of the History of the Men or Times in which He writes, to take care that his Heart be altogether pure and disengaged from Passion and Prejudice, otherwise he will not have it in his Power, to make use of a noble Author's Motto, *Not to dare to conceal a Truth, or to publish a Falshood:* His Mind therefore ought to be wholly dispassionate and loose of all kinds of Byas and Inequality. I set out with no personal Prejudice against Captain *Mackheath*, he has never taken a Shilling from me or mine upon the Road; but as he has robb'd many whom I know, and goes on still publickly to plunder, I rather *Advertife* than Write againft him; and I hope the Captain, when he thinks cooly on this Head, will not afperfe me as a Libeller, or call this my Publick Spiritednefs, Malevolence. I hope I fhall have Courage enough to bind my felf down to the Rules of Candour and Truth in the following *Memoirs*. I fhall confine my felf not to talk againft the Man, but his Crimes; and therefore I fhall not, according to the Cuftom of Biographers, fet down the minuter Circumftances of this Gentleman's Birth and Education, as I think the Obloquy of his evil Actions, or the Merit of his good ones, fhould rather reft on himfelf than on thofe who brought him into the World, or were concern'd in the Education of him afterwards: and becaufe nothing is fo frequent as for bad Men to degenerate from their Blood and Principles,

ciples. What principally determined me to publish these *Memoirs*, was, an honest Inclination I had to undeceive my Fellow-Citizens, before whom he has been lately set upon the publick Stage as a Character of Heroism, if not of Virtue. The Dramatick Writer has indeed dress'd him out to Advantage, he stands erect the first Piece in the Canvas, and has gained much popular Applause; he has made him the Lover and the Warrior, he is the Darling of the Fair, and the Glory of the thievish Heroes who surround him: He is a perfect, polite, modern fine Gentleman, and *Dorimant* in Sir *Fopling*; tho a Person of equal Morals, is not a more accomplish'd Rake. He commits his Robberies with an Air of Authority and Gallantry, the common People mistake his Vices for Virtues; and those who are not in his Gang, applaud him.

IT is the Purpose of this little Treatise, if my poor Endeavours may
be

be bless'd with Success, to check this popular Applause so injurious to the Publick; nor am I the first who have taken the Alarm: our Reverend Guides and Spiritual Directors *have cry'd aloud and spar'd not*; they likewise have publish'd the Dangers which visibly threaten our Morals, when the People are used to behold a notorious Robber set up thus in a Point of Light, where all the Horrors of his Trade, where the dark Lanthorn, the Pistol, the Dagger, and the Ruin and Spoil of the Poor are concealed; he appears upon the Stage, not only surrounded with Pleasures and Glory, but even with Power, at the Head of a well arm'd and a vicious Crew, and is at last repriev'd by the Poet, even from the imaginary Punishment. When therefore a Person really Infamous, and an Instrument of much Evil to his Country, shall receive so much Encouragement and Applause from the People, and from those who are accounted of the better Sort too; for many

many such are to be found among his Admirers. It is worthy our Labour to look back a little, and to enquire into the Reason of the present Degeneracy of our Morals: Let us see then how, and by what Degrees, a brave, a great, and a generous People became so corrupt, to be capable to look on and laugh at Fraud and Rapine, and to mistake a Highwayman, for a Heroe.

B   CHAP.

CHAP. I.

AFTER the Death of King *William*, of immortal Memory, and that long and expenfive War that fucceeded in the Reign of Queen *Anne*, when we were deliver'd from the Fears of becoming Slaves to *Lewis* XIV; when his Scheme of Univerfal Monarchy was broke by our Arms: The People, who had with moft incredible Labour and Patience, and at a moft prodigious Expence of Blood and Treafure, fuffered all the Fatigues of a long and honourable War in the Defence of their Religion and Liberties; no fooner felt the Warmth of Repofe, and the Indulgence of Peace, but they gave themfelves wholly up to it, and began now to think of nothing fo much as Wealth and Eafe. Firft, there arofe among us a general and uncommon Defire of Money, and after this an extraordinary

nary Appetite for Power; the two great Fundamentals of every Evil. Avarice immediately overthrew all Probity, and Trust, and mutual Confidence; and in consequence, every ingenious and praise-worthy-Art shared the same Fate; and, in their stead, Pride, Ambition, Inhumanity, and venal and mercenary Desires of all Kinds took Place: Friendships and Enmities were now made as Interest only directed. It was thought Praise-worthy to deceive your Neighbour, and he who had more Fraud, was deemed to have more Understanding than his Fellow-Citizen. This insatiable Thirst after Power and Wealth became now contagious, and invaded the City like a Pestilence: every one may remember in what Manner the chief Magistrate and the Senate were drawn in to indulge the Madness of these avaritious Men. I should have pass'd in silence, that *fatal and destructive Scheme* that let Men loose upon one another; and I beg leave only to mention it now, to mark the Origin of this great Folly, and to shew that after this the People never recover'd their Integrity. After this extraordinary Change of Property, Virtue seem'd to become Vice, and Vice, Virtue; and all Men inclined to think, that if they had Wealth, they had a Right to every thing; therefore that, and that alone, became the general Study: and this Poison having thus mixed with the Blood and Spirits of the People, they became weak and enervate: the Desires of Mankind after Wealth being insatiable, were not to be diminish'd either by Want or Abundance. After this follow'd Rapine, Injustice, a general Dissolution of Morals; and in each Man was found a Desire after the Goods of his Neighbour, and the Rich oppress'd the Poor without Modesty or Moderation. Perhaps too, this Remissness in the Manners of the People, might at this time receive Encouragement and Example from their Superiors, whom they beheld rioting in all manner

ner of Wealth and Luxury: and those of the middle Rank finding themselves raised to great imaginary Wealth, copy'd those above them as far as they were able; like their Superiors, they came at once into the Expences of Women, Pictures, Jewels, rich Furniture, and magnificent Villas; costly Wines, and the dearest Excitements to vicious Palates were purchased from every Country: In a word, they fell into every thing that could indulge the most luxurious Inclination.

ABOUT this time, Honour and Wealth became Terms of the same Signification; and accordingly, Glory, Government, Power, were only to be found with the Rich: Virtue hung its Head, Poverty was every where accounted criminal; and the Man, whose Morals and Conduct in this corrupt Multitude were unblameable, was shunned and look'd upon with Malevolence by his Fellow-Citizens. Wealth, as I have said, did not only produce
Luxury,

Luxury, but tainted the Morals of our Youth with Avarice and Pride, Rapine and Waste: At the same time, a Profusion of their own Property, and a Desire after that of others, there was a general Neglect of all manner of Probity, Moderation, Humanity; nor had they the least Regard for Things Human or Divine. Enfeebled thus by Luxury, an unaccountable Supineness seem'd to have taken Possession of the Minds of many of the People; and those whose Spirits were enough awake, busy'd themselves in doing mutual Wrongs; so that at this time, having the Power to do Wrong, and doing Wrong were inseparable, each Man fancy'd himself in Possession of Millions: Accordingly the Foundations of costly Palaces were laid, they raised themselves to the most visionary Heights, and the lowest of the Vulgar were purchasing Titles in Heraldry, and fixing Nobility to their Names. The Appetites of Hunger and Thirst were anticipated, and Luxury prevented every Call

Call of Nature: In this Situation, thofe among our Youth who were unfuccefsful at the publick Gaming-Table, and yet lived in the Profufion of thofe who fucceeded, were reduced to Poverty, and by Poverty incited to attempt every thing to fupply the Neceffities of Luxury. When the Mind is thus tainted, it is not eafily recover'd to Virtue.

CHAP.

CHAP. II.

IN so great and so corrupt a City, as I have described, Captain *Mackheath*, as well as many other Gentlemen, at the same time, dissipated both his Morals and his Fortune. He saw the Spoilers of the People in quiet Possession of their ill-gotten Treasures, and look'd upon them as so many Civil Pirates, who prey'd upon their Fellow-Creatures under the Sanction of a Law. He often declared in his dissolute and immoral way of uttering his Thoughts, that he contemn'd those Laws, and that Society, who could only punish those who broke the Laws, not those who *broke thro'* them; and by virtue of which, the Poor had very little Protection against the Oppressions of the Rich: Laws, said he, that serve only to feed fat their numerous, and never to be satisfy'd fy'd Profeſſors: He ſaw no Reaſon why Property ſhould be ſo unfairly diſtributed, and this unequal Diviſion of the Goods of Nature ſeem'd to him like the over-weening Partiality of a fond Mother who lov'd her worſt Children beſt; that theſe Conſiderations had determin'd him to excommune himſelf, to leap the Pale of the Society, to run wild again, and remit himſelf to the Original State where all Men had a Right to all Things; and this Way of Proceeding, he flatter'd himſelf was Honourable and Juſt: And he declar'd, if he ſhould be taken by any of the Society, from whence he had excluded himſelf, he ſhould only look upon himſelf as conquer'd by an Enemy; he accounted his Robberies only ſo many Acts of Hoſtility, and confeſs'd the Conqueror had a Right to uſe the Conquer'd as he thought fit. But this Project of running wild ſoon vaniſh'd, and made way for what he conceiv'd to be much more commode and natural. He began to imagine,

gine, very unjuftly, as Men who fuffer their Reafon to ftray are foon loft, that not only the whole Community, but any Part of it, had a Right to diffolve it felf and to erect another; and to form fuch Regulations or Laws for the Society as they fhould think proper. Here he thought fit to fix, and having contracted an Intimacy in thefe Times with feveral diffolute and undone Perfons, much in the fame Circumftances with himfelf, he gather'd together a large and formidable Body; or rather their common Wants affociated them as Creatures of the fame Kind. Some were under Contracts they were never able to fatisfy; others, who had thrown away their Patrimonies at the Public, or at private Gaming-Tables; and many who had confumed their Fortunes in Riot, and were unable to ftand the Attack of their lawful Creditors: and befides thefe, there were fome who had already enter'd themfelves in Felonies, and in Wickednefs almoft of every Kind; thefe these were his Familiars, not his Intimates; for we must observe, the Captain chose those only to be nearest to him, and in his Council and Confidence, who were Men of weak Understandings; or if his Confidents had Abilities, they were always Men who could be credited no where else, and whose Morals were not to be depended upon even in a Confederacy of Thieves.

AS I am now to draw the Character of the Captain, and to give my Reader a View of his Person, before I publish his Actions; I beg leave to observe, that this Gentleman has been extremely misrepresented by the Author of the *Beggars Opera*; he has indeed taken, I think, too great a Poetical Licenfe: for since he descended to draw a living Highway-man, a Highway-man of the present Age, for such he is; however the Vulgar, by the Poet's imperfect Draught of him, may mistake him, he ought to have

have confin'd himself a little more strictly to Truth. Very few of the Captain's Irregularities with the Fair Sex have ever come to my Knowledge: or if he has had any criminal Amours, I never heard him charg'd with Perfidy to a Woman; and *Betty Flareit*, with whom the Captain has sometimes deign'd to amuse himself, and while away an idle Hour or two, has often declar'd he was a very innocent Lover. Neither would the Captain's Constitution at all bear any sort of Debauch in Brandy, or strong Spirits. So that here again the Dramatist has wrong'd him, to make way for a drunken Sonnet or two at his going off.

LET us now see what Figure the Captain will make as he really is, without the Flourishes of a Poetical Pen.

THE Captain descended from an antient and virtuous Family in the North

North of *Ireland*, or as others will have it, in the North-West of *England*. In his Youth, he discover'd an uncommon Vigour of Mind and Body; and which, if rightly apply'd, might have been of Service to his Country; but his Understanding, and his Person, as he grew in years, became obtuse, and were rather Clumsy than Athletick: he understood the Art of Wheedling perfectly well; he knew to apply to the general Passion of Mankind, and gain'd much by giving much away. Indeed, after he had made himself Master of this new Band of Pirates, he became by frequent Excursions Master of great Wealth; but even then, his Intemperance in acquiring it, could be equall'd by nothing but his Intemperance in consuming it; and he was the Bubble of every Projector, Painter, Toyman, Architect, and Virtuoso in *Europe*: Nothing fills this Part of his Character, but the *Rapti Largitor* of *Tacitus*. He had a laughable, frank, pleasant Manner among his Acquaintance

Acquaintance and Dependents, an eafy and flowing Utterance, and delighted to colour his bad Defigns and pernicious Projects with plaufible Pretences.

WHEN he was at any time publickly attack'd, or charg'd with Partiality, or Corruption, he took Flame immediately; he became in an Inftant paffionate and difconcerted, violent and jealous; and then, and then only, it manifeftly appear'd, that the two chief Ingredients in the Captain's Compofition were Arrogance and Avarice. I have heard the Captain's Courage difputed, and it has been reported that he has fometimes been bafhful in Action; but this I take to be a malevolent Afperfion only, fince he has pufhed on now for many Years, and committed feveral notorious Depredations with eminent Succefs. If he has had the Art to cover himfelf from the Punifhment of the Civil Magiftrate; if by Craft, or by Corruption, he has at any time got fo far into the Favour

vour of the several Headboroughs, Constables, Beadles, Goalers, and other the little *Satellites* of the Civil Power, to skreen himself and his Followers from the Hand of Justice, I think no Imputation ought to fall upon the Captain's Courage on this Account; we ought rather to consider him as a wise General, who never trusts any thing to Fortune that he can possibly avoid, and always parries with his Wisdom, the ill Effects of his Temerity.

CHAP.

CHAP. III.

IT will not, I think, for several Reasons, be necessary in this Place, to give a particular List of the Names of those Persons who were concern'd with the Captain, in many of his enormities: first, I do not find in my self any manner of Inclination to turn Evidence, as I fancy my self above the Temptation of the Reward offer'd by Law for such Services; and am unwilling, whatever Affection I may have for the Publick, to oblige it at the Expence of my own Character; for in this Age, the Person who attempts to mark those whose Actions are apparently detrimental to the Society; such as Smuglers, Owlers, Sharpers, Bambouzlers, Bites, Runners and Thieves of every Denomination, not only goes into an apparent Hazard of suffering in his

his Perfon, but likewife of perfonal Abufe and Scandal; and I queftion, whether I my felf fhall have any Thanks from fome Men for thefe my officious Memoirs: but the Confcioufnefs of difcharging my Duty outweighs every other Confideration. Befides, thefe daring Offenders, and their Dependents and Relations, are very numerous; and therefore likewife a Man ought to be very cautious how, or in what manner he declares himfelf their Enemy. Thefe People too, who are not only very mifchievous, but very artful, have got a Trick of crying *Thieves* at the fame time with you; and always endeavour by the Confufion and the Buftle they make, to change Perfons and Characters with their Accufers. There is yet another and more forcible Reafon than any of the former, why I do not think it proper to name feveral Perfons actually concern'd with the Captain: I hope fome of them may amend their Lives, and become good Citizens and Subjects

Subjects again. I my self, have heard of others, who are now ready and willing to reform their Errors; and having fully repair'd, by their Alliance with the Captain, their shatter'd Fortunes, would return to the Society, if they might be assur'd of Indemnity for what is past, and Freedom from all Resumption and Restitution; two Circumstances as necessary to preserve their Integrity when they take it up again, as their Engagements with the Captain were to re-establish their Fortunes before. But I know not how it is, now the Captain is at their Head, he maintains himself there with great Authority; he has the whole Body intirely under the Menage.

I HAVE known some, who from Reason and Conviction, have been utterly asham'd of their Conduct; and who have enter'd into a Resolution, whatever became of themselves, to deliver up this great Offender into the Hands of Justice: Yet when the Captain has

has at this time accidentally fallen in their way, I have seen them in half an Hour after return with pleased, and satisfy'd Faces, and determined absolutely to proceed in the same Measures; so Insinuating hath been his Discourse, so weighty his Arguments. This iniquitous Society is indeed now so establish'd, that it is thought among them to be difficult, dishonourable, dangerous, ungrateful, and even unjust to quit him; tho the Captain sometimes in the Wantonness of his Pride, and to shew his Power, commands them to perform Offices very mean and unmanly: yet tho every one blames his Conduct, not one of them dares to dispute his Authority.

HERE we may observe, how necessary it is for every Man who would preserve his Fame, or his Virtue, to avoid all sorts of Commerce with Dishonour, lest he should find himself, even before he is aware, involved

ved and intangled in a Labyrinth of Villany: From which, whatever Detestation he may have of it, he will find it difficult to disengage himself.

THE Captain thus establish'd, and firmly confiding in this League of Interest, went on in his Enterprizes from Day to Day with Bravery and Success: And tho among his Followers, most of them were incouraged to abide by him only in the Hope of a faithful Dividend of the Booty; yet some there were so wretchedly poor in Spirit, who obey'd him out of, I know not what Desire, of a poor Dominion or Command under him; provoked by no other Want, stimulated by no other Necessity, and among whom, none of the Plunder was ever shar'd.

THE Society, in the great Confidence they had in their Captain, unani-

unanimously made him their Cashier, and intrusted the just and equal Distribution of all the Booty to his Care and Fidelity, and received their several Shares from time to time from his hands only. They had indeed taken care for a Resource against Accidents, as they were all Soldiers of Fortune, in this manner: They purchased a strong Iron-Chest, with a Slit on the Top, into which every Man was obliged to drop every Day a certain Proportion of the Booty of that Day, if it amounted to more than the Day's Expence; and this was to be esteemed a sacred Deposit never to be touch'd but on the most important Occasions: Such as to provide for any of the Members in Sickness, to bribe a Jury, to take off an Evidence, and to prevent a Conviction, to pay a Lawyer, or a Goaler's Fees, or to support a Member in Prison, until he should be deliver'd by due Course of Law. The Key of this Chest was never to be produc'd, produc'd, it was never to be open'd, but on some or one of these Occasions. How it happen'd, I am not inform'd; but there was a general Rumour, that the Captain had not observ'd this Law, but had embezzled some Part of this sacred Deposit, which had like to have bred much ill Blood.

THIS Society had, by the Captain's wise Management, neglected nothing that was thought necessary for its Security.

IT had been frequently cemented with Oaths, as well as every other Obligation, which bad as well as good Men think necessary to bind one another; for without Faith, or the Appearance of it, no Society of any Kind can subsist. Among the rest of the Captain's Abilities, and which he valued himself most upon as necessary to keep his People together, was what he called *Eloquence*; he had been flatter'd, flatter'd, and flatter'd himself, that his Talent of this Kind was extraordinary: He talk'd much, and he lov'd to talk; and it was his Custom, when they met together, to declaim strongly, but particularly in his own Praise. About this time he thought fit to summon them; they convened accordingly, and in a private Room in the remote Parts of his House, the Doors being shut, he harangued them in these, or in the like words.

" IF the Courage, the Conduct,
" the Honour, the Fidelity, or the
" Zeal of any one of us to the o-
" ther were not well known, and
" often try'd and approv'd; if they
" were liable to the least Suspicion,
" the glorious Opportunities we have
" of possessing, and enjoying the Wealth
" of those from whose Tyranny and
" Injustice we now defend our selves
" by our Arms, must be immediately
" snatch'd out of our Hands; and
" we

" we fhould be deliver'd up to the
" Chaftifement of him whom our Ene-
" mies have the Affurance to call *The*
" *Civil Magiftrate.*

" Inftead of this, we have the Sa-
" tisfaction to meet one another this
" Day in Peace and in Safety, to
" tafte the mutual Joy and Delight
" which every Man receives who be-
" holds his faithful Ally and Compa-
" nion, united to him by the fame
" Ties of Intereft and Neceffity: for
" to have the fame Inclinations, and
" the fame Averfions, is the great
" Bond of Unity, and the very Foun-
" dation of mutual Benevolence and
" Friendfhip.

" WHEN therefore I behold you
" thus together, my Heart is lifted
" with uncommon Joy, when I con-
" fider the Hardfhips you have un-
" dergone, the Battles you have
" fought, the Blood you have fpilt,
" the Fatigues you have fuffer'd, and
" the

" the continual Perils to which your
" Lives and your Fortunes are now
" and at all times expofed for the
" Good of the Community. I look
" upon you as an illuftrious Band of
" Heroes, who have by your own
" Virtue deliver'd your felves from
" Slavery and Oppreffion, who have
" glorioufly recurr'd to your Right
" in the Laws of Nature, have fha-
" ken off the Yoke which burthen'd
" you, and fought your Liberty in
" Arms and Policy.

" We are in full Poffeffion of al-
" moft every thing we have to wifh,
" an uninterrupted Courfe of Victory
" hath attended our Arms; whatever
" Orders or Injunctions, or Decrees
" we pleafe to make, are heartily
" and unanimoufly obey'd. We collect
" Money from whom, and when,
" and where we pleafe; we are fub-
" ject to no Authority or Laws but
" what we make our felves. In a
" word, we are the Terror of our
" Ene-

" Enemies, and the Support and Comfort
" of our Friends.

" AND I affirm, Gentlemen, since
" I have been intrusted with your
" Cash, no one Shilling, I repeat
" it, not a Shilling has been em-
" bezzled, or squander'd or laid out,
" but in the Service of the Com-
" munity: I declare you could no
" where have found a Cashier so know-
" ing in Accounts, or so faithful and
" thrifty a Manager; and I challenge
" all Mankind to say the contrary;
" I defy the little invidious Scandal
" and dirty Aspersions which have
" been thrown, as if I had broke
" open the Iron-Chest, and squan-
" dred the Money my Friends have
" intrusted me with: but this Scan-
" dal is to be despised, as it takes
" its Source from yours and my Ene-
" mies.

" I DO not at all question, but by
" my Courage and Conduct, I shall
" live

" live to see you a flourishing Soci-
" ety; we have many and rich Friends
" in yon regular Community, they
" come over to our Principles daily;
" and no doubt, they will one Day
" inlist their Names in our Rolls:
" Who knows to what an Height
" you may arise? Our Enemies, they
" who talk so precisely of Right and
" Wrong, argue in a most ridiculous
" manner about unalterable Right and
" Property: Surely the *Macedonian*
" Youth had no more Right to the
" Dominions of *Darius*, than I had
" to the Purse and Periwig of old
" *Civicus*. And we have most unde-
" niably as good a Title to levy Mo-
" ney upon those who travel the
" Road, as *Cæsar* had to levy Mo-
" ney, without the Authority of the
" Senate, upon his Fellow - Subjects:
" but were it otherwise, we are not
" here to dispute about the Legality
" of our Profession; no, let us leave
" that to our Enemies: if we should
" ever unhappily fall into their Power,

" I fear we have little Mercy to ex-
" pect. Let us then unite as one Man,
" and let no Man boggle at coming
" thorowly into whatever the Interest
" or the Necessity of our Affairs shall
" require. What you have often wish'd
" you enjoy, Wealth, Honour, Glory,
" the Reward of happy Victors: But
" as the Thoughts of securing these
" Blessings to you, and yours, must
" more forcibly stimulate you to the
" Care of preserving them than any
" thing I can say; I shall conclude on-
" ly with reminding you, that Wealth
" is to be preferr'd to Poverty, and
" Liberty to Servitude.

THE Assembly now broke up, extremely pleas'd with the Captain's De-
clamation, and much comforted that
they had so good and so Praise-worthy a Cause. One does not know
how to account for it, but there is
something in the Captain's averring and
confident Air, that while he is speaking, does to some People of slow
Parts

Parts look like Sincerity and Truth, two Qualities that he is too much a Politician ever to suffer by. But as there is in the Mind of every Man conscious of great Crimes, an Instability and Fear, that works thro' all the affected Jollity and Ease of the most tranquil Heart, a guilty Flush will now and then dart into his Features, and discover that all is not quiet within. I have observ'd the Captain, when he has caught a Man's Eye upon him, whom he suspected to be his Enemy, turn pale and shake, and immediately all the Muscles in his Face have confess'd every thing he could be accus'd of; so unquiet a Companion is a bad Mind.

CHAP.

CHAP. IV.

THE Captain was now perfectly pleas'd with himself, and satisfy'd in his Abilities, he rais'd his Crest; he plumed himself in the Fulness of his Power and Sun-shine; he would compare himself by Turns to the greatest Generals: Now he was *Hannibal*, now *Scipio*, or *Fabius*. And when he would number himself among those who were fam'd in civil Polity, and the Arts of Government, he was *Ulysses*, *Lycurgus*, *Solon*, *Cicero*, *Richlieu* and *Mazarine:* but above all, the Visions that vapour'd his Brain, his most delighting Dream was, that there was an exact Similitude between him and Cardinal *Richlieu*, for the Name of *Mazarine* he held in Contempt. How so unproportion'd an Idea could seize his Head, I know not; but *Bob Brazen*, an old Servant of the Captain's, tain's, and one who when he pleas'd, would take Liberties, as being in the Depth of his Secrets; when the Captain was one Day vaunting thus, and drawing the Parallel between himself and *Richlieu.* Noble Captain, said he, you are quite out here, you shall give me leave to set you right; and when I have shewn you the Pourtraits of these two Ministers, *Richlieu* and *Mazarine*, perhaps, if you lay your Hand upon your Heart, you may confess you have no Likeness either to the one or the other; or if you have any Resemblance, it must be to *Mazarine.* Take an Ebauche of them then as follows.

JULIUS MAZARINE *was First Minister in* France, *and succeeded* Richlieu; *he went successfully thro' many and great Affairs, but with a little and mean Genius for Government.* Richlieu *had a large and extensive Genius; but as he was not thorowly confided in by the King his Master,*

Master, he found all *Business* more *embarrass'd in the Cabinet*, than if he had been to *direct in the Weakness and Confusion of a Minority*; Mazarine *acted without Controul, and the Councils in which he presided were uniform and firm.* Richlieu's *Prince would neither govern, nor be govern'd, and he was forc'd to serve him in spite of himself, and at the Hazard of his Life:* Mazarine *was industrious and insinuating, and knew how to draw People into his Party by their Interest, and insolently used to say,* No Man ought to be esteemed a good *Frenchman* who did not receive his Wages. Mazarine *got the better of his Enemies by Artifice and Stratagem,* Richlieu, *by open Force.* Richlieu *supported his Master's Character with Courage and Dignity,* Mazarine *govern'd, but not with Dignity; and those who were in his Pension had rather the Air of* well-fed Servants, *than of Gentlemen.* Richlieu, it is true, was haughty,

haughty, was imperious; but in every thing he discover'd an extensive, a great, and an exalted Spirit. Mazarine was fam'd for Finesse and Avarice; he had the Art of corrrupting the Manners of the People, till at last he render'd the French Faith ridiculous to a Proverb; he sunk their Courage, lessen'd their Honour and Credit, threw all into Confusion, and render'd the Royal Favours wholly Venal. There was nothing he really dreaded so much as Merit, and no body durst pretend to any Share in his Interest or Favour, who could not produce well-attested Memorials that they had Minds sufficiently debased to his Purposes, supple and capable of being instrumental in executing the vilest Projects: And as he had but little true Knowledge of Mankind, he always believ'd the worst of them; Honour, Integrity of Heart, and Purity of Manners, he look'd on only as a Poetical Fiction: He had indeed occasion for none, and had
none

none about him but busy artful Creatures, who could deceive, betray, project, and make Money of every thing: By these Means his Name became odious and detestable among the People; and yet this Lowness and Narrowness of his Mind display'd it self in nothing more, than in that hearty Contempt which he always discover'd for all the liberal Arts and Sciences, as if they could not possibly have been of any Use to any Government. Richlieu *lov'd Letters, and Men of Letters; and as he was learned himself, he lov'd to encourage Learning, and took every Occasion to excite an Emulation in the learned World.* Mazarine *had no real Regard for any thing, neither the Church, nor Letters, nor Arts, nor Arms, nor Virtue of any Kind; therefore it is not to be wonder'd, that a general Odium, both of great and little, rose at once against him.* Mazarine *affected the Character of a* cunning Minister, *whereas true Wisdom*

gives

gives Succefs always to open and honeſt Meaſures, not to thoſe conducted by little Artifices of Trick and Fraud. 'Tis a Sign of Weakneſs, and want of Capacity and Knowledge of the direct and broad Road, when a Politician thus gropes out a way thro' blind Lanes and Alleys.

THESE are, noble Captain, ſaid *Bob*, the true Characters, as I have collated them, of theſe two Miniſters; tho I really think it is Preſumption in you to pretend to riſe even to that of *Mazarine*, low as I have given it: you forget you are only a common Robber; you forget your ſelf and us too. Thus far *Bob Brazen* ventur'd to chaſtiſe his Maſter, who ſhook his Sides with a hearty Laugh, took all in good part, and went out to give his Orders with his uſual Frankneſs and Sincerity.

NOW the Night and Buſineſs came on, and the ſeveral Parties diſperſed and divided for the Road; some made Incursions on the Country, others were posted in the Cities of *London* and *Westminster*; they kept a strict and regular Correspondence, and as the Persons attack'd were generally fewer in Number than their Attackers, they commonly carry'd off much Booty. It must be confess'd by all who have had the Honour to be robb'd by them, that they collected in a very Gentleman-like manner; and when they were treated sometimes unseasonably and passionately with rough Language, they smiled only and rifled on, and minded Business: Nor were they ever known to come into any Acts of Inhumanity and Violence. But as frequent Robberies were now committed, and in the very Streets of *London*, some few of the Justices of the Peace issued out their Search-Warrants, the Alarm seemed to be taken, and yet no Discoveries were made, or at least not of any who belong'd to the Captain's Confederacy;

deracy: But among the Magistrates who most busy'd themselves, and labour'd most heartily to break this illegal Knot of Outlaws, who prey'd upon the Commonwealth, was *Probus*; *Probus*, an antient Magistrate of the City, and an Alderman above the Chair, an honest true-hearted Independent Whig; he was often seen to march himself at the Head of his venerable Patrole of Watchmen, a veteran honest Band, to try at least if he could have the Honour and Happiness of attaching any of this audacious Fraternity; but alas his Endeavours were never favour'd with Success: And what was very odd, several of his Brethren whose Assistance he desir'd, in order to make such an Inquiry as the Law commanded after these Plunderers of the Publick, told him that he was really too busy; that as for People of bad Characters, there were such perhaps, and always were, and must be such under the best regulated Police; but that the exrraordinary

Noise

Noise and Clamour he now raised, was only the Effect of Whim, ill Humour, Spleen, or an officious Vanity of appearing more diligent or more honest than his Neighbours; that he might remember the various and unaccountable Stories of the *Wild Irish*; and but a few Years were pass'd since the *Mohocks* put every thing into Confusion, when the whole Town was alarm'd, and in bodily Fear about the wild Frolicks of two or three drunken Rakes: they advised him to go home and to sleep quietly in his Bed, without disturbing his own or his Neighbour's Repose concerning the Welfare of the Publick: They assur'd him, that the Constables and Watchmen knew their Duty very well, and they were satisfy'd nothing could happen amiss; and that if he went on thus continually to cry *Thieves*, they should look upon him as a *Malecontent*, not at all satisfy'd with the Government of the City, as a Disturber of the publick Tranquillity: And in a word, that

that they would take care he should be left out of the next Commission of the Peace.

THIS odd Treatment of the old Gentleman alarm'd him extremely; but at the same time it warm'd him, and he reply'd, " That frequent Com-
" plaints of Robberies committed had
" been made to him upon Oath; that
" he believ'd the City was never more
" infested with these sort of Pirates than
" now; that there was most certainly a
" Confederacy of Men who lived upon
" Plunder, and that one *Mackheath* was
" generally reputed to be their Captain;
" that he thought it a Matter of great
" Concern to the City, and therefore he
" had exerted himself in his Province as
" he was authorised to do by Law; nor
" did he conceive that he was imperti-
" nently busy: And if the Alarms of
" the *Wild Irish* and the *Mohocks* were
" without any Foundation, he thought
" they ought not to be Precedents for
" Supineness or Negligence, and serve
" only

" only to lull them afleep when the
" Danger was real, left they fhould a-
" wake when it was too late ; that he
" was alarm'd not only for the publick
" Safety, but his own ; that he had
" much to lofe ; and altho he was very
" well content to part with the *laſt Shil-*
" *ling* in the Defenſe of the Laws of
" his Country, and for the Benefit of
" the Society, yet he could never con-
" ſent that any Man fhould fet up a
" Right to take a fingle Shilling out of
" his Pocket forcibly ; and which pub-
" lick Robbers might pretend a Prefcrip-
" tion to do, if they were permitted
" to go on thus with Impunity ; they
" will foon, faid he, miftake this In-
" dolence of yours for Indulgence, and
" plead Cuftom to their Crimes. That
" as to the invidious Name of *Male-*
" *content*, with which they were plea-
" fed to honour him, he defpifed the
" Character, as he was very confcious
" he never found fault but when he had
" reafon fo to do : and as to leaving
" him out of the Commiffion of the
" Peace,

"Peace, perhaps, Gentlemen, said he,
"that may not be in your Power; but
"if it is, I shall still have a Right to
"talk, and to complain too, when I
"find my self agriev'd, both as a Ci-
"tizen and an *Englishman*."

HOWEVER it was, this cooled the Hunt a little, and the Captain still pursued his old Measures: As we shall shew in the following Chapter.

CHAP. V.

HITHERTO we have shewn the Captain in the Fulness of his Joy, in the Shine of his happier Hours; when he appear'd jocund and gay at the Head of a strong and a well-arm'd Party; when his Foes look'd little in his Eyes, and his Companions exulted with him in his Prosperity. It is most certain, never any Man swallow'd popular Applause more greedily than the Captain: Yet tho he had generally a sort of hoity-toity Joy about him, that seem'd to keep him buoyant, even amidst the greatest Iniquities he hourly committed; a nearer View might discover a secret Horror and Cloud that clung around his Heart, and check'd him in the loudest Laugh. Nor is it at all astonishing, when we consider how many and what dangerous Enterprizes he every Day undertook.

took. The Attack, or seizing of the Booty, was not less dangerous than the disposing it after it was taken; and as the richest of the Plunder could not be sold here, he was oblig'd to send it to *France*, *Holland*, *Germany*, and many Parts beyond the Seas, where he always found People who dealt this way; but who always made him bad Returns, and to whom he was a constant Bubble: Tho among all his Correspondents, no one used the Captain so ill as Monsieur *Trapanté*, a *French* Merchant, so he styled himself; but he was in reality, only a famous Receiver of stolen Goods: To this Man the Captain consigned Gold Watches, Diamond Rings, Medals, and whatever other Remarkables fell into his Hands, and were judged by no means proper or safe to be exposed to Sale at home. But *Trapanté*, the most cunning and fallacious Man that ever took up the Mystery of Pawnbroking, never made him any Returns: And when he expostulated this Matter with him, Monsieur fieur invented many frivolous and idle Pretences to defraud him. Sometimes he wrote him word that he had been at great Expences in Hufh-Money; that he was under Apprehenfions of being impeach'd by a *Spanifh* Merchant, to whom he had confign'd fome Diamonds, which were difcover'd by a Jew at *Madrid* to have been the Property of a Man of Quality in *England*: At other Times he had Bills drawn upon him from *Vienna*, with Letters of Advice and Threats, and which he durft not refufe accepting, for fear of being impleaded. And when the Captain in thefe untoward Circumftances fometimes grew peevifh, and remonftrated to the *Frenchman* with fome Acrimony, the unjuft and ungentleman-like Treatment he receiv'd, and threaten'd never to employ him again as his Factor; the faucy *Frenchman* always took him fhort with Menaces to come over, and to turn Evidence againft him: He told him, he was fure of Pardon and Protection; and he fhould, if he continued to ufe him in this manner,

manner, begin to consider cooly both what his Interest and his Duty prompted him to, and drop the foolish personal Inclination that he had for him. In this Affair, I have heard his Companions say, the Captain was inexcusable, for that long before he dealt with the *Frenchman*, he was not ignorant of his Character, nor in what manner he had ruin'd several unhappy Gentlemen in this way before, and would most certainly betray him, as soon as ever he refus'd to feed his Avarice. Nor had the Captain much better Usage at Home, the watchful Cares, the anxious Fears, and the continual Disturbance and Hurry in which he liv'd, made his Post not to be envied by the lowest in his Confederacy. Those under his Direction were never satisfy'd, and it was observable, when he was, and he frequently was, partial in the Distribution of the Booty; the Person whom he thus favour'd, was always the very first who mutiny'd. So natural is it for Men of ser-
vile

vile Minds, to impute every thing they receive, rather to their own Merit than the Bounty of a Master.

THUS you see he had the Humours of Mankind, as well as their Necessities to administer to; and the first were as difficult to be govern'd as the last.

SOMETIMES his People would pretend Conscience, and the great Uneasiness they were under to continue in that way of Life: At other times they told him flatly, that it was better at once to dye, than to hang thus hourly in constant Anxieties and Fears. But whenever these penitent or anxious Brows appear'd before him, he had a certain and an infallible Remedy; he took them aside one by one into a private Apartment, mutter'd a few words, smiled and squeezed them by the Hand; and immediately after this, all-Despondence, and conscientious Qualms,

Qualms, and Murmurings, and Jealoufies vanifh'd away; and the Captain was declar'd a Gentleman of the firft Capacity, and the greateft Honour of any in *Europe*.

THESE I have mention'd, were but a few of the Difficulties that befieg'd the Captain daily; so dearly did he pay for being at the Head of this unlawful League: And I have heard, that he has often confefs'd to an Intimate, that he lamented his Situation; and if the Danger of defcending was not apparently greater than continuing where he was, he fhould with Joy change for the meaneft Condition of the pooreft Labourer in the Commonwealth; tho at the fame time when he talk'd to the Confederacy, he profefs'd to live and dye with them, and declar'd he had very little Regard to what any vulgar Wretches fhould write or talk concerning him.

MANKIND hunt Happiness, and pursue it thro' Paths where they are sure never to overtake it, and are very often oblig'd to return in Search of it to the very Spot where they first set out.

YET notwithstanding the Captain was now and then punish'd with a Qualm of this Kind; when his Spirits return'd, when his Companions surrounded him, when the Business of the Day provok'd him, or some new Prize was set in view, he always return'd cheerfully to his Iniquity.

IT is very surprizing, that the Captain, who has now been an old Offender, should never have been capitally convicted. The first Offence, as I remember, for which he was publickly question'd, was a Depredation committed in *Scotland* upon some
Farmers,

Farmers; who having fold their Hay and Corn at *Edinburgh*, were returning home: the Captain was accufed, and muft have been convicted, but for the Evidence of his faithful Servant *Bob Brazen*, whom I have mentioned before. *Bob* fwore the Captain was in another Place when that Fact was committed; and that he had no Knowledge of the Fact, or any Share in the Spoil: and when this Teftimony feem'd not to have its full Weight with the Jury, *Bob* took the Crime upon himfelf, and fwore he committed it fingly and alone; and what is yet more furprizing, *Bob* was never queftion'd for this afterwards. This Service the Captain has upon all Occafions, and does, as I am inform'd, to this Hour acknowledge: And indeed this was a particular Mark of Friendfhip, and fuch as is not often to be met with in this degenerate Age.

H   IT

IT would be an endlefs and a trifling Labour to recount the Particulars of every Affair that the Captain has been engag'd in from time to time: Some were gallant, fome were rafh, fome dangerous, and others only gainful or whimfical: His manner of ftealing the feveral Quart and Pint Pots out of every Publick Houfe in a large Market-Town, and obliging the Inhabitants to pay a Penny a-piece for every Pot before they were deliver'd, was for fome time the Subject of Mirth; as was likewife the odd Method he took to levy Contributions upon a whole Fleet of Colliers at *Newcaftle*.

SOME People were mightily pleafed likewife with the Difappointment he met with, in the Execution of a rafh and irregular Scheme he had form'd, form'd, to attack a Parcel of brave and generous Seamen, who he had wrong Information were such a Day to receive their Pay; but *Jack-Tar* was so well prepar'd to meet him, and stood so resolutely to his Arms, that the Captain was oblig'd to drop the Project, and leave him in quiet Possession of his Property.

SOON after this, he was grown so daring by Impunity, that it became dangerous to walk the Streets of *London* after it was dark, so frequent and so open were the Robberies; when his Majesty, by his most gracious Proclamation, at once dissipated the several Gangs, and the Fears of his People.

CONCLUSION.

I HAVE gone thro' as many Circumstances concerning the Life and Manners of Captain *Mackheath* as have occur'd to me; and, I hope, no body will from the Title of this little Tract, expect to be let into the more minute Particulars of his Life and Conversation; I have only endeavour'd as strongly as I could to mark the Character of this Man's Mind, and to shew my Readers by this Example, that the direct Paths to Happiness are Integrity and Content, however Mankind are led astray in the Search of it, among the Glare of Wealth and imaginary Dignities.

I KNOW it is a very difficult, a very invidious, and a dangerous Task, to write the Actions of evil Men

Men while they yet live, however true, or juft, or impartial fuch Writings may be: But as I thought this Endeavour of mine might not be wholly unufeful to the Publick, I refolved to do my Duty as a good Citizen; and at the fame time, I confefs by my prefent Joy at concluding this little Book, that I did not refift the Temptations of my Vanity as a frail Man.

AS I profefs'd in the Beginning of thefe Memoirs, to conduct my felf impartially, I hope the Captain will acquit me as to that Part of the Performance: What remains is, to exhort him, which I do in the moft hearty and pathetick manner, not to go on ftill to behold himfelf in a falfe and a flattering Mirrour, and to glorify himfelf in the Glare of thofe Rays which his Profperity only hath
thrown

thrown around him; the Defolation and Ravages he daily commits are recorded and laid up againft him, and Punifhment furely, tho flowly, ftalks behind him: he muft be equally blind and vain to imagine that his Flatterers, now his little Minions, will attend and dance around him in his adverfe Hours. Can he who never loved or trufted any Man, but as he was ufeful to him, indulge himfelf in the fond Belief that he is belov'd or trufted by any Man, but for the Convenience fuch a Parafite finds in his Favour? or can he expect Integrity or Gratitude in a Creature, whofe whole Merit and Recommendation to his Service muft be the Want of thofe very Qualities? The fame Neceffity that introduced him into his Service, will fhew him the way out of it; he muft expect therefore when the evil Hour fhall come, to fee himfelf totally abandon'd: thefe

Flies

Flies of the Sunshine are not to be found in the Winter of Adversity; let him then look upon me as the only faithful and unbyass'd Friend he hath. I have rung out the Alarm-Bell, and warn'd him while the Day yet is, to repent of his evil Ways; I hope well he will receive the Benefit I intended him from these Memoirs. If this shall happen, I shall have the great Reward my Vanity propos'd. But should the Captain neglect or despise these my Admonitions, I desire him only to be so good to himself to repeat what the wisest Man hath said, "*He that be-* "*ing often reproved hardneth his Neck,* "*shall suddenly be destroy'd, and that* "*without Remedy.*"

FINIS.

A Trip to the Moon

Anonymous

Bibliographical note:

*This facsimile has been made from a copy in the
British Museum
(12350.e.5)*

*Verso half title B
Trip to the Moon*

A TRIP TO THE MOON.

By Mr. *MURTAGH Mc. DERMOT*.

CONTAINING

Some Observations and Reflections, made by him during his Stay in that *Planet*, upon the Manners of the Inhabitants.

Quæ genus aut Flexum variant Heteroclita sunto.
   Lill. Gram,

——*Ridentem dicere verum*
———*quid vetat.*   Hor,

Printed at *DUBLIN*:
And Reprinted at *LONDON*, for J. ROBERTS in *Warwick-Lane*. M DCC XXVIII.

(Price One Shilling.)

THE
PREFACE.

AM not ignorant to what Danger Treatises of this Nature are liable, on account of a Mistake that prevails among the more ignorant Sort, who deny the Transmigration of an Inhabitant of one Planet to another, as firmly as they deny the Transmigration of Souls from one Body to another. But tho' I do not take upon me to defend the latter, since I dare not pretend to argue better than Pythagoras has done, yet I hold the former, and bring the most convincing Argument for it, Experience. I went, I saw, I return'd; I ventur'd my Life many Times for the Information of my Countrymen, who, I hope, will shortly by their own Ingenuity, confirm what I have said. There is one Objection against this Piece, which I think ought to be remov'd. It may be said, that the Author never has been in the Moon, since he relates very little, but what is observable among us, for he talks of Plays, Coffee-Houses, Balls, Ladies, Tea, Intriguing, Pythagoreans, and other Things, which may be easily apply'd to our selves, and are in Use among us. To this I answer,

First, That to condemn a Man without sufficient Evidence, is contrary to our Irish Statutes, neither can such Evidence be had, till some Body arrives from the

A 2 Moon,

Moon, who I am sure will bear Witness to all I have set down.

Secondly, The Similitude of Manners is but a weak Objection. Does not every Body know that Nature in all her Works delights in Uniformity? Why then may not the Inhabitants of our secondary Planet be like us in their Behaviour? I doubt not, but if I had seen more of them I should have been able to describe Persons like some of our Neighbours. As to what is said concerning Government, let none misapply it: I had sworn Allegiance to King George the First of glorious Memory, before my Departure, and was always firmly attach'd to the Hanoverian Succession, against the base Pretensions of a cowardly, spurious, Popish Pretender; besides, a monarchical Government can never be applied with the the least probability to the Crown of Great Britain. In the next Place, let me make some Apology for endeavouring to account for some Things in an uncommon Manner.

The best Philosophers have been famous for their own Conjectures; some of which I have follow'd, and made bold to add my own, where they were not very positive. Other Accounts I have related according to the receiv'd Doctrine of the Moon, for which I am oblig'd to my dear Friend Tckbrff.

What has been said, may suffice to vindicate me from such Aspersions as evil-minded Persons may cast upon me, who look no higher than their own native Earth. It remains that I address my self to those of a more generous Disposition, who I hope will excuse small Faults, and impute them rather to my Ignorance, than to any design of imposing on the Publick.

A

A
Trip to the Moon, &c.

CHAP. I.

Containing an Account of the Author's *Defign to travel. His going to Sea. His Arrival at* Teneriffe. *His Afcent to the* Peak. *His being taken up by a Whirlwind. The Manner of his Journey towards the* Moon. *Some Reflections made by the Way. His Arrival at the* Moon, *and what happened thereupon.*

O fatisfy a violent Inclination which I always had to fee foreign Countries, and being incapacitated by my Circumftances to travel barely for the Improvement of my Mind, I thought it moft adviſeable to turn Sailor; and in purfuance to my Defign, I bound my felf to one *James Anderfon*, Mafter of the *Runner*, a Veffel of about 75 Tun, (tho' the *Cuftom-Houfe* had it but 70) belonging to *Dublin*, in the Year 1718. This I did againft the Will of my Mother, my Father being dead a little before, of which I have many Times fince repented, and obferv'd, that thofe who will not be directed by their Parents, meet with ill Succefs in their Undertakings.

On the 6th of *June* 1718, we fet fail for the *Canaries*, being loaden with Beef, Butter, Cheefe, Candles and Soap, and in a few Hours got clear of the Land. But here I cannot but mention the fad Condition my Mother was in at our parting; fhe accompanied me to the Side of the Veffel, and there,

with

with abundance of Tears, reprefented to me the Dangers of the Sea; but finding it was too late to detain me, fhe fwoon'd in my Arms. I then began to wifh my felf free, and could not forbear fhedding fome Tears. The Captain who was prefent at this Interview, being afraid my Mother's Tears would move him fo much as to part with me, like a good Man that wou'd avoid Temptation, went down to his Cabbin, and gave Orders to bring me aboard by force. His Orders were obey'd, and my Mother was left as dead upon the Shore. I had no fooner got aboard, but I was fet about fome of the hardeft Work of the Ship, and was comforted by being told it would make me forget my Mother. This I bore very patiently, having no Body to accufe but my felf for my Sufferings. The Reader muft excufe me if in this Voyage I do not give him an Account of our Courfes, fince I being unacquainted with failing, and fully griev'd for my Mother, did not much mind them.

On the 12th of *Auguft* following, we arriv'd at *Teneriffe*, being driven thither by ftrefs of Weather, for our Defign was to land at *Palma*, to take in Sugar; we got into *Santa Cruz* Bay, which is to the North Eaft of the Ifland, and rode in 17 Fathom of Water. The Storm continued for fome Days after we had providentially caft Anchor; during which Time, my Curiofity and Rafhnefs prompted me to afcend the *Peak*.

My Converfation with Sailors, and their Reports, had given me fuch ftrange and pleafing Ideas of remote Countries, during my ftay in *Dublin*, efpecially of *Teneriffe*, (altho' they vary'd a little in their Computations; and many, I am perfuaded, have affirm'd that they have been at the Top of the Mountain, when they never were within 1000 Leagues of the Ifland) that I refolv'd to be an Eye-witnefs of what I had heard.

The

The next Morning, I began to prepare for my intended Journey, juſt as the Sun was above the Horizon. I haſten'd Breakfaſt as much as I cou'd, and after I ſhifted my ſelf I begg'd the Aſſiſtance of two of the Sailors to ſet me on Shore, which I obtain'd, on Condition that I wou'd divide whatever I got, with them. I conſented and was ſet on Shore.

I was no ſooner landed, than I began ſeriouſly to reflect on my folly, (then not hearing the Noiſe of the Seamen, or Curſes of my Maſter) I remember'd my Mothers warnings, but above all her ſwooning: My Maſter's fair Promiſes before I was his Servant, and his hard Uſage after, which made me often wiſh my ſelf at home, and reckon my Stripes as my Deſerts. I went on thus melancholy, till I perceiv'd my ſelf to aſcend the Hill, and then I bent my ſelf wholly upon confirming what I had heard; but to my great ſurprize, I found ſcarce one Word I had heard to be true, except that the Mountain is very high. It is certain that it is very large too, and that many may have aſcended it; but then they may have aſcended by different Ways, and ſome may have met with more inequalities in their aſcent than others, which may have occaſion'd a Difference in their Accounts of its Height. I was wholly unprovided with Inſtruments to take its Altitude, having brought nothing along with me, but a Bottle of Brandy, a Piece of Cheeſe, and a few Biſcuits. I only obſerv'd, that I was 56 times weary in my aſcent; by which given Number, if my Health and habit of Body were now the ſame, I could eaſily find out the Number ſought for, viz. the Height of it. For by going up and down any Mountain of a moderate Height, till I was 56 times weary, and by finding out a mean Proportional between aſcending and deſcending, and by making allowances for Trips and Stumbles, and the Storm, I humbly conceive, an ordinary Mathematician may meaſure the Height of the *Peak* of *Teneriffe*.

(8)

With much difficulty I got within sight of the Top of the Mountain, (I mean so as to see every Part of it distinctly) where I sat down to refresh my self. I pull'd out a Biscuit and held it in my left Hand, whilst I employ'd my right in searching for my Cheese; but the Wind was so violent that it blow'd away half my Biscuit as if it had been a Wafer, which oblig'd me to hold my Head between my Legs, while I Eat what I thought proper; but I am not certain to this Day, whether the Biscuit was crack'd or not. At length I arriv'd at the very Summit of the Mountain, where I was oblig'd to discharge by Vomiting what I had lately eaten, that purer Air being very disagreeable to my gross Constitution; this made me think very meanly of my self, who in my own Country was constantly complaining of close and foggy Weather; when I found that such a Place was no more fit for me to breathe in, than Heaven is for habitual Sinners, if they might be permitted to go there without Repentance.

Whilst I was thus meditating on my own corrupt Nature, a sudden Whirlwind came, that rais'd me from the Place I stood on; I suppose, that by Vomiting, (for it was very violent) I had increas'd the bulk of my Body, by the swelling of its Parts in my convulsive Motions; so that it then became equal to more columns of Air than it was equal to before my Vomiting; besides it was become lighter by the discharge I had made, which might alone produce what follow'd. For since we know that Vessels at a Key float or lye adrift as the Tide comes in, or goes out, and learned Men have given us this Reason for it, *viz.* That at high Water, the subjacent columns of Water are greater, or at least equal to the Bulk and Weight of the Vessel, and at low Water the contrary; it follows, that there must be a certain quantity of Water, less than which wou'd not be able to sustain a Body of a certain Weight and Magnitude. This may be

easily

easily apply'd, by considering that Air and Water are both Fluids, and differ only in their Density, and some other Properties which I have no occasion to mention; so that it is probable in the last Degree, that my Body became then so proportionate to the subjacent columns of Air, that it easily sustain'd me. Or admitting, not granting, that this will not clearly account for it, I can yet have recourse to the Storm, which was then the Occasion of the continued Motion of my Body. But leaving such Disquisitions to the Learned, and confessing my own Weakness in attempting any thing of this Kind, I shall proceed to relate what happen'd in my Voyage to the *Moon*, (for so I may call it) having already hinted at the Analogy between Air and Water. After I had been rais'd from the Mountain, I was carried at such a rate for a while, that I almost lost my Breath; but the Force of the Whirlwind gradually abating, my Passage became more easy, till I came to a Place of Resting. This was a Space between the Vortices of the *Earth* and *Moon*, where the Attraction of neither prevail'd, but the contrary Motions of their Effluvia destroy'd one another.

Here I began to look about me, and deplore my Condition; I feared that when my Provision was consum'd, (for that I happen'd to have kept, being better secur'd than my Hat, which had been blown away,) I must inevitably die with Hunger, tho' I were secure from being crush'd by falling to either of the Planets: But my Pride soon prevail'd over this desponding Humour, when I consider'd my Circumstances in another light. I began to think I was too good for the Society of Mortals, which Opinion I was encourag'd in, by calling to mind every Action which I thought shou'd be rewarded, throwing the bad Ones entirely out of the Account: So that I now fancied my self made a *Star*, and that as my Body was to give Light to Men's Eyes, so my Actions which I accounted good, were to be set as an Example they shou'd imi-

B tate

tate. And altho' upon surveying my self, I found nothing Luminous about me, yet I was perfuaded thofe on Earth wou'd think otherwife, and that I was render'd incapable of perceiving it my felf at that Time, left being confcious of it I fhou'd become too haughty and unfit for that exalted Station. But then I began to confider, whether I might not derive the Light which I thought I gave from the *Sun*, and by the Motion of my Arms, and flowing of my Hair, be taken for a Comet. But this I rejected as erroneous, and wou'd not be oblig'd to the *Sun* for his Rays, fo that I refolved to be independent, and model my Courfe by my own Reafon. This I inftantly fet about, and refolving to be fingular, and make People gaze at me, I intended to move from S. S. E. to N. N. W. and to perform but one Revolution in a royal Period, whether it happened to be long or fhort, fo that I might be confulted about the Fate of a King, tho' I knew nothing of the Matter.

Pleas'd with thofe imaginary Profpects, and being well refted, I began to ftir, and put my Projects in Execution; but this I found fo difficult by means of the contrary Attractions, that my former defponding Humour return'd with an addition of Malice and Envy. I faw that I muft Die, and perhaps never be heard of if I continued where I was, fo that I ftrove with all my might, to throw my felf back to the Earth, hoping I might kill fome Body by my Fall, whofe Friends wou'd fpread abroad my Fame, tho' ignorant of my Intentions. To compafs this, after much Labour, I remov'd my felf fomewhat farther from the Verge of the Earth's Atmofphere, intending to fall with the greater Rapidity, and bring certain Death to any Mortal I fhou'd chance to light on. But this I fhou'd never have any hopes of obtaining, had it not been that a Cloud full of Hail was driven towards me by the Whirlwind. I laid hold on the Opportunity, and putting both my Hands againft it, by all Strength, I caus'd it to re-act upon me as much as I acted upon it, fo that I was quickly remov'd into the Sphere of

the

the *Moon*'s Attraction, more than I intended; for two thirds of my Body being attracted by the *Moon*, the reſt ſoon follow'd, ſo that I was carried with incredible ſwiftneſs, which ſtill increas'd in my fall towards that Planet.

It was my good Fortune to fall into a Fiſh-pond, which our ſharp-ſighted Philoſophers miſtake for a Part of the Sea, and call it *Sinus Rorum*; but I hope they will not be ſo bold as to deny what I ſay, ſince they all confeſs that they never were there. It is call'd in the Language of the *Moon Bragg-Ququs* becauſe it belongs to the King of *Ququs*. By good Fortune the King's Fiſherman was angling for the Diverſion of ſome of the Court, when I fell into the Pond, and the hook which was tied to his Line, got into one of my Button-holes, ſo that he was oblig'd either to draw me out, tho' my Fall had terribly affrighted them, or loſe his Rod, which wou'd have been puniſh'd with Death, for there they are oblig'd to perform whatever they undertake, be it never ſo difficult.

CHAP. II.

Containing an Account of the People's Care of him. His Surprize upon his Recovery. His manner of Learning their Language in a Night's time, with an Account for it.

WET and dirty as I was, and Dead in all outward Appearance, he drew me out of the Pond to the Amazement of all that ſaw me. I was carried to the King's great Hall to be conſulted on, and expos'd to publick View. All that ſaw me believ'd me to be a Land Animal, and that ſome Bird of Prey had dropt me, being tir'd with my weight; but their chief concern was to bring me to life, which was ſoon effected, by a few Herbs which they pounded, pouring the juice of them down my Throat, and applying the Leaves by way of Poultice to my Poſteriors. It may
ſeem

seem a little strange, that those Herbs shou'd be so powerful; but if we consider that the *Moon* has an Influence upon the Plants of the Earth, whence they derive their medicinal Qualities, it follows that the nearer any Plant is to that Body, it possesses those qualities in a more eminent Degree, and consequently that those which grow upon it must excel all others. The Fright I was in upon my first opening my Eyes, had like to deprive me utterly of that Life which they were so follicitous to preserve; and I will leave it to any Man's own Breast, whether he wou'd not be terrified as much as I was, to find himself among such a Set of Animals as I am going to describe, without knowing how he was introduced to such Company. The Assembly was made up of Brutes and half Brutes, there were Bears, Wolves, Tygers, Foxes, Monkeys, Cats and Dogs, &c. and those of several Kinds, with certain other Animals, very like the Pictures which I have seen of Beasts, in the *East* and *West-Indies*; others had only one or more Members of Beasts; but what amaz'd me most of all was, that those Brutes walk'd upright and spoke, which I am sure was enough to terrifie any Man that has liv'd since *Æsop*'s Days. The first I took notice of, was a Wolf, that held me by the Wrist; I apprehended that he wou'd instantly devour me, upon the Notice which I thought he had of an Earthy Smell about me, by the extraordinary fineness of his olfactory Nerves, whence he might judge me to be Dead; for I mistook the Poultice in my Breeches for something more offensive; but I afterwards understood, that he was only an eminent Physician, that had not always good Success, and was then feeling my Pulse. I found my self very weak, and was for taking a Dram, for I had still kept my Bottle, but my Doctor Wolf hindred me, alledging as I understood after, that my Distemper was not yet come to its Crisis. He was of Opinion, that the Humours of the Body insist as much upon Liberty and Property,

perty, and are as sensible of an Affront as an *English-man*, and that Distempers arise only from their striving to keep out Strangers; besides, the animal Spirits are design'd for a Standing Army to suppress Riots, and assist the weak Proprietor; but considering the great waste I had made of them, and that Brandy was a spirituous Liquor, he fear'd that a Dram wou'd be too powerful an Enemy for what was left of my animal Spirits, and that the Conflict wou'd end in my Destruction.

I was forc'd to submit to his Judgment without knowing at that time his Reasons, and was convey'd by a couple of Mastiffs in the Ticking of a Bolster, which they had emptied for that purpose, to a convenient Apartment. The Room where I was laid, was order'd to be kept dark 'till I cou'd learn their Language; and a Gentleman with an Ass's Head, appointed to instruct me. The Method which he took for my Improvement, was to make me repeat after him the Names of those Things I seem'd to have occasion for, and 'till I had done so, I was sure not to get the use of them. I improv'd daily to his great Satisfaction, 'till I thought I was able to walk abroad; but not knowing how to express my self to him so as to be understood, or why my Chamber was continually darken'd, I ventur'd to get up once before him, and grope for my Cloaths; but he imagining that I wanted the Chamber-Pot, brought it to me with great speed, crying out *Lmldnse*, which was the Name of it, that I might repeat it after him; but I was so provok'd at his Mistake, that I only answer'd in plain *English* B—d and W—ds; he thinking that I strove to repeat *Lmldnse*, when I curs'd and swore, and finding that I did not do it, imputed it to some Defect in my Tongue; upon which he instantly left me to go and advise with his Brethren. Not finding my Cloaths, I was oblig'd to lie down again, full of Indignation, and resolv'd rather to starve my self, than live as I had done much longer. But my Tutor

soon

soon return'd with a couple of Mules, who were to affift him in the fplitting of my Tongue with a Silver Three-pence. One of the Mules approach'd me with a Candle and a Three-penny Piece, whilft the other fecur'd my Hands, and my Tutor offer'd to open my Mouth, often repeating *Lmldnfe*. I thought at firft they had defign'd the Three-penny Piece for the fame Ufe to me that *Demofthenes* made of *Pebbles*, 'till they began to proceed to the Operation. My Tutor had made me roar fo much, and become fo uneafy, by an immoderate Expanfion of my Jaws, that I happily put out the Candle, which gave me fome refpite, and fruftrated their Intentions; for we were no fooner in the Dark, and that I was left to my felf, whilft the others were employ'd in lighting the Candle, and getting Ropes to tie me, than I rofe to put my felf in a pofture of Defence, fufpecting their Intentions, from the Ufage I remember'd to have feen *Magpies* meet with in my own Country. But they return'd before I cou'd find any thing which I thought proper for my Defence, fo that I refolved to repeat whatever they faid as diftinctly as I cou'd, hoping by that means to preferve my Tongue, which fucceeded as I cou'd wifh. For my Tutor, upon his Entry, was difcourfing very ferioufly with a young Man whom he brought to affift him, and among other Words, often mentioned *Lmldnfe*, which I repeated very diftinctly. The whole Company turn'd their Eyes upon my Tutor, who, appearing furpriz'd, left the Room. I ran to the young Man, whom I had not feen before, and by many obliging Geftures prevail'd upon him to ftay with me. They obferv'd my Fondnefs for him, and thought him to be the moft proper Perfon to inftruct me. *Tckbrff*, for that was his Name, accepted of the Office, and to my great Satisfaction, in a fhort Time, made me fit for Converfation. He was one that had been a Brute, but by applying to Learning, and confidering his Folly, he recover'd his human Shape; he was generally de-
fpis'd

spis'd by all Beasts, and by some reputed to be a Conjurer, since there were Beasts that affirm'd themselves to be more virtuous than him, yet were in no likelihood of recovering their human Form. He did not much mind their Aspersions, but employ'd himself chiefly in reclaiming such as he found most tractable. He observ'd that I was one of good natural Parts, and might probably arrive at Knowledge by shorter Methods than had been us'd with his Countrymen. The first Tryal which he made of me, was to make me perfect Master of their Language; and this he effected in a Night's Time, after the manner I shall relate. He took a large and correct Dictionary, and minc'd the Leaves of it; those he put into an Earthen Vessel half full of Water, and cover'd it so close that no Air could come into it; he plac'd the Vessel, with its upper Part parallel to the Horizon, upon a gentle Fire, where he let it remain thirty-nine Minutes. The Air which was inclos'd in the Vessel, being put into a violent Motion by the Heat of the Fire, together with the Motion of the Water, soon reduc'd the minc'd Leaves to a Consistence of Jelly. The Vessel had been cover'd so closely, to hinder any of the Letters from being carried off in Vapours, and that the Air in the upper part of the Vessel might act with the greater Force. He then set it by to cool, before he ventur'd to uncover it; and when it was perfectly cold, gave it to me to eat for *Sowins* with Whitewine and Sugar. This serv'd me for Supper, and I was order'd to sleep as soon as I had taken it; he wou'd not leave me that Night, but watch'd me as I slept, and assur'd me in the Morning, that he was wonderfully delighted to hear me break Wind in my Sleep; sometimes with all the force of Rhetorick, sometimes in the Tone of a Grammarian.

When I awoke, I receiv'd a particular Account of what he had done, and thank'd him with all imaginable Expressions of Gratitude. But I was very desirous to know whether the Mules intended to slit my

Tongue

Tongue or not, or if they did, what cou'd be their reason for it; to which I receiv'd this Answer; That I might observe, that in their Language four or more Consonants were often join'd in one Word without a Vowel intervening, and consequently requir'd a greater Volubility of Tongue than other Languages where the Case is otherwise, that Member being chiefly employ'd in the Pronunciation of Consonants: And in order to my more speedy and better learning their Language, it was thought advisable to divide my Tongue, that I might be able to pronounce two Consonants at once, since I had not been accustom'd to it from my Infancy; and that my former Tutor, mistaking my Meaning, (as I had inform'd him) had persuaded some as ignorant as himself to consent to the Proposal.

CHAP. III.

Containing an Account of his being sent for by the King. His Discourse with Tckbrff *about the King. His Manner of approaching him. Some Observations on his Courtiers. His Approach to him. His escaping being put to death; and what Discourse he had with* Tckbrff *about the People of his own Country, and the People of the* Moon.

THE King upon notice of my Recovery, gave Orders that I shou'd be brought before him; upon which I desir'd the Advice of *Tckbrff*: He told me first that the King, who was an absolute Monarch, was an ambitious Tyrant, he was one that never troubled himself about the Good of his People; but if ever their Interest interfer'd with his even unlawful Diversions, it was entirely neglected; he was a great Lover of Pleasure, and of every thing that was new, which he was pleas'd to call polite Learning, (tho' he was often fond of, and encourag'd the greatest Absurdities); an Instance of which he

gave

gave me, in the Preferment of one to great Posts of Trust, who had only propos'd to make the Rays of Light palpable to the Hands; out of which, when his Design was perfected, he intended that an Apartment for the King shou'd be built; and altho' the failing in a Project was to be punish'd with Death, where the Projectors were such Fools as to confess their Disappointment, yet this Man requir'd such a long Time, and so great Expences, that he was sure to outlive his Proposals. He had, however, amus'd the King with an odd Account of the Means he wou'd make use of, and made them so unintelligible by the help of the Mathematicks, that he was believ'd to mean honestly, and a Pension was settled on him for effecting his Design. The Rays of Light were to be let into a dark Room, one by one, thro' Holes equal to their Bulk, which he affirmed he was well acquainted with. Here was a Mathematical Demonstration of an Hour long, which I omit for the Reader's sake. They were then to be refracted ninety-nine times by passing thro' different Mediums, which wou'd weaken their Force so much, that they might be at length fix'd in a Liquor which he had prepar'd for that purpose; and when the vacant Interstices of the Liquor were fill'd with them, (for he asserted that there was a Vacuum) by Chymical Operations, he wou'd gather them into Vessels to be reserv'd, till he got enough of all Colours for erecting the Building. The Cement which he propos'd for them, was *Cartesius's* subtle Matter, which might be gather'd by Sheets daub'd with a bituminous Substance, compounded of the Effluvia of certain Bodies, whose Virtues he was well acquainted with. Those Sheets were to be hung in the open Air till the subtle Matter had cover'd them; then they were to be boil'd in Vessels hermetically seal'd 'till the subtle Matter had stuck to the Tops of them, whence it might be taken and laid by for use. This short

Account he gave of one among the many famous Men who were then at Court.

I defir'd to know in what manner I was to approach his Majefty; and was told, that fince I was a Foreigner, the moft proper Method wou'd be to walk upon my Hands with my Heels upwards, that the King might have the better Opinion of my Abilities; and was affur'd, that the Novelty of the Thing wou'd be very acceptable. I lik'd the Propofal, and was two Days in learning to walk in that manner; during which Time I pretended not to be throughly recover'd, and fed only upon learned Books in their Language prepar'd as before. I voided nothing by way of Excrement all the while I liv'd upon Books, but a few falfe Concords, which cou'd not fubfift within me, on account of a Meal I had made upon Criticifms.

When the Time came that I was to appear before his Majefty, I was conducted by *Tckbrff* to the Palace to wait 'till I was call'd for. While I was attending the King's Levee, I could not but make many Obfervations upon the ftrange Behaviour of the Courtiers, whofe different Paffions and Interefts I cou'd eafily difcern. I faw a Fox and a Calf accofting each other with great Civility, tho' I am certain that they were inveterate Enemies: But their manner of Salutation, which feem'd a little extraordinary, may perhaps be worth the Reader's notice. They bow'd moft courteoufly to each other at firft fight, which continued 'till they had the Happinefs to fhake Hands; I expected that a Kifs wou'd enfue, but it feems the Gentlemen were better bred; for, upon fhaking Hands, each apply'd his Nofe to the Pofteriors of the other; where, after they had regal'd their Senfe of Smelling for a few Moments, they began to exprefs their Hatred for one another in the moft obliging Terms. *Tckbrff*, as learned as he was, and to whom I am much indebted, cou'd not give me a natural Reafon for this manner of Compliment, which was peculiar to Men of high Rank; for the common
People

People affected Cleanliness in that Case, and made use of joining their Lips to those of their Friends upon meeting. He told me indeed, that the joining of the Lips of Friends was founded in Nature, and bore an Hieroglyphical Meaning. For since it is by what proceeds from the Mouth, that a Man is well or ill reputed of; and that we cannot judge of all Men by their Writings; that the greater part of Mankind know not how to write, it is evident that Nature, which operates by the most general and compendious Ways, hath taught us to join our Lips in Friendship, where two Persons should be resolv'd to agree in their Sentiments, and submit to the most powerful Reasons that shall be pronounc'd by either with respect to some Truth or Truths wherein they are both concern'd; as when two Brothers meet, they should both be resolv'd before-hand to agree in this, that the Welfare of their Parents was to be desir'd and promoted by them to the utmost of their Power; the joining of Lips intimating a Conformity of Opinions, which thro' the Lips were to be convey'd. But the Deference which *Tckbrff* paid to Courtiers, as being Men of Power and Learning, made him incapable of assigning a Reason for their smelling to the Back-parts upon meeting; and his Instructions had so far prevail'd upon me, that I dar'd not even to think, during my stay among them, so as that I might not be favourably understood by any indifferent Person, had I express'd my Meaning in Words. But since I came to my own Country, I began to think as freely as my Neighbours, and examine many Things in the *Moon* by *English* Rules, particularly the manner of Salutation among Courtiers just mentioned. I believe that they well knowing that thro' the Fundament the most stinking Excrement is convey'd; and that the Intention, as well as Habit of Body, may from its Smell, Shape, and Colour, be guess'd at, have, to avoid needless Expressions, such as *How do you do*, wisely made use of this Method to inform themselves

I am sensible that some ill-meaning Persons may say, that this Salute is very like that used by two *Irish* Curs, when each suspects the other to differ from him in Sex, and hopes he may prove a Bitch. But those Gentlemen may be pleas'd to consider, that both the Persons mentioned were really Brutes, and that this Compliment pass'd between them purely out of Complaisance; tho' I cannot affirm it for certain Truth; or else my own Solution of the Matter might satisfy, I think, an unprejudic'd Person.

But to return from this Digression: While I was entertaining my self with Reflections on the Behaviour of those People, notice was given me that his Majesty was at leisure to look at me; I instantly inverted my Body, and began to move upon my Hands after my Guide, but had much difficulty in my Passage; for the Courtiers press'd so hard to view me in this uncommon Posture, that they often trod upon my Fingers. At length I came into the King's Presence, where I met with different Treatment at first from what I expected; for after that I had made the greatest Protestations of my Fidelity and Readiness to serve him in the Court Dialect, he told me, with a Frown, that he took me for an Impostor, who, to carry on some Designs against the State, and prevent my being readily known, had appear'd in that manner. He added, that I must certainly be a *Scufmlr*, (which Word, in our Language, signifies a Man of *Law*, if you interpret it literally) or one that undertook to prove both Sides of a Question, since I had now made it doubtful, which End of a Man ought to be uppermost; and concluded that I should be rewarded accordingly; but the Time and Manner of it were yet to be consider'd of. I shou'd have inevitably died at that Time, had it not been for a Lie which I told; for I assur'd his Majesty, that all Foreigners of Distinction, as well as Ambassadors, approach our Kings in that Posture which he saw me in; whence he inferr'd, that it was difficult to know which

was

was the fure End of them, and when they were in earneſt. I was inſtantly order'd to refume my natural Poſture, and give a full and clear Account of my felf. To ſhew my Art in getting upon my Feet, I deſcrib'd with my big Toes the Portion of a Circle, whoſe Radius was nearly equal to the Length of my Body; I then anſwer'd all the Queſtions which were put to me concerning the manner of my coming into that Kingdom, and the Government and Cuſtoms of my own Nation. The great Knowledge which I had of their Language, ſupply'd me with ſuch Variety of elegant Expreſſions, that the King took me for a Perſon of an uncommon Genius, as he was pleaſed to term it, and told me that I ſhould find the Marks of his royal Favour; tho' I am inclined to believe he intended to make uſe of my Judgment and Parts to enſlave his People the more, if poſſible, and perpetrate his Cruelty with the greater Security.

However there was a Penſion ſettled on me for my Support, 'till a Place ſhould fall, which I might be thought capable of managing. *Tckbrff*, after we had withdrawn from the King, told me that he believed we were all honeſt Men in my Country, and could wiſh to be among them; for ſurely, ſaid he, none that has but the leaſt part of a Man about him, can diſobey thoſe moſt reaſonable Laws of that excellent Conſtitution, where the Intereſts of the King and the People are ſo blended, that it is impoſſible for the one to ſubſiſt without the other; and where the People muſt out of Gratitude love him whoſe chief and conſtant Care it is to preſerve them in their Rights and Privileges.

I cou'd not but ſmile at his Diſcourſe, and tell him, that notwithſtanding they enjoy'd all thoſe mighty Bleſſings which he had mention'd, they were perhaps the moſt refractory and rebellious People in the *Solar Syſtem*. He doubted my Veracity, 'till I explained to him, as well as I could, the Difference between *Whig* and *Tory*, *Proteſtant* and *Papiſt*, and told him with what

Zeal

Zeal every Man maintain'd that Opinion which he embrac'd thro' Ignorance, Prejudice, or Intereſt, without daring to examine his Principles by an infallible Rule, leſt he ſhou'd ſee any Reaſon for renouncing that Error he was ſo fond of, if it ſhou'd prove one. I gave him alſo an Account of their proceedings againſt a King, that thro' Faction and private Intereſt was put to Death, yet might have ſav'd his Life and his Crown if he wou'd conſent with wicked Miniſters to oppreſs his People. Here *Tckbrff* expreſs'd the greateſt Indignation and Horror mix'd with a Degree of Pity for the unthinking Contrivers of his Death; and ask'd me how I could preſerve my human Shape among ſuch a corrupted Multitude. I told him that we carried on our moſt wicked Practices, and encourag'd the vileſt Paſſions with the greateſt ſhew of Humanity, and beg'd of him to let me know if he could, how it came to paſs that his Countrymen, were ſo unhappy as to have their Thoughts prefigur'd in their Bodies; or why ſuch Metamorphoſes did not make them Honeſt? He reply'd, that the Reaſon why thoſe Transformations did not make them Honeſt, was owing to the Ignorance of their Deformity; for every Man judg'd favourably of himſelf by a Miſconſtruction of his Actions, and it was obſervable, that no Perſon who had any part of a Beaſt in his compoſition, cou'd with a ſlight View behold his own Defects, tho' he often ſaw more brutal Members in others than they really had, which proceeded from a Deſire they had that it ſhou'd be ſo; for they miſtaking Virtue for a relative Thing, imagin'd every Man to be Virtuous, than whom they cou'd find one more Brutal; never conſidering, that he, who wou'd deſerve the Character of a good Man, muſt obſerve to the utmoſt of his Power, an exact Conformity of every of his Actions to right Reaſon. As to the Changes which our Bodies are ſubject to, (continued he) the beſt Account which I find in Writings or Tradition is this; that our Fore-Fathers in the early Ages of the *Moon*, before

they

they had built them Houses; were oblig'd to live in Caves, and by that means were much conversant with Beasts of all kinds; and as the Principle of Self-love began to be misunderstood, they began to imitate and put in Practice the Dispositions and Actions of those Beasts which were most agreeable to their Inclinations; here they began to grow cunning and deceive each other, and each himself, with the Sagacity of Brutes, as their private Interest prevail'd. Now since we know that all Bodies, especially those of a more soft Texture, derive certain Qualities from those Bodies which are nearest to them, so as sometimes to appear quite different from what they really are; it is probable that different Men diligently attending different Brutes to observe their own, had their correspondent Members transform'd into those of the Brute they attended; but whether this was done by the Effluvia that proceeded from the Beast, as the Moderns hold; or by some natural Magick, as the Antients were of Opinion, I will not take upon me to determine; but 'tis said that the first Changes were thus made, which have continued for so many Ages.

I then ask'd him, how they came to be so negligent of the Education of the Heir apparent to the Crown, as to suffer him to ascend the Throne with any Members of a Beast; for I had taken notice when I was before the King, that he had the Head and the right Paw of a *Lion*. He answer'd that their King was elective, and that upon a King's decease, they crown'd one who was remarkable for the good Services he had done his Country, and for the Perfectness of his human Form; but the best they cou'd find, wou'd sometimes upon his being invested with so much Power, give a Loose to his irregular Desires, since he obtain'd all that he had so long wish'd for; and it was observable in the King I had seen, that his left Hand was inclin'd to be hairy, and that he never par'd the Nails of it, whence it was expected that it wou'd soon become like the other. Here I cou'd not but praise
our

our own King, who before his Acceffion to the Crown had fignaliz'd himfelf for his Valour, and often hazarded his Life for the Defence of his Country, and after his Coronation improv'd the good Qualities he was before poffefs'd of, to the great Joy of his People. *Tckbrff* wifh'd that their Government might be chang'd to that of the *Englifh*, for he often bewail'd the miferable confequences of unlimited Power in a Sovereign.

CHAP. IV.

Containing an Account of their Difcourfe about an Amour between Fribbigghe *and* Blmmfl. *Their Characters. He turns* Fribbigghe's *Rival. Makes a Speech to* Blmmfl. Fribbigghe *is difcarded.*

WE then began to difcourfe about an Amour that was much talk'd of, between a Tabby *Cat*, and a black and white *Lap-Dog*, and it was believ'd that it wou'd be a Match, from the Similitude of their Intellects.

The *Cat* which was the Male, was a noted Fortune-hunter, and one that had as little pretenfions to a Lady's Heart as any in the Kingdom of *Ququs*, if he was confider'd to be what he really was. He was one that laid out his fmall Fortune entirely upon his Cloaths, and contented himfelf with more ordinary Meals than an *Irifh* Footman wou'd do, when he eat at his own Expence. He was a great Pretender to Wit and good Senfe, tho' deftitute of both: This I affirm on my own certain Knowledge of the Man; but others proceeded fome what further, whofe Cenfure I fhall fubmit to the candid Reader. They faid that he was a Coward and had broke off the Point of his Sword one Day under a Pretence of fharpening it; but thofe Gentlemen may be pleas'd to confider, that a *Cat* (whofe Form *Fribbigghe*, for that was the Creature's Name) ufurp'd, does fometimes, force its Nails into a Poft in order to make them fharper, tho' it may by chance
meet

meet with one fomewhat too hard to be pierc'd, and break a Nail in the Experiment; why then might not *Fribbiggbo* run his Sword into a Beam, for none are pofitive as to the Manner of breaking it, and if the Blade prov'd bad, with a fafe Confcience leave a Bit of it in the Wood; or elfe he might defignedly break it to prevent Murder, fince he was often affronted? Others reported that he was a Fool, and had given out that he had kick'd a Gentleman, who it was believ'd had kick'd him, fince he always fhunn'd him; and that he boafted of Favours receiv'd from a Lady, who upon his Second Vifit had forbid him her Houfe. But what he hated moft of all to be told of was, the laying out of 3 *s.* and 7 *d.* which was all that he had at a certain Time: He gave 3 *s.* 3 *d.* to Chairmen on a dry Day, and after buying Snuff with 3 Pence more, referv'd but a fingle Penny for his Supper; when it unfortunately happen'd that he was oblig'd to Sup in his own Room. He never met with fo good Succefs in any Amour as he did in this I am fpeaking of, for he had often patiently born a Beating for his Impudence, which he call'd Gallantry, and began to be tir'd of the *Lap-dog*, becaufe he had met with fo little difficulty in his Addreffes, and valu'd her as he did all others chiefly for her Fortune. The *Lap-Dog* which was fo much taken Notice of in the *Moon*, wou'd not I am certain obtain the fame Character in *Dublin*: I rather think that fhe wou'd pafs for an accomplifh'd Lady; and that every Mathematical Figure which fhe would publifh in her Head-cloaths would be induftrioufly taken notice of, and fet forth in many different Editions. If I begin with her Motion, it was neither Natural or Eafy, for if it were, it wou'd be always the fame, and fhe wou'd not be fo choice of it. I have feen her in many different ways of paffing along a Walk; fuch as Ambling, Pacing, Trotting, and fometimes Running, and often in a *Je ne fcay quoy* Manner that was a Compound of feveral of the foremention'd: And have been told that when fhe has had has Viſitors to excuſe her, ſhe has call'd a Servant to reach her the Poaker from the other Side of the Fire. At all publick Places, ſhe only minded the various Appearances which others made; perhaps it may be hence concluded, that ſhe was a Lady of good Senſe and one that obſerv'd Mankind, to make her own Conduct the more Regular: But I aſſure you that ſhe only minded the Outſide, and could not ſmell a Beaux Brain's, for the Eſſence in his Wig, or diſcover a groveling Soul in a Brocade Waſtcoat; and People that did not much care for her, were wont to ſay that it was a Maxim with her, that much Powder on a Beaux Shoulders ſignified much Senſe; and ſmart Repartee, was denoted by an Hat, if I may ſo call it, made to be carried under the Arm. Yet this I may venture to ſay in her Praiſe, that ſhe always minded one thing in publick Places, and that was the Dreſs of others, which ſhe cou'd give a better Account of when ſhe came Home than of any thing that was ſaid; which will be an Argument of her good Judgment as long as a Philoſopher is held preferable to a Verbaliſt, or Obſervations on Subſtances better than Obſervations on Words.

  Her uncommon Character I confeſs, made me once turn *Fribbigghe's* Rival and pay her a Viſit under the Pretence of Courtſhip. I am juſtly ſenſible how much I expoſe my ſelf, in putting my ſelf in competition with ſuch a contemptible Animal as a Beaux, who has nothing but his being a Beaux to recommend him: But why may I not be allow'd this Liberty, as well as ſome of my Countrymen are allow'd to go to *Bawdy-Houſes* for Speculation. When I came to her Apartment I was introduc'd by her Waiting-Maid with much Ceremony, and deſir'd to ſit down directly oppoſite to her, I ſuppoſe that ſhe might view me the Better. But I cou'd ſoon perceive that ſhe did not like me, becauſe I made no gaudy Appearance: And I believe ſhe took me for a Fool, for ſhe ask'd me half a Dozen impertinent Queſtions before I got leave to make her an Anſwer to one of them; among the reſt, ſhe ask'd me what a Clock it was, tho' there was a Clock in the

Room;

Room; and she was seated more conveniently for looking at it than I was; she ask'd me besides, whether I had heard of a Duel that was fought the Night before, which unless I had been entirely Deaf I cou'd not but have heard of as I pass'd along the Streets, for the *News-boys* were very loud in proclaiming it. I told her Ladyship, that from the Moment that I had seen her, I became incapable of observing the most common Occurrences, being wholly taken up in contemplating her Charms. Here she began to look at me with a more pleasant Countenance, which encourag'd me to proceed.

I call'd to mind all the eloquent Jargon I had ever heard or cou'd think of, and resolv'd that Nonsense shou'd pass for Wit with my now adorable *Blmmst*; since I was persuaded that her Understanding was much about the same Size with that of most of our *Irish* Ladies, who never begin to believe that a Man loves them till he has told them such Lies as would startle any but themselves. I swore that my Body was like a Bundle of Matches, which was fir'd by the Lightning of her Eyes, and earnestly pray'd that a gentle Breeze of her Pity wou'd vouchsafe to cool my glowing Heart. Thou *Primrose* of Perfection, said I, were a Demiculverin let off within my Belly, it cou'd not discompose my Frame, more than a Frown from thine awful Brow. Alas! How often have I strove to rid my self of this hated load of Life, since the Magnet of my Soul holds its repelling end to me; but the cruel Fates deny me the Happiness of dying yet, especially in the Manner I wou'd chuse; I thought to steal from this unpleasant World: For what can delight me, when I do not enjoy what I most ardently wish for? I thought to entomb my self in the River, and assist the God of it with my Tears to supply his Urn. But my Flame was so great, so far beyond what can be imagin'd, that I made a greater Noise in my plunge, than the *Sun* does when he dips in the Straights of *Gibraltar*. The affrighted Fishes roar'd, the G*o*d frown'd, and the Nymphs

Nymphs threw me on the Bank again. I next attempted to swing by the Neck in my Garters; Fool that I was, to think that they'cou'd withstand the Fire that rag'd within me! They were soon consum'd, and I left almost in despair of dying; never were you, my Fairer than the fairest, more griev'd for the breaking of a Necklace: Yet I had a Sword, and resolv'd to make a new Passage for my Sighs, and wound this Heart of mine, which gave me such Uneasiness; but here my Attempt was vain, my Blade was melted, and my Fingers burn'd, for the Heat of my Breast exceeded that of the Sun-beams collected in many Glasses. How great was then the Anguish of my Mind? I rav'd and fann'd my Flame by repeating *Blmmst*. Then my good Genius appear'd, and bid me be comforted, and said, your Goddess's Heart is not made of Steel; she will consider your deplorable Condition, and as you deserve, reward you. 'Twas this embolden'd me to approach you, and made me hope, since I knew my own Sincerity, that I shou'd not be despis'd.

The Effect which this rapturous Bombast had on her, is almost incredible; she presented her Hand to me to kiss, and told me that she pitied my Sufferings; but I mistook her Meaning, and grasping it with one of my Hands, made bold to kiss her Lips; she seem'd a little angry at my Rudeness, but was pacify'd by my swearing that her Breath was sweeter than the Breeze which wantons in Amaranthine Bowers. I then repeated my Caresses with little difficulty, and persuaded her that I was all over Love, and she all over Charms. But *Fribbigghe*'s unlucky Stars sent him into the Room just as we were in a strict Embrace. It seems that she had lately permitted him to enter her Apartment without sending first to know whether she was pleas'd to be within or not; and this which he took for a Mark of her special Favour, prov'd his Disgrace. After he came into the Room, he stood for some time without Speech or Motion, and like a religious Man that is loth to believe his Eyes, often rubb'd them. *Blmmst*, who

who was ready enough to find Faults where there were none, was a little confounded at the Sight of *Fribbigbe*; but since I had sworn that I lov'd and suffer'd so much, she thought I absolv'd her from her Promises, and that *Fribbiggbe* was to be discarded: She took the Hint from his rubbing his Eyes, and told him that she believ'd he was not right awake; or else he wou'd not have the Impudence to come into the Chamber of one that shou'd command his Esteem, without first knowing whether his Visit was seasonable; and told him that for that Time she wou'd pardon him; but begg'd of him to be more discreet for the future. As great a Fool as he was, he cou'd not but perceive that he was ill us'd, and tho' he did not love her, yet his little Soul cou'd not bear to see her in the Arms of another: What, Madam, said he, is it thus that I am slighted? Are all my Sufferings and your Vows so soon forgotten? And have I seen you in the Arms of one whom of all living I shou'd never suspect for a Rival? But Madam you are fond of Rarities, or else you cou'd never leave me for such a Person. Here I was going to reply, but she prevented me, and told him that I was more than I appear'd to be; but for some Reasons which he shou'd never be acquainted with, had chosen that Dress, and desir'd him to be cautious in speaking of me. Madam, said he, I shall never think well of any that regard you, since you have blam'd me for what I have done with your Permission. Then turning to me, he told me that he wou'd remember me, and would be glad to see me in the Park at six that Evening. I assur'd him, that I shou'd be very sorry that he shou'd forget me, and as he was going down Stairs, lent him two or three Kicks for a Token to put him in mind of me. He was so much enrag'd, that he seem'd not to take notice of them, but walk'd off in some Disorder.

CHAP.

CHAP. V.

Containing an Account of Blmmſſ's *inviting him to drink Tea with her. A philoſophical Account of the Effects of* Tea, *with its firſt Riſe. His Departure from* Blmmſl; *and his Uſage towards* Fribbigghe.

AS ſoon as he was gone, *Blmmſl* invited me to drink *Tea* with her, over which ſhe oblig'd me in taking poor *Fribbigghe* to pieces. Then ſhe gave me the private Characters of all the beautiful Ladies in Town; but amongſt them all, there was not one that got a good Word; and as the *Tea* Leaves began to ſpread themſelves, ſo ſhe began to diſcover her Mind, 'till I became acquainted with all her Secrets. I have ſince enquir'd of many ingenious Gentlemen, to find out the true Cauſe of Ladies venting their Scandal over *Tea*; ſome of whoſe Opinions, with their leave, I ſhall ſet down.

One told me that Sympathy was the Cauſe of it; for, ſaid he, we may obſerve that the hot Water has the ſame Effect upon the *Tea* Leaves, that it has upon a Lady, for they both diſcover what was not ſeen before, upon taking it; whence he inferr'd, that a Woman's Soul was moſt like a *Tea* Leaf, of any thing it cou'd be compar'd to, becauſe it is ſo eaſily oblig'd to diſcover its Secrets. But I objected that Sympathy was exploded, and 'till he cou'd prove that the Soul of a Woman is ſurrounded by the hot Water upon drinking it, as *Tea* Leaves are in the Pot, his Similitude would not be juſt; which if he undertook to prove, he muſt inevitably place a Lady's Soul in ſome part of her Belly; but I adviſ'd him to take care how he aſſerted ſuch a thing, ſince thereby he might probably incur the Diſpleaſure of the whole Sex.

Another ſaid, ſince by the help of *Microſcopes*, we have diſcover'd certain Eminences upon Leaves, and certain Animals creeping, nay, running among them, as wild Beafts do in a Forreft, it is probable that thofe Animals, upon drying of a *Tea* Leaf, are dried too, and become hard, and are feemingly dead, as Swallows are in Winter; but when they are put into hot Water, they come to life again, and being taken along with the Water into a Lady's Mouth, they irritate the Nerves of her Tongue, and caufe fome Uneafinefs in that Member, which makes it then fo apt to defame others. He then defir'd me to confider the Finenefs of a Lady's Body, and how apt we are to give ill Language when we are vex'd. He added, that the Water might fometimes be fo hot, as to kill thofe Animals, which he took for a Reafon why fometimes a Pot of *Tea* might be drank without Scandal. A third was of Opinion, that it was the Voices of thofe Animals being fcalded with the hot Water, which we took for Scandal, tho' it was not, and defir'd me to confider how apt we were to be deceiv'd in many things, and why not in this? I muft confefs, that thefe Gentlemen have learnedly accounted for it, but not to my Satisfaction: For granting that there were fuch Animals upon Leaves, why do not thofe upon *Tobacco* produce the fame Effect, or why may we not hear thofe upon *Tea* Leaves roar before they get into a Lady's Mouth? Surely none wou'd be fo unmannerly as to blame a Lady for the crying of an Animal fo hard to be feen.

But the beft Account I cou'd meet with, is founded upon the Relation which is given by the Natives of the Country where *Tea* grows; they fay that this Plant was at firft held in no more Efteem than common Bufhes, and that the Leaves of it were never us'd, if they were us'd at all, but as Saw-duft or Chaff, 'till it happen'd once that a certain Animal among them, remarkable for its Pride and Ill-nature, came to fhelter it felf from the Heat of the Sun under this Shrub (they call the Animal *Namow*) where, as it lay a long Time fecur'd from the Heat, it had an Inclination to put forth its Excrement; or to exprefs the Matter more cleanly, to untruſs a Point, and thought no place ſo proper for it as that where it had been reſted. (This is mention'd as an Inſtance of that Creature's Ingratitude to its Benefactor.) In ſhort, it left ſomething at the Root of the Tree which did not ſmell very pleaſant in the Noſes of them who liv'd at that time. It had a ſtrange Effect alſo upon the Tree, for it made it retain its Smell, and inſtead of not affecting Peoples Noſes at all, affect them in a very diſagreeable manner; ſo that they made as little uſe of it for a long time after, as they do of *Hemlock* in *Ireland*: But ſucceeding Ages differ'd very much from their Forefathers; for it happen'd that a Lady, famous for her great Knowledge of the Virtues of Plants, (I am heartily ſorry I cannot remember her Name) took ſome of the Leaves of this Tree, and boil'd them to find out their Qualities, and after much Study aſſur'd her female Friends, that thoſe Leaves were very wholeſome, and that Water in which they were boil'd, contributed much to the dilating the urinary Paſſages, and by that means wou'd keep them from the Stone or Gravel; but the diſagreeable Smell and Taſte of 'em might be corrected by Ingredients fit to pleaſe thoſe Senſes which the *Tea* Leaves offended. Her Advice was follow'd by thoſe ſhe had any Influence on, and they choſe *Tea* Water for their Breakfaſt; but they took ſo much of it at ſeveral times in the Day, and put ſo much Sugar in it, that they began to be troubled with Diſeaſes which they might have been free from, had they never changed their Diet. But the Lady who recommended it to 'em, cou'd not bear that her Counſel ſhou'd be neglected, and at laſt perſuaded 'em that it had no diſagreeable Taſte or Smell at all, and ought to be taken with but little or no Sugar, if they intended it ſhou'd do 'em any good. They were eaſily inclin'd to believe her, ſince they were already great Admirers of ſeveral ſtinking Things, and valu'd 'em for ſtinking, ſuch as Cream-Cheeſes, Veniſon, &c. ſo that in a ſhort Time from a few, the Folly became epidemical.

This

This is an Account of the first Use of Tea, as it is now among the Ladies; but to give a Reason for the Scandal which attends it, must be the next Thing I shall mention.

I have already observ'd to you, that the Animal which gave this Tree its Qualities, was proud and Ill-natur'd; and it is very probable, if it could speak, that Defamation would attend such an evil Disposition; and since neither the Animal nor the Tree were endued with Speech, and that the Seeds of Defamation, as we may reasonably suppose, were transmitted from the one to the other, inasmuch as a bad Temper often depends chiefly on the Habit of the Body, it follows, that a Lady must speak for both, since she can do it, lest Nature might be said to intend an Effect, and not produce it, when and where she may. The only Objection of any Moment which this Account is liable to, is, that it is very strange that so remote a Cause should operate so strongly and universally upon Ladies, and not upon Men, who have not yet degenerated into Misses. But to this I answer, that the Delicacy of a Lady's Constitution renders her more capable of being influenc'd by a weak and remote Cause than a Man is; for surely there is a Difference between the Dirt which they are made of, and the Dirt of which the rest of Mankind is form'd, or else they would never take so much upon them. But to return whence I digress'd: I sat with *Blimnst* till it was near the Time that I was to meet *Fribbigghe* at. I was very glad that I was so near my Delivery; for I confess that I was heartily tir'd with playing the Hypocrite so long. I left her, seemingly, as much concerned as she was, and walk'd towards the Park, reflecting on her strange Behaviour and monstrous Credulity: I was surpriz'd to think that I had gain'd her Affections so much at the first Visit, when others had spent some Lunar Years in their Ad-

E dresses

dreſſes to her, without being favour'd with any thing that might give them Hopes. I could attribute my good Succeſs to nothing, but that I had hit the critical Minute, ſo much talk'd of in *Ireland*, when a Woman gives her Conſent.

I was no ſooner come to the Park, but two or three of my Acquaintance, told me that *Fribbigghe* had been there a long Time before, expecting me to fight him, and was reſolv'd to poſt me for a Coward for not meeting him. I aſſur'd them I was come ſooner than the appointed Time, and begg'd of 'em to aſſiſt me in looking for him, that I might uſe him as he deſerv'd. After we had ſpent ſome Time in looking for him; we were inform'd that he went with ſome Ladies to walk in a Green adjacent to the Town; thither we went and found him; but I am confident that he would have given any Conſideration to be remov'd ſome Miles from me when he ſaw me. He ſeem'd very earneſt in Diſcourſe with the Ladies, and wou'd fain not take Notice of me; but I call'd to him ſo loud, that he could not but hear me: Upon which he turn'd, and trembled. I call'd him aſide; though I muſt own it was a little rude to take him from the Ladies; yet I conceiv'd ſo ill of them all, upon *Blmmſt*'s Account, that I have never ſince paid them ſo much Reſpect as I did before. Upon telling him of ſome Truths, for which he ſaw I had Vouchers, he began to put them off with a Joke, and told me he would always eſteem me as a particular Friend, ſince, he aſſur'd me, that I had ſomething very engaging in my Countenance. The Offer he made me of his Friendſhip was as provoking to me, as any Thing he could have ſaid to me. I told him that I could not be by any Means perſuaded to keep ſuch a Fool, as I was ſure he was, Company, and that I was reſolv'd to make him as ridiculous as I could. I then pull'd off his Wig, and ſhook all the Powder in it upon his

Cloaths,

Cloaths, whilſt he was asking me all the while, whether that was Uſage for a Gentleman, and was telling thoſe that flock'd about us how much his Cloaths, which I had ſpoil'd, had coſt him. I confeſs'd that the Uſage I had given him was not at all fit for a Gentleman; and ſince he was ſo much troubled about his Cloaths, I would vex him the more. I took him accordingly, and led him to a Ditch full of Water, where I toſs'd him in as gently as poſſible. There I left him to be laugh'd at by the Crowd, which was very merry at his Expence.

CHAP. VI.

Containing an Account of his Obſervations on the Cuſtoms, Manners, and Religion of the People of the Moon.

THE next Day I intended to ſpend in obſerving the Cuſtoms, Manners, and Religion of the People: I had choſen that Day becauſe it was the Anniverſary of the King's Nativity. *Tckbrſſ* had promiſed to accompany me, and lay the Truth before me, where I ſhould happen to doubt, or miſunderſtand any Thing we ſhould ſee: Accordingly we ſet out about Ten in the Morning, intending to go to a Place of Worſhip not very far diſtant from my Lodging: We were no ſooner got into the Street, than I heard the moſt confuſ'd and deafening Noiſe that ever reach'd my Ears. It conſtantly increaſ'd, and I thought ſometimes that I heard articulate Sounds: I could not but expreſs my Fear and Amazement; for I believ'd it ſupernatural, and that for the Sins of the People God had ſuffer'd them to be plagu'd in that Manner. But upon Enquiry, I found that it was by this Means they deſign'd to perſuade their Monarch that they were joyful for his Nativity,

Nativity, and well affected to his Government, yet I could not imagine by what it was caus'd; for it was more loud and shrill than any Sound of Bells I had ever heard in *Ireland*. I was inform'd that they had no Bells in the Moon; and to supply that Defect, they, upon Days of Rejoicing, hir'd certain Persons, fit for nothing else, to foment Quarrels between Women, so as that they might scold: Those Women were immediately carried to the Tops of Steeples, where they were furnish'd with Liquors to enflame their Rage, and had those Fomenters standing by them, to take care that each should return the ill Language she receiv'd, tho' they were ready enough of themselves to continue their loud Reproaches; and that those scolding Women were what made such an horrible Din. *Tckbrff* further told me, that this Custom of putting the scolding Women upon the Tops of Steeples, had made them, for some Years, past keep their Tongues in more Subjection than they were wont to do, which oblig'd 'em to hire Persons to make them alarm the Kingdom. I could not but wish that all the loud-tongu'd Women in mine own Country were transported to the *Moon*, till I consider'd, that by that Means poor *Ireland* would find a great Scarcity of Wives, and perhaps in one Age be wholly uninhabited. I have since thought that Philosophers upon Earth might mistake this Noise in the *Moon* for Musick, which made them first talk of the Musick of the Spheres.

Before I had Time to reflect upon what I had heard, we met with a Company of Beasts, among whom we could not discover the least Remains of Humanity, except in one, who had preserv'd his Nose; but I believe that was owing to his not taking Snuff; for I did not see him take a Pinch during our Conference, as the rest did. Those were Persons, who to shew how ready they were to serve

their

[37]

their King, had made themselves so drunk, that they forgot how to help themselves; they rail'd at all that did not stagger, and pronounced them disaffected Persons. A Swine that happen'd to be next to me, had like to have thrown me down with a Reel which he took, tho' I happily kept myself from falling: The rest seeing me run from him, thought I had assaulted him, and sent an Hero to beat me for it. He came up to me, and aim'd a furious Blow at my *Cerebellum*; I avoided it, and he fell into the Gutter; the Company shouted as if they had obtain'd a Victory, while we made what Haste we could from them. How much better, said *Tolbrsy*, when we were got from them, would those Persons prove their Loyalty, if upon this Day each would apply with remarkable Industry to that which might make him useful in the Commonwealth, rather than, by wishing Health to our Sovereign, impair their own, and by utterly extinguishing their little Reason, if they had any left, render themselves so contemptible to all that are not in the same Condition?

He had just ended this Reflection when we enter'd the *Temple*. I had not, indeed, as yet enquir'd into the Belief of the Congregation I was now going to join with, which may seem a little strange at first Sight to any one who considers what a vast Number of Books a Man of my Parts might have devour'd since my Arrival; some of which ought to have taught me this Lesson, that when a Man willingly does he knows not what, he may be guilty of he knows not what: But this could not possibly be my Case; for I told you before, and you must take my Word for it, that I was a perfect Master of their Language; so that I could not be guilty of I know not what, in assenting to what I did not understand; besides, I was resolv'd for the present barely to observe what I saw, without any more Emotion

of

of Mind than if it had been my Fate to be a Statue for the Ornament of that Place. But here I will give the Reader some Account of the Belief of this Sect, which was the most numerous of any in the *Moon*. They were the Followers of the *Pythagorean* Doctrine; and whatever they practis'd, they confidently affirmed that they had his express Command for, or else they made him to mean Things as they serv'd their Interests, by giving his Thoughts a new Turn, and by making their Comments upon his Writings as authentick as what they were design'd to explain. Here it may be ask'd, how *Pythagoras* ever got into the *Moon*? But I think it may be ask'd with greater Propriety, how he ever got to the Earth? For by examining the Records in both Places, it will be found, that the first Body which he animated was in the *Moon*, and was the Body of a Corn-Cutter; He lived very poorly in that State for many Years, till he was set at Liberty by a Disease contracted by smelling stinking Toes. The next which he enter'd into was that of a Citizen, but in a short Time was scolded out of that Tenement by his Wife. He serv'd an Apprenticeship of five Years immediately after in the Shape of a Coach-Horse to a Lady of Quality, who kill'd him with going a-Visiting. He was then transform'd into a Spider, a Bailiff, an Whore, an Emperor, an Hangman, a Greyhound, a Kitchen-Wench, a Lawyer, a Fox, and a Mad-Man. In this last Station he set up for a Philosopher, and call'd himself *Pythagoras*. He was not always stark mad, but had his Intervals of right Reason; in which he gain'd so much upon his Hearers, that at length they took his mad Fits for nothing but surprising Flights of his Imagination. He gain'd so much Credit in a little Time, that the greatest Absurdities confirmed by an *Ipse Dixit*, were thought to be sufficiently

ently demonstrated. He us'd to harangue the People upon the Fallibility of their Senses; and by deceiving them sometimes with *Legerdemain*, in which he was very expert, brought them to believe, that their Senses, being rightly dispos'd, the Object at a proper Distance, and in a proper Medium, cou'd, and often did deceive 'em. So that if a Man caught him in Bed with his Wife, he wou'd before he got up deny the Fact, and then learnedly prove, that the Cuckold was either asleep, or somewhere else at the same Time; or else that himself was not *Pythagoras*, but the Man of the House; or else, if he was hard put to it, that he was both. Shou'd the poor Man, notwithstanding all this, still believe his Senses, and that he was a Cuckold, he would indict him for what he had said; and in case of Obstinacy (so great was his Power) put him to Death. He gave out that he had a Golden Thigh, which the common People understood literally; but the wiser Sort have found out, that he meant only that one of his Breeches Pockets was constantly full of that Metal; whence his Followers, in Imitation of him, spare no Pains to get it; and some have been so cunning as to pretend they never use any Money, that they might the more easily keep all they got, and be furnish'd with Necessaries *gratis*. He order'd his Followers to abstain from all kind of Flesh, and from Beans: What his Design cou'd be in the first, is thought to be only a Pretext to his Knavery, to deceive the People, by the seeming Austerity of his Morals. But his Followers could not play the Hypocrites so well, they could not abstain from Flesh altogether, wherefore they allow'd themselves the Use of it, except at some certain Times, when they thought Fish might be acceptable thro' Variety. Some think that by the Word *Fish* he understands all Animals; but this they reject,

and

and for a Reason, refer you to their own Comment upon that Paffage, where they have rendered it Land Animals. *Pythagoras* himfelf has given us a Reafon for abftaining from Beans, *viz.* becaufe they are like Mens Tefticles. He did not know but that a Man's Tefticle had as good a Relifh as a Bean, which if it fhould ever be found out, might occafion the Caftration of fome of his Followers, and by that means render them incapable of Pleafures which it was his Defire they fhould enjoy, and he forefaw they wou'd be much addicted to. By thefe few Inftances, the reft may be guefs'd at, and known, as well as *Hercules* by his Foot.

Pythagoras had certainly an odd Way of thinking; but his Succeffors have found out Things that he never dream'd of. He taught, that when the Soul leaves a Body, it becomes happy or miferable, according to the Circumftances of the next Body that receives it; But his Succeffors teach, that it is in their Power to continue their Kindnefs to their Friends, after their Separation from a Body; and to that End, have invefted certain Perfons with Power to know what becomes of others, and make their Sufferings have a fpeedy End; for they hold for their own Intereft, that their Friends are miferable after leaving the Body they were laft in, and will continue to be fo till they affift them. This plainly fhews, that *Pythagoras* was better natur'd than his Succeffors, who make their Gain of Peoples Mifery, which, tho' imaginary, wou'd become real, were it in their Power to make it fo. He indeed attributed much to Numbers, and was a great Proficient in the Mathematicks; but they fupport a bad Caufe by the Numbers that adhere to it: Whence it will follow, that he that cheats half the World, is an honefter Man than him that cheats only a fourth Part.

They

They are great Admirers of right Angles, and wou'd fain make it appear, that right Angles alone have more Efficacy than any other Figures that can be imagin'd; yet they cannot prove that *Pythagoras* was of that Opinion. In fine, they are so much taken up in admiring their Instructor, that they forget his Instructions. He orders them to worship the Gods; but they will worship him, or any Body else, as they please; nay, sometimes you may find them in so good an Humour, that they won't scruple to pay Divine Worship to a rotten Post.

Pythag or as liv'd in great Repute for a long Time; and having sufficiently establish'd his Doctrine, he shifted his Dwelling, and became a Foot-Soldier; but was oblig'd to forsake that Body by drinking Brandy: He had no sooner left the Army, but he was oblig'd to animate an Oyster, where he was allow'd the Liberty of Thinking, and compos'd his *Aurea Carmina*. He was soon taken up, and devour'd by a young Lady, who immediately became so Learned, that there was no enduring her. Many pursue him thro' several other Bodies; but their Accounts have so little to support 'em, that I rather chose to omit them, than set down any Thing but that which is founded upon the best Authority.

I shou'd now proceed to what I saw in the Temple; but as all what I saw was mysterious, and Mysteries are not to be divulg'd, I must be excus'd for not discovering what I saw. When the Crowd was gone, *Tckrff* took me to see the Rarities of the Place, and prevail'd upon one that belong'd to it, to shew them to us. We were led into a large Room full of Wonders; to recount all which, would fill a large Volume, yet I will set down a few which I remember above others. The first Thing he shewed us was a Frying-Pan with but one Handle, which was all the Houshold Goods of a certain famous *Pythagorean*. The next was a large Cup with two Handles; which was look'd upon as preternatural in the Age it was made, with an Inscription to this Purpose, *He is a Beast that drinks more at one Time, than he can lift with one Hand.* A small Bundle of Birch, consisting of eight Twigs and an half, with which a great Man was wont to keep down proud Flesh. A Gallipot, in which was to be seen some of the Brimstone which *Pythagoras* himself us'd to cure himself of the Itch: This is shewn to prove the Antiquity of that Distemper in the Northern Parts, where *Pythagoras* for a while resided. A three-legged Stool; which retain'd so much Virtue from the Person who us'd to sit upon it, that it wou'd cure Jealousy: The jealous Person was to sit upon this Stool three Hours, during which Time he was to believe firmly that his Consort was virtuous. An Horn, to drink out of, which would prevent Cuckoldom. A Stone which had been laugh'd at for speaking Nonsense, and had been ever since silent. These are a few of the surprising Things which I saw. When we had view'd them all, and were going away, the good Man who had shew'd them to us, took as much Water out of a Bason, that stood by the Door, as he cou'd hold in his Hand, and threw it in my Face. I apprehended that it was because I had given him nothing; and tho' I was angry, I gave him something for his Trouble, and and took my Leave of those renowned *Pythagoreans*. There were many other Sects of Philosophers in the Town, who all hated the *Pythagoreans*, as being notorious Cheats; tho' the *Pythagoreans* were even with them, by cutting their Throats, as often as they found Opportunity, and look'd upon murdering those that differ'd with them in Opinion, as a meritorious Action. *Tckbrff* desir'd me to go

and

and see a Fountain which was in the Midst of the Town, and which the *Pythagoreans* had often strove in vain to stop up. It was remarkable for the Purity of its Water, and for not suffering any Dirt to settle in it. The more the *Pythagoreans* labour'd to suppress it, the more it over-flow'd, and grew daily more famous, to their Shame and Confusion. The Reason of their Hatred to it was, that it had so much Virtue, that an hearty Draught of its Water wou'd make the ablest *Pythagorean* renounce his Principles, if Obstinacy and Prejudice had not usurp'd the Seat of his Understanding. It had restor'd many to their Human Shape, and prov'd an infallible Remedy again the Griping of the Guts; where the Pain was so great, that it made People look as if they were possess'd. It was under the King's immediate Care, who, upon his Coronation, had oblig'd himself to protect it; and well did it deserve to have a Royal Patron, since it was the greatest Blessing that ever had been bestow'd upon the Kingdom. It brought Peace and Plenty wheresoever it flow'd, and guided the People in the true Road of Happiness. It had a Guard continually surrounding it, which was made firm to its Interests by drinking of it. Many times did the *Pythagoreans* hazard their Lives and Fortunes to a Man, in Hopes of destroying it, and often caus'd such an Effusion of Blood upon its Banks, that it chang'd its Colour for a Time, tho' it never cou'd be corrupted. The Bodies of those that died in the Defence of it, were gently carried down the Stream that issued from it into a remote Country, where they receiv'd new Life, and enjoy'd endless Happiness.

Many had desir'd to draw off its Water into their own Grounds; and to that End, had secretly dug Passages under the Earth, thinking that the Fountain wou'd pour its Water into them, and by that

F 2 Means

Means they would become sole Masters of all its Benefits: But they were all disappointed; for in their Way they constantly met with some Fountain, which they mistook for the true one; and were so blinded with their own Conceits, that they could not see that they had not come near the Fountain which they coveted, and that the Water which they had got, had none of those good Qualities which made the other so desirable. Had they been content to enjoy its Benefits in common, it was sufficient to satisfy them all, let them be never so greedy: Yet each obstinately maintain'd that he was in the right; and to gain the Fountain he had found the more Repute, cry'd down the true one. I will not take upon me to say that all the Philosophers which we had upon Earth were first in the *Moon*, tho' I have been often tempted to believe it, from the Conformity of the Opinion of several earthly Philosophers to those religious Sects in the *Moon*; for I observ'd that there were *Platonicks* and *Cynicks* there: The former affected magical Transports, and pretended that they kept a Courier constantly to bring them Intelligence from Heaven: The latter differ'd from them in this, that they admir'd an extraordinary Simplicity in their Garb, which, tho' different from that of other People, was as fashionable as theirs; since it is Custom alone that alters Fashions, and they had nearly stuck to one Fashion for many Years. They were the most unmannerly People in the *Moon*, and were so politick, that they had persuaded many that they were in earnest, and that to be virtuous was to be unmannerly, and that we cannot be brought to Heaven with an Equipage. It is surprizing to reflect upon what a Multitude is misled, when all are allow'd to approach the sacred Fountain, and Persons appointed to take Care that those who come to drink observe Rules prescrib'd to them.

CHAP.

CHAP. VII.

Containing an Account of his going to a Coffee-House; *what he observ'd and heard there. His Design to go to a* Play-House. *An Account of what* Tckbrff *said to him before they went thither; what he observ'd and heard there; with a natural Account for a Man's becoming a Critick.*

THE next Thing I went to see was a *Coffee-House*, where we intended to trifle away our Time till the *Play-House* was open: We went thither, and took our Seats at a long Table, with a Design to settle the Affairs of the Nation; for I must confess, that upon my entering the *Coffee-House* I found myself insensibly turn Politician, and become more concern'd to find out the Designs of One a thousand Miles distant from me, than I was about returning to mine own Country, tho' I am sure that my own Affairs were but in a very bad State when I left it.

I had just lighted my Pipe, and read a Paragraph of a Paper, in quest of Truth, where I was certain that there was an hundred to one against my finding it, when my Thoughts were turned another Way by a Company that seated themselves next to us. But before I inform against them, I will set down the Substance of a Fragment which I met with in *Tckbrff*'s Library. It was a philosophical Account of Mens meddling with Affairs that do not belong to them, when they enter *Coffee-Houses*. It first prov'd that Coffee was of an hot and dry Nature, and took it for granted that it was much us'd in Houses that

took

took their Names from it ; as likewife that the finer Parts of the *Coffee* were floating in the Air which fill'd thofe Houfes. This was prov'd, if any doubted it, by People's fmelling the *Coffee* upon Entrance. It next enquir'd into the Nature of Politicks, and of the ordinary Difcourfe of *Coffee-Houfes*; both which it prov'd to be of an hot and dry Conftitution ; whence 'twas inferr'd, that *Coffee* was the Caufe of thofe Difcourfes from their Likenefs. It was further hinted, that this Hypothefis of the *Coffee* floating in the Air, might account for thofe People's Behaviour who were not able to purchafe a Difh of *Coffee*, fince it is fuppos'd that they are all endued with the Senfe of Smelling, and that every Body knows how near the Brain, the Seat of all Senfation, the Nofe is plac'd.

The Company juft mention'd confifting of an He-Goat, an Hedgehog, and a Porcupine, the Matter in Debate was, whether there was any fuch Thing as Love ; and whether any Perfons ever kill'd themfelves for Love. The Goat, by whofe Looks and Difcourfe I difcover'd that he was married, denied both the Queftions, and faid, That though Hiftory furnifhed us with many Inftances of People that run into another World to look for a Miftrefs, yet a reafonable Man is not obliged to believe one Word of it, when he can affign another Caufe for their fo fudden Departure ; as, that a Man may have his Pockets pick'd by a Female, and hang himfelf for the Lofs of his Money, as many have done ; or elfe, by watching for Entrance at a Back-Door, catch Cold, and fpit Blood, whence filly People might think his Throat was cut ; or, if a Man that was going to Sea had a Mind to learn to fwim with his Cloaths on, if he fhould chance to be drown'd in learning, why, forfooth, he was in Love. He then argued like a Philofopher, and a married one too, from his own Experience, that there was no fuch Thing as Love ; but what was fo call'd, might be refolv'd into a Defire

fire of Money, Intereſt, Eaſe, or ſome ſuch Principles of our Actions; and further, defir'd his Companions to conſider how heartily the moſt profeſs'd and ardent Lovers hated one another in the End of their Acquaintance. The Hedgehog affirm'd, that there was ſuch a Thing as Love, tho' not in the ſtricteſt Senſe, that is, that one Perſon alone can be the Object of the Defires of another; and argued likewiſe from Experience, that he had a Dozen Miſtreſſes at one Time, not one of which he lov'd above another: But it was his throwing down Apples in an Orchard, and then rolling himſelf among them, to make them ſtick to his Sides, that firſt made him be of this Opinion. The Porcupine was of his Opinion, with a Diſtinction, that is, that one may love a great many, tho' not in the ſame inſtant; and that if a Man ſhould chance to meet two or three of his Beloved in one Place, and at one Time, he muſt love none of them for that Time, becauſe his Love is divided, tho' he could murder himſelf for any one of them, conſider'd ſeparately from the reſt; and for Proof of this he ſwore, that he would kill himſelf the next Day, if the firſt of his Charmers which he met did not uſe him kindly. He then call'd for a Diſh of *Coffee*, and ſhot a Quill at the Wench who brought it to him; and, to confirm his Doctrine, lov'd her for half a Night, till her Maſter was getting up. The Clock ſtruck, and the learned Aſſembly, for Reaſons beſt known to themſelves, departed. I am not well able to determine the Cauſe of this Company's talking of Love in a *Coffee-Houſe*, unleſs it be that they were tir'd with Politicks, and, for Relaxation of their Minds, deſign'd to diſcourſe of a ſofter Subject. As ſoon as they were gone, we began to think of the *Play-Houſe*, and *Tckbrff* told me, that it would be proper to go thither early, that we might get a convenient Seat; for he believ'd that the Houſe would

would be much crowded that Night; and by this, said he, a Man may judge of the People's Inclinations. The Play which is to be acted to Night is one that extenuates Vice without condemning it, and that contains all the false Arguments that can be brought in Defence of Gallantry, which, if examin'd, will prove to be nothing less than fashionable Wickedness. The House is always full when Honesty is brought on the Stage to be laugh'd at, or when the shining Character in the Play be the Character of an harden'd Villain, that calls himself a fine Gentleman. This People forgets how Glory, and the Character of a fine Gentleman, was acquir'd of old. 'Twas Virtue, and a Love for their King and Country, that made the Gentleman. But now the Learning of the Age has turn'd the Dust of a Campaign into sweet Powder; and those which should weild a Sword, have now learn'd the fashionable Airs of managing a Snuff-Box. The Writers of Plays well know which Way the People's Affections tend; and, to comply with their deprav'd Humour, have always introduc'd Virtue and Innocence in the utmost Distress, as if Affliction were their inseparable Attendant, whilst Vice is generally brought in in Triumph, and by a false Gloss assumes the Appearance of Virtue. This is not to change Names, but Things, even Things of the greatest Consequence. But let us hasten to the *Play-House*, where, by the Acclamations of the People, you may confirm what I have said, as well as by what you will see represented on the Stage.

We went thither accordingly, and found all that *Tckbrff* had said to be true; for the House was soon fill'd, and by good Luck we got to a Seat were we could see all that was done in the House very distinctly. But as our greatest Pleasures have their Alloy of Bitterness, it here prov'd my Case; for I had propos'd a great deal of Pleasure to myself in

seeing

seeing a Play in the *Moon*, and probably would have enjoy'd it, had I not been seated where I was; for there was an Animal that sat next to me which gave me great Uneasiness, both by his Looks and Speech. He had a most frightful and meagre Countenance; and the Sight of him made me think, that whenfoever a Poet drew the Picture of Envy, he must certainly mean an Animal of this Species. I cannot compare him to any one Brute that I saw in *Ireland*; for he was a Compound of many Brutes, tho' a Cur seem'd to constitute the greatest Part of him. It were well for Children, and Women with Child, if he were oblig'd to wear a Mask, to prevent Miscarriages, and the frightening of foolish Children out of their Wits. During the whole Time of Action, he was railing at the Poet and the Players, and for the most part found Faults where there were none; and if any Thing was said which he was forc'd to acknowledge to be good, tho' that happen'd but rarely, he would curse himself for not being able to think so well.

When the Play was over, I enquir'd of *Tchbrf* who that Person I just mention'd was. He told me that he was a Critick, or one that is never pleas'd, if he is pleas'd at all, but when he is finding out real Faults in Writings, or making new ones. He is one that is hated by, and hates all Writers: His Observations are often trifling, and foreign to the Purpose: He would not think a Month ill bestow'd in finding out the Orthography of a proper Name, or upon what Syllable of it the Accent was to be plac'd: But he has this Curse attending him, that he can raise Spirits often, which he cannot lay; and after his greatest Labours, is generally more ignorant of what he enquir'd into, than he was at the Beginning. There are many Causes assign'd for a Person's becoming of this Class: Some will have ill Nature to be the only Cause of it; and alledge, that

G it

it is vifible in every Feature of his Countenance. Others think, that ill Nature, join'd to a Senfe of his own Ignorance, is the Caufe of it; which makes him ftrive to make others appear as ignorant as he is perfuaded that he himfelf is: But to this is objected, that Criticks are very conceited, or at leaft feem fo, of their own Abilities. The moft rational Account of this is founded upon an Explication of the natural Caufe of it, by the Obfervations which were made upon the Brain of one of thofe Animals: It was obferv'd that there were many little Animals not unlike thofe found in Books, which we call Book-Worms, running about the pineal Gland. From whence the Anatomift argues thus: Since the Seat of the Soul is in the pineal Gland, becaufe it is allow'd to be wholly in the whole Body, and wholly in every Part, or, to ufe their Words, who deny the firft Pofition, that it is *Totum in toto, & totum in qualibet parte*, it follows, that thofe little Animals which inhabit the pineal Gland, muft affect the whole Soul. But ftill the Queftion is, Why thofe little Animals, by thus affecting the whole Soul, fhould make a Man a Critick?

To which I anfwer, that bad Company will fpoil any Man; and foon make him of their Principles. Now every Body allows, that it is the chief Bufinefs of thofe Animals to make Holes in all the Books they come at, never confidering whether the the Book they lite on deferves fuch Treatment, or not; and that the Soul is continually affected by thefe Animals, may be thus proved: Experience convinces us, that it is poffible for larger Animals to get into the Brain; but thofe larger Animals muft leave a fenfible Mark of their Entry, which the Book-Worms do not. But why fhould we wonder that we do not perceive the Holes by which they enter, fince we cannot perceive the Holes through which the Rays of Light pafs? And to make this

appear

[51]

the more reasonable, it is held, that those Animals are taken into the Brain when they are very young, and much about the Size of a pretty big Ray of Light, which, by the By, is a Reason why a Man does not become a great Critick of a sudden, but daily improves, as those Animals grow up, and come to a worse Use of their Faculties. The Manner of their getting into the Brain is by Attraction through the Eyes; for when the Brain is heated by intense Thinking, it is allow'd to attract more strongly than when it is cool. This Opportunity is taken hold of for their Entry along with the Rays of Light through the Coats and Humours of the Eye, till they strike upon the Optick Nerve; in which there are insensible Holes for the Passage of the Animal Spirits, through which they are attracted into the Substance of the Brain. Those little Animals wander for some Time in the Substance of the Brain, till they come to the pineal Gland, to which they are invited by its pleasant Situation. It is to no Purpose to object, that if they were attracted through the Eyes in this Manner, they might blind a Man, since the same Objection lies against the Rays of Light; or to say, that they would eat the Brain, for lack of other Food, since it is more probable that they would rather chuse to eat one another than the Brain, whose Taste is quite different from that of Paper; and that it is reasonable to suppose that their Bodies are of a Taste not unlike it, as many nice Palates have assured us, since they were first bred in Ink and Paper. Besides, they are known to breed so fast, that two are sufficient to stock a Kingdom in a short Time, provided they be Male and Female.

G 2   CHAP.

CHAP. VIII.

Containing an Account of his Dream: Its Extravagance accounted for. His being awaken'd by People dancing; with some Observations upon a Ball.

WHEN *Tckbrff* had ended this Account, I took my Leave of him, and repair'd to my Lodgings, to go to Rest, being sufficiently tir'd with the Labours of the Day; but I must not omit that I supp'd before I lay down. I had not been long in Bed before I fell into a profound Sleep, in which I had the following Dream. I do not doubt but that lying down upon a full Stomach, might, partly by the Vapours which ascended from my Stomach to my Brain, contribute something to set my Imagination to work; and if the Vapours which ascend from the Stomach to the Head affect the Imagination, I can very well account for the Extravagance, and Incoherence of my Dream, since those Vapours must consist of something compounded of the different Sorts of Things which I eat: Yet, not to beg the Question, I will confirm the Doctrine of I know not what Vapours ascending from the Stomach to the Brain, by the Testimony of every old Woman that can order a Vomit for the Head-Ach; and as those Vapours were material, that is, compos'd of Matter finely prepared, and as all Matter must have some Form, it is certain that the Parts of Matter which constituted those Vapours were of several different Forms. Now it is confess'd that those different Forms of the Parts of Matter, is the Reason of the Difference which we perceive in Bodies by tasting, tafting. Experience alfo tells us, that by mixing Bodies we may alter what we call their Tafte, or *Sapor*: Now I will leave it to any Man to judge what a ftrange Confufion of Figures there muft be in that Man's Stomach, who fupp'd as I did before he lay down: I eat of Flefh of three Kinds, with five Modifications, or, as we call it in mine own Country, Ways of putting Sauce about it, and dreffing it. I muft be excus'd for not difcovering all that I know of it, fince I apprehend that it would encourage a new Sect to minifter to the Luxury of our modern *Epicureans*: I eat of two Kinds of Fifh, with four Modifications, with other Things which were call'd Eatables, tho' I am fure I could never make a Meal of them, that had above twenty feven different Modifications, which I counted; they were very like Sweetmeats. All this confider'd, plainly proves that thofe Vapours which were bred in Confufion, could never end in Regularity and Exactnefs, efpecially if we take into the Account the Variety of Liquors which I drank at my Meal, moft of which were very volatile. Surely no Philofopher will deny that the Soul cannot be as eafily, at leaft, affected in the Head, as in the Tongue, when he confiders the Texture of both, and that the Vapours which affect the Soul in the Brain, bear the fame Proportion to that which affects the Soul in the Tongue, that the Brain does to the Tongue.

But as Dreams are often very extravagant, there muft be no great Exactnefs expected in mine: I thought that I was feated in the *Play-Houfe* of *Dublin* upon the Earth, near two Criticks, (of the fame Shape with thofe above mention'd,) before the Curtain was drawn, who were in earneft Difpute; each anfwered the Doubts which the other propos'd, by raifing new ones; and they pafs'd from one Queftion to another fo faft, that they determin'd none. The Difpute was about the Curtain: One ask'd, whether

ther the Person who made it was a *Wig* or *Tory*?
Upon the other's answering that he was a *Wig*, he
affirm'd that he was a *Tory*, and a marry'd Man
too, since the Stiches of his Wife, who had a Hand
in it, might be distinguish'd from his. The other
alledg'd, that the Difference in the Stitches proceeded from a small Prick which he gave his
Finger, and that he sow'd it by Candle Light:
The other affirm'd, that it was by Day Light, since
one might see thro' it: To which was answer'd,
that the Holes which were in it, were the Effect
of the Taylor's Negligence in pressing it with a
too hot Iron. This was obstinately deny'd; and
then both quoted the Records of the *Play-House*,
for a Proof of their contrary Opinions. At length
they became so angry, by the Opposition they met
with from each other, that they forgot what they
first contended about, and proceeded to direct Abuse.

While these two were thus abusing each other, a
Gentleman, with a very thinking Countenance, address'd himself to me, and said, You see, *Sir*, how
those Persons dispute warmly about Trifles: It is
certain, that a Philosopher may learn a good Lesson from any Thing; but these two cannot hit upon the Method of it. If a Man must choose that
Curtain for a Subject, let him take the Actors and
Audience into Consideration also. You may observe, that in the Curtain before us, there are
three remarkable Holes, if we may call that Slit
in the Middle one: The two outermost, by bare
looking at them, discover that there was some
Pains taken with them, and the Rent in the Middle, seems to be at first begun by some Body's
Fury. Now to apply: May that those whom you
see walking behind the Curtain, be justly compar'd to the learned Part of Mankind, who often
look thro' the Curtain, to observe the Behaviour

of

of the Audience, which may be compar'd to the World: The Curtain itself may be compared to Ignorance, which hinders them from seeing what they desire to see, without some Trouble; for you see that a Man must either stoop to look thro' the the outermost Holes, or else lift up the Hole to the Height of his Eyes which he comes to. These Holes are like the Works of *Aristotle* and his Correctors, which we must turn over before we are allow'd to be Part of the learned World, or, to speak more generally, like the beaten Paths of Knowledge. Men that take all upon Trust, stoop down to peep thro' the Holes: Those are mere Drudges, fit for nothing else, but to carry the Burthen of another's Knowledge: Others somewhat superior to them, disdain to stoop, without Reason, to another's Sentiments, and by a Strength of Mind, raise the Hole to their own Height, yet are too cowardly to attempt uncommon Paths. The Rent near the Middle is the Effect of a Genius far above others, and plainly shews that Art had no hand in it. For it is torn, not cut, and has rendered the Veil above it capable of being rent in the same Manner, if Art does not interpose. To this the Celebrated of all Ages came; and it may be observ'd, that the Top of the Slit does not rise higher than the tallest Person's Head that comes to it. These are the Men that find Truth by uncommon Methods, and every one that approaches it stretches, if not breaks a Thread or two: Others being plac'd in a Way where they might find one of those Holes, thro' a Stupid Carelesness, despise them all, and intend to look at the World thro' the Distance of the Threads in the first Part of the Curtain they come to. To this End they push the Curtain somewhat before them, and if they see any Thing at all, they see it very confusedly; and tho' they remove the Curtain a little forward,

yet

yet it falls back again beyond its due Situation. We may next confider thofe that come to the Sides of the Curtain ; of which fome peep, others fhew their whole Body: The former are thofe, which would obferve the World and inftruct it, without being known; the latter dare ftand its Cenfure, and fhew their Perfon to give an Authority to their Writings. The Walking of thofe behind the Curtain to and fro, may be called the Difputes which are among the Learned, each of which would fain prove the reft Block-heads, thro' a vain Conceit, that two of a Trade can never agree; but cannot all the Learned much better——Here I was awaken'd, much troubled that I had not Time to ask this vifionary Gentleman fome Queftions.

I was awakened by a Noife that was made in the next Houfe to me: I arofe immediately, as well to fee what was the Caufe of this Noife which I heard, as to commit my fleeping Conference to my Writing, fince I was very diftruftful of my Memory. When I had taken this Abftract of my Dream, (for I dare not be very pofitive in faying that I heard nothing but what I fet down) I went out to the Place where the Noife was made. I was mightily furpriz'd at my Entry, to fee fo many People making Fools of themfelves by certain Rules, and dancing themfelves into Brutes to Mufick. They called this Affembly a Ball, by a Metaphorical Expreffion; for as in a round Piece of Matter, which is ufually called a Ball, all the Parts which make up this Ball are equally fubject to all the Motions that can be given to the Ball; fo in this Affembly, every one that came into the Room was equally fubject to be made a Beaft and a Fool of. And farther, fince a Globe fet upon a Plain, as Philofophers tells us, if once moved, would move for ever, if fomething did not hinder it; fo when
thofe

[57]

thofe People have once begun to dance, if their Strength did not fail them, they would never leave off. Befides, they call themfelves a Ball, from a Cuftom which they have of forming a Circle with their Bodies, as Horfes do about a Pond, when many go to drink at once. I could not but be griev'd, to fee People applaud each other for their Imitation of Beafts, fince every Motion of theirs was defigned to imitate fome Creature which they defpifed. The Creatures which they chiefly imitated, were Ducks, Horfes, and a Pack of Dogs playing after a plentiful Meal : Their Imitation of Ducks, which was flow, and waddling, they called *Drptxje*; it may be render'd, without much Straining, a Minuet : Their Imitation of a Trooper's Horfe, when he is exercifing, may be render'd Jiggs: And their Imitation of Dogs, Country-Dances. Their Jiggs were called *Cfdmmo*, and their Country-Dances *Glghdne*. There were fome who attempted to imitate the Flying of Birds; but thofe that could raife themfelves higheft from the Ground, were moft hurted in their Fall. It is but trifling to urge, that by Dancing we learn a graceful Carriage and genteel Behaviour, fince thofe Beafts which we imitate are void of both; and Reafon alone fhould direct us in acquiring them, tho' Cuftom is now the univerfal Director : But ftill the Difficulty is to account, for this Propenfity to imitate Brutes. *Philofophers* divide the *Appetite* into rational and fenfitive; the former is peculiar to Men, the latter we have in common with Beafts: When the Rational governs, all Things are well, and we live as we ought to do : But, from the Moment that the fenfitive gets the upper Hand, we commence Brutes Now the Soul is fuppos'd to have its rational End uppermoft, when Men do the ordinary Offices of Life, which they are obliged to: But this is a grand Miftake; for the Generality of

H Men

Men eat and fleep by mere Inftinct. Befides, I never heard tell of a Medium, which the Philofophers cou'd agree to, between Man and Beaft: Hence it is probable, that in a Man's learning to become a Fool, or to dance, that by the violent and frequent Motion of his Body, he fhakes the rational End of his Soul into his Heels, which being accuftom'd to govern, and impatient of Subjection, caufes fome Uneafinefs in the lower Parts, and keeps them always in Motion. Befides, it is no great Wonder, that thofe who have the Soul of a Beaft to direct their upper Parts, fhou'd be ftrongly inclin'd to brutal Actions.

CHAP. IX.

Containing an Account of his failing under Water: The Manner of it. The Boat's fplitting againft a Rock: Their being receiv'd into a fubterraneous Cavern: Their Reception. An Account of mechanical Poetry: Sactuff's Kindnefs to them.

Hitherto I had liv'd as happily as I could expect at fuch a Diftance from mine own Country; and now I began to think ferioufly of fettling in the *Moon* for the Remainder of my Life; and after ftudying a long Time in vain, how to get back to the Earth, I concluded that it was impoffible, tho' Experience has fince convinc'd me of my Error. How often have I at Night, gaz'd at the dear Planet I was born in? Whilft it difpens'd its Light and kind Influence to the *Moon*, I would oft, with the greateft Sorrow, call upon my Friends in it, as if they cou'd hear me, or lend me any Affiftance: Then would I reflect up-
its

on its Beauty, and blame myſelf for having once thought that it was leſs glorious than other Planets. At length I reſolv'd to find Contentment in the *Moon*, which is ſo hard to be found in the Earth, and make a Choice of Neceſſity. But cruel Fortune, whoſe Power reach'd even thither, envied me this Happineſs which I propos'd to myſelf, and reſolv'd to lead me into more Dangers.

Amidſt my firm Reſolutions to decline meddling with State Affairs, and innocently enjoy my moderate Penſion, *Tckbrff* came to me, and told me he had invented ſomething worth my ſeeing. It was a Boat to ſail in under Water. I immediately ask'd how we ſhould breathe; and he told me, he had provided ſeveral Bottles full of Animal Spirits, which he had gather'd by tying thoſe Bottles to Perſons Noſes that were dying. The Boat after we had enter'd into it, and diligently ſtopp'd all the Holes to keep out the Water, was to be fill'd with thoſe Spirits, which would abundantly compenſate the want of Air. I doubted what he ſaid, till he aſſur'd me that he had already made the Experiment, and had a ſufficient Quantity of Animal Spirits for one Day's ſailing. Upon this I went with him to the Boat, which cou'd contain but three Perſons with the Bottles. We took along with us an old Mathematician, to ſteer for us; who by his Skill, cou'd ſink the Boat to any Depth requir'd. When we had enter'd the Boat, and carefully ſtopp'd every Hole which might let in the Water, *Tckbrff* open'd the Bottles, one by one, as we began to want freſh Air; and indeed they made our Reſpiration very pleaſant, for the Spirits ſoon found a Paſſage into every Part of our Bodies, and caus'd all our Members to breathe, as well as perform other Animal Functions.

The next Thing we ſet about, was to ſink the Boat; which the old Gentleman perform'd in a very wonderful Manner: He began first to demonstrate, that there was a Principle of Gravity inherent in all Matter, which made it tend to the Center. *Tckbrff*, who knew the Part he was to act, would now and then deny something that he had said. The old Gentleman, to confirm his Assertion, would give a mathematical Thump to the Bottom of the Boat, which would cause it sensibly to descend; and thus he would sink it to any Depth requir'd. Whenever we had a Mind to raise the Boat, the old Gentleman would suffer his Hypothesis to be refuted, and withhold his Demonstrative Fist.

We sail'd very pleasantly for about a League, and saw all the Wonders of the Deep: There were three Windows in our Barge made of transparent Steel; one of each Side, and one at the Stern. My Veracity in this may be doubted; but when a Man considers that Bodies are made transparent when their Pores lie in rectilinear Directions, the only Difficulty will be to prove that Steel may have its Pores dispos'd in this Manner; and the best Way to prove this, will be to explain the Manner in which the Steel was made transparent. The old Gentleman, before mention'd, took three Pieces of Steel, and beat them with an Hammer till they were very thin: This Work indeed requir'd some Time. He then took the Steel Plates, and put each of them between two Fires of equal Degrees of Heat, and let them remain so long between the Fires, that the Particles of the opposite Fires, by their acting upon the Steel, and attracting each other, at length found a Passage through the Steel, which was made pliable by their uninterrupted Action on either Side. When he found that the Holes, through which the Fire had pass'd, were big enough to suffer the Rays of Light to pass through, he threw Water upon the Steel Plates, which cool'd them, and

made

made them hard: This being done suddenly, kept the Pores as wide when the Steel was cold, as it was when it was acted upon by the Fires. He did not venture, indeed, to polish the Plates, left he should stop the Pores by rubbing upon them. Through these three Windows we look'd into the Sea; for the Holes through which the Light pass'd were too small to suffer the least Particle of Water to enter at, and avoided many Rocks, as well as observ'd the Behaviour of the Fishes. I could observe some moving gently along for their Recreation, and others, with a more thoughtful Countenance, moving precipitantly, to dispatch some Business. There was a Fish taken Prisoner by two others at our Right Side: I judg'd that he was taken Prisoner, by his being seiz'd by the Gills, and forcibly carried back by the Road he came. His Crime, I suppose, was Theft; for he carried a Piece of Flesh in his Mouth, which he dropp'd as soon as he was seiz'd; but it was taken up by one of his Attendants. We were desirous to know what would be the Event of this that we had seen, and accordingly desir'd our old Gentleman to steer after them.

Happy had it been for us, if we had not been so curious; for our Pilot, instead of minding his Way, was taken up in considering whether he might not demonstrate a mathematical Problem by the Motions of those Fishes Tails. In this profound Contemplation he was so wholly taken up with observing the Fishes Tails, that he took no Notice of a Rock, which he should have left at the Larboard-Side, but drove directly against it, and split the Boat. I spy'd the Rock as we were upon it; but it was too late to prevent the certain Death which I immediately expected. Our Boat came with great Violence against the Rock, (for we made all the Way we could,) and split into an hundred Pieces: We should all have immediately perish'd, had it not
been

been for the wonderful Adventure which we met with.

Our Boat had no sooner struck against the Rock, but it open'd, and discover'd a large and lightsome Apartment: A very uncouth Figure came speedily to the Opening of the Rock, and pull'd us all in, to know what we wanted. As soon as we got safe in, he clos'd the Rock, and told us, in the Language of *Quqns*, that had he taken us into his Lodging to save us from being drown'd. Before we had given him an Account of our coming thither, he pitch'd upon the old Mathematician to speak for us, expecting that he would declare the Truth. Indeed he related Matters of Fact just as they happen'd; and our Treatment would have been more favourable than it was, had not he ventur'd to explain in his own Terms the Manner of sinking and raising the Boat. Our Host was confounded at this new Doctrine, and took us for Conjurerers: Upon which he order'd us to be chain'd, to prevent our doing any Mischief, and set a Guard to prevent our drawing Figures, which sat heavier upon the old Man than his Chains.

When we were thus confin'd, I had Leisure to observe the Place we were in, as well as the Behaviour of those that were at work in it; for there were several employed in Spinning, and working at Anvils. The Light which we had, was made by Pieces of stinking Fish, hung up and down; but I could by no Means guess at what they were working. At length I prevail'd upon a gentle Youth, that was set to watch us, to give me an Account of their Manner of working. He told me, that those at the Wheels were spinning Sonnets, Odes, Epigrams, and all the easier Kinds of Poetry. I was surpriz'd at this Relation, till he explain'd to me the Manner of their Spinning. They first took the Letters of their Alphabet, and set them down in all the

various

various Cases that they were capable of, in long Pieces of Paper, whose Breadth did not exceed half an Inch; they next twisted this Paper with their Wheels, till those Letters which appear'd on the Outside of the Thread were jumbled into a Poetical Line. Those Lines were carefully set down in a Day-Book by one appointed for that Purpose; from which they were transferr'd by others into another Book, and rang'd in harmonious Order, according to their Agreement or Disagreement. Whensoever it happen'd that a Thread was broke, they piec'd it with a proper Name, an old Proverb, or a Simile; of which they always had a good Store ready made for those Occasions. It is not strange that those Poets should make those Verses thus mechanically, to any one that considers how possible the Work is; for where the Vowels and Consonants are so variously mix'd, and such a Quantity of them on each Side of the Paper, it necessarily follows, that in Twisting some of the Letters must be hid, whilst those that appear'd on the Sides of the Thread as certainly must make Words, as that Words are made of Vowels and Consonants. I will not say that the uniform Motion of the Wheel, and the Squeezing of the Letters according to Art, contributed nothing to their Endeavours. Indeed, they could not find a Line which was good Sense upon every Thread, tho' upon some they found two or three, when the Spinster was skilful, and the Paper able to endure many Twistings. Abbreviations and Apostrophes were occasion'd by some Letters being hid in a Wrinkle, which did really belong to the Line, tho' the Skill of the Spinsters could not force them to shew themselves.

As to those at work at the Anvils, said he, they are employ'd in making Epick Poems: Their Hammers are of Leads, and their Anvils of Crab-Tree: They have all the Letters of the Alphabet written
severally

severally on separate Pieces of Paper: Those Pieces are generally square, and one of their Sides never exceed a Quarter of an Inch. Soft Clay is what they work at, with those Letters strew'd in it: They beat this Clay till a Line, or half a Line, may be read on some Side of it; which being written, as before, they begin to hammer afresh for another Line, and so on. This Work is, indeed, more difficult than the former, and requires great Art in managing the Hammer, and tempering the Clay; yet a skilful Man will beat forty Line, or more sometimes, out of one Piece of Clay. There are some who work at the Anvil that do not, as yet, pretend to beat out whole Lines, and are employ'd in making Epithets, Proper Names, and poetical Blunders. But, said I, to what End is all this Pains taken, since you have no Commerce with those upon dry Land. He smil'd, and told me, that I was mistaken; for it was to those Men which I saw at work, that the People in the Moon were indebted for all the Poetry which they had among them. My Master, said he, has certain invisible Messengers, which he calls the *Muses*; those he sends to vend the Wares as fast as he gets them ready for Sale. The Muses carry his Goods up to the Moon, and sell them there to the highest Bidder; but he rates his tolerable Productions so dear, that it generally costs a Man all that he is worth to purchase one or more of them, according to their Value, and the Buyer's Abilities; which is a Reason that those that are accounted the best Poets, are generally the poorest. I ask'd him then, why his Master sold any Poems that were bad? or why he did not claim all the Praise which was given to some of his Works, as his own proper Due? He answer'd, that his Master had Workmen of all sorts, and consequently some bad ones, which would have their Wages paid them as punctually as the best; and since he had

Hopes

Hopes that the worst would mend, be sold their Works to encourage them, and defray the Charges he has been at in maintaining them, and supplying them with Materials to work with. Besides, Money being what he chiefly coveted, he little minded Applause, which he knew would never maintain a Man, or even mend an old Shoe.

Here *Tckbrff* interrupted us, and told me, that I was very merry in my Confinement, and rather ought to consider how I might be set free, than ask Questions about my Keepers. I told him, that as our Entry into this Place was a little odd, so I believed would our Escape be, if ever such a Thing happen'd; and that I was perfectly resign'd to undergo any Thing which should be laid upon us, except starving; for I could not think of dying with an empty Stomach, without a Qualm. I know of no Method, answer'd *Tckbrff*, of setting ourselves at Liberty, but by sincerely promising to behave well, and be obedient to all the Commands of our present Master. I lik'd the Proposal, and willed to have it immediately executed; and in order to it, resolv'd to speak for us all, which, if it should turn to our Disadvantage, I would be only as blameable as those who had brought me to this Place.

I then prevail'd upon the young Man above mention'd to call his Master: As he was coming near us, I had Leisure to view him distinctly; and indeed he was a very uncommon Figure, and very strangely dress'd: His Nose was plac'd in his Forehead, and his Mouth was below his Chin; his Eyes and Ears, Legs and Arms, had chang'd their Places, and his Gate was between Walking and Flying. He wore a Mantle artfully wrought with many Figures, of Cupids, Monsters, green Fields, Caves, Armour, Gods and Castles, with here and there a Battle and a Wedding. When he was come up to us, I began to speak to him, and said, *Most mighty and puissant*

I

puissant Hero, thou Glory of thy Race, and Wonder of the Age, pardon the meanest of thy Servants that attempts to enumerate thy Virtues; but they are so conspicuous, that inanimate Things are ready to proclaim them: With which of thy good Qualities shall I begin; shall I first praise thy wonderful Knowledge in Arts, or rather thy surprizing Humanity towards us; that Humanity to which we owe that we are alive, and have an Opportunity of being astonish'd at thy glorious Mansions. Our greatest Ambition is to serve thee; and if we prove defective in any Thing thou commandest, let our Willingness to undertake it attone for it. But here thy Perfections dazzle me, and thy Virtues ought rather to be admir'd in expressive Silence, than unworthily enumerated. Never was a Patron better pleas'd with a Dedication from one that scarce knew him: We were immediately set at Liberty, and invited to Dinner. You may believe that this was very acceptable to us, when I tell you that we very hungry.

Our Dinner was of Fish, some of which I knew the Names of, but other Dishes, that were like Olios, I was an entire Stranger to. At Table I first gave a short Account of my Coming to the Moon, and answer'd some Questions concerning the Earth, and then was favour'd with the following Account from him, that entertain'd us. To relate, said he, all the Passages of my Life, would be too tedious, tho' they are, as far as I can see, no way inferior to what you have deliver'd concerning yourself, in being strange and surprizing: I shall only hint at Matters of less Importance, and give you a full Account of Principals.

CHAP.

CHAP. X.

Containing a brief Account of Sadtuff's Life, with the Manner of his coming there. Of his shewing them his Rarities, especially a Colour subsisting without a Body, and the Philosopher's Stone; with some Account of it.

I Was born in *Bakzil*, a City of *Poronis*, which is a Kingdom in the *Northern* Parts of the Moon: My Father enjoy'd a moderate Fortune, just sufficient for the Maintenance of a numerous Family; for he had four Sons, and three Daughters. My eldest Brother being the greatest Blockhead of the Family, was made a Merchant: In him was the old Proverb verify'd, that *Fools have Fortune*; for he became very rich. My second Brother and I were sent to School, and were design'd for a liberal Education. In my tender Years I discover'd the Marks of a comprehensive Mind; and was not a little proud of the Praise and Caresses of my Friends: This Humour so far prevail'd with me, that I thought myself perfectly knowing in many Things, which I was an utter Stranger to. I mightily affected Solitude, and was found often alone in the Fields, when my School-Fellows were assembled in Town at their Diversions. It happen'd one Day, as I was taking my Walk, I was wholly taken up in representing a long Scene of Prosperity to my Imagination, which I hop'd would befal me. So far was I transported with these Thoughts, that I had wander'd insensibly into a Wood at a good Distance from my Father's: Night was approaching, and I could not find the right Way; I then refolved to fpend that Night in fome Tree, and early the next Morning to go home. As I was looking about for a convenient Place to lodge in that Night, I chanced to fpy an old Man with this Mantle, which you fee me wear, caſt about him: His Eyes were funk in his Head, and his Beard was white, and half an Yard long; but when he fpoke I was wonderfully terrified. He approach'd me, and asked me by what Chance I was brought thither, or whither I propofed to go. I anfwer'd, that I had loft my Way, and begg'd of him to direct me, fince I believ'd he was no Stranger in thofe Parts. He told me that it would be in vain for me to attempt to get home that Night; and fince I had met with him, I fhould be welcome to fuch Entertainment as his Dwelling afforded: I thank'd him for his kind Offer, and went along with him. He led me through many By and *Unfrequented Ways* to a Cave in which he dwelt; but juft as I entred, he difcern'd in me a great Uneafinefs, and bid me be of good Chear, with an Affurance that no Evil fhould befal me whilft I remain'd with him. To comfort me, by moving his Wand, a Table heap'd with Dainties was fet before us by invifible Servants. I was at firft loath to tafte, till overcome with Hunger and his Intreaties, I prov'd it good and wholefome. After Supper I began to take a great Liking to fuch Entertainment, and defign'd to return home no more, if I could live where I was. Here *Tckbrff* interrupted, and faid, he could not believe that any Man had Spirits at his Command; for, faid he, if the Devil be fo very proud as we are told he is, how is it confiftent with his Pride to fubmit himfelf and his Retinue to the Caprice of every one that is willing to employ them? It is faid, indeed, that thofe to whom he is thus fubject for a fhort Time, become his Vaffals for ever; but if he had no Way of peopling his Territories, but by being firft a Slave him-

[69]

himself, there might be some Grounds for this Opinion; yet since we know that in every Company, even the smallest, he has, for the most part, one or more Deputies, by whose unwearied Diligence, he might expect in a short Time to people the very Deserts of his Empire, though he never stirr'd abroad himself: It is not reasonable to suppose that his Pride would brook with such a voluntary Subjection.

All this, reply'd *Salhuff*, I will readily grant you, (for that was our Host's Name;) and will shew you, as far as it is lawful for me at present, how a Conjurer performs his Works: A Conjurer, in the vulgar Acceptation, is taken for one who has made a League with the Devil; but I assure you that it only signifies a Philosopher, or one that is a curious Observer of Events, and their true Causes; from which Observation he foretels Things that must happen, as if they were Contingencies: By this Means, Wars, Eclipses, Storms, &c. are foretold. But the working of Miracles, which is falsly ascrib'd to them, is no more than the Effect of their cunning Delusion: For those Men, by their unwearied Diligence, find out Qualities unknown to the Vulgar in the commonest Bodies: They will transform a Body (as they say) by deceiving the Sight, or substituting another in the Room of it; and this is done either by the Help of some Effluvia which they transmit to the Eyes of their Spectators, or by placing the Body to be transform'd in different Lights, which every one knows will alter the Colour, if not seemingly the Form of the Body. I have myself, a Powder, which will hinder the Rays of Light from being reflected from any Body, and so make it invisible; and likewise a Bottle of Spirits, which will hinder a Man from seeing Bodies of such Colours as I do design to conceal, except their Eyes be anointed with something which I have prepar'd, to hinder

the

the Operation of thofe Spirits. I dare reveal no more at prefent, but fhall proceed to inform you of mine own Adventures as briefly as I can.

After Supper, I confented to ftay with him, on Condition that he wou'd inftruct me in his Art; which he in a fhort Time perform'd. I liv'd with him thirty nine Years, for the moft Part pretty pleafantly, tho' in the Beginning I did not much care for the Converfation of Perfons I could not fee; for he kept many Servants, who were firm to his Intereft on Account of the good Wages which he gave them, and who were not to be feen by any Stranger, for fear of a Difcovery. He fupply'd them with Money by the Help of the Philofopher's Stone, which he was in Poffeffion of, and generally kept one Perfon invifible to buy him Neceffaries. During the firft three Years, I was employ'd in grinding Powders, gathering Herbs, and boiling them for Ufe; and fometimes was allow'd to fee the Manner of fome of their Performances. When I had attain'd to this fmall Knowledge, I began to think myfelf as expert as my Mafter, and refolv'd to give him a Proof of my Skill, upon the firft Opportunity.

But fee how Fortune favour'd my Defign: I was order'd one Day to make a certain Powder; and to this End, I was firft to wafh a Piece of Wood in a Chymical Liquor, and then hammer it it till I had broke the Continuity of the Parts: All this I did; and above my Orders, I wet the Powder in this Liquor, purely to fee what Effect it wou'd have, and was a little amaz'd, that the Powder upon being wet became invifible, the Bulk of it ftill remaining the fame, as I obferved by feeling it. I immediately concluded that the Colour was latent in the Liquor, fince the Wood had loft it; and thought, that to extract the Colour from the Liquor, wou'd be a fufficient Proof of

my

my Art. Accordingly I took the Liquor, and plac'd it in a Glafs Veffel over the Fire: This Veffel I cover'd with three Folds of fine Linnen, and over it plac'd a Retort, to receive the Liquor as it fhou'd be carried up in Vapours: After it had remain'd for the Space of three Hours over a gentle Fire, I perceiv'd that the Liquor was entirely forc'd into the Retort; and then I took it off to cool. When I had feparated the Veffels, I faw the Colour (with no fmall Joy) fticking to the Linnen: This I artfully took from it, and laid it by, to be preferv'd for a Rarity, which I will prefently fhew you.

Perhaps you may wonder how a Body may be depriv'd of all Colour; or how Colour, which is only a Property of Body, can fubfift without a Body; but this is not to be marvell'd at, when you confider that it is as poffible for a Property to fubfift without a Body, as for nothing to have any Property. Yet fome have affirm'd that nothing hath Properties, when they fay that a Shadow is a *Nigrum Nihil*, or a Black Nothing. When I had effected this, I brought my Performance to my Mafter, who was very much delighted with it.

From that Time I was no longer kept in Ignorance of the moft myfterious Part of his Art: I was firft fworn to obferve certain Articles, and then inftructed in many Niceties of Art: I was taught to gather Lightening, and preferve it for Ufe; to make wholefome Bread of Hail-Stones, and Tarts of driven Snow; to make Clocks of Radifhes, and Buff-Belts of Nut-Shells; with many other Things too tedious to recount. In fhort, I was taught to act Impoffibilities, and find out Things that never had a Being. Thus I became a ufeful Servant to an indulgent Mafter, who repofed more Confidence in me, than in any of his Domefticks; and, in his
Life-

Life-time, as well as at his Death, let me feel his Bounty.

A little before his Death, he was very much indispofed, and thought that he would be in a fair Way of Recovery, if he removed to this Place where we now are : Accordingly he took me along with him, and we both arrived here fafe by the Help of a Diving-Bell, which he kept for that Purpofe. We were no fooner arrived than his Sicknefs increafed, which fhortly made an End of him. About an Hour before he died, he called me to him, and fpoke to me like a kind Father, advifing me, and bequeathing all his Poffeffions to me.

I know, faid he, that the Hour of my Death is at hand; and now I bid Farewel to all the gilded Vanity which Men fo eagerly purfue. Mark well my Words, and do not fufpect a dying Man of Falfhood : I now am old, and fraught with Experience and Obfervation, which may be of ufe to you that are young : I have feen Fortune loaded with Gifts and Honours, fmilingly courting me to enjoy her ; yet, juft when I hoped to poffefs her, fhe hath frown'd ; and not only baffled my Hopes, but deprived me of fome fmall Favours which I before quietly enjoyed. This Treatment convinc'd me that fhe was giddy, and armed me againft her Smiles, as well as Frowns : I oppofed her with a fuperior Power, and call'd Virtue to my Aid, who is conftant to her Votaries : She led me far from Noife and Tumult, and brought me Contentment in Solitude. There I exercifed my Mind, and improved it ; and made Difcoveries in Nature ufeful to myfelf and others ; yet here Fortune was kind, and difcovered her Blindnefs, by tempting one that was out of her Power. Her Shadows could not draw me from the real Subftance ; neither could Abundance of Gold make

me

me forget that I was a Man. If Riches could free a Man from Death, what Treasures cou'd I offer, were I unwilling to die? But I refign my Breath in Quietnefs, and my immortal Part thirfts after new Happinefs. The Thoughts of certain Death made me ftudy to die well; and that my lateft Hours fhould not be full of Horror and Remorfe; all my worldly Goods I give to you, who will, I hope, rightly ufe them. Care and Difquiet attends the Abufe of them, whilft Men look upon thofe Things which are, at beft, but convenient, and often fuperfluous, as neceffary.

More he would have faid, but his Strength fail'd him; and, to my inexpreffible Grief, he gave up the Ghoft. He now lies buried in one End of this Cave in a Tomb, which I took Care to adorn, that being the only Way by which I could profefs mine Efteem for fo indulgent and fo kind a Mafter.

When *Sacluff* had made an End of Speaking, we requefted of him to fhew us fome of his Rarieties, efpecially the Philofophers Stone, of which I had heard fo much before, with but little Certainty. He confented, and firft produc'd the Colour fubfifting without a Body: It was a pale Red, fufpended, I know not how, in a little Box; it touched no Part of the Box, neither could it be felt, or eafily removed.

When we had wondered a while at this, he fhew'd us the Philofopher's Stone. It was a little Piece of compounded Earth, fomewhat refembling a Man: It was improperly call'd a Stone, and had that Name on Account of its Infenfibility. Its Arms were extended, and its Paws were ready to grafp at any Thing: Its Countenance was pale and meagre, and looked like one almoft fpent with over-watching, and prey'd upon by Cares. It ftood upon an Heap of Gold, attended by feveral Phantoms

Phantoms: Avarice, Fear, and Discontent, were its inseparable Attendants, which laboured to increase, as well as preserve the baneful Store. The Phantom of Avarice was constantly commending the Possessions of others, and proposing Means to bring them to this useless Lump; while that of Fear would raise imaginary Doubts, and rack her Invention for Difficulties. Those two were at continual Discord; for Avarice would bring in Security to its Aid; but Fear opposed it, by setting forth, that it was unguarded and dangerous. All this while Discontent sat brooding over their Jars, and by the Assistance of Despair found out Means to foment them. Pleasure once came, and offered them his Service; but they unanimously rejected it, urged on by Fear, who shewed them all the Extravagancies which Pleasure was liable to. Notwithstanding those Domestick Broils, they all concurred in increasing the Store; and to this End they employ'd two other Phantoms, the Desire and Necessity of others. Those brought Meterials convertible into Gold, whilst the others causing them to undergo many Changes, at length made them *Sterling*.

CHAP.

CHAP. XI.

Containing an Account of the Author's hammering out a Poem. The Poem. Saffuff's Form and Mantle. The Author and Tckbrff's Escape thence; with their Arrival at a strange Country. An amazing Sight: The Reason of it; with the Manner of their learning their Language. Their Appearing before the King; and their being made Correctors-General to the Book of Fame.

IN the next Place *Saffuff* led us to fee his Men at Work, (whose Manner of working I have already describ'd,) and complied with a Request of mine, in suffering me to hammer out a Poem. In order to this I wrote the Letters of the *English* Alphabet upon Pieces of Paper, as above, and then proceeded to down rightHammering: After some little Labour I collected the following Poem, which I here set down with the Alteration of but two Words since it left the Moon. When I had made the Poem I hammered for a Title, and could find no other than that which is perfixed to it. The making of the Poem had like to prove the Cause of my Confinement, since it made *Saffuff* conceive too well of my Ability, to become serviceable to him.

RODOMONTADO BEMBUZ.

THE happy Pa-Gods of the gloomy Seas,
  Shall make the World with Taratantara blaze,
When Indian *Firelooks sends us* Dumplins *home,*
And wond'rous Woodcocks *have forgot to roam.*

The British *Widows in the* Indian *Trees,*
With Hairs difhevell'd danggling on their Knees:
In magick Noife *behold the glimmering Froth,*
And in my Pockets Pitchers *full of Broth.*
The fwearing Dewlap *of the fnowy Herd,*
And Pigs *fweet finging with a downy Beard*:
But now behold what's done beneath the Main,
The ftarry Tritons, *and the gilded Bean*;
While thund'ring Pifmires *clog the fable Brain,*
And wond'ring Echoes tumble o'er the Plain.
In lolling Numbers I fhall ne'er begin
To tell the Prowefs of a lighted Gin.
Thus Keckerman *and* Crakanthorp *forget to die,*
And Peter Fiskifon *fhall ceafe to fly*:
We'll echo Murmurs with a Hunting Horn;
And ftartle all the Children yet unborn:
Of Shoeing-Horns I'll fing the Praife,
And on their Afhes Pyramids *will raife*:
Nor fquabbling Papifts, *or the frighted* Moor,
Shall e'er make Derby *pifs behind the Door.*
The Deeds of Atlas, *or fome pretty Swain,*
Are now, alas! alas! they're all in vain!
In Hemlock *Rays, I'll fwagger to the Sky,*
And make the Whirlwinds *in fweet Numbers fly*:
While groveling Criticks *wallow in the Mire,*
I'll foar aloft to tune my warbling Lyre.

When I had finifh'd this Poem, I fhew'd and explain'd it to *Sactuff*; who immediately offer'd me a confiderable Penfion to affift him in his Work: I did not pofitively refufe him, but begg'd a little Time to confider of it. We remain'd in this Cave fixteen Days; during which Time we had good Entertainment as the Place afforded; and we were conftantly confidering how we fhould efcape. After *Sactuff* had told us that he was pleas'd with our Company, one Time, when we were all cheerfully converfing, I took Occafion to ask him fome Queftions

tions about his ſtrange Form. He told me, that at his Birth he was unlike other Children; but could never aſſign any Cauſe for it, other than ſome ſtrange Conceits, and Miſmanagement of his Mother, while he was in her Womb. I do not, ſaid he, repine at mine uncommon Form, well knowing that my Body ſhould be the leaſt of my Concern, ſince my Deformity cannot hinder the Operations of my Mind. Whenſoever, indeed, I appear abroad, I cover myſelf cloſe with this Mantle, which was very wonderfully made: It was made by my Maſter of a Salt Wave, artfully dried in Smoke: He firſt infus'd a coagulating Liquor into it, and then ſpread it upon a Frame till it became dry, and afterwards he painted it.

It was now almoſt Time to betake ourſelves to Reſt, when I call'd *Tckbrff* aſide, and propos'd to him a Method of eſcaping. I had before enquir'd of ſome of the Servants where the Chimney open'd itſelf, and was told, that about a League thence it open'd into a Cave, but was impaſſable, on account of the Smoke and craggy Rock that ſurrounded it: Yet I believ'd that if we aſcended when the Fire was out, we might, with ſome Difficulty, eſcape. *Tckbrff* was of my Opinion, and willed inſtantly to ſet about it; but the old Mathematician would by no Means venture himſelf into it; for, ſaid he, I can perceive near the Mouth of it a great many acute Angles, which my Fleſh has a natural Averſion to. However, ſince you are reſolv'd to venture, I will keep them from lighting a Fire as long as I can, and wiſh you Succeſs.

When we had taken our Leave of him, he retir'd to his Bed, and left us waiting till we ſhould think they were all aſleep, at which Time, when it came, we reſolutely aſcended. We had not got far when we were minded to go down again; and certainly would, had we not perceived our Paſſage to grow lefs fleep. Never did Knight in enchanted Caftle fuffer more than we did in paffing through this gloomy Labyrinth; our Cloaths and Skins were much torn, and our Mouths filled with Soot. When we had climb'd about a Mile, our Paffage became more eafy, which encouraged us to proceed, till after much Toil and Vexation we faw the Light, and could walk upright; we were then within fifty Yards of the Mouth of the Cave, which was very large, and open'd into a pleafant Field.

We were no fooner come out, than we return'd God Thanks for our Delivery, and wafh'd ourfelves in a River that was near; then we laid down to refrefh ourfelves in the Field, before we went any further, and confulted upon Meafures to be taken in this ftrange Place. We had fcarce fat down, when a vaft Quantity of Smoke iffued out of the Cave: We fuppos'd that *Sactuff* had caus'd a larger Fire than ufual to be made, in order to ftifle us in our Flight: But if that was his Defign, it was fruftrated. After we had refted a while, we rofe, and made towards a Town that was not very far thence.

In our Way thither, we met with an amazing Sight, a Field full of little Children, with their Heads juft above Ground: I was mov'd with Horror, when I faw them to be too young to deferve fo fevere a Punifhment, as I thought that was. However, we went on till we came to an Houfe fituate at one End of the Town: We went in, the Door being open; but could fee no Body; befides, we could fee no Locks on any Door, but every Thing expos'd: We fear'd to meddle with any Thing, left, being caught in the Fact, we fhould be impal'd alive; for we had form'd ftrange Notions of this People's Cruelty. We left this Houfe, and went to another; where we found the Inhabitants within, who receiv'd us with pleafant Looks, and caus'd us

to

[79]

to sit down; but what they said we were not able to understand; yet we suspected Treachery to be couch'd under this Civility. That Night we were well entertain'd; and the next Morning several Foreigners were brought before us, to find out one that could understand us: Such a one at length we found, who interpreted to the Hearers what we said, as well as gave us to understand that the People were kindly affected towards us. Our chief Concern was next to learn their Language, that we might be able to converse with them, and find out their Manner of Living.

It was our good Fortune to have some of the Money of *Quqns* about us, with which we hir'd a Person to instruct us in the Language. His Method, tho' uncommon, prov'd successful; for in seventeen Days Time we became perfect Masters of their Language: He caus'd us to wear every Night Paper Caps upon our Heads, closely shaved, and on the inner Side of those Caps was wrote part of their Language. He then gave us a Potion to make us sleep foundly, and sweat; by which Means, when we awoke the next Day, we understood every Thing that was wrote on our Night-Caps.

For when the Pores of our Heads were open in sweating, the Spirit of the Words was attracted by the Brain, in which it was embrac'd by the Soul, which every Body allows to have a Thirst after Knowledge. That Words have a Spirit, is plain from the wonderful Effects which they produce, which the dead Letter would never be able to perform. Thus by sleeping with the Language about our Heads, we soon understood it.

When we were capable of conversing, we found that we were not to be maintain'd always at others Expence; but if we design'd to live among them, we must prove useful to the Publick. To this End we consulted, growing suspicious that their Favours

would

would shortly ceafe, when we had told them of all our Adventures that were pleafing to them ; for the People were of an itching Temper, fond of Novelty, and quickly cloy'd with their choiceft Delights. They liv'd under a wife King, that preferr'd their Safety before his own ; and murmur'd at all his Proceedings, when they were not fully fatisfied of every Thing that induc'd him to take any Meafures for their Welfare ; tho' they knew him oblig'd by all Ties, divine and human, as willing alfo, to provide for their Happinefs and Security.

Now that we were able to converfe with them, I enquired into the Meaning of that Sight of young Children, which we had feen as we came to this Place ; and was told, that many eminent Politicians, from nice Experiments and Obfervations made upon the Body Politick, had infallibly predicted a great Diftemper in it, which wou'd require a more than ordinary Effufion of Blood, in order to cure it : To this End, Orders were given for fowing two thoufand Acres with Men, which fhou'd be ready to bleed when Occafion requir'd. Befides, this way of producing them was much more fpeedy, than that of being born of a Woman. They had a certain Plant growing among them, of whofe Berries, laid in Hot-Beds, Children were thus form'd.

But as I faid before, beginning to be tired of our Dependance upon thofe whom we thought unwilling longer to maintain us, we went directly to the King, and offer'd him our Service as Soldiers, and Perfons whom Experience had confirm'd in many Things ufeful to a *Commonwealth* : We were well receiv'd, and upon Examination anfwering fome Queftions, were fettled into fome Places which we could manage, with a Promife of Preferment if we rightly behav'd.

The

[81]

The Place aſſign'd me, was to be Corrector-General of the *Book* of *Fame*, which was deliver'd to me. In it I set down every Report that was spread; and by comparing the different Accounts that were given, I form'd some stated Opinion, which every one was oblig'd to aſſent to, under the Penalty of having some very scandalous Report divulg'd and confirm'd upon them.

The Deſign of this Office was to prevent the Loſs of Time in uſeleſs Speculations on their Neighbours Actions, as well as to restrain a licentious way of speaking of others, which had been the Cauſe of many Disturbances. Now whenſoever I declar'd on any Story, if it was but some trivial Matter, I omitted ſuch Circumstances as might not be favourably understood by all that heard them; by which means, in a little Time, the People made Allowances for the Infirmities they were ſubject to, and began to cheriſh a brotherly Love among them.

I publiſh'd among them, a Multiplication Table, by which they might be capable of diſcerning the Growth of any Story, and diſcover in what ſort of Minds it acquir'd any Thing. I laid down alſo ſomeRules for diſtinguiſhing the ſimple Reports from the compound; as alſo for being acquainted with the arithmetical Progreſſion of a Tale, and diſcovering its Age by its Size and Complexion: As oft as any noted Piece of Villany was laid before me, I publiſh'd it with all the aggravating Circumſtances that ſhou'd deter others from the like Practice; yet this, however uſeful, had like to have been my Ruin, as ſhall be told in its proper Place.

Tckbriff was my Aſſiſtant in my Office, and ſhar'd with me both in the Trouble and Penſion. We liv'd in this Manner for the Space of two Years; and when we were at Leiſure, we ſpent our Time in obſerving the Behaviour of the People.

L   CHAP.

CHAP. XII.

Containing an Account of the People. The Author's and Tckbrff's *Banishment. The Author alone prepares to return to the Earth: The Manner of his coming. His Arrival at the Land of Parrots: Their Kindness to him. He destroys some of their Enemies. In return, they lend their Assistance to set him on the Coast of* Guinea; *whence he sail'd to* London.

THE Generality of them were kind and affectionate to each other, which produc'd in them an Openness of living, whereby they held all Things almost in common. When they went abroad, they left their Houses open, and knew not what a Lock was. It was usual with them to assist each other in their private Concerns, without the Expectation of any Reward, other than the like Kindness, if requisite. In their Marriages they never us'd any tedious Courtships; but when a Woman was marriagable, her nearest Friend advertis'd it, with her good and bad Qualities, if she had any, and invited Persons to come and treat with them about her, that so if their Inclinations were the same, they might speedily be join'd. Upon the Decease of an Husband, the Wife, if inclin'd to Marriage, hung out a plain Black Flag, to signify her Resolution to have a second Husband. Sometimes a Widow wou'd hang out a Black Flag, with a Death's Head in the Middle of it, thereby declaring her Aversion to Marriage; as

by

by the same Arms Pyrates declare their Enmity to Mankind.

Here, again, I believed that I was settled for Life; but I soon found my Miſtake, and happily found out Means to return to the Earth. The Occaſion of my leaving them was this: There was brought before us one Day an Account of a certain Nobleman, who, by a baſe and underhand Dealing, had drawn off many of the King's Subjects from their Allegiance: This was confirmed to us by ſome whom he had corrupted. I immediately enter'd it, and publiſhed his Crime, with ſome Conſiderations upon Rebellion, which render'd them odious to the People. As ſoon as this was publick, he found out thoſe who had turned againſt him, and, by Promiſes of Security and Bribes, caus'd them publickly to recant, and, further, to declare that we, out of Malice to the Nobleman, had hired them to accuſe him. All that we could ſay could not clear us; for the King believed our Accuſers honeſt, and ſentenc'd us, within twenty Days to depart from his Dominions.

Tckbrff propoſed to return to *Quqns*; but I ſaid we had not Money ſufficient to bear our Charges thither, ſince we would be obliged, on Account of ſome vaſt Mountains, to go round-about a great Part of the Moon, to arrive at it. What (ſaid he) will you then remain here to be put to Death? I anſwer'd, that I had form'd a Deſign of attempting a Return to the Earth, and would be exceeding happy if he would bear me Company thither: He replied, that it ſeem'd to him impracticable; Beſides, if it ſhould ſucceed, he would not deſire to live among ſuch Inhabitants of it, as I had deſcribed to him; yet, ſince we muſt part, ſaid he, I will aſſiſt you, if I can, while I ſtay here: But ſurely you don't intend to truſt to a Whirl-Wind a ſecond Time? I confeſs'd that I did not like

L 2 ſuch

such Travelling, but intended to go thither after the following Manner.

We already know, said I, the Height of the Moon's *Atmosphere*, and know how Gun-Powder will raise a Ball of any Weight to any Height: Now I design to place myself in the Middle of ten wooden Vessels, placed one within another, with the Outermost strongly hooped with Iron, to prevent its breaking. This I will place over 7000 Barrels of Powder, which I know will raise me to the Top of the *Atmosphere*. I should here observe, that there were several Mountains out of which they dug Gun-Powder, which was made fit for use, as Salt is on the Earth, by exposing it to the intense Heat of the Sun in some Parts that are very near the Equator. The Mountains were called *Pfefwhthbz*, or the *Devil's Warts*. But before I blow myself up, I'll provide myself with a large Pair of Wings, which I will fasten to my Arms in my Resting-Place; by the Help of which I will fly down to the Earth.

Here he objected that both the Vessels and I would be set on Fire. To this I answered, that I had a Remedy to prevent that; for, said I, between the Vessels I will pour a Quantity of Water, which will prevent the burning any but the Outermost, by boring Holes in the Sides of all the Innermost, excepting that in which I stand, thro' which the Water may freely pass to quench the Outer, which, I believe, will be fir'd; that which is in the Middle shall have no Holes in it, that so the Water may not come near me: The upper Part of my Tubs I will cover with two Plates of Tin, between which I will place a Quantity of wet Sand to prevent the lowermost Plate from setting the Wood on Fire: This Cover shall be fastned by me on the Inside, so as that I can throw it off when I think that I am got out of the Smoak. I'll supply the Want

[85]

Want of fresh Air by some Bottles of animal Spirits; and will prevent the Vessels from touching each other, by placing Pieces of Lead between the Sides and Bottoms, which upon the Approach of the Fire, will melt and fall off before they can do any Harm. I believe that my Motion will be pretty swift; but I am used to travel Post, and by this Time can bear to be hurried. I provide my self with Wings, to prevent my too rapid Fall to the Earth; for I believe, were I not thus provided, I should not escape so well as I did in my Fall to the Moon.

Tckbrff said, that the Design, though rendered a little feasible, might not succeed, and many unforeseen Accidents might cause it to miscarry. As to that, said I, I must rely upon Providence, which I hope will send me with News to my Countrymen, whose Ingenuity may, in Time, find out a more easy Method of maintaining a Correspondence with other Planetary Inhabitants.

Immediately I set about preparing for my Departure, and in about a Week's Time had all Things ready for it. The Morning before I was blown up, I took my Leave of *Tckbrff*, and my other Friends, with the utmost Regret. He presented me with a Tobacco-Stopper; and in return, I gave him an *Irish* Bottle-Skrew. He would not be a Spectator of my leaving 'em, for he could not believe that I would survive it.

In short there was an Hole dug in the Earth for the Powder, and a Train laid of about a Mile long. When I enter'd my Tubs, as soon as I saw the Fire approaching me, I covered my self, and in a short Time was carried with great Rapidity far out of Sight; and with the Loss of mine outer Tub, I arriv'd safe between the *Atmospheres* of the Earth and Moon; where I sat a while to refresh myself, and tie on my Wings for the Remainder of my Journey.

While

While I was fitting here, there came a Flock of *Woodcocks* from the Moon, and alighted on my Tubs, where after having refted a while, they made towards the Earth. It was of great Ufe to me to obferve their Flight ; for they being acquainted with the beft Roads, were a Guide to me: They did not fly directly down, but going before the Wind, defcended obliquely, to prevent, as I fuppofe, their being hurried down. I placed my Feet againft my Tubs, and made after them. I could not keep up with them, fo that in a little Time I loft Sight of them.

I flew very pleafantly, till I chanced to come to the *Southern* Parts of *Africk*, where I had like to be knock'd down with the Top of an high Mountain, as the Earth was revolving; but I timely perceiv'd it, and got over the *Ethiopick* Ocean. In that I durft not alight, but flying more to the *South*, I alighted on a pleafant Country; fituate in *Terra Auftralis incognita*, where in a delightful Grove I fell afleep, being much tired with my flying, and almoft roafted with the Sun. I know not how long I flept, but I was awaken'd by a Number of *Parrots* that were fitting in Trees about me. When I began to ftir, they made a great Noife, and feem'd to be afraid of me, I believe, on Account of my Wings and Size. I then took but little Notice of them, but went to the Top of a Mountain, in order to look out for fome Town, to which I might refort ; but feeing none, I could not tell what would become of me. The *Parrots* ftill followed me, and by Degrees became lefs afraid of me ; for I fuddenly laid hold on one of them ; upon which the reft made a prodigious Noife ; but when they perceived that I ufed it very gently, and let it go again, they came about me in great Numbers.

As a Return for my civil Treatment, they called to me by the Name *Crammrick*, and went before to a

Cave

[87]

Cave where they repofited their *Winter's Store*, which confifted in Abundance of different Sorts of fine Fruits, which were laid upon broad dry Leaves fpread over a Mofs. One of them prefented me with a Bunch of Raifins, and another with fome other choice Fruits, till I had eaten plentifully: This was my daily Entertainment for many Days, till I one Day found by chance a kind of Grain, not unlike Peafe, which I dried, and pounding it between two Stones, I mixed it with Water, then I moulded it into a thin Cake, and bak'd it in the Sun. This I ufed for Bread, neither was it unpleafant, and eat it with the Flefh of fome fmall Animals common among them, after I had dried it by the Sun. After every Meal I made, I had a Collation of fine Fruit brought me, and might have lived entirely upon it, had I not feared that it would not agree well with my Conftitution, and perhaps breed a Famine among thofe that were fo kind to me.

By Degrees I came to know the Names of feveral Things in their Language, and could falute thofe that I met, and in a little Time was able to converfe with them. The only Fault that I could find with them, was, that they were too talkative, like Women, conftantly afking impertinent Queftions. They lived under a Monarchial Government, and obferved a lineal Succeffion. They had certain Feftivals in Honour of their King, which they celebrated by regular Flights in the Air, and Songs in the Praife of their Monarch; but thofe Feftivals were attended generally with a great Slaughter of them, occafion'd by fome Birds of Prey that ufed to watch this Opportunity to deftroy them, and plunder their Fruits. They complained to me of this Calamity, and afked if I could provide a Remedy againft it. I afked in what Manner they attack'd them; and was told, that they purfued them whitherfoever they

fled,

fled, till they were tired of deftroying them; and then they went to their Store to plunder it.

I promis'd my Affiftance; and accordingly, when the Feftival was come, I cover'd my Face and Head with a Cap made of ftrong Bark, only I left Holes in it for my Mouth and Eyes, and placed myfelf with a Club in my Hand by the Store. The Birds of Prey arriv'd, and after a great Fight went to vifit the Store: They did not come all at once, but in fmall Companies; moft of which I deftroy'd, though they made what Refiftance they could, and the reft fled away. I number'd near an Hundred that I had kill'd, to the great Joy of the *Parrots*, who fpent the Remainder of the Day in praifing me for the Victory, and proffering me their Service in any thing they were able to perform. I thank'd them, and promis'd to make ufe of their Affiftance in going to mine own Country; which they, with fome Relunctance to part with me, at length confented to.

I firft with fharp Flints, and a Knife which I had in my Pocket, cut down as many fmall Trees, as I, with much Labour and Difficulty, made a pretty large Boat of, not unlike thofe made ufe of in the North of *Ireland*, fave that it was not covered with Skins, inftead of which I made ufe of Gum, of which there was great Plenty, with which I daub'd it all over, fo that it would keep out the Water, and bear me without Danger. When this was finifh'd, I twifted as many Twigs together as ferv'd me inftead of feveral Ropes: Thefe I faftened to the Stem of my Boat, and begg'd of the King, that he would lend me as many of his Subjects as would be able to draw my Boat to the neareft Country that was inhabited by Men.

At length he comply'd, and allow'd us a fufficient Quantity of Provifion for our Voyage. We put off early in the Morning, after Abundance of
Ceremony

[89]

Ceremony at our parting. The Birds which came along with me, took hold of the Twigs faſtened at the Stem of the Boat; and being many in Number, in ſixty Days Time we got ſafe into the *Trade-Winds*, which in ſeventeen Days more drove us on the Coaſt of *Guinea*. The Birds would not come aſhore with me, but left me pretty near it, ſo that I did ſwim out, while they carried my Cloaths and Wings, and dropp'd them down to me, but would not alight: They went back again to the Boat, where, after a moderate Repaſt, they went away.

There was ſo great a Number of them, that they reliev'd each other very often, and ſail'd with little Trouble.

When I was arriv'd at *Guinea*, I ſought for *Engliſh* Merchants, and found a very civil Gentleman, one Mr. *Jacob Broome*, who hir'd me for a Sailor towards *England:* But I rather liv'd like a Paſſenger than a common Sailor; for Mr. *Broome* was ſo taken with my Adventures, that he exempted me from the Office of a common Sailor, and made me his Companion, while I gave him an Account of my Travels.

Our Voyage was very eaſy; for we met with but one ſmall Storm, and were chas'd for a Day by an *Algerine*. In our Road home I ſaw the Peak of *Teneriff*, which brought many Things into my Mind, which griev'd me in the ſuffering, but pleas'd me in the remembering of them. Thence we ſail'd to *London*, and on the 12th of *September*, 1720. landed there. My Maſter furniſh'd me with what Money bore my Charges to *Dublin*, upon promiſing that I would publiſh mine Adventures. I arriv'd at *Dublin* the 27th of the ſame Month, where I was inform'd that my Friends were remov'd to the *North* of *Ireland*: Thither I follow'd them, being ſufficiently tir'd with Rambling; and there I reſolve to ſpend the Remainder of my Days in,

M   Quiet

Quiet, if Fortune has not some unforeseen Trouble in Store for me.

Thus in the Space of two Years, three Months, twenty one Days, I view'd a great Part both of the Earth and Moon: There are few, I believe, would run the Risque that I did, though they may be desirous of seeing what I saw; for a *Whirlwind* is not the easiest Vehicle; and being blow'd up, it but little better. If I have said any Thing to displease the Ladies, let them go on to drink *Tea*, and kill themselves out of Spight: If the Beaux are angry, I care not; and the Criticks may go hang themselves, e're they shall vex me: Besides, let them all consider, that what is here spoken is of the Inhabitants of the Moon. Well-meaning Persons I esteem, and to their Censure I wholly submit, who, I am persuaded, will not expect the greatest Exactness, and much Rhetorick, from a Sailor, studious to deliver the Truth.

The End of the First Part.

THE

THE
DEDICATION.
TO THE
Worthy, Daring, Adventurous, Thrice-renown'd, and Victorious Captain LEMUEL GULLIVER.

SHALL a Poet find a Patron, and not a Lunatick? Let it not be said, *Gulliver*'s alive, or the *Laputians* had e're now crush'd us, by coming down to mourn him; yet his Lustre dazzles; he cannot be conceal'd: His Fame rings loudly in the MOON: *To Clods of Earth I tell it.*

Thee

The DEDICATION.

Thee, *Gulliver,* I ftile moft worthy; and as I believe thee averfe to Flattery, as free from Pride, I am perfuaded that you will not be offended at a *Dedication* in the *Rear,* but approve of, and accept, if what goes before be worth your Notice: Accept it according to your wonted Candour, and believe me to be,

With all due Refpect,

Your moft Devoted
9 JA 56
Humble Servant,

Murtagh Mc. Dermot.

THE

THE CONTENTS.

CHAP. I. *Containing an Account of the Author's Design to Travel. His going to Sea. His Arrival at* Teneriffe. *His Ascent to the Peak. His being taken up by a Whirlwind. The Manner of his Journey towards the* Moon. *Some Reflections made by the Way. His Arrival at the* Moon; *and what happen'd thereupon.* Page 5

CHAP. II. *Containing an Account of the People's Care of him. His Surprize upon his Recovery. His Manner of learning their Language in a Night's Time; with an Account for it.* 11

CHAP. III. *Containing an Account of his being sent for by the King. His Discourse with* Tckbrff *about the King. His Manner of approaching him. Some Observations on his Courtiers. His Approach to him. His escaping being put to Death. And what Discourse he had with* Tckbrff, *about the People of his own* Country, *and the People of the* Moon. 16

CHAP. IV. *Containing an Account of their Discourse about an Amour between* Frib-

CONTENTS.

Fribbigghe *and* Blmmſl. *Their Characters. He turns* Fribbigghe's *Rival. Makes a Speech to* Blmmſl. Fribbigghe *is diſcarded.* Pag. 24

CHAP. V. *Containing an Account of* Blmmſl's *inviting him to drink* Tea *with her. A Philoſophical Account of the Effects of* Tea; *with its firſt Riſe. His Departure from* Blmmſl; *and his Uſage towards* Fribbrigghe. 30

CHAP. VI. *Containing an Account of his Obſervations on the Cuſtoms, Manners, and Religion, of the People of the* Moon. 35

CHAP. VII. *Containing an Account of his going to a* Coffee-Houſe; *what he obſerv'd and heard there. His Deſign to go to a* Play-Houſe. *An Account of what* Tckbrff *ſaid to him before they went thither; what he obſerv'd and heard there; with a natural Account for a Man's becoming a Critick.* 45

CHAP. VIII. *Containing an Account of his Dream: Its Extravagance accounted for. His being awaken'd by People dancing; with ſome Obſervations upon a Ball.* 52

CHAP. IX. *Containing an Account of his ſailing under Water: The Manner of it. The Boat's ſplitting againſt a Rock: Their being receiv'd into a ſubterraneous Cavern: Their Reception. An Account of mechanical Poetry:* Sactuff's *Kindneſs to them.* 58

CHAP. X. *Containing a brief Account of* Sactuff's *Life; with the Manner of his com-*

ing

CONTENTS.

ing there. Of his shewing them his Rarities, especially a Colour, subsisting without a Body; and the Philosopher's Stone; with some Account of it. 67

CHAP. XI. Containing an Account of the Author's hammering out a Poem. The Poem. Sactuff's Form and Mantle. The Author and Tckbrff's Escape thence; with their Arrival at a strange Country. An amazing Sight. The Reason of it: With the Manner of their learning their Language. Their appearing before the King; and their being made Correctors-General to the Book of Fame 75

CHAP. XII. Containing an Account of the People. The Author's and Tckbrff's Banishment. The Author alone prepares to return to the Earth. The Manner of his coming. His Arrival at the Land of Parrots: Their Kindness to him. He destroys some of their Enemies. In return, they lend their Assistance to set him on the Coast of Guinea; whence he sail'd to London. 82

Adver-

Advertisement.

SINCE I thought of making this Publick, I met with an Account of Travelling in *Whirlwinds*, not unlike my Passage into the MOON, which is here inserted, taken from *Dickson's* NEWS-LETTER, as follows:

Reading, June 5. 1727.

YEsterday a *Whirlwind* took up into the Air, near 100 Yards from the Ground, four Hay-Cocks in a Field near this Town, each weighing 200 Pound, and carried them to another Place half a Mile off.

N. B. Perhaps some may imagine my being in the MOON to be only a mere Dream; but why one should not be as likely as the other, I shall leave it to the Judgment of the Reader after he has read the Foregoing *TRIP*, &c.

The Adventures of Abdalla

by

Jean-Paul Bignon

Bibliographical note:

This facsimile has been made from a copy in the Beinecke Library of Yale University (Hfc31 376)

THE ADVENTURES OF ABDALLA,

Son of HANIF,
Sent by the
Sultan of the INDIES,
To make a Discovery of the
Island of *BORICO*,
Where the *Fountain* which restores *past Youth*
is supposed to be found.

Also an Account of the
TRAVELS of *ROUSCHEN*,
A PERSIAN LADY, to the *TOPSY-TURVY* Island, undiscover'd to this Day.

The whole intermix'd with several Curious and
Instructive HISTORIES.

Translated into *French* from an *Arabick* Manuscript
found at *Batavia* by Mr. de SANDISSON:
And now done into ENGLISH
By *WILLIAM HATCHETT*, Gent.

Adorn'd with CUTS.

LONDON:
Printed for THO. WORRALL at the *Judge's-Head* over against
St. *Dunstan's* Church in *Fleet-street*. 1729.

Advertisement.

HE *Letter that* Monsieur *de* Sandisson *wrote, when he sent me the Works of* Abdalla, *is so instructive, that it may serve instead of a Preface to this Translation. I thought proper therefore, after having made some small Amendments in the Style, to incert it; and so shall content myself with making here some proper Remarks on my own Performance.*

I have often been at a great Loss how to give a right Version to those Passages, which are quite different from our Customs; and I have as often been tempted to adapt them all after the French *Fashion. I try'd, indeed, to accomplish it, but whether it be Prepossession, or that the* Eastern *Histories, when disguis'd, lose of their Beauty, I know not, my Endeavours al-*
                                                    ways

Advertisement.

ways seem'd Unsuccessful. I then imagin'd it would be best to keep a Medium, to soften certain Places, and to explain others by short Notes.

I have taken a particular Care to set in a true Light, all that regards the Religion of the Indians, and the Opinion of the Mahometans touching the Genii. The Accounts we receive from all the noted Travellers, who have visited the Indies, and treated on the Manners of the Indians, have long since, furnish'd us with Expressions convincing enough to prove the Superstition of that People. It is true, few of those Travellers have taken Notice of the Indian Theology, as pertinently as the Story of the Widow deliver'd from the Fire; which very thing renders the Works of Abdalla more valuable and curious. As to the good and bad Genii, and the different Things they meddle with, according to the Credulity of the Arabians and Persians, those who have read the Oriental Works of Monsieur Vattier, and who read those which Messieurs Petis, de la Croix, and Galland, daily communicate to the Publick, with so much Success, cannot but be pretty well acquainted with them.

Some Readers may perhaps readily object against

ADVERTISEMENT. iii

gainst the Word Ginne, because I have not alter'd it from the Original; but I beg they'll consider, there are Genii of both Sexes, and that to distinguish them, nothing is more easy than to say, Genius and Ginne: Whereas, in being confin'd to the Term only of Genius, there would be a Necessity of saying, Genii Male and Genii Female, which in the Course of a Story somewhat long, would prove very troublesome; besides, I cannot think but it would be equally disagreeable to the Ear to say, Genii Female, when it must be attributed to so many Female Creatures of that Kind.

If the Word Fairy had signify'd the same Thing, I might have imploy'd it instead of Ginne, but it implies a quite different Signification: the Fairy neither being the Female of the Genius, nor the Genius the Male of the Fairy. A Fairy is not a Creature of a superior Order: Those who were of that Opinion are mistaken; she is an ordinary Woman, which may be easily prov'd by all the Narrations of the Antients. Among these Narrations one may know the Fairies, not only by themselves, but likewise by their Kindred. But not to be confuted by the Authority of the old Oriental Books: The Fairy Morgan, whom the History of Lancelot du Lac speaks of, was she not the Sister of King Artus? The Fairy that

Guerin

Advertisement.

Guerin Mesquin *examin'd, and all those whom he found with her in the obscure Grotto's of the Appenine Mountains, were Women, and sinful ones; 'tis he himself makes mention of it, in the Book which bears his Name.* The Genealogy of the Fairy *in the Island of* Hircania, *is describ'd in the History of* Palmerin d'Olive, *and his Children. In that of the Knight of the golden Star* (Stella de Oro) *is prov'd, that the Fairy in the Valley of Shades, was a Woman of this World. It would be insignificant to expatiate any farther on this Subject, therefore I return to the* Genii.

According to the Mahometan *Authors, the World before the Creation of* Adam *was inhabited by the* Genii: *The one call'd* Divs*, *and the others* Peris: *The first was* Bad, *and the latter* Good. *This Opposition of Inclinations caus'd a continual Discord; but* Adam, *who was to give the Universe new Inhabitants, in Exclusion of the* Genii, *had no sooner appear'd, than a much greater Division arose between them. The* Peris, *who were submissive to* God *in every thing, not only augmented their hatred against the* Divs, *but even a new Faction*

---

* *This Word l'v, ought to be pronounc'd like a Consonant, in* Dive.

broke

ADVERTISEMENT.

broke out among the Evil Genii. *Several of their Legions open'd their Eyes to the Truth, and went and eſtabliſh'd themſelves in the Mountain of* Kaf, *under the Conduct of* Surkhrag, *their Chief. The other* Genii *continu'd living together, notwithſtanding their Diviſions; and ſurrendring up to Mankind almoſt all the Earth, they inhabited that Part which they call after their own Name, the* Ginniſtan. *Under the Reign of* Solomon, *a great Number of* Divs *was again converted; others, likewiſe follow'd the right Path, by hearing, as* Mahomet *ſays, the* Alcoran *read. As to the* Peris, *we never heard of their changing; nor that they had even the Thought of ſeparating themſelves, till the Time of Queen* Feramak.

This little Expoſition ſeems neceſſary for the better Underſtanding of this Work, which ſuppoſes a great Knowledge of the Oriental *Fables. I ſhall obſerve farther, that I found as much Difficulty in Regard of the* Peris *and* Divs, *as I had done on Account of the* Genii *in General. You meet with both Sexes among the* Peris *and* Divs; *for that Reaſon, I've been oblig'd to add to their Names a Termination that may diſtinguiſh them. I call therefore the* Peris *and* Divs, *ſimply,* Males; *and their Companions the* Periſes *and* Dives, Females.

The

ADVERTISEMENT.

The Peris *and* Divs *have Disciples. The Women, instructed by the* Peris, *are properly speaking,* Fairies; *and the Men, Disciples of the same* Genii, *are call'd* Sages: *Such as* Alquif *and the Knight* dell'Isola Serrata. *Those of both Sexes, who subject themselves to the* Divs, *are call'd* Sorcerers *and* Sorceresses.

If, in reading the Preliminary Letter, you meet with any Obscurity in the Adventure which follows these Marks * * * *, *that Intricacy will be unravell'd, by reading the History of the* Persian Lady Roufchen.

Monf. de Sandisson's
LETTER
TO THE
TRANSLATOR,

Written at BATAVIA the 13th of December, in the Year 1703.

S I R,

DO not underſtand *Arabick* enough to know the true Worth of the Memoirs I ſend you; be ſo Good, therefore to excuſe me, if I intreat you to put me in a Condition of becoming ſomewhat a Judge of it. To requeſt ſuch a Favour, is, if I miſtake

mistake not, advising you to translate them into *French*. I wish you may find them curious enough to ingage you in the Performance of it.

The learned *Arabians*, to whom I have communicated them say, there is a great deal of Difference between the Style of this Work, and that of the *Alcoran*. They assert that the Language of *Abdalla* is mixed with *Usbeck* Expressions, and *Indian* Terms, which would be looked upon at *Mecca* and *Medina* as wretched *Barbarisms*.

In the main, I find them much divided in their Sentiments: Some cannot believe what *Abdalla* says he saw with his own Eyes; others give Credit both to that, and almost all the rest. For my Part, I am inclinable to be much of the same Opinion with the Latter, though I never could attain but a very superficial Account of the principal Adventures. I will give you my Reason for such a Belief, after I have related to you what I know of the Author.

Hanif, the Father of *Abdalla*, was a Man much esteemed at Court, and in the Army of *Gehan-Guir*, who preferr'd him to the Post of *Kobat-Kan*, that is to say, of Commissary General of his Horse. He became suspected fufpected by *Chah-Jehan*, in the Troubles which attended his Elevation to the Throne. This Prince's Sufpicions were perhaps ill-grounded, but however they were, *Hanif* was divefted of his Employment, and a Part of his Eftate. Notwithftanding this Difgrace, he ftill reforted to Court, and always appear'd there among the reft of the *Omerahs* with Grandeur, till he ended his Days, which happen'd about two Years before the Departure of his Son. *Abdalla*, a great while after his Return, was fent by *Chah-Jehan* to *Batavia*, in order to fet on Foot a Treaty of Commerce with the *Eaft-India* Company's General. During his Negociation, he died at Monfieur *William Berkuys*'s Houfe, where he, with the chief of his Attendance, had been lodged. It was reported that he poyfoned himfelf, but the Truth is, his Death proceeded from an Excefs of Chagrin, which the falfe News of his Mafter's Death had caufed him. He imagined that *Chah-Jehan*, who had always deferred taking the Water of the Fountain of *Borico*, which *Abdalla* brought him, had made Ufe of it in his Abfence; and that for want of duly obferving the Circumftances requifite for the drinking it, he had render'd that Liquor fatal, which otherwife was of a heavenly Nature. If he took any, it was

a 2 but

but too true in one Senfe, fince it rais'd fo great a Ferment in his Humours, as to make him appear Lifelefs for fome time, which was the Reafon his own Children took immediate Poffeffion of all he had; and that *Aureng-Zebe*, who remain'd fole Mafter, depriv'd him of his Liberty. It does not belong to us to ask why *Chah Jehan*'s recocover'd Health fo foon relaps'd after his Confinement, but we may judge by the long Life of *Aureng-Zebe*, that his Father left him when he was dying, fomething more valuable than all the precious Stones, which *Begum-Saheb* * made him a Prefent of in a golden Bafon. *Aureng-Zebe* would undoubtedly have advanc'd *Abdalla* to the higheft Employment of the State, had he been courageous enough to have furviv'd the Report. Upon his Death-bed, he left thefe Memoirs to his Landlord, and made him fome other Prefents more confiderable. This *Berkuys*, now living, is the Son of *William* of that Name. He was a good big Lad when this happen'd, and fo remember'd thefe Particulars which he related unto me, when he put the Manufcript into my Hands.

* Begum-Saheb, Aureng-Zebe's *Sifter, tended on* Chah-Jehan *during his Imprifonment ; and when he was dead, fhe made* Aureng-Zebe *a Prefent of a large golden Bafon, which contain'd all* Chah-Jehan's *precious Stones, and her own.*

I now

I now return to the Motive of my Credulity. I muſt own, the ſudden Changes from one Place to another, and the ſurpriſing Adventures which happen at the ſame time, are the moſt difficult Incidents to be credited in the following Memoirs; but he, for Example, who receives for Fact the Travels of *Rouſchen*, would appear very ridiculous to raiſe Scruples on the reſt of the Book. Now this is exactly my Caſe. I can't well doubt of the Reality of the Travels of *Rouſchen*, ſince I myſelf was carry'd away as ſhe was, and detain'd at leaſt two Hours in the Academy of the *Topſy-Turvy* Iſland.

* * * * * * *

You are ſenſible how ſolicitous I've ever been in procuring Books of *Fairies;* ſince you have been ſo good hitherto, as to ſend me all thoſe that have been publiſh'd. One Night about nine a Clock, as I was in my Cabinet, concluding the Peruſal of the laſt Volume of that Parcel of Books, which were convey'd to me by your Correſpondent at *Surat*, I perceiv'd, about ſix Yards from me, a fine old Gentleman, dreſs'd in blue, whoſe grey Beard touch'd his Knees, and who carry'd in his left Hand a Net, reſembling that which Fiſhermen call a caſting Net. *Argamaſſe*, ſaid he to me, firſt Queen of the blue *Peris,*

Peris[a], and *Aligand* her Spouse, this Day[b] risen from the Dead, are about to put an End to two important Affairs. They have made Choice of you to assist at the Decision of them, and to communicate it to the rest of Mankind. I was, as you may well imagine, very much astonish'd and affrighted; but I had not a Moment allow'd me to recollect myself. The old Gentleman cast his Net over me, and after having sufficiently secur'd me in it, he carry'd me on his Back into my Garden; and from thence through a vast Space of Darkness, very thick and cold, into an Amphitheatre full of People. I did not know where I was, neither could I ever tell, till the History of *Rouschen* since inform'd me: The Amphitheatre where I was being the same she describes. My Carrier presented me to the blue Queen, who plac'd me at her Feet, speaking these four Words: *See, hear, retain* and *publish*.

A Moment after we heard a great Sound of Kettle-Drums and Trumpets coming from the white Gate. I did not know that Instant, whether it was best to seem pleas'd or melancholy; but the Assembly appearing the former, I very readily comply'd with their Disposition. The Sound of these warlike

---

[a] *Good* Genii.   [b] *This Mystery is explain'd at length in the History of the* Persian Lady.

Inſtruments augmented more and more: In a Word, twelve wing'd Kettle-Drummers, and as many Kettle-Drum Carriers, enter'd like Birds, and contributed the more to our Pleaſure, as it was oppoſite to their Nature either to ſoar up in the Air, or even to ſupport themſelves there at all. The *former* were downright *Bears*, produc'd in the new *Zembla;* and the *latter*, the greateſt *Aſſes* that ever came out of *Arcadia* or *Mirabilis*. The Trumpeters that follow'd them were no leſs extraordinary: Imagine with yourſelf; twelve large Eels, about the Bigneſs of two Men, holding in their Mouths twelve Silver Pipes, eighteen or twenty Foot long, and twelve little old Men ſqueezing their Tails with their Fingers, to oblige them to blow ſofter or harder, as requir'd. The Eels ſupported the old Men in the Air, and were ſuſtain'd themſelves by the Aſſiſtance of four great Wings, which by the Make and inimitable Variety of Colours, reſembled thoſe of a Butterfly.

Then there came in a ſpacious Chariot drawn by four *Dragons*, who had all the Beauty of Beaſts of their Kind, without having their Fierceneſs. Their Wings appear'd to be *Gold*, and their Scales of *Emerald*. The Creſts they wore on their Heads were of ſo beautiful a Colour, that they might paſs for a precious Pile of Rubies. Their long Tails mov'd in Cadence at the Sound of the Kettle-Drums and Trumpets. The Chariot was of Filigreen enamell'd, fix'd on Bars of Gold, and interspers'd with Saphires so nicely wrought, as gave a natural and lively Representation of all Sorts of Flowers and Birds. The fair *Glaftine* was plac'd majestically in it. There was so nigh a Resemblance between *Argamaffe* her Grandmother, thrice remov'd, and herself, that I could have known her without being told it by any Body. A very melancholy Prisoner who had a Book under his Arm, on which he now and then cast sad Looks, was ty'd behind the Chariot, and chose rather to be dragg'd by than to follow it. After he was gone past, I perceiv'd something wrote upon his Back, where I read these Words: *The Count of Gabalis, a noted Impoftor.* The Kettle-Drummers and Trumpeters rang'd themselves at the Extremities of the *Area*, and the *Dragons* plac'd *Glaftine* and her Chariot exactly in the Middle. This *Perife* salu ed those risen from the Dead, and then spoke to the Queen *Argamaffe* to this Effect The Presence of the Prisoner already declares the Success of one Part of the Commission I was charged with, and I have not been less diligent and exact in discharging the other.

I was

I was ordered to infpect all the new Books that treat about us: I have not fail'd doing it; but I am very much diffatisfied with what I have obferved in them. No Body fcarce has wrote well on our Subject, ever fince the Death of the faithful *Galerſi*. We fee nothing Now-a-days publiſh'd, but trifling Books, unworthy of us. I ſhall prove what I fay by one Sketch alone; for to make an entire Lift of thefe infipid, forc'd Works, and to give a Detail of the many Impertinences they contain, would be making you unneceffarily undergo the fame Pains I have been at.

Did you ever hear talk of *Obligeantine, Bienfaifante, Rancune, Tranquille, Bourgillone, Plaifir,* and *Berlinguette*? What Sort of People Name you there, faid *Argamaſſe*? *Periſes*, or as they call them in *Europe, Fairies,* reply'd *Glaſtine.* There was never any of that Name, anfwered *Argamaſſe*. I grant it, refumed *Glaſtine;* they make them likewife equal to the Gods, that never were fo: For Example, they unite *Runcune* with *Pactolus.*

The Moveables, which thefe pretended *Fairies* make ufe of, are no lefs oppofite to Probability: Such as, *Sofas of Avanturine Couches of Azuli Stone, Stools of Cornelian,* and *Canapies of Amber.* Don't you admire the Choice of thefe Materials? If thefe Goods be be delicately wrought, they are very brittle; but yet if they were clumsey and massy, how could they be removed? Not to mention the eminent Danger would accrue to the Canopy of Amber * from its too near approach to the Fire. What will you say of the *Buildings of Nacre,* of the *Affiotat Wine,* and of the *Onix* Stone, belonging to these said *Fairies*? I assure you, interrupted *Aligand,* these must be Women different from the rest of their Sex, who undertake to write such fine Things. I was not willing to inform myself too much about it, continued *Glaftine;* but if these are Women, they feel *a Father's Love,* for the Works they are Mothers of. Are these Charming *Fairies* that you have named us, resumed the blew *Peri,* in good repute with honest People? O dear! Yes, said *Glaftine:* Their Princes and Princesses are very excellent Persons: As the *Queen of Cabbage Lettices,* the *Prince Small Pea,* the *Princess Beancod.* Upon which, there was an agreeable murmuring made in the Company, and I heard the major Part of the young *Peris* say to one another; Certainly Men must needs think all that's charming of this little crowned People, for they are most delightful to the Eye. Here are others, continued *Glaftine,* whose majestick

* *Yellow Amber dissolves in the Fire.*

Names

Names will inspire you with more reverence. As, *King Coquerico*, *King Peudaquet* and the *King of Dunces*; are not these Potent Princes? As she affected to pronounce these ridiculous Names, with an Air of Gravity, the Assembly burst into a Fit of Laughter, which continued for some Time. At last, she cried out, after having laugh'd as well as the rest of the Company, Let me entreat you, at least, not to contemn the Heroes and Horoines, which these illustrious *Fairies* think to protect: Being, *a little Pig*, but *the prettiest little Pig that ever was seen; a Sea Princess, whose Hair is of the finest White that ever was heard of;* and *a Swallow*, but *the most beautiful little Swallow that ever was seen.* Say no more, Daughter, interrupted *Aligand*; how could so many Absurdities enter into your Head? I've no more to say on this Subject, replied *Glastine*, it now lies in the Queen's Breasts, to see what Remedy must be applied to suppress the itching Mind, every Body is possessed with, Now-a-Days, to become Authors. If they are suffered to proceed, all the World will at last suppose us to be like the *Obligeantines* and the *Bourgillones*: Nay, they'll even believe that some Part of the *Cabalistick* Islands is still existing, and that this Wretch, looking on *Gabalis*, is Captain of the *Philosophers*, who are suppos'd to inhabit therein. It

It's highly neceffary, faid *Argamaffe*, that we maturely confider on putting a Stop to all petty Scriblers, and on punifhing *Gabalis*. By thefe few Words fpeaking, fhe difpos'd the Queens to give their Advice, and went even in Perfon to know it. After this fhe refum'd her Place, and clos'd the firft Affair by this Sentence.

Whereas we have been informed, that Perfons of different Ages and Sexes meddle with compofing Books ; wherein they attribute many Things to us, which we are mere Strangers to, and wherein they unjuftly confound us with Chimerical *Fairies:* We *Perife* and *Argamaffe*, ancient Queens of the blew Palace, after having taken the Advice of the five Ruling Queens, have refolved in our Academical Council, that fuch Authors, as are found guilty fhall receive Punifhment, though with Clemency for the firft Tranfgreffion. If fuch Offenders happen to be Women they fhall be addicted to Sluttifhnefs; fometimes troubled with frightful Dreams ; and at other times poffeffed with the Spirit of Talkativenefs to Excefs. If the like Difafter befal Men, they fhall be plagued with a ftinking Breath, during the Space of three Years ; and they fhall affect to live after fuch a Manner, as will make them be pointed at by every Body. And to the End that all such Disorders, which may arise hereafter, be effectually suppressed, it is enacted and ordered, by the Advice of our said Council, that the Nails of either Sex, who shall inconsiderately imploy their Pen on our Subject, be immediately changed into Claws, and that a continual Itching affect the minutest Part of their Bodies. Moreover, we expresly forbid all Persons, of what Denomination soever, and even those whom we shall have deputed to transmit our Actions to Posterity to make Compositions by themselves; but we strictly enjoin and expect Men shall consult with able and ingenious Women, when their Off-springs require masterly Sentiments and Amendments; and that Women likewise shall shew their Productions to Men of good Sense and Penetration, who shall take particular Care to cleanse them from all Contradictions, Exaggerations and Tautologies. For such is our Will and Pleasure.

This Sentence being pronounced, they passed to the Judgment of *Gabalis*. The Queens thought proper that he should make his Speech. The Order was signified to him by *Glastine*, and he made it in the following Terms.

Since my ill Fate has so decreed that I should fall into your Hands, and that in
spite

spite of all my Knowledge and Cunning, I shall not be able to escape them; it behoves me to employ all my Thoughts to excite Compassion, and endeavour by a sincere and hearty Acknowledgement, to mitigate the Punishment due to my Crimes. I must confess therefore, I have used my utmost Efforts to give a new Gloss to an Art, which you have thought fit to condemn; and that I have neglected nothing to establish myself in the good Opinion of the World. I have endeavoured to make the Black Art, a Science taught by the *Divs* * pass for true Wisdom; and as for myself, I sometimes borrowed the Title of a *German* Count, and at other Times went under the Name of the Captain of the Philosophers, that lived in the *Cabalistick* Islands. When first I took up the scribling Trade, I strove to confound you with the *Divs*, but without Success; because it was impossible for Men either to discern you through the *bad* Actions of the *Divs*, or to distinguish those by your *good* Ones. Thus I was deluded to undertake what chiefly drew upon me your Indignation; and further, supposing the Existence of the four elementary People, endeavoured to engage the Publick to attri-

* *Evil* Genij. *In the Word* Div, *I'v ought to be pronounc'd almost like an* F.

bute

[xv]

bute thofe Prodigies to them, which in reality belonged to you; and to believe you were fubject to us. I might in fome Meafure, extenuate my Crime, by reprefenting to you, that I am not the Author of the *Sylphes*, *Gnomes*; *Nymphes*, nor of the *Salamanders*, of whom *Paracelfus*, *Vigenere*, and fome others have treated on before my Pupil; and that his too great Facility to give Ear to my Difcourfes, did but too much encourage me to impofe it on him; but you are equally acquainted with what remains to clear me, as with that which renders me guilty in your Sight.

Gabalis fetch'd a great Sigh, and bow'd down his Head, after having finifh'd his Speech. His Punifhment was deferr'd till he had declar'd all the Secrets of the black Faction, which he was look'd upon to be the Chief of at that Time among Men. *Argamaffe* commanded therefore, the Prifon of the Academy to appear, in order to lodge the Criminal in it. She had no fooner fpoke but the Earth open'd about ten Yards from *Gabalis*, and difcover'd a moft terrible Monfter. He was as big as fix *Elephants*, and his Body was only cover'd with a wrinkled Skin without any Hair on it. His Eyes were large but hollow, and the prodigious Width of his Mouth refembled the Brink of an Abyfs.

His

His Belly touch'd the Ground, and was only supported by four huge Paws, forasmuch as it was necessary to move very slowly. What a Prison that Belly must make! The Monster approach'd *Gabalis* by Degrees, and when he was at a very little Distance from him, he open'd his Mouth, and receiv'd this Wretch into the Bottom of his Entrails. After this Expedition, which fill'd me with Horror, the living Prison repair'd to the Place from whence it came out, and the Earth clos'd of itself. Thus ended the second Affair.

As soon as the Assembly broke up, my Carrier, dress'd in blue, cast his Net over me, took me on his Shoulders, and carry'd me back again to my Cabinet, where he left me, repeating the two last of the four Words, that *Argamasse* had said to me; *retain* and *publish*. Some Moments after this it struck twelve a Clock.

It would be somewhat difficult, Sir, not to remember such a strange Adventure as mine was. To make it perfectly known to the World, the best way would be to print it, if all Books that are published, sold well enough for being publickly censured. To conclude, I hope now you'll no longer wonder at my Facility in believing the Prodigies contain'd in the Memoirs of *Abdalla*; so I finish my Letter by assuring you that I am, *&c.*

A

A TABLE

OF THE

HISTORIES and STORIES

Contain'd in this BOOK.

MONSIEUR Sandiffon's *Letter*.
The *Beginning of the Adventures of* Abdalla *Son of* Hanif.   Page 1
The History of Almoraddin.   9
The Adventure of the Indian *Lady delivered from the Fire.*   18
The Adventure of the Indian *Virgin carried away by the* Fakirs.   23
The first Story of Loulou.   31
The History of the King *without a Nose*.   33
The History of the Persian *Lady, with her Voyage into the* Topsy-Turvy *Island.*   39
The World *reversed.*   51
The History of Ajoub *of* Schiras.   61

A TABLE, &c.

The Continuation of the History of the Persian La-
dy. 67
The Resurrection of Queen Faramak *and* Gian *her
Husband.* 74
The Sequel of the History of Ajoub *of Schiras.* 80
The second Story of Loulou. 84
The History of Prince Tangut *and the Princess
with a Nose a Foot long.* 88
The third Story of Loulou. 115
The Continuation of the History of Almoraddin. 116
The Adventure of the Father *of the Pilot.* 117
The History of the Giant Hardoun *and the beautiful*
Nour: *As also, that of the* Genius Feridoun *and
the Princess* Cheroudah. 121
The Adventure of the Santon, *Husband of the young
Woman.* 135
The Adventure of the first of the young sorrowful
Santons. 138
The Adventure of the second of the young sorrowful
Santons. 142
The Adventure of the third of the young sorrowful
Santons. 148
The Adventure of the old Santon *at the Queen of
the Mountains.* 153
The Sequel of the History of Almoraddin *and Queen*
Zulikhah. 163

THE

THE ADVENTURES OF ABDALLA, Son of HANIF.

 Owards the Conclusion of the *Ramadan*[a], in the sixth Year of the Reign of *Chah-Jehan*[b], Pillar of Faith, *Oglouf-Kan*, Captain of the Palace Guards, came into my Chamber, a little while before the second Prayer[c] began, and spoke to me in the following manner. *Abdalla*,

[a] The Ramadan *is the* Mahometans *Month of Fasting, during which solemn Fast, they neither eat nor drink from the rising of the Sun till the Stars begin to appear. They abstain likewise, till that Moment, from lying with their Wives.*

[b] Chah-Jehan *the great Mogul, Father of* Aureng-zebe, *and Son of* Jehan-Guir, *Son of* Ekbar, *Son of* Houmayous, *the seventh Descendant of* Tamerlane.

[c] *The* Mahometans *are oblig'd to pray five times a Day, namely, a little after Sun-rising, just after noon Day, before Sun-setting, at Sun-setting, and very late at Night.*

Son of *Hanif*, I wish the Command I am going to execute, may prove advantageous to thee. Give me thy Sabre and follow me to the Sultan's, for such is his Pleasure. The Moment I heard these Words, I fell prostrate, and after having ador'd God, *Oglouf-Kan*, answer'd I, put thy Hand upon my Head; the Sultan is Master of my Life; and I am his Slave. At the same Time I deliver'd him up my Sabre and follow'd him. There were ten Guards posted at the Bottom of the Stairs, who environ'd me; and with this Attendance I pass'd thro' all the Courts belonging to the Palace, and at last was brought before *Chah-Jehan*.

This Monarch had no other Company with him but *Emir-Gemla*, Son of *Gabdol*, who was General of his Forces at that Time, and the venerable *Fazel-Kan*, Son of *Hafam*, Chief of the *Imans*[d]. *Oglouf-Kan*, who went before me, presented him my Cimeter, and said: Light of the Faithful, *Abdalla*, without the least Resistance, has submitted himself to thy Orders; may thy Enemies imitate his Example. Tho' I was not conscious of being Criminal in any thing, yet I felt an extreme Fear and Dread seize my Spirits: However, I arm'd myself so as to prevent any Appearance of it in my Countenance. The Sultan's Eyes were no ways fiery, but that was not sufficient to assure me; for, what occasion is there to shew Wrath only to destroy a Shrub? As soon as he saw me at his Feet, Son of *Hanif*, said he to me, let us pray; let us fall down before him who never dies. These Words encreas'd my Terror. The Sultan, the General, the Iman, the Captain of

---

[d] Mahometan *Ecclefiasticks, who have the Care of the Mosques.*

the Guards, the Guards that attended at the Door, knelt down, bow'd their Faces towards the Ground, and glorify'd the Prophet. Uncertain of my Fate, I invok'd this faithful interpreter of the Will of the Almighty to be my Protector. My Soul communicated her Meditations to him thus: Messenger of God, if I've always detested the three Heresies; [e] if my Resolutions were sincere, when I went to pay Honour to thy Shrine, and to bedew with my Sweat the holy Mount *Arafat*[f]; if I have made it hitherto the chief Delight of my Mind, and the Attention of my Eyes, to read over the divine Book, be then my support. The Computation of my Days will soon perhaps be expir'd. I see already the dark and frightful Angels [g] ready to receive me. Remember how much Faith I repose in thee; there is but one God, and thou art his Prophet.

The Prayer being ended, the Sultan rose up, and turning towards me, said, Son of *Hanif*, I have resolv'd on making thee undertake a long Voyage, bow down thy Head. Father of *Muffelmen*, answer'd I, with a pretty bold Accent, the Voyage will be certainly long, and without return, which

[e] *The three principal Heresies among the* Mahometans *are,* First, *That by Grace we are saved independently of the Law.* Secondly, *That by Truth we are sav'd independently both of Grace and the Law.* Thirdly, *That all Religions are Good. Those who maintain this last Principle are burnt as soon as discover'd. Nevertheless,* Mahomet *himself has taught this Doctrine:* " Every Man, *says he,* that practises virtue, *Jew,* " *Christian,* or other, who quits his Religion to embrace " another; every Man, who adores God, and does good " actions, will be sav'd. *Alc. az.* 2.

[f] *A Mountain not far from* Mecca, *where* Adam *and* Eve'*s Eyes were open'd, according to the* Mahometan *Fables. The Pilgrims that go to* Mecca *run up it.*

[g] Monkir *and* Quarekir, *dark Angels, to whom the* Mahometans *are deliver'd after Death.*

we muſt all expect to make at different Times; may the moſt mighty and merciful God multiply thy Years. When I had pronounc'd theſe few Words, I comforted my ſelf on my Knees, and ſtretch'd forth my Neck. He drew out my Sabre, which he had not let out of his Hands, even during the Prayer, and extended his Arm; but inſtead of ſevering my Head from my Body, he ſheath'd the Blade again; which unexpected Clemency exacted from the Aſſiſtants loud Acclamations of Joy; I open'd my Eyes, which Darkneſs, the Forerunner of Death, had already clos'd. How great was my Surprize! *Chah-Jehan*, with a pleaſant Aſpect, came and rais'd me from my former Poſition, embrac'd me, and avow'd he was as much charm'd with my Courage, as with my Obedience. Then he order'd *Oglouf-Kan* to retire with his Guards, plac'd me between *Fazel-Kan* and *Emir-Jemla*, over againſt his Sopha, and made Signs to *Emir-Jemla* to ſpeak to me.

My Lord, ſaid *Emir-Jemla*, I have ſeen and talk'd with a Man that was 340 Years of Age, and who had ten more to live. He was found oppreſs'd with Chains, in the King of *Golkonda*'s Camp, after the Defeat, and the Victory which you obtain'd over him, procur'd this ſame Perſon his Liberty. I detain'd him three Days, which hardly ſuffic'd to relate the Revolutions that he had ſeen, during the Courſe of his long Life. I did not think it fit to keep him any longer, ſo I gave him the Sum of ten Roupies[h], with his Liberty to go where he pleas'd. He was a Native of *Bengal*, and was call'd the old Man of that Place. His Eyes were very much ſunk in

[h] *A Piece of Silver, worth about thirty Pence,* French Money.

his Head, his Voice was clear, his Hair and Beard very nicely comb'd out, and as white as Snow. Tho' his Visage was full of Wrinkles, yet it wore a fine fresh Colour, and one might easily discover in it a Gaiety that naturally accompanies a perfect Health. He seem'd to have been bigger than he was, and his Body being thus shrunk, cou'd scarcely be brought to stoop. The Nerves in his Neck appear'd likewise to be contracted, and to have drawn his Head nigher to his Shoulders; nevertheless he walk'd nimbly, and without any thing to support him. Being ask'd what means he us'd to attain so very advanc'd an age, he told me, his Father, who was 350 Years old, had bequeath'd three Dozes of the Water brought from the Fountain of the Island of *Borico*, and that by virtue of which, he had been thrice restor'd to his former Youth. I cautiously desir'd him to tell me in what Part of the World this Island was, and whether it was permitted to fetch any of the Water contained in this blessed Fountain of Life. He protested he could not answer either of the Questions, and that he had even several times propos'd the same Demand to his Father, but could never be satisfy'd in them. I then press'd him very strenuously to inform me, by what means his Father came by so surprizing a Liquor: He always made answer it was a Present made him by *Vichnou*, [i] a God, whom he had for a long time sacrific'd to. Thus, my Lord, you have heard all I cou'd gather from this *Kafar*.[k] So fabulous a Conclusion as that was, did not a little contribute to make me despise him; for after

[i] Parabaravastou, *the Chief of the Gods, created, as the* Indians *say, three inferior Gods, namely,* Bruma, Vichnou *and* Routren.
[k] *Or* Kafer, *wicked, treacherous.*

B 3   what

what Manner foever I queſtion'd him, he ſtill perſiſted in the ſame Story. *Emir* having finiſh'd what he had to ſay, *Chah-Jehan* turn'd towards the Son of *Haſam*, who with the moſt profound Reſpect, mov'd his Hand to his Forehead, and ſpoke in the following Manner.

Sacred Defender of the Faithful, may the Sword of the deſtroying Angel [1] grow ruſty in thy Favour. I have neither conceal'd my Sentiments from thee, nor diſguis'd what our Books have taught me. *Amrou*, Son of *Gigim*, ſays, in his Hiſtory of the World, in the Chapter where he treats of thoſe Parts obvious to our Knowledge, tho' we don't know preciſely where they lie, that the Iſland of *Borico* is ſituated by it ſelf, ſurrounded by a vaſt Extent of Sea; that Days and Nights are of an Equality; and that Trees bear Fruit all the Year there, becauſe the Alteration of the Seaſons is imperceptible. He alſo makes mention of the Water that gives youthful Vigour to Bodies impair'd by Weakneſs and old Age; and aſſures us, that a ſmall Piece of Building environs the Fountain. The chief Prieſt, who alone has the keeping of the Key of this Edifice, diſpoſes of none of the Water, but after certain Directions, which he preſcribes. The Natives even of the Iſland are depriv'd of it, and only allow'd to make uſe of what conveys itſelf into the Out Parts, which has nothing nigh the ſame Virtue. It fortifies indeed, but the Source only can reſtore Youth. The Water of the Fountain taſtes like the moſt exquiſite Wine, and is of ſuch Strength, that the leaſt Exceſs of drinking it kindles a Fire in the

---

[1] *His Name is* Adriel, *he deſtroys all Mankind. According to* Mahomet, *he will be chang'd into a Sheep at the End of the World, and will kill himſelf between Hell and Paradiſe.*

Veins,

Veins, which is not to be extinguished but by the Loſs of Life.

But who inſtructed *Amrou* ſo well, interrupted *Chah-Jehan?* and from whom had he this Relation? My Lord, reſum'd the Chief of the *Imans*, he does not ſatisfy us as to that Article, but I fancy he muſt have had it from ſome Traveller; for he adds, that ſeveral Foreigners had in vain attempted to take the little Edifice by Force. " An Army of Phantoms, *ſays he*, ſuppreſs'd
" their Temerity. Some were menac'd by Lyons
" and Dragons in Wrath; and others were re-
" pell'd by huge Giants, ready to eat them up.
" Some felt the Earth quake under their Feet;
" and others again had like to have been con-
" ſum'd by blazing Cataracts of elemental Flames.
" All the Natives came pouring down likewiſe
" in Arms upon them; inſomuch, that thoſe
" who cou'd ſooneſt reach their Veſſel, eſteem'd
" themſelves moſt bleſs'd with God's divine Aſ-
" ſiſtance.

Its very probable, My Lord, that the Son of *Gigim*, who neglected no Opportunity of cultivating his Underſtanding, heard a Deſcription of what I've juſt now related, by ſome of thoſe who made their Eſcape.

The Sultan, perceiving *Fazel-Kan* had given over ſpeaking, broke out into an Exclamation, ſaying thrice together, what a Treaſure would the Water of that Source be! Then he look'd ſtedfaſtly on me, and ſaid; *Abdalla*, if the Voyage I ſeem'd to threaten thee with cou'd not make thee afraid, how ſhouldſt thou dread going that of the Iſland of *Borico* in my Service? I was extremely rejoic'd at laſt, to know what my Adventure was likely to produce. Moſt potent of Kings, anſwer'd I, I fear none but thee on Earth.

This Inftant I'll range the Seas, and cut me to Pieces if I don't bring thee what thou defireft. Depart inftantly, reply'd *Chah-Jehan*, for the Years thou fhalt annex to mine, fhall prove as many happy ones to thee. Defpife the Phantoms of *Amrou*, his Recital of them is fuperfluous. A refolute and arm'd People was fufficient to fubdue thofe who have impos'd on this Author. I receiv'd my Orders with the moft profound Humility. The Sultan ftrictly charg'd us to conceal the Secret, and deputed *Emir-Jemla* to fupply me with what was neceffary for the Voyage. Then I withdrew full of Joy and Inquietude.

The next Morning at peep of Day, I left *Agra*, and difpos'd my felf to join a Caravan that was juft going to *Cambaye*. I had no Equipage but an ordinary Suit of Cloaths on my Back, tho' I carried about me, in Gold and Jewels, to the Value of a Town. I commonly let the Company I met with pafs by me, on purpofe that I might have the more Liberty to think on the Means of executing my Commiffion. I was very penfive; I thought there was no Poffibility of Succefs, and look'd upon my Expedition as a Banifhment. I am going, faid I, to wander I know not where, in queft of an Ifland that perhaps is no where to be found. Nothing is more certain than my incertitude of the Road I ought to take. However, I began at laft to arm my felf againft the difcouraging Thoughts my Soul had fuggefted, and to take fuch Meafures, as fhould either make me fucceed contrary to all hope, or convince me my Search was vain. A Day's Journey from *Bargant*, I perceiv'd I was not the only Perfon that had avoided Company to indulge Reflection. A young Man, well mounted, of a very agreeable Afpect, feem'd to be much in the fame way of thinking

with

with my felf, which I was convinc'd of by the feveral Obfervations I made of him. His melancholy Air having infpir'd me with Curiofity, I follow'd him pretty brifkly. When I was fomewhat near to him, I heard him fetch a great Sigh, and fay pretty high, fuppofing himfelf alone; *Oh! if fhe now efcapes, I am irretrievably loft.* The Noife of my Horfe interrupting his Refvery, we faluted each other. The Converfation at firft was carried on with Indifference, till at laft we both became interefted in it. I found Means to infinuate my felf into his Confidence, and therefore he made no Difficulty to relate me the Subject of his Inquietudes, in the following Manner.

The Hiftory of ALMORADDIN.

MY Name is *Almoraddin,* and I am the only Son of a Merchant, who was about three Years ago, one of the Richeft of *Cambaye.* His Excefs of Love and Tendernefs for me, has reduc'd him into very indifferent Circumftances; and for the fame Reafon, perhaps, he is juft on the Brink of confuming what little Subftance he has left. Alas! how wretched am I, to be both the Caufe of his Misfortune and my own! I've deluded him into an Abyfs of my own making, where Love and Vanity have continually precipitated me, and where Defpair now plunges me a third Time. Some Relations Sons of our Bufinefs, refolving to apply themfelves to Commerce, and to go a trafficking Voyage to *Siam,* made me an offer to forfake Pleafures and Idlenefs, as they
had

had done, in order to fee the World, and to acquire Riches. I was eafily prevail'd upon to comply, and as eafily brought my Father to give into it. He equip'd me a fine Ship, loaded it with rich Merchandife, and after having recommended Vigilance and Fidelity to me, and given me his Bleffing, I had his Leave to begin my Voyage. We coafted all the Ifthma of *India*, without meeting with the leaft bad Weather; but the Wind changing, when we had fail'd Part of the Ifland of *Ceylan*, we ventur'd to enter into the Streights of *Malacca*, and thought it beft to coaft round the Ifland of *Sumatra*. One Day, as I was amufing my felf on Deck, I efpied a fine Sea-Port, and adjoining to it, a Town moft delightfully fituated. I immediately afk'd the Pilot the Name of it, and exprefs'd at the fame Time a vaft Inclination to go afhore there. That Town, anfwer'd he, is the capital City of the little Kingdom of *Barroftan*, which is govern'd at prefent by Queen *Zulikbah*, one of the beautifulleft Princeffes in the Eaft. She has made a Law, which has been already the Ruin of numberlefs imprudent Youths. If you follow my Advice, you'll look upon her Port as a dangerous Rock, and we fhall purfue our Voyage.

What does that Law enjoin? anfwer'd I, your Difcourfe furprifes me. This Law, reply'd he, obliges every Commander of a Ship that enters her Port, to lie one Night with the Queen. If any Familiarity happens between them, he muft of Neceffity become her Spoufe; but if he does not anfwer the warm Expectations of *Zulikbah*, his Veffel, Men and Cargo, are confifcated, and himfelf banifh'd from her Dominions the next Day. Were my Life even to lie at Stake, refum'd I, I am refolv'd to try whether Fortune
will

will favour me more than thofe you have been fpeaking of, and to experience their Deficiency in pleafing fo very amiable a Princefs. The Pilot wou'd fain have continued his Remonftrances, but I compell'd him to obey; when we enter'd full fail into the Harbour. Upon my landing, a Crowd of Courtiers met me to pay their Compliments; the Populace look'd upon me in the Streets I pafs'd thro', with a Kind of Admiration, and her Majefty gave me a very gracious Reception. The Moment I accofted her, how did her fhining Eyes inflame my Soul! Such charming rofy Lips! accompanied with fuch regular Features, as can only be imagin'd! what a heavenly Complexion! how delicate a Shape[a]! what Sweetnefs, and what Majefty united together! to fee all thefe Charms center'd in one Perfon tranfported me. I moft willingly receiv'd the Impreffion they made, in Expectation of enjoying them immediately when the happy Opportunity approach'd. *Zulikhah* took me by the Hand, and having feated me nigh her, fhe afk'd me, with all the Affability imaginable, if I was acquainted with the Laws of that Country? Fair *Zulikhah*, reply'd I, your Laws are not unknown to me; could I but merit the Happinefs they impofe as an Obligation! There can't be any fo fweet in the World; nor fo feverely obferv'd, refum'd fhe, fmiling. After that fhe chang'd the Converfation, and afk'd fome Queftions concerning me and my Voyage. All I was capable of faying on that Score, feem'd to afford her a Deal of Pleafure. Our Supper was ferv'd with the utmoft Magnificence, follow'd by a Ball, all the Ho-

[a] *Throughout all the Eaſt Country, a fine Shape is what gives the Name of Beauty.*

nour of which I engrofs'd, according to the Judgment of the Queen, who could not forbear admiring me perform the Dance ᵇ of the *Parſes*. When it grew late, ſhe conducted me to her Apartment; a handſome Slave brought us Sweet-meats and Liquors; we undreſs'd our ſelves, and the Moment we were in Bed I fell a Sleep. Next Morning, two arm'd Men awoke me, and ſaid in a rough Manner, mind thou obſerv'ſt the Law. I open'd my Eyes, examin'd the Place the Queen had quitted, I curs'd my bad Fate for ſleeping, dreſs'd my ſelf with all Expedition, and then the two Men thruſt me out of the Palace. No Language is extenſive enough to expreſs the Fatigues I underwent in traverſing the Iſland. At laſt I reach'd *Achen*, where I found a Veſſel oblig'd to touch at *Cambaye*, ſo ſhip'd my ſelf on board of it, in the Quality of a common Sailor.

Being arriv'd in my native Country, I went directly to one of my Friends, who hardly knew me again, being ſo much disfigur'd. I made him believe my Ship was loſt upon a Rock, and deſir'd him to acquaint my Father with my Shipwreck and Arrival. This was ſending him the Diſeaſe and the Remedy at the ſame Time. He did not regard the Loſs of a third Part of his Riches in the leaſt, but haſten'd to meet me where I was. Oh Son! ſaid he, embracing me, let us rejoice and be of good Comfort; the Sea has left us the moſt valuable of our Treaſures, by preſerving thy Life. He led me home, where I found every thing that might engage me to forget the reſt of the World. Some time after that, my Companions arriv'd alſo laden with vaſt

---

ᵇ *The Deſcendants of the ancient Inhabitants of* Perſia, *who ſtill ſubſiſt in ſome Parts of* Indoſtan *and* Perſia.

Riches,

p. 1. 2

[13]

Riches. I related to them my pretended Misfortune, which they feem'd fenfibly affected at. If you are difpos'd, faid they, to venture again to Sea next Spring, we will keep in Company the whole Voyage, and your Lofs fhall be doubly repair'd. I needed not many Perfuafions to bring me to a Refolution of leaving *Cambaye* a fecond Time: The Idea of the charming Queen of *Barroftan* being forcible enough to make me accept the Propofition.

When the Winter Seafon was almoft fpent, my Father, taking Notice of my Penfivenefs, prefs'd me to tell him what troubled my Mind. Can you be ignorant of it, replied I? I fhall die with Grief, if I don't find fome way or other to repair the Lofs you have fuftain'd by my Misfortune. My dear Child, refum'd he, don't think of expofing your felf to frefh Dangers. Let us rather peaceably enjoy our little Certainty at home. This is entirely my advice; but if you are fully bent on courting Fortune a fecond Time, I love you too well to make any Oppofition to it. I burft into Tears of Gratitude, which ferv'd to compleat his Tendernefs. He prepar'd a Veffel for me, much richer laden than the former; he renew'd his Inftructions, and I joyfully fet fail along with the reft of my Friends. I had no fooner difcover'd the fatal Ifland. but I let the Company Ships make the Streights of *Malacca* before me; and backening my Courfes till Night, I bore away in fpi.e of them. As for the Ships Company, it was fruitlefs for them to oppofe my Defign. With what Regret did the faithful and experienc'd Pilot refign his Care of the Rudder, and with how much Joy did I immediately take the Management of it, and fteer that Courfe which blind Love directed me. I was much more

carefs'd

carefs'd now than the firſt Time of my Arrival, I being the only Perſon that ever return'd thither a ſecond Time. The divine *Zulikhah* ſtrove to charm me by additional Graces, which ſhe made to ſhine before my Eyes; but alas! how ill did I repay her kind Advances! A jealous Devil lull'd me to ſleep as ſoon as we were in Bed. When I awoke in the Morning, my Aſtoniſhment and Deſpair exceeded all Bounds, and nothing cou'd equal them, but the Hardſhips I endur'd in my Journey to *Cambaye*.

Here a thouſand Sobs interrupted *Almoraddin*'s Diſcourſe. I confeſs, ſaid I to him, your Misfortunes exact Tears, but ſtill you are happy in having learnt both how to avoid Dangers, and to overcome your ſelf. Such Knowledge is never too dear bought. Alas! cry'd he, I have pay'd the Price, without acquiring it. How unfortunate am I! I have loſt two Ships and valuable Cargoes with them; my Father commiſerates the ill Fate of my ſecond pretended Ship-wreck, and even conſents to run the Hazard of a third, which perhaps will reduce us to the laſt Extremity of Want. We have converted all the little Stock we had left into Merchandiſe. Even my Father's Liberty ſtands at ſtake: He has borrow'd of the wealthy *Mamut* of *Aden*, the Sum of ten thouſand *Roupies*, upon Condition of becoming his Slave, if he does not pay him the ſaid Sum again in a Years time.

The eaſy to be wrought on Goodneſs of the Father, and the Obſtinacy of the Son, excited very much my Compaſſion. As all Countries were indifferent to me, for what I had to do, I made an offer of my Service to accompany him in his Voyage. I'll unravel, ſaid I to him, what prov'd the Cauſe of your Miſcarriages; you muſt certainly

p. 15

certainly have acted void of Precaution. He readily accepted my Proposal, with all the Transports of Joy imaginable: Thus we continu'd travelling always together. I discover'd to him whom I was, and what Reasons had induc'd me to forsake my own Country; attributing only that to my Caprice and Curiosity, which I had never undertaken but by an Order, that strictly enjoin'd me to secrecy. If I may judge of his Thoughts by my own, I fancy we were both equally surpriz'd at the whimsical Motives of our Voyages; and that whilst I was accusing him within my self of *Madness*, he was wondering the same Time at my extravagant *Folly*.

One Day towards Evening, as we were travelling before the Caravan, and entertaining our selves as usual, we heard a sad and lamentable Outcry come from the Ruins of an old Mosque, encompass'd with Trees, and pretty distant from the high Road. We immediately hasten'd that Way, and after having ty'd up our Horses to a Tree, we pass'd thro' a Thicket to the Place, where the Cries, which augmented more and more, were heard. There presented to our View a Gang of *Bramines* [e] and *Fakirs* [d], who were using Violence to two young Creatures of their own Religion. Tho' four of these Ruffians were employ'd to hold each of them, whilst two of the Chief of the Gang strove to satisfy their Brutality, yet still they made a laudable Resistance. As became true *Musselmen*, we fell upon these infamous Villains, Sword in Hand. Detestable Rascals, said I to them, I'll punish your Impu-

[e] Bramines *or* Brahmens, *religious* Gentiles, *much respected, but great Cheats.*
[d] *Another Sort of religious Idolaters.*

dence

dence and Hypocrify, and Death fhall be the only Attonement of the foul Crime you attempt to commit. The three that were next me foon experienc'd the Fury of my Arm: The reft, quitting their Hold of the Women, form'd directly a fmall Battalion, and having drawn their *Canjars*[e] from under their Robes, they difpos'd themfelves being thus arm'd to attack us, uttering forth moft dreadful Howlings at the fame Time. Thefe hideous Shouts had not their defign'd Effect; for inftead of terrifying us they prov'd fatal to them, drawing almoft all the Soldiers belonging to the Convoy of the Caravan to our Affiftance. Four more of thefe Villains had fallen by our Hands when this Succour came up to us; the reft were furrounded and cut in Pieces without any Quarter. I was not wounded in the Action, but *Almoraddin* was flightly in one of his Shoulders.

During the Combat the Women had hid themfelves, but as foon as it was ended, they came from the Bufhes that had ferv'd them as an Afylum. They proftrated themfelves before us, greatly acknowledging us for their Deliverers and Mafters. We did not fuffer them long to remain in this Pofture: Praife God, faid I to them, and honour *Mahomet* his Prophet, whofe Slaves we are; for his invincible Sword has deliver'd you. As the approach of Night did not permit us to ftay any longer in that Place, we took up the Women behind us, and went, after having diftributed fome Money among the Soldiers, who equally divided the Spoils of the Slain, to look for Lodgings.

We were fo much fatigu'd, that however curious we might be to hear the Adventures of our

[e] Canjar, *a fhort but very broad Poniard.*

fair

fair Captives, we gave way to sleep immediately after Supper was over. They pass'd the Night in the same Chamber, much admiring our Modesty; but they were ignorant of *Almoraddin*'s Heart being too deeply engag'd at *Sumatra*, and that for my Part, I had resolv'd never to embark my self in any Pleasure that might give me too great an Attachment. The next Day, we provided them with Horses, and pursuing our Journey, we desir'd them to inform us how they came to fall into the Hands of those Villains we deliver'd them from.

The eldest of the two, who was very richly drest, drew from her Bosom a little Parcel, which she presented to me, saying: It is highly just that I should give you some Proofs of my Gratitude, and that the Plunder, which the Hypocrites thought to make, should devolve on you. I made a decent Refusal of her Present, as did also *Almoraddin*. You are not sensible, reply'd she, of what I offer you. She open'd the Parcel, which prov'd to be a considerable Quantity of Diamonds and other Jewels, very nicely wrought. Since you have, said I to her, so luckily preserv'd this Treasure, it would be as barbarous in us to deprive you of it. Be so good, added *Almoraddin*, as not to delay gratifying our eagerness to hear you, and in doing that, you'll make us all the Return we require. The generous Answer of this Merchant, considering the present Posture of his Affairs, enhanc'd very much my Esteem of him.

The Adventure of the INDIAN LADY, deliver'd from the Fire.

NOT long ago, resum'd the Lady to those present, I was the happiest Woman in all *Kitcur*. My Husband was both young, handsome and complaisant; his Relations shew'd me the most tender Regard, and each Day produc'd a new Scene of Delight. I was married a twelve Month, and I scarce thought it one. At last, a terrible Fit of the Cholick unhappily put an End to my Husband's Life and my own Felicity, which the most skilful Physicians try'd in vain to preserve. When he gave up his last Breath, I was sitting down at the Head of his Bed in a most deplorable Condition; his Relations were all in Tears; the *Bramines* invok'd the assisting Spirits, and conjur'd the Day Star to send the Rays of Light to re-animate the then lifeless Body. But alas! that dear Portion of the Divinity was already too far flown from its Matter to be rejoin'd, it was united to its Source. I fell into a Swound, from which I was no sooner recover'd, but a strange Delirium seiz'd me. I can't tell what my Disorder might make me say at that time, but when my Spirits were settled, I found my self upon my Bed, encompass'd by *Bramines*, who seem'd by their Gestures and Singing to be exceeding Gay.

Their Folly did much augment my Grief. I passionately ask'd them what was the meaning of their Mirth? Their Chief, an aged Man of great Authority, impos'd silence on the rest, and kissing my Hand, in spite of me, said: 'Tis your heroic

heroic Virtue we celebrate, your conjugal Tenderness, your faithful Love, a divine Fire, which the purest Flames that ever proceded from Balm or Cinnamon, are unworthy to be mix'd with. Oh happy deceas'd! continued he, raising his Voice, blifsful Soul! bright Spark that augments the Lustre of the Day be no longer agitated! Thy faithful Confort will be shortly rais'd to join and mingle Glory with thee. Whilst he was delivering this fatal Difcourfe [a], which I too well comprehended, I endeavour'd to make my Efcape; but the cruel old Man, and those who were fubfervient to him, confpir'd to detain me, continuing to overwhelm me with their deceitful Praifes. You are the Glory of your Country, faid they, you are the Support of our Religion, a Prodigy of Courage, and a worthy Example to the Memory of fucceeding Ages. By you, all Widows will learn to follow their tender Hufbands into the other World, and to purify their Charms in the facred Fire. How delightful is it to blend our Afhes with thofe we formerly cherifh'd, and to fly to the Center of Light to celebrate new Nuptials!

I am unworthy of all thefe Honours you heap upon me, cry'd I; my Spoufe will be fatisfy'd with my Tears; I fhall rejoin him as he quitted me, when Fate ordains it. But you have chofen, reply'd they all together, to end your Days after a more glorious Manner; your Soul is rais'd above it felf. *Oh dearejt of Hufbands!* did you fay, *I cannot, will not furvive thee.* You faid it, and our Ears heard it; don't therefore op-

---

[a] *The* Indian *Women are oblig'd to be burnt alive with the dead Bodies of their Hufbands, if, in their Grief, they happen to fay they'll die for him. The* Mahometans *endeavour as much as poffible to abolifh this Cuftom.*

pose any longer a pretended Modesty to the Praises you merit. We have inform'd the Magistrates of it, your Relations, all your fellow Citizens; they have deliver'd you up to our Zeal, and we will not fail to see the Execution of their Desires. I represented that I had not been heard, and that if any Expression slipt from me, worthy of Death, I said it during my Delirium. Notwithstanding this, they listen'd not to my Allegation. My Frenzy was judg'd as a supernatural Condition, and capable of acting with Reason in it. My Persecutors did not suffer me out of their Sight, whilst my Husband's Corps was washing, and the Pile of Wood making ready. My Complaints being fruitless, I resolv'd, out of Despair, to refuse taking any Sustenance, and to keep in a continual Silence. This Conduct even was look'd upon as a marvellous Effect of my Virtue, as my infamous Panegyrists would insinuate: The half of my Soul, said they, was already with the Sun, and the other disdain'd the common Weaknesses of human Nature.

The Chief of these *Barbarians*, who found me agreeable to his Inclination, and had a conceal'd Design, was very much alarm'd at my Resolution. The Night before my intended Obsequies, instead of exhorting me as usual, he whisper'd me, and said, *Fear not, fair Lady, I'll find means to save you. The Gods mov'd at my Prayers, resign you up for some time, to their Minister, and command you not to abridge a Life, that even the Flames revere by Hunger.* I greedily swallow'd the Hope of it, without examining too much the Price the Deceiver set upon my Deliverance. I eat, I reeiv'd the Congratulations of my Friends, and all the Commissions they gave me for the other World without Concern. The next Day they drest me in in the richeft Apparel I had, and conducted me by the Sound of Inftruments to the Pile, that was erected at an extraordinary Expence, without the City Gates. I enter'd the Lodge that was prepar'd for me, and my Hufband's Body was laid crofs my Knees, according to the Cuftom of *Kitour*. As foon as the Entrance of the Lodge was ftopt up, the Pile was fet on Fire, and the Air eccho'd with the mournful Sound of the Flutes, and the Acclamations of the Populace. At the firft Appearance of the Flames, I was repoffefs'd of all my former Terror; efpecially when the combuftible Matters I was fitting on, funk down with me on a fudden under the Earth. The Meafures were fo well taken, that my Defcent prov'd fuccefsful. Two *Bramines*, whom I faw not, but heard, immediately remov'd my Hufband's Body from me, and having drawn it up again into the Lodge that was all on Fire, they ftopt it up with Materials proper for that Purpofe. After that, they convey'd me thro' a long and obfcure Paffage that led into a Vault, where they fhut me up.

The Ceremony of my funeral Rites being over, and the Night fucceeding, the *Bramines* and their Chief repair'd to the Place where I was. My Vault being pretty large and very light, the Brothers made a very fplendid Entertainment, were exceeding merry, and did not a little pun upon the eafy Credulity of the People. When Supper was ended, they divided themfelves by the old Man's Orders, fome going under Ground, and the others without, to put the finifhing Stroke to the Reparation of the Place where we defcended from the Pile, that the Knowledge of their Artifice might not be perceivable by the moft difcerning. I expected now to be attack'd by the old *Bramine*,

he

he remaining alone with me; but whether he had a Mind to win me by feign'd Respect, or rather, that he did not think the Circumstances suitable, I can't tell; nothing however was offer'd at that Time, but an exaggerated Representation of the Favour he had done me. Six *Bramines*, whom he probably repos'd a particular Confidence in, came back again to us before Day-light, provided with Horses and Provisions. Just after I had taken all the Jewels off my Cloaths, they disguis'd me in a long Robe, like those they wear certain Days in the Year. Thus we set forward, I not knowing whither they design'd to carry me.

The farther we left *Kitour* behind us, the more clearly my odious Lover declar'd in what View he had procur'd my Deliverance. We met Yesterday at *Maffan*, a Company of *Fakirs*, who having a Waggon, travell'd more commodious than we. As these Sort of People commonly keep a very good Understanding with each other, their Chief readily accepted the Proposition ours made him to unite Companies. We left our Horses at *Maffan*, and I was plac'd next this virtuous Lady, who was expos'd to the same Danger as my self, and the *Bramines* and *Fakirs* sat one among another. Their Chiefs, despairing to bring us to a shameful Consent by fair Means, resolv'd to effect their Designs by having Recourse to the last Extremity; when, luckily for us, the vile Accomplishment of them prov'd abortive, in the Place, that ought to be hereafter the Theatre of your Glory.

We were sensibly touch'd at the Account this charming *Indian* gave us of her Delivery. *Almoraddin* made an offer of his Service to shelter her at his Father's House, well knowing she was no longer safe at *Kitour*. She return'd him many
Thanks,

Thanks, telling us, she had an Uncle at *Amadabat*, who was a *Muſſulman*, nam'd *Ali-Bajou*, that would protect her from all future Danger. It were ſufficient, ſaid I to her, to be a *Muſſulman*, to do ſo good an Action. Then we beheld, as deſignedly, the other fair Maid, who with a ſmiling Countenance, ſaid to us: Generous Defenders of my Life and Liberty, the beginning of my Misfortunes was not ſo tragick as that which you have heard this Lady ſay ſhe underwent.

The Adventure of the INDIAN VIRGIN carried away by the FAKIRS.

I Come from a large Market Town that lies on the high Road, about a Mile and a half from *Amanabat*. We ſhall paſs thro' it, ſo muſt beg you'll pleaſe to leave me to the Care of my Relations, who live there. About four Days ago the Feaſt of the God *Ram* [a], and the Monkey *Innuman* [b], was celebrated there. This Day is always ſolemniz'd with great rejoicing, in Memory of the Victory they obtain'd over the Giant *Ravanem*, and the Deliverance of *Sidi*, Wife of *Ram*, whom the ſaid Giant had detain'd in his Iſland of *Serandib* [c]. There was a great Concourſe of Strangers in the Streets, who either reſorted there out of Devotion, or a Deſire of partaking of the Diverſions which that Place affords on ſuch

[a] Ram, *is the God* Vichnou *made Man*
[b] *The King of Monkeys. 'Twas he that firſt found out the Raviſher of* Sidi, *and ſupply'd* Ram *with an Army of five hundred Millions of Monkeys.*
[c] *It is the Iſland of* Ceilan *that* Ravanem *was King of.*

Occasions. The Inhabitants were mingled among the rest, who amus'd themselves in beholding a thousand different Spectacles. Upon the Market-Place there were Comedians, who diverted the Publick by little Scenes of Buffoonry; Posture-Masters, whose Dexterity was astonishing; Dancers, who were admir'd for their Agility; and Musicians, who sung the grand Chorus. The *Fakirs*, whom you so deservedly punish'd, drew likewise about them a great Number of Spectators, by representing, in a very moving Manner, on their Waggon, which was drawn along, the carrying away of *Cariavarti*, Daughter of *Bruma*. The youngest among them, dress'd in Women's Cloaths, acted the Part of the Goddess. At her first Appearance, she sat on the Front of the Waggon, in a very negligent Posture, amusing her self in making a Nosegay of various Flowers, and singing harmoniously at the same Time. Whilst she was thus imploy'd, the God *Bruma*, plac'd at the hind Part of the Waggon, express'd, in Presence of his *Andis*[d], the Violence of his Passion for his Daughter; and they advis'd him to metamorphose himself into a Stag, to surprize her, and to ravish her, since she refus'd to extinguish the Conflagration she had rais'd in his Soul. *Bruma*, receiving their Advice, plac'd a huge Pair of Buck's Horns on his Forehead, and, with the Assistance of his Favourites, seiz'd on *Cariavarti*, carried her away, and conceal'd her under a large Silk Coverlid, that represented a Forest[e]. Then the Waggon mov'd. The Goddess was very strangely agita-

[d] *The* Andis, *of an* Indian *Divinity, are those who perform great Penances in his Honour.*
[e] *The God* Bruma *ravish'd his own Daughter in a Forest, transform'd into a Stag.*

ted,

ted, and fill'd the Air with Cries. She was heard, by Intervals, fay thefe lamentable Words: Alas! They are carrying me away! Where are my Relations? Oh *Vichnou!* Oh *Rutren!* Will the Traitors live long without Punifhment? *Bruma* and his *Andis* readily mimick'd, in a very comical Manner, all her Geftures; and repeating her Words with different Accents, they form'd an Harmony that made the whole Audience laugh.

Unhappily for me, I was fo much pleas'd with this Spectacle, and follow'd the Waggon fo confiderable a Time, that the God *Bruma* took particular Notice of me. Towards Evening, after the laft Reprefentation, he pull'd off his Mafk and Horns, bad the Spectators give Attention, and faid: Adorers of *Ram*, we efteem our felves very happy, in having afforded you any Diverfion by this our Performance. But do ye think you are acquainted with all we can do? No, no, you fuppofe we take time in ftudying our Tones and Geftures; and it is therefore neceffary for us to undeceive you, by renewing fome other agreeable Scene. Whilft he was fpeaking thefe Words, he gave a Signal to his Companions, who very probably were accuftom'd to fuch like Crimes. The *Fakirs* jump'd down upon the Ground, feiz'd me, threw me upon their Waggon, and wrapp'd me in *Cariavarti*'s Coverlid, all which was done in the twinkling of an Eye. I began to ftruggle, to fquawl out, and to call Men and Dogs to my Succour; but thefe Mirrors of Impudence mimick'd exactly what they faw me do, and drown'd my Complaints in their ridiculous Sounds. This deceitful Mufick anfwer'd the End the pretended *Bruma* propos'd to himfelf; all the Affembly was diverted, and the Waggon began to move. Thofe who knew me, imagin'd, after one Turn round

the

the Market Place, I should be set down again in the Place from whence they took me, but the *Fakirs* had no such Design. They redoubled their Movements, till by Degrees they had convey'd me out of Town; which was no sooner done, but they drove the Horses in such a Manner, that the Waggon seem'd to fly. They got into a Wood about Midnight, where they would not have stopp'd, but to feed themselves and their Cattle. Till that Moment, the Fear and Confusion they were in, had hinder'd them from making me any Overtures; but then, their Chief began to declare himself openly my Lover, to tire me with his Importunities, and to urge his insolent Solicitations with more Fervency. I summon'd all the Presence of Mind I was Mistress of to repel them; but, alas! what Impression can the most skilful Argument make on a lustful Man, whom I was resolv'd not to condescend to? The most cruel Menaces had been already utter'd, when this agreeable Widow became my Companion in Distress; and Threatnings would have produc'd far more direful Effects, had not you, Gentlemen, render'd them void, by seasonably coming to our Succour.

The subtle Villainy of the *Fakirs*, in this second Adventure, appear'd so horrible in our Eyes, that we could not help loading them with a thousand Imprecations, tho' they were Dead. Had it been in our Power, we should have brought them to Life again, on Purpose to sacrifice it with more Torture and Satisfaction a second Time. We deliver'd the *Indian* Virgin up to her Parents, who embrac'd her with inexpressible Transports of Joy, and we no sooner reach'd *Amadabat*, but I conducted the fair Widow to her Uncle *Ali-Bajou*,

Bajou, who afterwards inſtructed her, and put her in the Paths of the Prophet.

Cambaye is a City too well known to need a particular Deſcription of it; but as it was there, I began ſeriouſly to diſcharge my ſelf of the Commiſſion *Chah-Jehan* had honour'd me with, it will be proper, in as few Words as poſſible, to give an Account here of the Method I took to procure all my Reſearches. The Moment I alighted in any Place, my firſt Care was to inform my ſelf, if there liv'd there or thereabouts, any very aged Perſons, famous learn'd Men, or celebrated Travellers; and if I found any, I ſpar'd nothing to make them talk with all the Franknefs imaginable.

When an old Man told me his Health was puny and wavering, I aſk'd what had reduc'd him to that imperfect State of Health; and when, on the contrary, he ſaid it was no ways impair'd, but found and vigorous, I begg'd him to tell me what Secret he made uſe of to preſerve his Strength. The major Part of them poſſeſs'd no ſuch Secret: Some anſwer'd, I eat but one Meal a Day; or, I never take Phyſick; or, I avoid what Fatigues the Body too much; or, I accuſtom my ſelf to very little Sleep. Others again, made quite oppoſite Anſwers: I eat four Meals a Day; I take a Purge every Month; I love Exerciſe; and I ſleep very much. The old Man of *Calicut*, aſſur'd me, his long Life was owing to the Care he always took in keeping his Head and Feet dry; and he of *Barroſtan*, attributed his to the natural Averſion he ever bore to raw Fruit and fat Victuals. Others alledg'd the Cauſe of their Health to proceed from avoiding Paſſion and Sadneſs; but never a one of them made the leaſt mention of the Iſland of *Borico*, or the Water that reſtores paſt Youth.

The

The learned Men behav'd with a vaſt Deal more Reſerve; but however, Money for the moſt Part reconcil'd me to thoſe, whom Praiſes had not Effect enough on. I propos'd to them various Queſtions on the Evacuations that happen to human Bodies, and on the Means to repair them. They made very fine Diſcourſes on that Head. They prov'd that the Preſervation of Bodies was nothing elſe but a perpetual Re-eſtabliſhment. They computed the Age of certain Trees [f] and Animals [g], ſuppos'd to live long, becauſe they die without being taken notice of. They added to the Liſt of theſe Animals, a much larger of Men and Women, whom they aver'd to have liv'd many Ages. The Accounts they gave me were well atteſted, and they were ignorant of nothing relating to theſe very aged People, but the Means that had preſerv'd them ſo long in the World. The Reaſons alledg'd on that Score tended to Infinity. At laſt, being urg'd to come to a Concluſion, they all avow'd their Ignorance, except the *Alchimiſts*, who could not be brought to agree that any was yet in Poſſeſſion of what they term, with Emphaſy, *The Sweet Enemy of Uglineſs, of Poverty and of Death*; but were continually hoping how to diſcover it. I don't rank the Lovers of ſupernatural Sciences among the Number of the learned Men by Profeſſion, becauſe they are of a ſuperior Order.

I have always grounded my chief Hopes on them and Travellers. Was not the old Man of *Bengal* a Traveller? and was not the Son of *Gigim* inſtructed alſo by Travellers? Whether I hap-

---

[f] *An Oak Tree is a hundred Year before it comes to its full Growth, it flouriſhes as many more, and decays the ſame.*

[g] *A Raven, a Crow, a Stag*, &c.

pen'd

pen'd to fojourn, or to be on the Road, I question'd thofe who had feen the World, without any other View but Curiofity, concerning what furprizing Things they had feen and heard of during their Travels. They did not require much Entreaty; for I always obferv'd, they were as fond of recounting their Adventures, as I was of hearing them. They were fo much the Reverfe of the learned Men, that they would even have pay'd me for liftening to, or rather admiring them; for, in the main, it's Admiration they want. I propos'd my felf two Views by exacting thefe Narrations: I was in hopes either naturally to hear fome News of the Motive of my Voyage, or elfe to come by the Knowledge of fome *Sage*, in unity with the *Genii*. Such was my Conduct where ever I pafs'd, fo fhall difpence my felf, at prefent, from purfuing the Thread of my Hiftory.

Almoraddin's Veffel being all in Readinefs, we put out to Sea. Our Paffage was both longer and more dangerous than the Seafon of the Year feem'd to promife. We were feveral Times oblig'd by bad Weather, to put in along the Coaft of the main Land, and even to ftay near a Month at *Calicut*, whilft our Ship was repair'd of the Damage fhe met with at Sea. There happen'd to be in the Town, at that Time, a *Perfian* Lady, the Relict of a Merchant of the fame Nation. This Lady's Name was *Roufchen*[h], who had a Daughter between eight and nine Years of Age, of a lively Wit, call'd *Loulou*[i]. Her Houfe was very much reforted to on Account of the many curious and furprizing Things which were talk'd of there. What moft excited my Curiofity, was the Voyage, fhe faid, fhe had made to the *Topfy-Turvy* Ifland, where

[h] *Shining.*   [i] *Pearl.*

fhe

she had been an Eye Witness of such Wonders, as no Mortal ever saw before her self. But when we arriv'd at *Calicut*, she had for some Time left off relating any thing about her Voyage thither, because she perceiv'd they had not Faith enough to believe it, and that the most Part of the Strangers, who frequented her House, look'd upon what she said concerning the *Peris*[k], and *Divs*[l], as meer Fiction. The Adorers of *Issa*[m] regarded her Notions as the Effect of Madness, and the rest did not know what to make of her.

I should have been sorry to have miss'd so favourable an Opportunity of becoming acquainted with so extraordinary a Person as she was; since the Name *Topsy-Turvy* Island gave me such a lively Idea of that I was in search of. We paid her several Visits, which she receiv'd with so much Civility, as left us no Room to believe our Company was disagreeable. She reason'd with such a Fluency of good Sense, upon all Sorts of Subjects, that my prejudice against all the Women of her Country began to dissipate. The young *Loulou* promoted likewise Conversation according to her Capacity. When we made our first Visit, I began to run in Praise of her fine Eyes and Eyebrows; upon which, *Roufchen* interrupted and said: *Daughter! make appear your Wit deserves far greater Encomiums.* I shall, answer'd *Loulou*, by telling these Strangers the Story of the three great Fishes.

[k] *These are good* Genii.   [l] *The Name of the bad* Genii.
[m] Jesus Christ.

The first Story of LOULOU.

YOU must know there was formerly a Pond in the Kingdom of *Staphilin*, which extends it self along the Coast of the *Grey* Sea, that was renown'd for producing very fine Fish. These Fishes were reserv'd for the King's Use only, and whosoever of his Subjects should presume to meddle with them, incurr'd his high Displeasure. He even forbid any should be caught for himself, during a considerable Time, which augmented the Growth of three of these Fishes to so preposterous a Size, that they lorded it over the whole Pond. As Fishes have their different Inclinations, as well as Men: So the first of them was very *couragcous*, the second very *cunning*, and the third very *slothful*. These Tyrants became, at last, so nice in their eating, that they turn'd up their Noses at their usual Food, and in short, nothing would go down with them but their Fellow Fishes, which depeopled the Pond in a very short Time.

As all vile Actions come to light one time or another, their rapacious Gluttony came at last to the King's Ears, who resolv'd to have them caught and to eat them. He sent therefore his Fishermen one Night to the Pond, ordering them to have their Nets in Readiness for the next Day. They repair'd thither accordingly; and as they were talking about their Commission, a Frog, not far from them, over-heard all they said, and went immediately to carry the fatal News to the three Fishes, who were at Supper together that Night. They made a Jest of what the poor Frog kindly forewarn'd them, and only thought of engaging his Company at Table, where they sat till Midnight,

night, and then fell asleep. As soon as the Sun was risen, the King went in Person, and order'd the Fishermen to environ the Pond with their Nets. The watchful Frog hearing what was in Agitation, thunder'd out his croaking, in order to awake the three Fishes, who were still asleep. The *courageous* and *cunning* ones awoke: The first made the best of his Way to the Mouth of a Brook that ran into the Pond, where he broke through the Net, and sav'd himself. The second counterfeited himself dead, and floated on the Surface of the Water, as though he had been poison'd. The Frog call'd the *lazy one* several times, but in vain; there was no such thing as stirring him, though the Sly-boots heard well enough all the while. He indulg'd himself so long, till at last the Fishermens Nets made their Approaches. They took up the *cunning one* that was floating, into their Hands, but smelling the pestiferous Matter he had rubb'd his Head with, they threw him into the Pond again as a rotten Fish. As for the *slothful one*, he had scarce open'd his Eyes when he was caught and carried away. Nay, I have heard it averr'd for Truth, that he even yawn'd several Times before the King, and ask'd, with his Eyes clos'd, what a Clock it was? This Prince perceiving he was fat and in extraordinary good Case, order'd the Officers of his Kitchen to open him, to cut him into Slices, and to dress him into several Sauces for his Breakfast. It is so true, added the little Story-teller, that a lazy Criminal never escapes the Punishment due to him.

We very much applauded the Subject and Manner, which the agreeable *Loulou* told it with. She related to us after that, several other such like Stories, which were learnt her, as we afterwards found out, by a *Portuguese* Slave, who had

the

the Care of her Education. But to return to the Mother. Our Friendſhip with her becoming now more familiar, we entreated her to pleaſure us with a Deſcription of her Voyage. She readily comply'd with our Requeſts, on Condition, each of us, in return, would likewiſe relate an Adventure as true and ſurpriſing as her's was, and that one of us two would begin firſt. Not to fail anſwering your Expectations, ſaid I to her, as to the Wonders, would be only to repeat your own Words; and for the reſt, we hope you'll be ſatisfy'd, charming *Rouſchen*, with our perfect Submiſſion to your better Judgment.

Almoraddin choſe to begin. The trueſt and moſt ſurpriſing Hiſtory obvious to my Knowledge, ſaid he, is that of the King without a Noſe. I was told it by *Scheikh-Alſem*, whom God be merciful to.

The *Hiſtory* of the King without a *Noſe*.

A Magician, that took upon him the Name of the Sage *Becolhan*, went one Day to the Court of *Fion*, King of *Gor*[a], where he met with ſo affable a Reception, that he reſolv'd to remain there ſome time. Notwithſtanding the kind Treatment was ſhewn him, he could not forbear exerciſing his *Ill-Genius*; he fill'd the whole Kingdom with an unheard-of Multitude of venemous Crea-

[a] Gor, *an ancient Kingdom, ſituated near Mount* Caucaſus, *which bounds it* North *and* Eaſt: *It is now a Province in the Kingdom belonging to the Great Mogul.*

tures,

tures, and threw a vaft Number of Perfons, of all Conditions, into incurable Difeafes, by his diabolical Enchantments. Upon his Arrival, he publickly foretold, couch'd in obfcure Terms; that the Kingdom was juft upon the Brink of Deftruction. King *Fion*, perceiving the Prophefy, he before ridicul'd, in a Difpofition to be accomplifh'd, thought no body more proper to redrefs the prefent Calamities, than he, who alone had the Foreknowledge of them. He intimated to him therefore his Reflections on that Exigence, and fervently defir'd he would not refufe affording his Affiftance in it. *Becolban*, tranfported to fee the King caught in the Snare he had laid for him, faid: Prince! I have already been ftudying fome time to difpel what difturbs thee; for I know thy Inquietudes. Tho' I were not as naturally inclin'd to Generofity as I am, yet the civil Ufage thou haft fhewn me, would fo much affect my Gratitude, as to make me undertake any thing with Pleafure that difcover'd the leaft View of ferving thee. 'Till now, fome unlucky Conftellation has oppos'd the good Difpofition I feel on this Occafion; but as foon as ever the dire Caufe ceafes to obftruct its Influence, I'll fignify to thee what Courfe muft be taken. *Fion* was extreamly fatisfy'd with this Anfwer, which very much augmented the Veneration he poffefs'd in Favour of the pretended Sage.

It is the Cuftom for the Sovereign of that Country to fleep every Day two Hours after Dinner, encompafs'd by his Nobles, who follow his Example. To make court to Sultans, in other Parts of the World, confifts in accofting them in a handfome Manner, in faying fomething that's agreeable and witty to them, and in ftriving to become ferviceable to them; but there it confifts

in

in sleeping with them, which is done with great Ceremony. The Monarch and his Courtiers are very magnificently dreſt to paſs thoſe two Hours, extended at their Eaſe, on Sofa's very rich and commodious. About eight Days after the Interview I have mention'd, *Fion* fell into a Dream, when aſleep in the midſt of his Courtiers. He thought he ſaw erected in the great Square of *Gor*, a large Column of black Marble, with a Statue upon it reſembling *Becolban*, which held a little Scroll of Paper in each Hand: In one was wrote, *Heaven deſtroys*; and in the other, *I cure*. He thought likewiſe that a vaſt Multitude of ſick Men and Women went and touch'd the Column, and were perfectly reſtor'd by it; that the languiſhing Flocks of Sheep, under the Care of their Shepherds, approach'd it, and were alſo re-eſtabliſh'd; and laſtly, that Millions of Serpents and Dragons came in their Turn, to the Feet of the Column, and were all deſtroy'd by it. When *Fion* awoke, he told his Dream to thoſe preſent, who advis'd him to ſend for the Sage to give the Interpretation of it. Thoſe deputed to go for him, knock'd a long while at his Door without any body anſwering. At laſt, as they began to be impatient, *Becolban* look'd out of his Window, and ſaid to them in a great Paſſion; that he knew well enough what they came for; that they might go back again; for the Dream was expreſſive enough of it ſelf. This wicked Man did not ſay an untruth, in aſſuring them he knew the Reaſon of their coming, for he was the Author of the Dream.

The Anſwer being brought back to the Prince, he call'd a Council, which was of Opinion, that the Statue of *Becolban* ſhould immediately be erected, after the Model of that which had appear'd to *Fion*, as alſo, that divine Honours ſhould

should be pay'd to the Prophet. The Queen was the only Person that oppos'd this Deliberation, but her Sentiments were rejected. The rest of the Dream was accomplish'd as soon as the Edict was executed: Men and Cattle recover'd, and the venemous Beasts that infested the Kingdom, were all destroy'd. The detestable *Becolban*, who was proud of the Success of his Practices, no longer appear'd in Publick. He was proclaim'd God of *Gor*, every where Hymns were sung in his Honour, and in as many Places Vows were made him.

But his Glory was likely to be very short liv'd: He knew the Ills he had done were more real than their cure, and that those who imagin'd themselves restor'd to a perfect State of Health, would soon relapse into a much more deplorable Situation than before. This very Consideration compell'd him, much against his Inclination, to think of quitting the Place in an abrupt Manner. But however, the Day of his Departure being come, he was willing to take leave of *Fion*. This Prince, sleeping as usual in Publick, thought *Becolban* appear'd again to him, and said: King of *Gor*! Thou hast caus'd my Statue to be erected, thy People have honour'd me, I am highly satisfy'd with my Treatment, and must find out some way or other to recompense thee for it. I don't think it a sufficient Retaliation to have preserv'd thy Subjects and their Flocks from perishing, it is very just that thou also shouldst partake of my Vigilance and Liberality. Thy Kingdom is powerful in Men, and fertile in Product, but still it is destitute of Gold and Silver. Follow me therefore, and I'll lead thee to a Treasure that the Gods have reveal'd unto me. *Fion* thought he saw this pretended Sage making ready to depart in the Quality of his

Guide,

p. 37

Guide, that he follow'd him, and that, after having paſt Mountains, Rivers and Woods, they came, at laſt into a ſpacious Field, cover'd with Pomgranate-Trees. When they were got to about the middle of it, *Becolhan* pointed to one of them with his Finger, ſaying, under that Tree the Treaſure was actually hid. How ſhall I know it again, anſwer'd *Fion*; for this Field is large, and all the reſt of the Pomgranate-Trees reſemble that you have ſhewn me? Cut off a Branch like this, reply'd *Becolhan*, bending him one, and that will ſerve you as a Mark. *Fion* took hold of the Branch, drew out his Knife, and cut it off; upon which, the Magician burſt into a Fit of Laughter, and diſappear'd.

King *Gor* was ſeiz'd that very Moment with the moſt piercing Pain! and the very Hall, ſet apart for ſleeping in, echo'd with the terrible Groan he gave, when he awoke from his Dream. All his Courtiers open'd their Eyes at this grievous Complaint, and were much aſtoniſh'd to ſee their Maſter cover'd with Blood, holding in one Hand his Knife, and in the other his Noſe, that he had juſt cut off. Perfidious Villain, cry'd he, doſt thou laugh at my Misfortune, and think'ſt thou ſhalt eſcape the Puniſhment due to thy Crime? No, no—— Quick, Fly to the Place where *Becolhan* lives, ſecure the Traitor, and bring him inſtantly before me. His Nobles and Officers ran immediately to the Magicians Houſe, but he was gone. They diſpatch'd a Hundred young Men, well mounted, with Orders to ſtop the Criminal wherever he paſs'd, but as ineffectual. The King finding *Becolhan* had eſcap'd his Rage, both his Pains and Anger augmented. He related his unhappy Adventure to his Courtiers, and then order'd the Queen to be call'd, who was the on-

D 3   ly

ly Perſon that had conceiv'd a bad Opinion of the Magician. But alas! ſhe was neither to be found in her Apartment, nor throughout all the Palace, which produc'd freſh Matter of Deſpair to the unfortunate Prince, who ſuſpected her Guilty of the worſt of Treachery. He was ready to run diſtracted; and his Attendants were oblig'd to keep him in their Sight, the reſt of the Day and the following Night, leſt the Exceſs of his Tranſports ſhould prompt him to make away with himſelf. The next Day, he order'd *Becolban*'s Statue to be pulled down, drawn about the Streets, and burnt to Aſhes. He likewiſe commanded the whole Street, where this inhuman Wretch liv'd, to be demoliſh'd, and would be at the Execution of it in Perſon.

The Magician's Houſe was the firſt they began to demoliſh, but before they proceeded to the reſt, they heard a great Noiſe in the Air, and ſaw a great black Cloud deſcend from thence, and ſettle it ſelf upon the Ruins, where it open'd and diſcover'd the moſt beautiful Creature that ever was beheld. She addreſs'd her ſelf to the King, ſaying; behold my Features and remember them! though thou haſt ſeen them far leſs handſome. The Moment ſhe had ſpoken theſe Words, both the King and People knew her to be the Queen of *Gor*, which ſtruck them into ſuch a Confuſion, as hinder'd them from teſtifying their Admiration any other way, but a profound Silence. I had condeſcended, continu'd ſhe, to become a Woman of this World to make thee happy, but thou haſt render'd thy ſelf unworthy the Embraces of a *Periſe*. Thou waſt not ſatisfy'd with contemning my Counſels, but thou muſt farther hearken to infamous Suſpicions. Now thou ſhalt judge if they were well grounded: I have taken Revenge, in thy Cauſe, of an *Impoſtor*, and to revenge my ſelf of an *ungrateful* Perſon, I have condemn'd thee never to ſee my Face more. At theſe Words ſhe diſappear'd, the Cloud diſpers'd, and then they ſaw, with greater Aſtoniſhment, the Magician confin'd and burning in a Cage of red hot Iron. Thus King *Fion* paſs'd the reſt of his Days in Sorrow and Affliction, without a Noſe, and without a Wife; and the Magician's Puniſhment laſted as long as this unhappy Prince liv'd. *Scheikh-Alſem* added, that to this Day, might be ſeen at *Gor*, the very Place and Ruins where *Becolhan*'s Houſe ſtood.

This Adventure, ſaid *Rouſchen*, deſerves to be written in golden Letters. How well can I diſtinguiſh the oppoſite Characters of the *Peris* and *Divs* in it! But, *Almoraddin*, did not your Author give a Deſcription of the Queen of *Gor*, after her Victory over the *Divs*, that were ſubject to *Becolhan*? No Madam, reply'd he. I am ſorry for it, reſum'd *Rouſchen*; for certainly I muſt have ſeen this admirable *Periſe*, and I think I know her. You believe you know her, Madam, interrupted we, you ought to know her! The Hiſtory, reply'd ſhe, I am going to tell you of, will perhaps ſolve the Doubts I perceive you are in.

The Hiſtory of the PERSIAN LADY, *with her Voyage to the* Topſy-Turvy *Iſland*.

THEY ſay true Friendſhip is rarely to be found among Brothers, and for my Part, I believe it leſs frequent among Siſters: I never had but one, and there was no Poffibility of agreeing with her. The poor Year fhe was older than I, made her ufurp an Air of Superiorty over me, that was infupportable. She was continually in an ill Humour, but it never appear'd in fo ftrong a Light, as the Night before her Nuptials. Tir'd with bearing her repeated Infults, I was provok'd, at laft, to fpeak in my Turn; which I did, in the moft picquant Manner I was Miftrefs of: *Koutai*, faid I to her, if Reproaches could make me grow lean, thou wouldft certainly overwhelm me with them ftill. Am I the Caufe, if Fate has not thought proper to form me after thy Refemblance? The Rage that thefe Words rais'd in her Soul can't well be imagin'd, much lefs exprefs'd. She flew at me to tear my Eyes out; but I left her in that Feud, and fought fhelter in a Garret, that laid over her Chamber. She made fuch a terrible Noife, that alarm'd the whole Houfe. Father, Mother, Slaves, and every body ran to her Room to fee what the Uproar was; and found her Pale, full of Tears, and reduc'd to the laft Degree of Defpair. She related the Quarrel to her own Advantage, and protefted, if fhe had not Satisfaction for the dreadful Infult I had given her, fhe would take fuch Meafures as would not be very pleafing to them. My Father and Mother immediately promis'd to fatisfy her in every thing fhe could wifh, and afk'd her, what Punifhment fhe thought I had deferv'd? I fhall be at Eafe, faid fhe, and *Roufchen* will be fufficiently punifh'd, if fhe be deny'd going to my Wedding. I faw and heard every thing was faid, thro' a little Crevice in the Chamber-Floor. Every body prais'd her Moderation, and an old Slave, who never lov'd me, readily fignaliz'd her Zeal, by haftening to lock me up in the Garret.

Finding

Finding myself thus close Prisoner, I did nothing but sob and cry. *Koutai*, said I, foresaw well enough my Revenge would be too much gratify'd if I made my Appearance at the Hymen, Her Apprehensions of it are now over, and her Want of Beauty, in my Absence, will be less conspicuous. What Joy to her! and how much Vexation to me! I pass'd the rest of the Day, and a part of the Night in such like Reflections, and then fell asleep. During my Slumber, I had a very extraordinary Dream. Methought I saw before me an immense Space of Land and Sea, that discovered, at a Distance, a very high blue Island, from the Top of which arose two large Clouds, wash'd with Silver, that advanced towards me, attended with an Infinity of others. All these Clouds dispersed themselves into two Lines, and form'd between the Island and me, the longest and most glittering Alley can be imagined. Another Cloud, that seem'd to be of burnished Gold, fill'd up the Extremity of the Alley towards the Island; and a little Girl, much like *Loulou*, being placed upon it, this Cloud, on a sudden, took the Shape of a Throne, and mov'd of itself.

As it advanced, the silvery Clouds transform'd themselves, on each Side, into Guards richly dress'd, who, with Sword in Hand, saluted the little Girl with all the Marks of a profound Respect. But how great was my Surprise, when this extraordinary Person, who, coming out of the Island, seem'd but as a Child, had not got half the Way, before I perceived she had the Face and Air of a Woman of 40 or 50 Years old. The nearer she approached, the more she appear'd advanced in Age, and when she was nigh at Hand, she discover'd herself to be but a little, wrinkled, stooping, grey-hair'd Creature: She look'd on me with an Eye of Friendſhip, and ſaid to me, in a trembling Voice; My well-beloved *Roufchen*, I know thy Sorrows; hope every thing from the Affiftance I am able to afford thee: See thou rememberest the Words I am about to impart to thee, and fail not to repeat them in caſe of Extremity: *Wife* Lutfallah! *Lady of the green Palace! Wife* Lutfallah! *Wife of* Millan-fchak! *What's the Sword of* Gian *doing? Where is his Buckler?* She had no ſooner finiſh'd theſe Words, than ſhe diſappear'd with all her Attendance.

I can't ſay whether I immediately awoke or not, but the ſtrong Idea of my Impriſonment returning, I ſaid, ſighing, Oh that what the powerful *Lutfallah* has juſt now told me, may prove true! *Wife* Lutfallah! *Lady of the green Palace! Wife* Lutfallah! *Wife of* Millan-Schak! *What's the Sword of* Gian *doing? Where is his Buckler?* At that Inſtant, I found myſelf undreſs'd, and lying in a very fine Bed; I rubb'd my Eyes with my Hands, I felt about me, I examin'd myſelf, and was aſſured I ſlept not. I then drew open the Curtains, and ſaw, with an extream Surprize, my Garret chang'd to a very ſpacious Chamber, adorn'd with the richeſt Tapeſtry, with a Looking-glaſs infinitely larger than I had ever ſeen any, and with two Pots of Maſſy Gold, whence iſſued a moſt exquiſite Perfume. In the Middle of the Chamber ſtood a Toilet ready prepared, and near it a Table, on which lay a rich Suit of Cloaths. I was about to riſe directly, but happening to caſt my Eyes on the great Looking-glaſs, I perceived what my Siſter and all about her were doing, naturally repreſented in it; ſo I choſe to remain ſtill in Bed, as well to amuſe myſelf in beholding ſo agreeable a Spectacle, as to repair the Fatigues of the Night. It is not ſo proper to relate all I ſaw there; let it

ſuffice

suffice then to say, that this miraculous Mirrour discover'd to me all that pass'd at the Feast, from which my Sister excluded me. Her Husband's Aspect did not a little contribute to my Satisfaction; for he was tall and meagre Faced, of a fierce Look, and who, even, that Day, had more the Air of a Tyrant than a Husband.

At last I arose, designing to make use of the Presents *Lutfallah* had made me, when a handsome Pair of Slippers came of their own accord, and offer'd themselves at my Feet. The first Step I took towards the Table, all the Cloaths, that lay prepared for me there, advanced and did their Office; and I felt at the same time some Body spare me the Labour both of combing and dressing my Head. I bore notwithstanding every thing done to me with Patience, and resign'd myself entirely up to the Care of the Queen of the *Peris*, thinking of nothing else but returning her my hearty Thanks for all that happen'd to me, and viewing myself in my Toilet-looking-Glass, (the other only representing absent Objects.) Though every thing they deck'd me with, made an extraordinary Appearance, yet it was seldom Gold, Silver or Jewels contributed towards it. Nothing gave so singular a Mark here of *Lutfallah*'s great Power, as the Colour of my Robe, which changed each Step I took. I walked about a considerable time, to admire this agreeable Prodigy at Leisure. During this Interval, the necessary Ceremonies were preparing at the *Iman*'s and *Cadi*'s House. After their Return, the two Halls, design'd to celebrate the Feasts in, began to fill with Guests. I did not much amuse myself in observing the Men; my Sister and her Friends engross'd all my Attention. *Koutai* seem'd to be very hungry, but the more eager she was to eat, the least Haste

she

she could make to do it. All the Dishes she touch'd disappear'd, and were set on a gilt Skin, that some unknown Hand had spread in my Chamber. It is impossible to express the prodigious Consternation this famish'd Bride and her Company were in. As I was as hungry again as she was, I left nothing scarce of the first Dishes set before me. As soon as ever I had done with them, they disappear'd; I cast an Eye in the Looking-glass, and saw the Remains I had left before *Koutai*, who was devouring them. This convinc'd me, that she, who had thought me unworthy of presiding at her Feast, was now condemned not to be satiated, but with my Refusals. I commiserated at last the Condition she was in, and acted like a good Sister during the rest of the Entertainment.

Towards Evening they went into the Baths, whilst execllent Voices sung, according to Custom, gay *Aganis* [a]. When that Ceremony was over, they disposed themselves for dancing. As I had always a strong Inclination for that Diversion, so my not partaking of the Pleasure of it, as well as the rest, began to chagrin me. I can't sit still any longer, cry'd I: *Wife* Lutfallah! *Lady of the green Palace! Wife* Lutfallah! *Wife of* Milan-schak! *What's the Sword of* Gian *doing? Where is his Buckler?* I must dance. So you shall, Child, answer'd one behind me. I look'd round and saw the ancient and powerful *Perise*. It's very much my Desire, continued she, you should appear in such good Company; I did not order you to be dress'd lightly, but with a View of making you assume a better Air in dancing. A *Perise* would fain have cover'd you all over with Jewels, resembling *Moëtader* the

Songs, Persian *Airs*.

Tabarcis,

Tabarois, but I never expose those I love, to get Pleurisies after such a Manner. Come along, Child, follow me.

Methought the Looking-glass, which that Moment represented the Hall, was now become the Door. We went in, and *Lutfallah*, who was only visible to me, placed herself nigh my Sister. I saluted the Company, and fell a dancing all alone. The Justness of my Dance, and still more, the continual Variety of my Clothes, astonish'd the whole Assembly. What they admired before was now become applauded: Acclamations of Joy and Praises were heard every where. *Koutai* was not able to brook my Glory any longer. Fury took Possession of her, and without any Regard to the Company present, she flew towards me, with her Fists in the Air like a Mad-woman. But the invisible *Lutfallah* prevented her approaching me, by touching her Chin with the End of a Rod made of Ebony, saying, *Fair Bride, meddle with no Body but yourself.* That Instant, the most compleat black Beard ever was seen, adorn'd the half of *Koutai*'s Face, which gave her other Employment than to think on me. After this Accident, *Lutfallah* convey'd me out, order'd me to enfold her, and then carry'd me away, with an unconceivable Swiftness, in a direct Line, towards the Sun.

After we had continu'd ascending for a very considerable time; You may now, said she, repose yourself: There is not thick Air enough over our Heads, to make you fall. I must confess it was with an aking Heart I quitted my Hold of *Lutfallah*; but what Pleasure did I not feel, when I found, without any Difficulty, I could both ascend and descend; go backwards and forwards, as though my Body were become immaterial! I cast my Eyes upon the Earth, which, at so vast a

Distance,

Distance, neither appear'd very obscure, nor yet very bright. If my Conductress had given Leave, I should have imploy'd myself in making some curious Observations, as the Place was so commodious for taking them; but she oppos'd it, saying, The Moon will presently make her Course over the Place we are in, and produce such Quantity of Air, that whilst the Sea is receiving its Flow, you may probably be stifled: Besides, I promis'd to be at home betimes; embrace me, therefore, and let us begone. The Part we descended from the Earth gave a tolerable Reflection, because it presented nothing to our View but the vast Plains of the Ocean: The more our Descent approach'd it, the more it seem'd to encrease in Bigness and Darkness; but when we came within Observation of the different Parts of it, I perceiv'd directly under us, in the Midst of the Waters, a very spacious Island, which I knew to be the same blue Island I had seen in a Dream, and which is called by the *Peris*, the *Topsy-Turvy* Island. It appear'd blue to me before, because of the Distance I was from it, but when my Approach was nigher, a thousand various Colours crowded upon my Sight. However, I did not fix my Eyes much on these new Objects, because my Attention was already taken up with something much more surprising.

Lutfallah, whom I held embrac'd, had transform'd herself during our Descent. Her grey Hairs were now become of a light Chestnut Colour; and the more we advanced towards the Island, the smoother and more beautiful her Complexion grew. Her Shape visibly form'd itself, her Neck was admirably long, her Arms round and taper, and her Hands plump and of a delicate Whiteness. How charming she was, when we had

pass'd

pafs'd two thirds of the Way! She ftill continu'd to grow younger, the nearer we approach'd the Earth: The Colour of her Hair became gradually lighter, till it was perfectly white; her whole Body deminifh'd, without lofing any thing of its Beauty or Proportion; and when we were about one fourth of a League from the Mountains of the *Topfy-Turvy* Ifland, I held no more than a Child of ten Years old in my Arms; fomewhat graver indeed, though nothing more charming and agreeable.

We landed in the Middle of the Ifland, about a hundred Yards from a River, that ferved inftead of a Moat to a pretty large Town. Seeing neither Draw-bridges nor Boats, I afk'd the Queen if we were to crofs it in the Air, and whether I was to difpofe myfelf as ufual? They pafs this River differently from what you imagine, anfwer'd fhe, throwing her Rod into it. At that Inftant, the Waters overagainft the Place where we ftood, fwell'd, forfook their Bottom, and form'd a tranfparent *Portico*, above Two hundred Yards high. This aftonifhing Elevation of the Waters did not however prevent their continual Running; and the Fifhes they were full of, made by their Sallies the moft agreeable Ornament of the *Portico*. How did they fport out of their Element! How often did they dart themfelves, fometimes up to the Top, fometimes down to the Bottom, and fometimes from the Sides of the Arch! Their Motions were alternate: One was no fooner loft to our View, than another appear'd the next Moment. The Flood, after quitting its Courfe, difcover'd a magnificent *Porphir* Stair-Cafe, above an hundred Steps down to the Bottom, which was illuminated by Lights from the Walls, and the great Gate that ftood at the Foot of it. As we were

were going down, *Lutfallah* inform'd me that the Illumination we saw was no more than a natural Cause, proceeding from a Vernish, the young *Peris* compose of the Skins of certain Fishes and Tails of Glow-worms, infused three Weeks in the Essence of rotten Wood, extracted without the Assistance of Fire. When we came to the Gate, we heard a horrid Croaking; and when both Sides of it were open, we saw an overgrown Frog, as big as a Goat, who moved on her two hind Legs, in order to receive the Queen, and deliver her up the same Rod I had seen her throw into the River. After she had taken it, and we had walk'd some Turns in a vast large Hall very light, being inlaid with *Ascra* [b] Stones, and such shining Flints as sometimes fall down with Thunder-bolts, the Frog retired very humbly towards the Door, which we shut after us, and then set up a second Croaking more hideous than the former.

This Signal was follow'd by a prodigious Noise of Drums and Trumpets: Then casting my Eyes round the Hall, I perceived Twenty-four Caverns very artfully cut out in the Wall, fill'd with as many Animals of an enormous Size, and of a Figure altogether strange to me. It was from them the Noise proceeded; each of these monstrous Beasts having a Drum or Trumpet, on which they play'd in a Manner proportionable to their Bigness and vast Strength. My Conductress told me they were *Mites* [c] of that Country, which, when I examin'd more nearly, I found had indeed the Resemblance of those I had seen before. We pass'd through a long Gallery, where an infinite

---

[b] *The Translator confesses he neither knows what* Ascra *Stones are, nor the Flints that accompany Thunder-bolts.*

[c] *An Animal scarce perceptible, whose Figure can only be discovered through a Microscope.*

Number of *Acudias* [d] and other shining Flies, sporting in the Air, diffus'd a pleasing Lustre from their Wings. From thence we came to a pair of Stairs, much like those we had descended at our Entrance, which conducted us to a great square Court, paved with greenish Marble: At each Corner were fine Lodgings built of the same Matter, and in the Middle a Fountain, whose Bason was more than thirty Foot Diameter, tho' cut out of but one entire Emerald. About twenty little old Women, and as many old Men, dress'd in Green, play'd here and there round the Court; some at Chuck-farthing, others at Shittle-cock, or at Cockal. As soon as *Lutfallah* appear'd, they gave over their Diversions, running to her, caressing her, and giving her the Title of Grand Mamma. The little Queen receiv'd them with so grave and prudish an Air, that I could not forbear laughing to see Old age so frolicksome, and Youth or rather Infancy so austere and commanding Respect. *Roufchen*, said *Lutfallah*, what you see undoubtedly surprises you. The Things I behold, answer'd I, would even be frightful to me, if I did not take them all, especially these rediculous old Women and Men, for so many Phantoms. It's the Effect of Prejudice and Ignorance that makes you think so, reply'd she; all that gay Youth exists as really as you do. Cast your Eyes upon this Looking-Glass, giving me a little Pocket one; and as I was just going to open it, she left me. I shudder still whenever I call to mind what I saw there, in seeing myself.

How great my Consternation! How sudden my Terrour! and how ready was I to sink down,

[d] *Little Volatiles very shining. There are Numbers of them in* America.

E   when

when I beheld my Cheeks flabby! my Eyes hollow! my Lips chopp'd and pale! my Mouth fall'n in! my Nose red and big at the End! my Chin picked! my Forehead full of Wrinkles! and my Hair as white as Snow! I ran hastily to see myself in the Fountain, still hoping the Effect of the Looking-glass might only prove an Illusion; but, alas! it brought the unwelcome Confirmation of what I had already seen, and made me cry out so terribly that all the ancient Populace gather'd together about me. My Affliction was so great, Words are not half forcible enough to express it. I became stupid and insensible, and remained in that wretched Situation, a considerable time, stretch'd on the Ground, leaning upon the Edge of the Emerald Bason. Being, at last, recovered from my deep Lethargy of Grief, I gave Vent to Tears and Complaints, crying out, Cruel *Lutfallah!* is this the Usage I was to hope from thy Protection? Hast thou conducted me here, only to make me feel the worst Effects of thy Indignation? Canst thou pretend to love me, and at the same time oppress me with the most dreadful of Ills? Couldst thou revenge thyself after a more barbarous manner, were I even thy profess'd Enemy? Oh happy *Koutai!* How do I now envy thy Beard! And how trivial do I think thy Misfortune, when compared with mine! The old Men and Women put the finishing Stroke to my Dispair, by their silly Conversation, and striving to compel me to drink some of the Fountain-water; but however they were prevented, by the Voice of a young Man, who came towards me from the other Side of the Square. He looked only to be about fifteen Years of Age, though he moved with a grave and majestick Air. His Visage wore a certain Reservedness, yet nothing of Austere in it. When he had

accosted

accosted me, he ask'd me, with a great deal of Affability, if I had ever heard speak of the *Peri, Milan-Schak?* The Perusal of our Annals, reply'd I, has given me some Idea of him. I am the very Person, answer'd he. Is it possible, resum'd I, much surpriz'd, that you can still look so young, considering how old you were, when you defeated the Monster *Ouranbad* [e], in the Mountain of *Aherman?* *Milan-Schak* shook his Head and smiled, and then offer'd me his Hand, with a vast deal of Complaisance, in order to conduct me to his Appartment. After having ascended a Jasper Stair-Case, we pass'd through two Anti-chambers, set off with Landskips, and guarded by two well made Youths, unarm'd, and came into a spacious and magnificent Chamber, all richly hung with green and gold Tapestry: From thence we went into a Cabinet, adorn'd with precious Furniture, whose Ground was Green, curiously embossed with Gold, and enrich'd every where with fine Emeralds. The Wood that was imploy'd there, resembled the Colour of those precious Stones; and in the Middle of the Cieling, there was a Carbuncle of the Bigness of a Pine-Apple, that gave a vast Lustre.

The World Revers'd.

DEar *Roufchen*, said *Milan-Schak*, when we had plac'd ourselves, there is such an Opposition between your World and ours, that it's impossible to imagine a greater, between Things essentially

[e] *A blood-thirsty Monster, that* Aherman, *Chief of the Divs, made use of, instead of a Hangman.*

the fame. Your great Trees are with us but fmall Herbs; and, on the contrary, a little, tender Plant with you, is, in this Countrey, the largeft of our Trees. The Fruits of the Earth are oppofite in the fame Proportion: Though our Corn does not differ from yours, as to its Nature, yet it furpaffes it fo much in Bignefs, that an hundred Perfons would not be able to confume ten Grains of it in a Month. As much Contrariety is found between Animals as Plants: We have none fo large among us as thofe you call *Infects*, nor none fo fmall as *Elephants* and *Crocodiles*. Your Flies are our greateft Birds, and *Eagles* are here almoft imperceptible. As for what is of a reafonable Size with you, is much the fame with us. You fpeak particular Languagues, the Fruit of Mens Invention; ours is fpoken univerfally, and as naturally, as *Seeing*, *Hearing*, and the reft of the Faculties are alike made ufe of by all Nations. The Knowledge of this Language is kept from the reft of Mankind; in Vain all your learned Men ftudy to find it out: It is only to be attained by fuch as vifit this Ifland, and unlefs they become a *Peris*, they lofe the Memory of it the Moment they depart. In your World, no Body ever rofe from the Dead, but by a Miracle; in this, we rife naturally every hundred Year, to live again the Space of one Day: You'll fee an Example of it after to Morrow. With you, Men are born with tender Bodies, juicy Limbs, and a foft Skin without Hair: Thus it is we die in this Empire; whence it will be eafy to infer, that we come into the World with Wrinkles, and all the Appendages of Old-age. As there are but very few handfome old People, neither *Lutfallah* nor I pretend to pafs for fuch; but you, charming *Roufchen*, who imagine yourfelf frightfully ugly, now appear as beautiful in our Eyes, as you did in those that beheld you at *Schiras*. Nothing, I assure you, can be more transporting to us, than those agreeable Wrinkles, which our Climate has adorn'd your Visage with; nor nothing more capable of enslaving us, than that flowing Hair, which dazles with its Whiteness. Every time we visit your Countries, we appear there as we should have done, had we been Natives thereof; here we look such as we really are, but according to our Way: An old Man speaks, dear *Roufchen*, and converses with a young Person, that's scarcely come to the Use of her Reason! The several Forms *Lutfallah* took, whilst with you, might, one would think, have sufficiently prepar'd you to bear yours with Intrepidity. All Men that set Foot in this Kingdom, must undergo the Laws of it; and such as are no longer dispos'd to stay there, only exchange them, to be subject to others. Deluded by Appearances, I found you giving yourself up to a thousand unjust Regrets, when I arriv'd with a young Man of your Countrey, who had invok'd me. The Queen overheard all your Reproaches, and was almost offended at them, but still her Affection is not at all diminish'd: I deliver'd her up my Charge, and then undertook to acquaint you how far it extended. If it does not suit you to embrace my Proposals, you'll be sent back again to your World, and all future Correspondence with us will cease: If on the contrary, they are weighty enough to engage your Compliance, you shall be rais'd to the highest Dignity a mortal can hope to acquire. In one word, we require nothing but your Consent to adopt you a *Perise*. If the Power of transforming Bodies, and doing the most surprising Miracles by one single Wave of a Rod; if a Life, that's almost infinite, is capable of moving you, follow me to the Fountain of Emerald:

rald: How few Drops foever you fwallow of its Water, all your Ideas will be reconciled, and they'll reftore you to the happy State of Infancy.

Generous *Milan-Schak!* reply'd I, I muft own, you have fkreen'd me from iminent Danger, by removing me from that fatal Water. I love my Reafon and my Countrey, and cannot prevail on myfelf to forfeit either of them. I am perfectly fatisfy'd with my own Condition; let it fuffice, therefore, I befeech you, that I admire yours. This *Peri* feem'd more furpriz'd at my Anfwer than difpleas'd at it; he fhrunk up his Shoulders, and look'd earneftly at me, as though I excited his Compaffion. During this mute Interval, there appear'd, at the Cabinet-Door, Six Green *Cats*, whofe Eyes fhone like as many Flambeaus, lighting along *Lutfallah*, who enter'd with an old Man, faying, *Ajoub*, whom I bring with me, perfifts ftill in his obftinacy; and *Roufchen*, reply'd *Milan-Schak*, is as opinionated. I threw myfelf at the Queen's Feet, imploring her Forgivenefs of my Weaknefs, in letting flip fo many indifcreet and unguarded Words in the Height of my grievous Complaints. *Ajoub* fell proftrate before *Milan-Schak*, befeeching him equally to pardon his Blindnefs. Old Peoples Anger againft Young, does not continue long, faid the Queen, rife up therefore, and fince it's fo decreed that we muft part, employ the little Time remains for you to ftay in my Empire, in obferving well the Laws of it. Pleas'd with the Profpect of our Liberty, we immediately rofe up from our Poftures. After that, we were told Supper was upon Table.

Proceeded by the fix Cat Flambeaux, we came into a large Hall on the fame Floor, wainfcotted with green Ebony, and adorn'd with Birds and
Feftoons

Festoons of Gold in Relievo: Four and twenty green Cats, and as many Lynx of the same Colour, plac'd on an equal Number of Stands of burnish'd Silver, darted from their Looks such a Radiance, as almost equall'd the Sun in its Meridian. There were two Tables: One supply'd with Pots of Perfume, and the other with a great Variety of Dishes. The Lady of the green Palace, *Milan-Schak*, four Queens, their Husbands, and those *Genii*, that were the most distinguish'd of their Families, plac'd themselves at the first of these Tables, and were magnificently serv'd with Perfumes, which are the ordinary Nourishment of *Peris*, born in the *Topsy-Turvy* Island. *Ajoub* and I, with a great Number of Guests, Proselytes from our World, and *Peris* by Adoption, fill'd the other Table. The first Course [a] was compos'd of large Fricassees of Pheasants, each Dish containing five or six hundred; the second was of Ortolans as big as Geese, accompany'd with Boars and Stags, spitted on Scewers, as *Europeans* do Larks: And the third presented us with two Ants Tongues, two Pasties made of the Thigh of the same Animal, which were of an excellent Taste, and several Plates of Artichokes and Melons as big as the green Peas of *Schiras*. They brought for the Desart, two Straw-berries, one Goose-berry, and two great Bowls of Squirrels Cream. The chief Part of the Dishes at Table I was unacquainted with at that time; but the Princess *Indgi-Mergian* inform'd me what they were the next Day. After Supper, my Countrey-man and I, having each a Cat allow'd to conduct and light us to our Chambers, a *Pabinc*, very well shap'd, undress'd me, and retir'd assoon as I was in Bed.

[a] *In the Original* Arabick, *the Courses of this Entertainment are serv'd without any Order, like the* Persians *and* Moguls.

My Cat having extinguish'd the Light by shutting her Eyes, I feasted Imagination with all my past Adventures, and methought I felt something, I know not what, seize me, that made a far stronger Impression on my Mind, in Favour of *Ajoub*, than all the other surprising Objects I had seen. 'Till that Moment I had liv'd free from Inclination, and was such a Novice in Love, that when I found my Heart first give way to it, I burst into a Flood of Tears. What can be the meaning, said I, of my thinking of that little Monster, whom I never saw before to Day? Why did I apprehend that *Lutfallah* would over-perswade him? Oh! I feel no longer an Indifference for him; and if what his Sight has inspir'd me with, can't properly be call'd Love, it is something very nearly ally'd to it. Oh! my Heart has betray'd me! It is flown away without my Consent! After all, continu'd I, this young Man's Figure is not frightfuller than my own: What Crime then will it be in me to love him? We share the like Fate with one another, and why should not that be a Motive inducing enough to create a stricter Unity between us? I even fancy he thinks already as favourably of me as I do of him: There's the Point that requires most Dexterity to be examin'd into, but how shall I be able to penetrate the inmost Meanings of his Soul, without discovering my own, unless my Freedom with him was somewhat greater? Sleep, at last, appeas'd all my Inquietudes. The *Pabine* awoke me, and made me rise as soon as Day appear'd. I was scarce dress'd, when I saw *Lutfallah*, *Milan-Schah*, and the Princess *Indgi-Mergian*, their eldest Daughter, whom they presented me to, ready to enter my Chamber. The Queen and her Spouse ask'd me, smiling, how I had pass'd the Night?
I made

I made Anfwer, with the moft profound Acknowledgment and Refpect, that I had flept very quietly. The Queftion, we propofe, includes the whole Night, reply'd they, and you only inform us of the latter Part of it. Thefe Hints prodigioufly furpriz'd me: I faw too well I had been overheard. Our Penetration ruffles her, faid *Milan-Schak*; come to a Refolution, *Roufchen*, do not balance any longer in it, nor delay faithfully embracing the Laws of the *Topfy-Turvy* Ifland. When he had finifh'd thefe Words, he took out of one of his Attendant's Hands, fomething like a Beet-Root, and holding it by the Leaves, he gave me a Bodkin, and commanded me to run it into the Place mark'd with a little black Spot. I obey'd him: That Moment the Root gave a terrible Shriek, and my Fellow-Companion in Fate ftood there inftead of it. His Face was all bloody, his Forehead pierc'd, and the Bodkin ftill remaining in his Wound. Oh! deareft *Ajoub!* cry'd I, embracing him, deareft *Ajoub!* whom my Soul loves more than Life, what have I done! How barbarous, or rather how unhappy am I! Was there no other Hand but mine to accomplifh *Milan-Schak*'s Will and Pleafure! Oh *Peri!* How could you make choice of me to fpill the Blood of one, for whofe Safety I fhould be ready to facrifice all my own? The wounded look'd upon me without much concern, and feem'd to fmile. *Lutfallah, Milan-Schak,* and the Princefs, fell a laughing in good Earneft, and faid to one another merrily, don't you think fhe has made the Declaration in Form? Has not fhe obferv'd all the Rules? There appears to be fome Sincerity in it, faid *Ajoub*, but we muft not too much depend on the firft Tranfports of Women, whofe Natures are variable. If I were fully perfuaded of the

Conftancy

Conftancy of *Roufchen*'s Love, I don't fay I would not—— but in faying nothing, I teftify too much for the firft Time. As I was preparing to thank him, and likewife to continue my Lamentations for the Hurt I had done him, *Milan-Schak*, who had all this Time gently held him by the Hair, now withdrew his Hand, and took the Bodkin out of his Forehead, without leaving the leaft Orifice. *Lutfallah* afk'd me, pretty ferioufly, what was the prefent Difpofition of my Heart towards him, whofe Misfortune had apparently exacted fo much Compaffion from me? You know, great Queen! I love him, anfwer'd I. Now, Child, you fpeak right, refum'd fhe: The Uncertainty you were in Yefterday, as to your Paffion, is directly oppofite to the Cuftom of my Kingdom, where Women make the firft Advances. I fhould deem it a very laudable one, reply'd I, did the amiable *Ajoub* think my Affiduities worthy of his Regard. You have both fulfill'd our Laws, anfwer'd the Queen; but fince you had rather live fubject to thofe of your own Countrey, it is my Will that you refume this Moment your former Shapes. Let the Influences that reign here, continu'd fhe, touching us with her Rod, ceafe operating upon you. *Lutfallah* did not give us time to return her thanks, but went out with her Attendants, leaving only with us a *Pabin* and a *Pabine*, who were decently plac'd on each Side of the Door.

Here the beautiful *Perfian* broke fhort, and afk'd us if we were not curious to know what thofe *Pabins* and *Pabines* refembled. The *Pabine*, that undrefs'd you, did indeed excite my Curiofity, faid *Almoraddin*, but I was unwilling to interrupt the Thread of your Story, by afking impertinent Queftions. The *Pabins*, refum'd *Roufchen*, *schen*, are Animals that serve the *Peris*, that are distributed into Cantons, and who cultivate the Lands of the *Topsy-Turvy* Island. No Creature on Earth has so much the Appearance of Man. Were you to see them drest or otherwise, you would be ready to swear they were Men and Women; nothing is wanting to make them so but a rational Soul. They have not only this Advantage over the rest of Animals, but they likewise speak the universal Language, like the *Peris*; whereas the others have but their particular ones. To conclude, the *Pabins* whole Discourse runs upon eating, drinking, working, and other Subjects relating thereto, and consists only in simple Propositions. They are active, robust, laborious, tractable, and great Imitators. All other Beasts revere and serve them, except *Monkeys* and *Fleas*: The first being in perpetual Contention with them for the Superiority, and the second, being huge wild Creatures of that Country, are very rapacious after the Flesh of these almost human *Pabins*. In every Village there is a Kind of a Storehouse set apart for the *Pabins*, to carry daily a certain Quantity of *Amber-Grease* of *Benjamin*, of *Incense* of *Aloes* Wood, and other Provisions. When the Place is full, it is convey'd invisibly to the City the *Peris* live in, and distributed in their several Habitations. The *Pabins* seldom divert themselves but at the Expence of other Animals, which they often set together by the Ears. They are delighted above all with the Wood-lice, when contracted like Bowls [b], they roul against each other. These immeasurable Bodies make such a hideous Noise in their Justling, that one would imagine

---

[b] *It is the Property of the Wood-lice to contract themselves into a Form perfectly round.*

them

them broke in a thousand Pieces, but immediately after it appears no more with them than an innocent Play-Game.

After this Digression, the *Persian* would have resum'd her Discourse, if the Fear of fatiguing her too much, had not oblig'd us to entreat her deferring the Continuance of it till next Day. We were of different Opinions, touching the Account she gave us, when we return'd to our Lodgings. *Almoraddin* was inclin'd to be incredulous, but for my Part, I was not far from giving Faith to all she had told us. However, our Sentiments agreed in doubting our own Judgments, and in feeling an equal Curiosity to hear the Sequel of the History. In this Disposition we repair'd to *Roufchen*'s next Day, who, after the usual Compliments, gratify'd our Impatience, in the following Manner.

As soon as the Queen and *Milan-Schak* had left us, we ran to the Looking-glass, where we enjoy'd the Pleasure of beholding our selves once more in our proper Forms; and felt, at the same Time, our Inclinations resume their natural Channel. I thought *Ajoub* agreeable; he esteem'd me infinitely more charming. Madam! said he, with the utmost Respect, how dare I, without an extreme Confusion, presume to appear before you, knowing what's past? Would to God, reply'd I, we had lost our Memory with all the Gifts of this Island; or that I had, like you, only too much Reserve to reproach my self with! In the Name of our common Countrey, interrupted *Ajoub*, let us live now, as tho' we remember'd nothing! I've so high an Idea of your Generosity and Goodness, as to believe you'll restore me that by Justice, which I'm in danger of losing, by your being depriv'd of that Instinct, which first caus'd you to love

love me. Equity, said I, recompences only Merit; and to merit is not the Work of a Day. Inform me, pray! whom you are, and what brings *Ajoub* of *Schiras* hither? As yet I know no more of you than your Name and Countrey. When I had thus spoken, I desir'd him to sit down by me, whilst he gave me the History of his Adventures.

The History of AJOUB *of* SCHIRAS.

I Am, said he, Son of *Ajoub* the Physician. You are not unacquainted, amiable *Roufchen*, that all the Youth of *Schiras* delight in dancing and playing on some Instrument. One Evening, when the extream Heats of the Season oblig'd every Body to turn the Night into Day, I left my Father's House, designing to take the fresh Air of the Streets, as I play'd along them with a Flagelet I had carry'd with me for that Purpose. After having strol'd thro' a great many, and repairing Homewards, I heard the Door of a fine spacious House open, and a Voice proceed from thence, which said: *Is it you?* Promising myself some good Fortune would prove the Issue; I made Answer, yes 'tis I. Pray come up then, resum'd the Voice. Without considering the Consequence, I readily ventur'd to follow it, which led me thro' a Hall-door that was half open. I was no sooner enter'd, than three young Men that lay in wait there, surrounded me with their drawn Sabres, and said: *Expect this Instant, to wash with thy Blood, the Stain thou hast cast on our Family, by deluding our Sister.* Finding myself engag'd in so sudden and powerful an Attack, I thought it most Prudence

not

not to put myself in a Posture of Defence, lest it should farther provoke their Rage. My Lords, said I, do nothing with Precipitation; let not Innocence fall a Victim to your Revenge tho' unluckily I am found in the Place of the Guilty. These Words suspended a while their Fury: Who art thou then, reply'd one of them hastily, if the infamous Villain we wait for be not thou? My Name, answer'd I, is *Ajoub*, I live in such a Place, and my Relations are well known there. Upon that, an old Gentleman, who was conceal'd in a dark Closet hard by, came forth, leading a most beautiful young Creature, very richly dress'd; whose Head and Eyes were fix'd on the Ground, and who let fall Abundance of Tears. *Gauber*, said he to her, pointing at me, is that the vile Wretch who has unlawfully feasted on thy Charms, and robb'd thee of thy Honour? *Gauber*, at this Question, became as fresh as a Rose newly blown, and looking in my Face, answer'd, I was not the Person. The old Gentleman, convinc'd of the Mistake, made a thousand Apologies to excuse it, and was just going to conduct me down Stairs again, when one of the young Men posted himself between me and the Door with his drawn Sword, and swore, that as I had been let into the Secret of the Dishonour of their Family, I should not escape. The other two said he was much in the Right of it, and held it absolutely necessary to dispatch me. Dear Children! reply'd the good old Gentleman, let not a blind Passion have too much the Ascendant over you! It would be the Height of Injustice, were your Revenge to take Place on the Innocent, and we might certainly expect that every Drop of his Blood would cry to Heaven for Vengeance, which would not fail, sooner or later, to fall down upon us. *Ajoub*, continu'd continu'd he, taking me by the Hand, make the beſt of your Way, and let not your Tongue betray what this Adventure has diſcover'd to you, if the Life I now preſerve be any ways dear to you. You will eaſily conceive with what Joy I receiv'd the News of my Deliverance, and how little a while I ſtay'd in the Houſe after it was given me. I was equally as preſſing to reach home, but juſt as I was opening our Door, an Arrow paſs'd whiſtling by my Ear, which made me jump. I look'd back and perceiv'd a Man make towards me, arm'd with a Bow in his left Hand, and a long Javelin in his Right, crying out to me: *Traytor! Tho' I have miſs'd thee once, have at thee a ſecond Time!* Seeing him alone, I took Courage, and ſaid, I muſt fall by thy Hands, if it be ſo decreed above. I drew my *Ganjar*, and having happily parry'd his firſt Offer, I encloſ'd him, wounding him twice in the Breaſt. He dropt down that inſtant, and begg'd his Life. I was not only generous enough to ſhew him Mercy, but telling me he was the Son of the Baſhaw of *Schiras*, I likewiſe ran immediately to a Surgeon, and ſent him to his Aſſiſtance. That done, I repair'd to my Father's, where I ſtay'd no longer than to provide myſelf with a Horſe and Money, and without taking Leave of any Perſon, left the City, having every thing to fear from the Fury of a Man, who doubtleſs, would have made me expiate, by a ſhameful Death, the Crime of his Son.

   I travell'd without following any certain Road. Towards Midnight I came to the great Lake of *Babu*, which was ſo calm, as if Heaven took a Pleaſure to contemplate its infinite Perfections in it. I rode a conſiderable Way by the Side of it, till, at laſt, I reach'd the Town that bears the ſame Name. I knock'd at the firſt Door I met with,
but

but no Body anfwer'd, except a great Maftiff-Dog, fet loofe in the Yard, that made fuch a terrible Barking, as awoke the reft of the Dogs of the Place. In a Moment, all *Babu* echo'd with the Noife thefe Animals made, ftill none of the Inhabitants feem'd in the leaft difturb'd at it. I went likewife and thunder'd at a neighbouring Door, but with the fame Succefs as before. Defpairing, at laft, to find any Shelter there that Night, I purfu'd my Journey, curfing all the fleepy Natives of *Babu*. As Nature was overwelm'd with Fatigue, and requir'd due Repofe, I quitted the high Road, defigning to look for fome kind Retreat, fuitable to indulge it. I took a Path that divided two fmall Mountains, which directed me to a Wood, where I rufh'd in, and made Choice of the Foot of a large wild Palm-tree for my Bed. I flept there till *Aurora* vifited the Earth with her glittering Rays; when, awaking, I was very much furpriz'd to hear, at a little Diftance from me, the Voice of a Man, who fpoke in the following Terms.

This is the precious Hour, Child: The *Peris* call'd it the wonderful one. Now it is the good *Genii* gather the powerful Herbs that transform irregular Men into wild Beafts; now it is every thing in Nature obeys their Orders, and that their myfterious Words prove moft efficacious. The Sun even when rifing, admires them; either becaufe they are profefs'd Enemies to the Children of *Ifriet* [a] and their Confederates, or that they overthrow all the vain Projects of the *Magicians*. In a Word, now it is the *Peris* appear under different Forms to Princes, that delight in executing Juftice, and to Tyrants who deferve Punifhment.

[a] *A Genius far more Cruel than the ordinary Divs.*

Oh

Oh Child! if thou couldſt foreſee this Moment as well as I, then would'ſt thou behold, ſome employ'd in the dark Shades of *Mazanderan*[b], to drive the *Lions* and *Tigers* from their Dens, in Defence of the Innocent in Oppreſſion, and admire the Facility of the others, in rendring the *Hydras* and *Griffins* Tame and Familiar.

  I had not Patience any longer to liſten to ſo ſtrange a Diſcourſe, without having a Curioſity to ſee the Perſon that held it. So advancing ſoftly from one Tree to another, I came to a pretty thick Grove of Laurels, where concealing myſelf, I had the Advantage of diſcovering without being perceiv'd, a grave old Man, habited in a long brown Robe, and a young Maid ſitting near him, with a blew Veil that cover'd every Part of her, except her Face and Hands. She had her Eyes fix'd very modeſtly on the old Man, whom ſhe ſeem'd liſtening to with great Attention. I ſhew'd myſelf, and by my Preſence interrupted their Converſation. At my Appearance, the young Maid drew her Veil over her Face, and the old Man roſe and met me. Having accoſted him, you behold, ſaid I, a Traveller, diſtreſs'd by Hunger and Wearineſs, compell'd to importune you. By *Ali!* reply'd he, you are moſt welcome, the *Sages* were never unhoſpitable. The Charity I ſhew you, will ſerve as a new Inſtruction for my Daughter. Go! refreſh yourſelf in our Retreat, we will rejoin you in an Hour. He ſhew'd me, at the ſame Time, a little Path, which I following, conducted me, after ſeveral Turnings, into a Grotto.

  Tho' the Entrance was very narrow and obſcure, yet it was light enough within, extreamly neat, and contain'd ſeveral ſpacious Chambers.

---

[b] *The Hircania of the Ancients.*

A Slave, to whom I declar'd my Diftrefs, and the charitable Intentions of his Mafter, brought before me Raifins, Piftachoes, frefh Dates, white Bread, and excellent Metheglin. Whilft I was thus agreeably employ'd, I defir'd him to go in fearch of my Horfe, defcribing, as well as I could, the Place where I had left him. If you expect I fhould obey you, anfwer'd the Slave, promife not to quit this Apartment till my Return, or my Mafter's. I readily oblig'd my felf fo to do, but after I had eat and drank, I was poffefs'd with fuch an irrefiftible Curiofity to examine the Dwelling of a Perfon like him I had feen, that it was impoffible for me to keep my Word, and I left no Part unfearch'd. The moft remote Cavity of the Grotto form'd a Cabinet full of Books, *Talifmans*, and Figures of all Sorts of Plants and Animals. I amus'd myfelf here more than in any other Part; and perceiving on the Table a Parchment unrowl'd, on which was fomething wrote in green Letters, I took it up inconfiderately, and read thefe Words: *Peri Milan-Schak! Lieutenant of the green Palace! Peri Milan-Schak! Hufband of Lutfallah! what's the Sword of Gian doing? where is his Buckler?* The Moment I had pronounc'd the laft Word of this Invocation, *Milan-Schak*, whom you know, appear'd to me, and carry'd me away, without fpeaking a Word. You are doubtlefs fenfible, beautiful *Roufchen*, that it was he who brought me to this Ifland.

The

The Continuation of the History of the Persian Lady.

AJOUB having had the good Nature to give me the real History of his leaving *Schiras*, I thought myself oblig'd, in Point of Honour and Gratitude, to relate also what had befallen me. He then gave me to understand that I was not unknown to him, that he had been one of my Admirers for a long Time, and that our Conditions being pretty near equal, he flatter'd himself with the Hope of being happy with me, by the Consent of our Parents. I gave Ear to what he said, without repulsing him too severely, or testifying too much I lov'd him. The Conversation lasted till Dinner, after which the Princess *Indgi-Mergian* led us into the Gardens. She was the most beautiful of all the *Perises*: Her Hair was the finest black in the World; her Eyes large and full of Vivacity; her Complection cannot be describ'd, without comparing it to the Lillies and Roses; to all this, she had an Air of Majesty worthy of her Birth, and knew how to explain herself with an admirable Grace. Since you are on the Point of leaving us, said she, when we were in the *Parterre*, it is necessary I should finish instructing you. Can you tell what these Flowers are? We told her we were charm'd at the Beauty of those we saw. The obliging Princess was pleas'd to give herself the Trouble to name them us, one after another. I say nam'd them us, for we knew them already, but without the Assistance of *Indgi-Mergian*, our Knowledge of them would have prov'd of little Service to us, except those of a middling Size. In Effect, how could we imagine to see a Violet, when we had a Flower before our Eyes as big as a Sun-Flower? and who would think of looking for Lillies, on Stems about the Bigness of a Pin? This agreeable Amusement did not hinder the Daughter of *Lutfallah* from telling us several other Things touching the Religion of the *Peris*, and the holy War this generous Nation had for so many Ages, maintain'd against the *Divs*. She likewise enlarg'd upon many other Particularities of the Island, which had not been treated on in the Instructions we receiv'd from *Lutfallah* and *Milan-Schak*.

Beyond the Parterre, there was a large Square of Water, in the middle of which was erected a most beautiful little Pleasure-house, built in the Form of a Castle. We intreated the Princess to favour us with the Sight of this delightful Edifice, who was complaisant enough to comply with our Request; and only call'd out pretty loud, ho *Mor!* ho *Mor!* when *Mor*, an old violet colour'd Water-Rat, with a great Beard, and as big as a Bear, immediately unchain'd a *Gondola* from the Foot of the Pleasure-house, and brought it over to us. We pass'd the Water in it, and landing, we enter'd into a little, tho' perfectly enchanting Recess. We cast our Eyes round, when to our great Astonishment we miss'd *Indgi-Mergian*, who that Moment was with us. I blush'd, and was very much confus'd to find myself thus alone with *Ajoub*. Give me a Proof, said I to him, of the Sincerity of your Affection, by the Respectfulness of your Behaviour; for nothing can be so much engaging to a Heart like mine as Modesty. *Ajoub* gaz'd upon me with such an Earnestness, as tho' he wanted the Power of Utterance; and when I had ceas'd speaking, his Lips and Hands mov'd, as if they were directed to me; but far from hearing

ing what he said, I could not distinguish even the Sound of his Voice. Then I look'd upon him in my Turn with equal Surprize: *Ajoub*, reply'd I, your Silence wounds me: What Presages all these Signs? What would you say to me? Here his Lips began again their Motion, and he resum'd all the little Gestures the Head and Hands commonly make use of, to give the proper Action to a solid Discourse, still, not a Syllable that he seem'd to pronounce, affected my hearing more than the first Time. I thought myself the Subject of his Derision, and he, probably, imagin'd the same of me; for we frown'd upon each other with such a Disdain as can't be express'd. During this Scene, the Daughter of *Lutfallah* re-appear'd, laughing immoderately. You injure both your Passions, said she to us, by a mistaken Resentment: 'Tis by a particular Virtue appropriated to this Summer House, that cuts off all Conversation between Lovers; because, as the young *Peris* resort there pretty often, the Queen did not judge proper to suffer it, lest a mutual Declaration of Tenderness, should prove instrumental in corrupting them. The Moment there's a Simpathy between *Hearts*, the *Ears* are render'd incapable of their Function. But however, your Grimaces and little Disgusts have afforded me too much unexpected Diversion, not to think myself oblig'd to you for it, and to allow you the Liberty of asking me any Question you shall be pleas'd to propose.

Having plac'd ourselves on a little *Sofa* below her's, we remain'd in Silence a considerable Time, to recover the Confusion our Spirits were in. Then I deliver'd myself as follows: Powerful Princess! I humbly entreat to know why our Sex govern in this Island. *Lutfallah* I perceive is acknowledg'd Queen, yet *Milan-Schak* claims not the Character of King. The other *Perifes*, whether Queens or Subjects, have equally a Superiority over their Husbands, which gives me much Matter of Wonder. May I, with Submission, farther ask if this Custom be introduc'd to compensate the Assiduities of the *Perifes*, whilst in a Virgin State? In our World, young Men before Marriage, pay their Mistresses the utmost Deference, Humility and Complaisance; but when that Ceremony is over, their former *Devoirs* are converted into *Authority*. Our Laws, resum'd the Princess, are much preferable to yours, and are grounded upon these three Reasons: The first is, the *Perifes* have infinitely more Understanding than the *Peris*, and are as naturally superior to them as those are to common Men, or these latter to the *Pabins*, and so on by Degrees. The second is, that Strength is added to their Wit; whereas Men are only Masters in your World, but because they are stronger. And the third is mysterious. Only observe, that Fertility is the Source of all Things, and that it can't be too much honour'd.

Indgi-Mergian having discontinu'd speaking, *Ajoub* kept up the Conversation, and said: As there's but little Probability of our being suffer'd to remain Time enough to make sufficient Remarks of this City, therefore I believe *Roufchen* will not be displeas'd if I beseech you, charming Princess! to give us some Idea of it; for, as yet, I know not so much as its Name. This City, answer'd the Daughter of *Lutfallah*, is call'd *Gianire*. After the Death of *Gian*, Sovereign of all the *Genii*, the War, that seem'd to be at an End towards his latter Years, being renew'd between the *Peris* and *Divs*, there arose such terrible Disorders throughout all *Ginniftan*, that made *Gian*, only Son of that good King abandon it, with his Family, and four

others

others of the moſt Illuſtrious of the Nation of the *Peris*. This great Deſign produc'd a very happy Event, by the Succour of *Feramak* his Conſort, who render'd the Vigilance of the *Divs* of no Effect, and conducted her triumphant Band into this Iſland. The Town was built in a very ſhort Time, which *Feramak* call'd *Gianire*, from the Name of her Huſband. To preſerve an eſtabliſh'd Peace in her new Colony, ſhe ſhar'd her Authority with the four Mothers of the Families that had accompany'd her, and ſince that Time, *Gianire* has always been govern'd by five Queens. Theſe our Anceſtors, made Choice of five different Colours to diſtinguiſh themſelves, their Subjects, and even their Deſcendants. Theſe Colours were *Green*, which is ours, *Blew*, *Yellow*, *Red* and *White*. There are five broad Streets in the City of *Gianire*; one End of them coming into the Market-Place, and the other leading to the Front of a Palace. The Queens Palaces are built of Marble of the ſame Colour their Arms are of; the ordinary Houſes take their's from the Palace they are dependent on; and thoſe are inhabited by *Peris* of the ſecond Claſs. I will ſhew you to morrow, both the great Market-Place and the Academy, which is the moſt ſumptuous Piece of Building in the whole Iſland. But how great ſoever your Admiration may be, at the Sight of ſo magnificent an Edifice, the Reſurrection of *Feramak* and *Gian*, my Anceſtors, and thoſe I have been telling you of, will, undoubtedly, aſtoniſh you much more. When *Indgi-Mergian* had finiſh'd the Deſcription, ſhe roſe up, and we croſs'd the Water again together. After that, we walk'd a conſiderable Time in a Wood of lofty Strawberry-trees, which, at that Seaſon, could ſcarcely ſupport the Weight of that delicious Fruit. They wafted a
moſt

moſt grateful Air, and ſuch an exquiſite Odour, that the hymenial Perfumes can't be compar'd to it, without rendering the Compariſon odious. The next Morning, a little before peep of Day, the whole Town was rais'd from their Sleep by a moſt harmonious Symphony, that was heard in the Air over the Academy, where People began to repair from all Parts.

Being very deſirous to be of the Number of the Spectators, I went down into the Court-yard, where I found two Wood-lice, about thirty Foot long, and large in Proportion, very richly harneſs'd, and who carry'd on their ſpacious Backs commodious and magnificent Lodgings, compos'd of a Chamber and two Cabinets: The one imploy'd the Forepart, and might contain twelve Foot ſquare; and the others, one of which ſerv'd as an Anti-chamber, were about ſeven Foot long, and ſix broad. Theſe moving Apartments were hung with green Velvet, the reſt of the Furniture anſwerable to it. Tho' theſe valuable Moveables, as well as all other Riches, ſtand the *Peris* in nothing, yet the Nicety of their Taſte and Judgment in adorning the Lodges of *Lutfallab* and *Milan-Schak*, was almoſt the chief Thing to be admir'd in them. I can't forbear acquainting you, now I am about it, that no Carriage whatever is comparable to thoſe, either for Safety or Conveniency. A Wood-louſe is of a ſurprizing tractable Nature, and always attentive to the Directions of his Conducter, whoſe Seat is plac'd as it were on the Head of this Animal. He goes as faſt as one pleaſes, without abating any thing of the Uneaſineſs of his Pace. If by Chance he lames himſelf in one of his Feet, it is not perceivable, becauſe he has thirteen more to ſuſtain him. His Shells are all ſpotted, and ſhine like thoſe of the

great

great *Indian* Tortoises; and their two Horns are almost as useful to them, as Trunks are to *Elephants*.

Lutfallah plac'd me nigh herself, and *Ajoub* accompany'd *Milan-schak*. We pass'd through a very long Street, cross'd by five others, at an equal Distance between each other. All the Houses we saw were built of green Marble, with such a Symmetry as did not fatigue the Sight by too near a Resemblance. We came at last to a very spacious, round Place, in the Middle of which was an Edifice, built also round, that has not its Fellow in the World, being the same *Indgi-Mergian* had told us of. It serves the *Peris* both for an Academy and a Temple: It is cover'd with a Golden *Cupilo*, whose Lustre did not seem lessen'd, even by the Sun's, which was then rising. Five Porticoes of *Agate*, each of different Colours, and adorn'd with twelve fine lofty Columns, give the Entrance into this magnificent Temple, and which face the five principal Streets of the Town. The Orders of Architecture are so regularly observ'd, that nothing we see in these Parts, can possibly convey a stronger or more grateful Idea. I took Notice that the Chapters of all the Columns are compos'd of four Figures, representing the Heads of Lobsters, the Contours of whose Horns, on the Top, produce a very agreeable Effect. The Portico we enter'd into, was of green *Agate*, spotted with White, on the Frontispiece of which was wrote the illustrious Names of *Feramak* and of *Gian*, in large golden Letters. We went up nine Steps of Serpentine Marble, into a Theatre divided into five Parts. All the Stages of each Part were full of *Perises* and *Peris* of different Ages, and dress'd in the same Colour with their Queen, whose Throne was fix'd quite on the Top.

The Resurrection of Queen FERAMAK, and GIAN her Husband.

IN the Middle of the Amphi-Theatre, there lay two Vessels of Crystal, in the Figure of Eggs, which contain'd two little dead Bodies of different Sexes. Just when we enter'd, the four Queens and their Husbands were sitting on the Ground about these Vessels, and contemplating them with a most surprising Attention and Modesty. *Lutfallah* and *Milan-Schak* join'd them; and *Ajoub* and I were conducted up to the Top of the Amphi-Theatre, by a private Stair-Case, and plac'd near the green Throne. There reigned such a profound Silence in this numerous Assembly as made it frightful. A quarter of an Hour after, *Feramak* and *Gian*, who were inclos'd in the two Vessels, began to shew all the Marks of Life; the transparent Eggs clove assunder, and were converted into green Cloaths to cover their Nakedness. These Bodies, risen from the Dead, grew to the same Bigness they were of in the Flower of their Age: Then they rose by degrees into the Air, the *Perises* and *Peris* surrounding them; and being come to the Height of the Thrones, they stopp'd there a Moment, casting their Eyes all round, as it were to examine the Company. After that, they sunk down, without the least Motion, towards the Middle, where I was, and plac'd themselves by each other in the green Throne. Nothing but Death itself could ever terrify me more than did the Approach of these People, who were just come from the other World. Those of both Sexes, that had accompany'd them thither, saluted them in the most profound Manner,

ner, and then went, taking the same Road in the Air, to fill their Thrones over the Band of their Colour. *Lutfallah* and *Milan-Schak* sat at the Feet of *Feramak* and *Gian*. The two risen from the Dead, wore a very grave and serious Air, as though they were meditating on Affairs of great Consequence. *Feramak* had a delicate fair Complexion; *Gian* a swarthy one; his Eyes were lively, his Beard and Hair jet-black, and look'd like a severe and courageous Man. His Wife pronounc'd the following Discourse, in a very distinct, easy Manner, and with a very elevated Voice.

The purify'd Shades, that came to visit us in our peaceful Mansions, since our last Expiration, have, from time to time, appris'd us of such Passages and Transactions, as would have oblig'd us to hasten our Return much sooner, had it been in our Power to accomplish it. It grieves me to tell you, my dear Children, that the Glory of our Nation degenerates by little and little, and that the detestable *Divs* are insensibly becoming conspicuous on our Ruin and Decay; a Misfortune the more fatal, as you are almost unprepar'd to receive it. Whence proceeds this passive Neglect of our Wel-fare? From a Want of due Reflection on the End, for which we are rais'd above the rest of Mortals. We trifle away our Time about Nothings; for such I esteem all Prodigies, done without having an absolute Necessity, or an apparent Advantage in view.

Do you imagine the most essential Glory of our State consists in building Palaces, adorning them with rich Furniture, dressing in magnificent Habits, giving a false Gloss of Beauty to Persons, whose Natures are opposite, filling Coffers with Pearls and Diamonds, inspiring Men with the Knowledge

ledge of the various Languages of Birds and other Animals, favouring the infignificant Paffion of fome amorous Trifler, and transforming Bodies from one Shape to another? All thefe Wonders, in our Power, are not eftimable in themfelves: they ought only to be made ufe of, as Means to arrive at a higher Degree of Perfection. If we propofe no more than the Performance of them, we abufe the moft fublime Gifts, render ourfelves ufelefs to the Univerfe, betray our Virtue, and refign up our Right of Empire to Enemies unworthy of it.

How can a few vain Applaufes footh us, when fo many impending Ills hang over our Heads? Ought we, alas! to purchafe a fading Admiration at fo dear a Rate? Where are the Ages, not to mention thofe of my own Time, which my grand Niece *Lutfallah* and her Spoufe render'd fo famous by their firft Exploits? Then our Sciences not only contributed to the Glory of the *Sams-*[a] *Nerimans*, the *Zals-Zers*, the *Roftams*, the *Kaicobads*, the *Asfendiars*, and a numerous Multitude of other Heroes, but at the fame time made Virtue alfo triumphant. Then we beheld nothing but great Enterprifes, Queens deliver'd from the Hands of their Ravifhers, Magicians vanquifh'd, Giants trod under Foot, Monfters defeated, Tyrants difpoil'd and put to Death, and the ftrongeft Enchantments of Vice happily brought to an End. Then the *Divs* [b] *Nerez* and their Difciples durft not prefume to appear, or if they had the Temerity to do it, they receiv'd the juft Punifhment of their Crimes: But alas! that happy Time's no more! The World feems now a days to be fill'd

---

[a] *Warriours very much boafted of in Romances, and as much fung in the* Perfian *and* Arabian *Poems.*
[b] *The true Sur-Name of the evil Genii.*

with *Genii*, only to do childish Actions. *Feramak*, in uttering these last Words, let fall some Tears, which the whole Assembly appear'd to be greatly mov'd at.

Your Sighs, pursu'd she, would make me judge I have a little too far exaggerated your Faults, but I hope my Reproaches will be of such Service as to engage you to remark what's most reprehensible in your past Actions, and put you more on your Guard for the future. As our Time is short among you, let the Youth of the second Class immediately begin their Exercise, that they may deserve our Praises.

That Moment the *Perises* and *Peris*, Subjects of *Lutfallah*, rose up and repair'd to the *Area*, in order to commence the Exercise of the Elements. The Chaos was the first thing represented; then they divided the Matter into two Parts, and after that into four. Each Part produc'd its proper Effects; as the *Fire*, Light'nings, Thunder-bolts, Conflagrations, and *Ignis Fatuus's:* The *Air*, Winds, Thunders, and ordinary Star-fallings. The *Water*, Tempests and Monsters; and the *Earth*, Earthquakes, new Mountains, Abysses and Forests. All these Things were shewn in Miniature, which gave a great Proof of the green Band's Dexterity, they having observ'd, with the greatest Nicety, all the Rules of Proportion.

The yellow and blue *Peris* assembled together to imitate rural Diversions: Their first Representation was, a surprising Prospect of Rocks, Rivers, Meadows, and all sorts of Cattel feeding therein, even with their Shepherds and Shepherdesses. The Scene was concluded by a witty Game: Three young Shepherds, and as many Shepherdesses, accompany'd with the oldest of their Profession, of each Sex, belonging to their Village, sate together under the Shade of some Trees. Each Shepherdess accus'd her Shepherd with a Defect; and each Shepherd attributed to his Shepherdess a Perfection. All the Shepherds prov'd, by a little pleasant Argument, that one reigning Quality of their Shepherdesses, was capable of effacing all the Failings they might otherwise be guilty of; and all the Shepherdesses plainly demonstrated, that the principal Imperfection of their Shepherds only serv'd to brighten the Lustre of their fine Qualities. The ancient Woman impos'd Silence on the Shepherds, as did the old Man on the Shepherdesses; and then they declar'd which of the Sheperdesses and Shepherds had argued best, according to the Opinion of the Company. Immediately after the Decision, they were created Queen and King of the *Dance*, which was perform'd by the Sound of a Bag-pipe and Tabor, which the old Man and Woman play'd upon.

The red and white *Peris* exercised next together: They built Cities, Castles, Palaces; made Furniture, Jewels, Cloaths, *Menageries*, Fountains and Singing-Birds: They represented likewise *Sultans* with their Courts; Princesses of all Ages and Nations, with their Attendants; and Mosques, Doctors, *Vizirs* and *Cadis*.

They were all so perfect in their Parts, that at each Motion of a Rod, every thing, that Moment, was presented to our View. *Feramak* and *Gian* openly applauded the Dexterity of their Performances. The Companies, transported with the Praises given them, re-united to treat the Assembly. In a Word, the whole Edifice was fill'd, in a Moment, with the most exquisite, rare and nourishing Perfumes. When the Entertainment was over, the Queens with their Spouses form'd a Circle in the Middle of the Amphi-Theatre. The

two

two risen from the Dead descended softly, till they came to the Centre, where *Gian*, who had kept Silence till then, said three times, with a loud and majestick Voice, *Let the Sword of* Gian *glitter, and his Buckler wound Ifriet*. As soon as this mysterious Proclamation was issu'd, *Feramak* and *Gian* insensibly diminish'd, and became Eggs again. Then they rose from the Ground as high as the Thrones, and hurrying through the Air with Rapidity, they went out of the blue Portico, and drew after them the whole Assembly. I was carry'd away as well as the rest; we flew over the Houses of the City, and having travel'd about eighteen Miles, we came to a Mountain of black Marble, which had a great Opening in the Middle. We enter'd into it, following the two Eggs, that conducted us down a continual Descent, through easy Paths, into a vast large arched Palace, where there were more than two thousand Eggs, exactly resembling the others. As my Eyes were attentively fix'd on them to see whereabouts they plac'd themselves, a Drop of Water fell on my Face from the Arch, which was so cold, that it depriv'd me of all my Senses. What Form or Figure I assum'd, I know not, but I am positive in this, that I found myself in my Father's House at *Schiras*, lay'd in a Bed, all over in a Sweat, and almost famish'd with Hunger.

I call'd for something to eat, which they gave me, with such Moderation, that I easily perceiv'd they imagin'd me seiz'd with some Indisposition. My Father, Sister, and Physician, who were present, assured me I had been three Days without any Motion, and almost any Pulse. I told them, it was certainly some Phantom, in my Shape, that had led them into such an Error, and then related to them my Adventures at length. The

Sighs

Sighs of my Father, the Nods of my Sister, and the certain smiling Air the Physician affected, convinc'd me they gave but little Credit to what had befallen me. My Sister's Beard might perhaps have gain'd Belief upon them, had she been still plagu'd with it. I call'd in vain for my changeable Habit, and as fruitless did I invoke *Lutfallah:* I hope, said I to them, you won't deny but the Son of our Bashaw was very dangerously wounded by young *Ajoub*; still they held my Assertion groundless. I was obliged to submit both to their Incredulity and the whole Town's. Fatigu'd at last with so general an Unbelief, I obtain'd, as soon as I was thought recover'd, Leave of my Father to go and live some time with an Aunt I have at *Oormus. Ajoub* paid me a Visit there, when I had almost forgot him. Indeed I could scarce recollect myself to have seen him, at his first accosting me; but he answer'd the Questions I ask'd him, so very particularly, that I no longer doubted it was he. After that, I entreated him to tell me, how he left the *Topsy-Turvy* Island.

The Sequel of the History of Ajoub.

MADAM, said he, your Departure and mine proceed from the same Cause: A Drop of Water, that fell upon me from the Top of the Vault, benumb'd all my Limbs. When my Spirits began to resume their former Functions, I found myself stretched on a Bed of dry Leaves, at the Bottom of a Grotto. I perceiv'd it to be the same where I had been order'd to go, by the Sage of *Babu*, but it was so empty and Desart like

then

then, that it look'd as though no Body had ever dwell'd there. I only found in the Recefs, that was set apart for the Sage's Cabinet, a Paper, where I read these Words:

"*Ajoub!* your Temerity, that deserv'd an exem-
"plary Punishment, has perhaps procur'd your fu-
"ture Happiness, unless a fatal Untowardness bring
"you here again. If you chance to return hither,
"the Situation of this Place shall remind you of
"your Fault. A Sage's Revenge extends itself
"no farther. Far from carrying his Resentment
"to the Extremity ordinary Men do, he kindly in-
"forms you, that the Person you wounded at
"*Schiras*, is become now one of your best
"Friends."

The Perusal of this Writing afforded me a great deal of Pleasure. I rose up and went directly out of the Grotto, where, contrary to my Expectations, I found my Horse ty'd to a Tree, whom I mounted upon, and proceeded with all Haste towards *Schiras*. As soon as I enter'd the Town, I went to an *Iman*'s [a] House of my Acquaintance, where I alighted and wrote a Line to the Bashaw's Son, who immediately sent back word to desire I would favour him with my Company. When I was by his Bed's-side, he said, looking pleasantly at me, and pressing my Hand, I have taken such good Precautions, as to prevent this Accident reaching my Father's Ears. My Wounds, though large, are not mortal; so that, neither you nor I have any thing to fear. Then I begg'd he would make me sensible in what I had incurr'd his Hatred. Jealousy, reply'd he, was the Motive that inflamed the Fury you saw me in, and which would certainly have prov'd fatal, had not your

[a] *A Mahometan Curate.*

Generosity disdain'd taking the Advantage, your superiour Skill had given over it.

The Occasion of my coming to such Extremities with you, was this: The happy Night of my Assignation with the charming *Gauher* being come, and waiting impatiently the much wish'd for Minute, I perceiv'd you pass under my Window, making the same Signal I had agreed to give her, in a Billet I had sent her for that Purpose. I did not take much Time to deliberate on such an odd Incident, but directly follow'd you. I scarce had overtaken you, when I saw you enter my Charmer's Doors. Your staying there so considerable a while, made me readily conclude she was become false, and that you had robb'd me of the only Treasure I possess'd in the World. How did Rage, Revenge and Despair torture me by Turns: I saw you at last come out, when I ran after you, attack'd you, and you know with what Success. My Innocence, reply'd I, deserv'd Fortune's Favour at that time. I grant it, resum'd he; yesterday one of *Gauher*'s Slaves inform'd me, that my last Letter to her had been intercepted by her Brothers, and describ'd likewise the dangerous Adventure had happen'd to you on my Account. I was very much surpriz'd, you must believe, at this News; but still more terribly shock'd, when the Slave added, that my Soul's Inspirer was condemn'd to fall the Victim of my Love, e'er two Hours elaps'd. Without losing a moment's time, I wrote to her Father, intimating, that my Conversation with his Daughter had only an honourable View, and that nothing in this World could render me so happy as his immediate Compliance to put it in execution. I sent this little Billet, which produced the very Effect I could wish. *Ajoub*, continu'd he, let our Friendship

ship be inviolable for the future, and begin to convince me of it, by going, this inftant, in my Name, to confirm the Promife I have given. I quitted myfelf of this agreeable Commiffion with as much Joy as they felt, who, fome Days before, imagin'd their Revenge gratify'd, by having me in their Power. The Night following I was feiz'd with a violent Fever, occafion'd by the Agitations and Fatigues I had endured. I kept my Bed for a long time, without feeing any Body, and was not even pafs'd Danger, when the welcome News of your Return reach'd my Ears: But, alas! how tranfient was the Happinefs that Thought gave me! Your Departure for *Ormus* foon fucceeded, which certainly would have cut my Thread of Life, had not my Father apply'd other Remedies than his own to reftore me. I difclos'd to him my Difeafe, which till then I had conceal'd, and likewife whom the fair Author was that I hoped would have Charity enough to heal the Wounds fhe had given. Upon this open Declaration, he had immediate Recourfe to your Father, moft adorable *Roufchen!* And after fome Conference together on that Head, the Life-reftoring Refult of it was this;— Prefenting me a Letter from my Father, wherein I read, with a Satisfaction and Pleafure I could not difguife, his Approbation of the Bearer becoming his Son-in-Law. How eafy is it to be dutiful, when it's agreeable to the Inclination! Our Marriage was folemniz'd with all the ufual Ceremonies; after which, *Ajoub* follow'd Merchandizing. I muft beg, Gentlemen, you'll difpenfe with me from proceeding any farther: I accompany'd him every where he went, and I think Death was very cruel to feparate us.

Loulou endeavour'd here to divert the Tears of her Mother, by a little witty Flight that came into her Head, or rather that she was Mistress of at Pleasure. Dear Mamma! said she to her, the *Portuguese* Slave, perceiving me cry and in a very melancholly Posture this Morning, told me a Story that has somewhat mitigated my Grief: I have it still fresh in my Memory, and if you please to give Attention to it, I hope it will prove as efficacious to you. The beautiful *Persian* could not refrain smiling, and said to her, If the Fable you speak of be not of too tedious a Length, I give you leave to relate it. Upon which she gave a Glance at me as though she was going to tell me something very surprising. I shall now, said she, inform *Abdallah*, why Men grow older as they live, whereas Serpents become younger.

The Second Story of LOULOU.

A LITTLE after the *Perises* had shewn their Power and Friendship to Men, they were sollicited to grant them a Gift. Let us know, answer'd the *Perises*, in what the Gift consists, and it shall be given to you. That we may always remain, reply'd the Man, in the full Vigour of our Youth, without ever feeling the Incommodities of old Age. Let it be according to your Wish, said the *Perises*, we all agree to it, but mind you be careful in preserving the Privilege we are about to grant you; for if once you lose it, expect to fall again into your former State.

Some time after this, a young *Peri* was dispatch'd to the Men, charg'd with Letters Patents, for perpetual Vigour, wrote in very good Form. As soon as they were deliver'd, all the old Men resum'd refum'd their former Youth, their grey Hairs fell, the Specks in their Eyes difappear'd, their wrinkled Skins grew fmooth, and they became, at laft, as handfome and ftrong as they had ever formerly been. How did the old Women then hold up their Heads! And with what Difdain did not they now revenge the Contempt had been fhewn them?

Some Years after this Condefcenfion of the *Perifes*, the War between the Men and the wild Beafts, happen'd to break out again, on Account of certain Forefts that the Men had ufurp'd. Each Power made War-like Preparations, and difpos'd themfelves to give Battle. The Men, having committed the Care of their Baggage to *Affes* and other tame Animals, began very hard Marches towards the contefted Forefts. The Enemies, on the contrary, did not all repair thither, but felected out of their Army a certain Number of *Serpents*, *Foxes* and fome other Creatures they judg'd moft cunning, to lye in Ambufh on the Roads, with ftrict Orders to maintain refolutely all difficult Paffes. Skirmifhes were continually happening between both Parties, without any apparent Advantage on either Side, till one Rencounter, the Men had the Misfortune of lofing all they efteem'd valuable, their Privilege; and that, through the Negligence of the Afs, who was loaded with it.

This ftupid Creature coming to the Side of a River, and Defigning to pafs it, a huge Serpent that was pofted there to obftruct the Paffage, faid to him, that if he had Thoughts of purfuing his Journey, he ought firft to quit his Load. The Afs, upon this, was going to turn back again, but being very thirfty, he ftoop'd down his Head to drink, before he fet forward; yet ftill the Serpent opp .'d his Defign, and coming up clofe to him, faid, What needs flattering, I fwear you fhall not tafte one Drop of it, unlefs you directly refign me up your Burthen. Thefe Waters, I am Keeper of, are very frefh and cool, and ought not to be drank but at Leifure; which you well deferve, after the Fatigues you have undergone. Unload yourfelf therefore, and take Refrefhment, then you'll find how gaily you'll go and rejoyn your Fellow-Travellers. The Afs, prefs'd both by Drought and Fear of ftaying too long behind his Companions, yielded, at laft, to this deceitful Speech, and threw off his Load. Whilft he was drinking the Serpent feiz'd the Panniers, and finding the Privilege in them made off, and communicated it to the reft of the Serpents. Since that time, Serpents caft every Year their old Skins, and take new ones. Men, on the contrary, hourly decay, till they attain old Age, which, at laft, puts an End to their Days.

I had all the Reafon imaginable to fufpect, that the *Perfian* and her Daughter had been appris'd of my Undertaking, and that this Story was levell'd at me. I affured the Mother, as did alfo *Almoraddin*, that nothing had ever fill'd me with more Admiration, than the Hiftory of her Adventures. She feem'd perfectly fatisfied with the Reflections we had made, and as we were about to take our Leaves, gave me an obliging Summons to difcharge that Part of the Convention which regarded me, as foon as poffible. I could wifh, Madam, faid I, I had already quitted myfelf of it, as *Almoraddin* has done; for what can I prefume to recount after all the wonderful Things I have heard?

We did not return our Vifit for many Days after the Converfation broke up. *Almoraddin* was taken up in haft'ning his Work-men, and ex-
changing

changing such Goods as he thought were superfluous, for those he had occasion for. Instead of Gum-*Arabick*, Amber from *Souffel*, and white Linens from *Cambaye*, he had Diamonds from *Visapour*, Pearls from *Coromandel*, and *Canara* Pepper, which is most esteem'd in the *Indies*. Tho' these Exchanges were very advantageous to him, yet the Profit that accrued from them, was far less sensible to him, than the Pleasure he felt in the Hope of presenting them to the beautiful *Zulikhaa*, whether his Attempt succeeded or not. And for my part, I did not want Employment. The more Questions I ask'd, the more I was convinced of the Difficulty of my coming to the Knowledge of the Oracle I was in search of. The Adventures of the *Persian* Lady, at first, gave me a Glimmering of Hope; but then when I had heard the Catastrophe of them, and found that she had not the least Correspondence with the *Peris*, I condemn'd my too great Facility in having conceiv'd it. As we return'd from paying our last Visit, *Almoraddin*, still more prejudic'd than before, said to me: We have both acknowledg'd our Admiration of *Roufchen*, but for my part, I only praise the Order of her *Refveries*, and great Simplicity in regard of *Ajoub*. And you, *Abdalla*, what is it you admire? Her Discoveries, answer'd I cooly. What you term as such, reply'd he, are not then gross Imaginations? Sure you are not still inclinable to believe *Roufchen* was ever in the *Topsy-Turvy* Island? I am persuaded, resum'd I, that her Body never was there, but as for her Soul, I find it possible; since the Voyage a Soul makes, may be no less true, than those perform'd by Souls and Bodies join'd together. Did not our Prophet go from *Mecca* to *Jerusalem*, and from thence to Heaven? Did not he traverse the Iron

Heaven, the *Brass* Heaven, the *Silver* Heaven, the *Golden* Heaven, the *Pearl* Heaven, the *Emerald* Heaven, the *Ruby* Heaven, and the *Opal* Heaven; tho' there is as much Distance from one Heaven to another, as would take an ordinary Man a thousand Years travelling? Did not he penetrate the five-hundred and forty Spaces of *Water*, *Snow*, *Hail*, *Clouds*, *Darkness*, *Fire*, *Light* and *Glory*, which reach from the *Opal* Heaven to the Throne of God? Did not he return to *Mecca* the same Way he went? And did not the Prophet perform this vast Voyage in one Night, imperceptibly to the fair *Aischa*, whom he was in Bed with? She could not be sensible of it, as the most celebrated Doctors assert, because the Body of *Mahomet* remain'd in Bed with her. *Almoraddin*, who was no very great Scholar, cast down his Eyes, and I did not judge it proper to augment his Confusion. The next Visit we paid to *Rouschen*, I discharg'd the Obligation I lay under, by relating the following History.

The History of Prince TANGUT, *and the Princess with a Nose a Foot long.*

THERE reign'd, in one of the Vallies of the great Mount *Dalanger*, a King, Widdower, very poor, and very old, who had three Sons, whom he spoke to one Day in these Terms: My Ancestors call me, but before my Departure, I think it my Duty to reveal a Secret to you. Know then, a little before my Marriage, I went in Pursuit of a *Bear*, and being very much fatigu'd with the Chace, and benighted, I sought Shelter and

Rest

Reſt for my weary'd Limbs, in a Cavern of the yellow Mountain. Next Morning, a very handſome young Man appear'd to me, and ſaid: *Aboucaf!* beget pretty Children! and when thou art juſt upon the Point of bidding adieu to the World, ſend them hither! I had not time to thank the Youth, before he became inviſible; but I have ever retain'd his Sayings to me. Repair, Dear Children! therefore to the yellow Mountain; perhaps you will find there an Inheritance more worthy of you, than that I am able to bequeath you. The three mountain Princes delay'd no Time to depart, and being come to the Cavern, advanc'd almoſt to the further Part of it, where they perceiv'd the Foot of a Stair-Caſe, which had been conceal'd till then. They went up above a thouſand Steps, and at laſt came to a ſquare Place cut in the Rock, but ſaw nothing there except a little Baſket made of Ruſhes, that contain'd a leathern Purſe, a Horn, ſuch as Shepherds make uſe of to recall their ſtray'd Flocks, and a Girdle made of coarſe Mohair. I can't ſay, ſaid *Hiarkan*, eldeſt of the Brothers, but our Father acted a very wiſe Part, not to be ſo very forward in communicating to us this Treaſure; however, let us ſhare it between us; ſo I'll take the *Girdle*. And I the *Horn*, ſaid *Xamor* the ſecond Son. The *Purſe* then conſequently falls to my Dividend, reply'd the youngeſt, who was call'd *Tangut*. As *Hiarkan* was unfolding his Girdle, a little Scroll dropt from it, wherein he read theſe Words: *What Part of the World wilt thou be tranſported to?* The other two, being curious to know whether they ſhould find any ſuch Writings encloſ'd in what they had, immediately examin'd; one his Horn, and the other his Purſe. *Xamor* found ſuch another, which imported: *What Number of Forces doſt thou wiſh to command?*

command? And the youngest drew one equally from his Purse, which said: *What Sum of Money hast thou need of?* If nothing oppos'd our being obey'd, cry'd they all together, but wishing, how happy were our Conditions now! It's very easy, said *Tangut*, to verify these Prodigies, by my making the first Experiment. Then he shut his Purse, and said: I have occasion for a thousand Pieces of Gold. That Instant, the Purse swell'd, and grew so heavy, that it dropt out of his Hands. He open'd it upon the Ground, empty'd it, and told over the very Sum he had just before call'd for. Imagine the Joy the Brothers conceiv'd at this Spectacle. *Aboucaf* could not participate of it, because he had just expir'd, as they got home again. After this good Prince's Obsequies were over, the Ceremony having been perform'd in a Manner suitable to his Rank, they all agreed to conceal the Secret, and to quit their barren Countrey in Quest of more fruitful Climates. *Hiarkan* and *Xamor* were the first that began their Progress; but I shall omit relating the Particularities of their Adventures, tho' I am perfectly acquainted with them, and only observe to you, that the very Year of their Departure, they founded the two Kingdoms and Cities, which bear their Names [a] to this Day; my Design being to confine myself to what befel *Tangut*.

He set forward, directing his Course towards

---

[a] *The Kingdom of* Hiarkan *is bounded on the* North, *by Mount* Magog; *on the South, by Mount* Caucasus; *on the East by the Kingdom of* Xamor; *and on the West, by the lesser* Thibet *and* Giagatai. *The Kingdom of* Xamor *is bounded on the North, by the* Tartarian Kalmuks; *on the South, by the Kingdom of* Belor, *and the greater* Thibet; *on the East, by that Part of* Tartary, *subject to the Emperor of* China; *and on the West, by the Kingdom of* Hiarkan.

the

the *South*, and after having travell'd a long Time, came at laſt to the ſpacious City of *Kemmerouf*, Metropolitan of the Kingdom of *Aſſan*. The Situation of that Place pleaſing him extreamly well, he determin'd to ſtay there a conſiderable Time, and therefore made uſe of his Purſe, to provide himſelf an Equipage, becoming the Rank of a great Prince. The prodigious Expence he was at, and the Richneſs of his Attendants, ſoon made him diſtinguiſh'd at Court. Nothing was talk'd of now at Sultan *Fadhel*'s Levee (for ſo was the King of *Aſſan* call'd) but the great Generoſity of *Tangut*. The *Emirs* not only courted his Friendſhip, but likewiſe his ſimple Acquaintance. The Ladies invented a thouſand Stratagems to rival each other's Views; for Youth, Beauty, and an Affluence of Fortune, Perfections ſeldom found together, were all united in his Perſon. *Tangut* made Profeſſions of Eſteem to all the Beauties of *Kemmerouf*, tho' in his Soul, he deſpis'd ſuch as were too flexible to them. The Charms of the haughty *Dogandar*, only Daughter to the Sultan, were alone capable of triumphing over his Heart. He did more for her in vain, than would have ruin'd the great *Kan*, and impoveriſh'd the Emperor of *China*. The Sultan and Sultaneſs, pleas'd with the conſtant Aſſiduity of this generous and opulent Stranger, and not doubting but he was of an illuſtrious Deſcent, order'd the Princeſs, at laſt, to receive him with leſs Diſdain, and at leaſt out of Gratitude, to liſten to his reſpectful Addreſſes. *Dogandar*, upon this Reproof, immediately chang'd her Conduct, and affected a beſeeching Air of Tenderneſs, which the Sultan took for a Mark of Obedience, and *Tangut* for the greateſt Proofs of Love; but they were both ignorant of the Motive that induc'd her to behave after such a Manner.

One Evening, after some few Expressions of her pretended Passion, she took Occasion to speak thus to her Lover: I have Reason to doubt the Sincerity of your Affection, since I'm still a Stranger to the Monarch that gave you Birth. The inexhaustible Treasure of your Mind speaks you a great Prince, but that's what the very Dregs of the People can distinguish as well as I: Is not it therefore the more surprising I should not know you better than the Commonalty? No, it is plain you cannot love me, and behave with such Reserve. But supposing it were so; what would not I then study to revenge the Mystery, that has so much disturb'd my Peace of Mind? These last Words being pronounc'd with an Air of Passion, the transported *Tangut* began to be terrify'd at them. Alas! Madam, cry'd he, what have I done, that you accuse and condemn me at the same Time? Let me know my Crime, that I may strive to amend it. What have I kept as a Secret from you? It is true, you were in the Right to judge of my Birth by the Appearance I make; for to my Father I owe the Source of it, as thro' his Means I came by the Purse, I now always carry about me. Can it be possible, resum'd *Dogandar*, readily changing her Accent, that all the Riches you squander away, should only proceed from a Purse so easily carry'd? Oh! it can't be! you still continue to deceive me! Madam, reply'd *Tangut*, I'll instantly convince you of it by Experience. Upon which he drew forth his Purse, open'd it several Times, and as many laid the golden Product at the young Princess's Feet. *Dogandar*, seiz'd with an insatiable Desire of becoming Mistress of such an admirable Purse, made Answer, fwer, she would not believe her own Eyes, unless she had first made the agreeable Proof of it herself. In so saying, she snatch'd it out of *Tangut*'s Hands, as it were in a Jest, hid it in her Bosom, ran away with it, and shut five or six Doors after her. Whilst he thought his Charmer only did it out of Diversion, he waited her Return with all the Patience such an Accident would Cause, that was done without Design; but when the Eunuch told him roughly to withdraw, by *Dogander*'s Orders, he began to foresee his approaching Misfortune. The next Day, and a great many Days after, he repair'd to the Sultan's, but with the same Impossibility of speaking to the Princess. He saw her, indeed, once or twice, and she likewise cast her Eyes upon him, but with this Difference; they were before engaging and full of Tenderness, now as cool and full of Contempt. Never was Trouble and Vexation equal to *Tangut*'s: His Affection for her detain'd him, and his Impossibility to support the daily Expence he was at, compell'd him to depart. After a great Struggle with himself, he resolv'd at last the more willingly on the latter, as his Disease was not incurable, if one of his Brothers would but assist him in it.

He left *Kemmerouf* without the least Formality, and travell'd till he reach'd *Xamor*, whom he hop'd to have more Influence over than *Hiarkan*. Brother, said he, the greatest of Misfortunes has befallen me; an unworthy beautiful Princess has robb'd me of my Purse. Let me entreat you therefore to lend me your Horn, that I may go incessantly and make her restore it. *Xamor* was very much surpriz'd and troubled at his Loss; however, after some Reproaches, which were rather the Effects of Love than Marks of Indignation,

tion, he granted his Brother the Favour he demanded.

Tangut, possess'd of the Horn, made the best of his Way towards *Kemmerouf*, fully bent on besieging it, at his Arrival there. When he came within Cannon-Shot of the Town, he sounded his Horn six Times, when fifty thousand Men block'd up each of the six Gates thereof. These Men were both stout and hardy, perfectly well arm'd, and distributed into Companies, Regiments and Brigades, all under the Conduct of prudent and intrepid Commanders. Neither Provision, Ammunition, nor any other Machines, useful to gain a Siege, were wanting. Whilst strong Detachments of Horse forag'd and laid the Countrey waste, the Foot play'd upon and undermin'd the Fortifications. *Fadhel*, and the Inhabitants of *Kemmerouf*, finding themselves attack'd by so formidable an Enemy, without knowing who they were, whence they came, or what Pretensions they made, were fill'd with the utmost Consternation. Several Spies were sent into their Camp, but all taken. They try'd likewise to repulse the Assiegeants, by showering down great Stones upon them, and making vigorous Sallies but in vain. They soon found what invulnerable Soldiers they had to deal with; and the Sultan perceiv'd he must either resolve to perish, or implore the Clemency of an Enemy he was a Stranger to. He look'd upon the last Task to be the least Insupportable, therefore summon'd his Family and Court, in order to throw themselves at the Feet of the Conqueror. As soon as they were out of the Gate of the Town, a strong Guard conducted them to *Tangut*'s Tent, before whom the King fell prostrate, with his Attendance, and did not dare to lift up his Eyes.

I can't

I can't tell, mighty Lord! said he, sighing, whether you are Man, or something more; but certain it is, that I have provok'd your Indignation, since I feel the terrible Effects of it. Whether you are resolv'd to pursue the Dictates of your Wrath, or that you have fix'd some Bounds to it, I hope you will not disapprove the humble Step I have taken to appease it. Pronounce, powerful Lord! the Sentence of our Deaths, or pardon us the Crimes, we have offended you in: Here we lie at your Mercy, and ready to undergo what you shall think proper to inflict on us. Should we be treated as Criminals, may we beseech you to let us know, wherein we have had the Misfortune to fall under your Displeasure.

Whilst the Sultan spoke, his Attendance were all in Tears, with their Eyes bent downwards, except the charming *Dogandar*'s, who tho' she cry'd like the rest, could not forbear now and then giving a Glance at *Tangut*. She remember'd him again, which fill'd her with fresh Courage and Hope. *Tangut*'s Eyes equally met her's, and could not resist taking their former Impression. His Heart throbb'd, and was again melted into Tenderness; insomuch, that the small Remains of Anger and Revenge he had left, was a Burthen to him, and only serv'd to change his Countenance. He rais'd the Sultan from the Ground, saying, he would soon clear up the Resentment requir'd, and then suddenly withdrew again, to conceal the Confusion he was in, and consult with himself what he had best say or do in that nice Point. In vain were all his Consultations: Whenever he study'd what Measures to take in his own Justification, Love, whose Power he felt anew, still had the upper Hand, and persuaded him to accommodate the Slights and Injuries his Charmer
had

had shewn him. In that View, he invited the Sultan, the Princesses, and the Chief of the Emirs to dine with him. *Dogandar* was not the only Person then that knew him again, still no body durst seem to own it.

    The Princess, having more Resolution than the rest, ventur'd, at last, to speak to him, in the following Manner. If it might be presum'd, my Lord, to declare our Thoughts freely, I'm positive we should find it no hard Task to convince you your Anger is unjust. Madam, reply'd *Tangut*, I know no body less Capable of such an Undertaking than yourself. These Words were pronounc'd with such Timidity and Faintness of Speech, that the penetrating Princess easily perceiv'd she still commanded Awe; and taking Advantage of the happy Discovery, said: Tho' you are so much prejudic'd, as to imagine me in particular incapable of making good the Assertion, yet none but myself shall prove, that you have resented as heinous, what I only meant as an innocent Piece of Raillery; and look'd upon my Conduct as insulting, when 'twas only design'd as a Tryal of your Constancy. Had I in the least thought you so violent in your Nature, I should have behav'd with more Circumspection. You gave me Protestations of your Love, and I was willing to convince myself of the Sincerity of them, by a harmless Method, that even you were the Author of; but alas! how Fatal has it prov'd! The Moment after, you abandon'd me, and was heard of no more, till you appear'd Sword in Hand ready to sacrifice me. How could I foresee so sudden a Departure, or expect so cruel a Return? Confess then, my Lord, my Innocence, and blame the Impulse of your own Passion.

Tangut

Tangut remaining speechless at these Words, *Fadhel* broke Silence, and after having blam'd his Daughters Imprudence, and entirely disapprov'd her want of Conduct, concluded his Reproofs, saying: Prince, If my inconsiderate Daughter still deserves any Place in your Affections, to morrow she's yours. Why, interrupted the Sultaness, should an Affair of such Consequence be deferr'd so long? This Moment, therefore, I dispose of my Daughter to the brave *Tangut*; let him accompany us, and give Peace to his own Subjects. This was too agreeable an offer for the Son of *Aboucaf* to refuse. He readily condescended to attend them into *Kemmerouf*, but conditionally, that he should be guarded by such Persons as he thought proper to pitch on, and remain likewise Master of one of the Gates of the Town. The Terror of the Inhabitants soon chang'd into an universal Joy, at the Sight of *Tangut*. He sometimes entertain'd himself familiarly with the Sultan, and sometimes with the Princesses; and always had the Precaution not to shew the least Sign of Anger on his Countenance. He now became Thoughtless of what was past, and was capable of no Reflection, but the pleasing Idea of possessing the charming *Dogandar*. The Sultan entertain'd him with the utmost Magnificence, at Supper that Night, in a Garden, where all the Trees were burthen'd with Flambeaux, which gave as much Light as at noon Day.

After Supper, *Dogandar* join'd *Tangut*, and led him some Distance from the Company. We are in a Place now, said she, where we may discourse without Restraint. How happy do I think myself, in being bless'd with a Lover and Spouse, who is the most powerful Prince in the Universe! I am so much amaz'd at your second surprising

H Expe-

Expedition, that I'm not yet recover'd from the Aftonifhment. No Potentate whatever can carry on a War without Money; the Source of your Treafure I am in Poffeffion of; notwithftanding which, you have found Means to raife an Army, able to give Laws to the whole World. What's more amazing ftill, your March was fo fudden, and fo well regulated, that we were furpriz'd and attack'd, before we dreamt any thing of the Matter. I fhall fay nothing of your Soldiers, who kill and cannot be kill'd. For my part, that's a Myftery beyond my Comprehenfion; but durft I hope any thing from your Complaifance, I would extend my Curiofity much farther. She fpoke that with fuch a tender befeeching Air, a Softnefs fhe was Miftrefs of at Pleafure, that he was incapable of the leaft Reflection, and drew forthwith the Horn out of his Pocket, faying: Madam, I might juftly be term'd one of the moft ungrateful Monfters upon Earth, were I to keep you any longer in an irkfome Sufpence. By this Inftrument alone, I have found the Army you now fee, and had I occafion for a Million more, it would equally produce them. The Moment I found it, and mention the Number of Forces I require, that very Inftant I am obey'd. It is incredible fure, cry'd the artful Princefs; how do I feel my Admiration and Curiofity augment! For Heavens fake, let me try if this miraculous Horn will be as efficacious when I blow it. In fpeaking thefe Words, fhe very dexteroufly took it from him, and retir'd five or fix Paces, in a toying Manner; then fhe put it to her Mouth, and demanded a hundred thoufand Men. In an Inftant, the Town, Palace, and even Garden, were full of new-rais'd Soldiers. Thofe belonging to *Tangut* difappear'd, becaufe the Enchantment was fuch, that the Effect produc'd duc'd by a second Person, destroy'd the Work of the first. It was as much as this unhappy Lover could do, to prevent the Orders taking Place, his Mistress had given to seize him. He left the Garden immediately, and by the Favour of the Night, made his Escape out of the nearest Gate he came to.

When he got some Distance from the Town, he curs'd his bad Fate, and abhorr'd his own Complaisance, with the Perfidy of *Dogandar*. The Dread of being taken made him not cease travelling, 'till he was in a Place of Surety. When he thought himself past Danger, and had Time to reflect more seriously on his Misfortunes, and how to remedy them, he conceiv'd nothing but one expedient to be depended on; which was in procuring his eldest Brother's Girdle. But alas! he despair'd surmounting so difficult a Point; and not only dreaded a Refusal, but likewise ill Treatment from him; for *Hiarkan* was of a hasty proud Temper, ill-natur'd, and unwilling to do good Offices: However, he resolv'd to put him to the Trial, whatever should be the Event of it.

Having reach'd *Hiarkan*'s House, and knowing his Foible, he immediately threw himself at his Feet, with Tears in his Eyes, and said: Would to God, dear Brother, I had follow'd your prudent Counsel. You have ever treated me with the Tenderness of a Father; how unhappy am I then not to have return'd the dutiful Obedience of a Child! There's, dear Brother, my chief Failing, and the Source whence springs all my Miscarriages; for tho' the Loss of my Purse, and *Xamor*'s Horn, justly reproach me with all that's criminal and stupid, yet such Losses, to weigh them duly, are only the Consequences of my want of Adherence to your Advice. Tell me, generous *Hiarkan*, what Sorrow is capable to expiate my Crime? If such will not suffice, name my Punishment; but don't refuse, I beseech you, the only Succour left to retrieve the Honour of a Family, bless'd by your being the Supporter of it. When I entreat you to lend me your Girdle, I am in hopes three Motives will engage you to grant the Request, which can only restore what I have been robb'd of. How great would the Happiness be, after that, if I might be suffer'd to pass the rest of my Days along with you, and endeavour to edify as much by the many Precedents of Prudence and Wisdom, you will not fail to set before me, as hitherto I have been blindly Remiss in emulating them.

Hiarkan stood immoveable as a Statue, and did not seem in the least touch'd at his Brother's Tears and penitent Declarations; but, on the contrary, this Insensibility was succeeded by so violent a Passion, that poor *Tangut* thought himself absolutely lost; yet was it to that Hurry and Confusion of Spirit he ow'd his Safety; for the Rage of *Hiarkan* being evaporated, he reproach'd himself with having been too severe, and at last granted him the Girdle. *Tangut* had no sooner put it on, than he wish'd to be in a *Mosque* at *Kemmerouf*, and immediately was transported thither. He conceal'd himself there till after Midnight, and then, every Body being in a profound Sleep, he nam'd the Chamber of his Mistress, and as quick as thought was in it. When approaching her Bed, *Tangut* beheld her in all the native Charms of sleeping Beauty, the Indignation he had conceiv'd against her, was in great Danger of being converted into a Desire altogether the Reverse. Not all the gross Impositions *Dogandar*

had

had been guilty of, were capable of ſtifling the Love he bore her: Ah *Hiarkan*, ſaid he to himſelf, were you in my Place! But, recollecting that he had been twice deceiv'd by her, and that it was the laſt Stake he had now to manage, he became aſham'd of his great Weakneſs, and flung open the Curtains, throwing down a Table which happen'd to ſtand near them.

The beautiful *Dogandar*, ſtartling, waked in the utmoſt Terror, and without daring to open her Eyes, demanded the Occaſion of that great Noiſe? A Lover, replied *Tangut*, injured by your Artifices, is to come to ſhew how much is yet in his Power to do for Vengeance and Redreſs: He ſtill, however, retains too much Generoſity to execute the one, provided you offer him the other. It is *Tangut* ſpeaks, continued he, deliver me inſtantly therefore the *Purſe* and *Horn* you have defrauded me of, for I have but a Moment to ſtay in your Apartment. The Voice and Name of this too eaſy *enamorato* diſpelled great part of the Fear *Dogandar* had been in. She preſently found in what Manner it was beſt for her to behave; ſo looking on him with a Languiſhment, ſhe knew well how to aſſume, replied; I might have imagined, none but you were capable of ſurpriſing People thus. I do not reſent the Miracles you perform, were they to happen every Day; but indeed, methinks you might contrive a more ſeaſonable Hour for their Operation, than the very Minute I was drowned in Repoſe. Let me know, I intreat you, the Cauſe of this new Tranſport: I cannot tell whether it is a Dream, what I have heard you ſay juſt now, or no; but it is certain, I am ſtrangely amazed at ſuch extraordinary Language.

She leaned on her Elbow in a careless Posture, while she was speaking, and two perfum'd Tapers casting their Lights directly on her Face and Neck, disclos'd to the admiring Eye Ten thousand Charms, which the Formalities of Dress conceal'd. *Tangut* had never beheld her in this inchanting Negligence, and was ravish'd anew with the Pleasure it gave him. All his Anger and Resentment vanish'd, and Love alone had the Possession of his Soul; Pardon, Madam, said he, with a Voice trembling between Hope and Despair, the Presumption of a Lover, who only intreats, with the greatest Respect, to know why you have twice deceiv'd his longing Expectations. Forbear to insult me, interrupted the Princess, nor keep at a Distance, which, if you lov'd indeed, must be painful to you. He obey'd her Commands and drew nearer, with what Joy at so unexpected a Condescension, it is very easy to imagine. Of what Deceit, continued she, do you accuse me? What mean you by Reproaches so unjust? Did I not justify my Behaviour concerning the *Purse?* And in Regard of the *Horn*, methinks it is your Interest to be silent, unless you would wish me to remember the most unworthy Action a Man could possibly be guilty of: It is you alas! have deceived me. I, Madam, cried *Tangut* hastily? Yes, replied *Dogandar*; did you not abandon me, at a Time when I had consented to all you wished, and by that Contempt, exposed me to the Laughter of the whole Universe?

I raised a new Army, which obliged that of yours to disappear: Ah Prince, how weak a Cause was this for your forsaking me! Were not the Troops I called, as much yours as the *Horn?* Or to speak more justly, was not she, who innocently

cently made the Experiment of that wonderful Inftrument, yours alfo?

This well diffembled Tendernefs had fuch an Effect on the foft Difpofition of *Tangut*, that he threw himfelf on his Knees, demanding Pardon, a fecond Time of the Princefs; who immediately raifed him, and looking on his Girdle, what new Mode have you brought us here? It feems, faid fhe fmiling, to be after the Manner of the *Hob-goblins*; but if it be, they are neither fo rich, nor fo ingenious as the Idea we conceive of them. This of yours is coarfe, and meanly wrought, if I am not greatly miftaken; but draw near, that I may be farther convinced of it. *Dogandar* could never have thought of a happier Expedient to fatisfy her Curiofity, in difcovering this new Secret, than by the Queftions fhe propos'd. Madam, anfwered *Tangut*, advancing towards her, I know not the Nation of the *Hob-goblins*, nor that a Girdle is one of their Habiliments; but am certain, mine is of an ineftimable Price, and infinitely dear to me, fince it has procured me the valuable Bleffings I now enjoy. While he was fpeaking, the fubtil Princefs unty'd the Girdle, and drew it infenfibly from him; faying, how got you hither then? Whence come you? And how much Time has your Journey taken you up? I have travelled, fays he, more than three Hundred Leagues in one Inftant: When this miraculous Girdle is bound about me, I but Name a City, and am tranfported immediately to it. But, Madam! What is it you are doing? I think you are robbing me of it. *Dogandar* had drawn as much of the Girdle from him, as went round her Waift, when he perceived the Fraud. Inftead of anfwering him, fhe wifh'd to be convey'd to the *Sultan*'s Chamber,

Chamber, and was readily obey'd. That Moment, *Fadhel* order'd his Guards to make diligent Search, which allarm'd the whole Palace. Happy it was now for *Tangut*, that his frequent Visits there, had brought him acquainted with the moſt private Avenues to it. A little Pair of Back-ſtairs happily afforded him with the Means of his Eſcape into the Streets, through which he ran, until he came to the Place in the Fortifications, ſomewhat out of Repair, and couragiouſly jump'd down it. After he had a little taken Breath, and had Time to conſider on his miſerable Condition, he endeavoured, not as formerly, to eaſe himſelf by bitter Complaints and Imprecations; but delivered himſelf up with a kind of Tranquillity to Deſpair; deſiring now, no more than to dye.

To the Weſt of *Kemmerouf*, there are many dreadful Mountains, which form a vaſt Deſert, void of any Water, and ſo barren, that even Animals, accuſtomed to live on the moſt unfruitful Lands, durſt not inhabit there. *Tangut* purſued his Way to it, in Hopes that there his Life and Misfortunes would find an End. He wandered all that Night, and the Day following, endeavouring to haſten his laſt Hour, by adding to Hunger, the moſt inſupportable Fatigue a Mortal could undergo. Towards the Concluſion of Day, as he moved, tottering with Weakneſs, down the Declenſion of a Rock, he fell into a deep Swound; and his Body, deprived of all Senſe, rouled, for ſome Time, towards a Precipiece, where this unhappy Prince muſt have been inevitably cruſhed to Pieces, had not his Garments catched hold of the Branches of an old Fig-tree, which prevented his farther Fall.

This

This Tree might be called the Wonder of that solitary Wild; no other green Thing being to be seen there. *Tangut*'s Swound was followed by a long Sleep, in which he continued till the next Day was far advanced. Having opened his Eyes, the first Object that he saw, was the Branch that held him. Perceiving the Fruit of it very lovely, he was tempted to taste of it: I have resolved to dye, said he to himself, therefore of what Importance will it be, if I defer my Death one Day longer? Let me enjoy once more, the Pleasure of eating Figs, since Fortune has been so kind to offer it: I shall not be much the farther from Death. He raised himself with a great deal of Pain, and pulling to him the nearest Boughs, devoured all the Fruit he could gather from them, with an extreme Greediness. They were of such a pernicious Quality, that his Nose encreased a Foot long, every Fig he swallowed; and though he felt the frightful Effect of it, yet his Appetite was so violent, that he did not discontinue eating, till his Stomach was quite full, and his Nose grown to so preposterous a Size, that with much ado, he disintangled it from the Branches of the Figg-tree.

While the Pleasure lasts, the Ills that succeed make little Impressions, but it is not the same afterwards. *Tangut*, who just before had defied Fortune to render him more miserable, now experienced, by what had befallen him, that his Misfortune was capable of Augmentation. Sure I was born, said he, under the most malignant Planet! The other Woes I suffered were occasioned by my own Imprudence; but what have I done to draw upon me this? Oh let me fly so fatal a Tree, and its delusive Fruit, and not a Moment longer bear the shameful Load of Life!
Then

Then he wrapp'd his Nose round his left Arm, and charged with his painful and ridiculous Burthen, pursued his wretched Way. His Strength was so much repaired by the Figs he had eaten, that he was enabled to travel with fresh Vigour, and before Sun-set, he arrived at a Valley, a considerable Distance from the Place he left. Being sat down on a Stone, he cast his Eyes, by Chance, towards a Hollow, where he perceived, though the Shade from the Rocks rendered it pretty obscure, a second Fig-Tree, laden with most beautiful Fruit. This Discovery, instead of pleasing him, gave him so much Pain, that had his Weariness permitted, he would have gone farther from an Object, which seemed to invite him yet once more, to prolong his Life and his Nose; but turned his Head another Way, and fell asleep.

When he awoke, Hunger tormented him anew, and he felt something within him dictate: Yesterday's Figs are now digested; what Harm will there be to taste these others, which present themselves? What can happen worse than thou hast already? And why shouldst thou resolve to avoid them? Will not this Valley serve thee for a Grave? Gather therefore, and eat of this delicious Fruit, till Death Approaches. This Inspiration induced him to draw nearer the Tree; and taking the End of his Nose in one Hand with the other, plucked a Fig, and put in his Mouth, which he had no sooner swallowed than the Extremity of his Nose slipt from his Hold, and shrunk a full Foot. A second Fig had the same Effect, and a third convinced him of the Virtue of this excellent Fruit, till by Degrees with an Infinity of Joy, he reduced it to its natural Proportion. Being thus happily recovered, he contrived

trived a Stratagem for the Re-eſtabliſhment of his Affairs, which ſucceeded perfectly well. He took out the linen Lining of his Turbant, and filled one Part of it with Figs of this laſt Quality; then returning with all Speed to the firſt Fig-tree, gathered alſo a great Number of them, which he tied up ſeparately in the ſame Linen; and afterwards took the Road of *Kemmerouf*, where he arrived about Evening.

He lodged that Night with a poor Woman, who was ignorant of his Diſtinction. In the Morning, he beſmeared his Face with Clay, put on the Habit of a Peaſant, and having filled a little Baſket with Figs of that Sort which lengthen the Noſe, he covered them neatly over with Leaves, and paſſed ſeveral Times before the Palace of *Fadhel*. The chief of the Purveyors taking Notice of him, called and aſked what he had to diſpoſe of? They are little Mountain Figs, ſaid the counterfeited Peaſant. This is not the Seaſon for Figs, replied an Officer, uncovering them, though theſe ſeem to be ripe: How do you ſell them? Fruits growing upon Rocks are ſo much expoſed to the Sun, ſaid the Peaſant, that they ripen ſooner than others. He then propoſed a Price, which being agreed to, *Tangut* removed his Quarters, dreſſed himſelf in the Habit of a Phyſician, put on a falſe Beard, and in this Diſguiſe attended the Effect of his Figs.

The chief of the Purveyors had no ſooner bought them, than he haſten'd directly to the *Sultaneſs* and Princeſs, who were drinking Coffee together. New Fruits! cry'd he, I preſent you with the firſt Figs of the Year. The Mother and Daughter ran to the Baſket, and *Dogandar* ſeiz'd them with all the Eagerneſs imaginable, and went to the other Side of the Room to eat them
with

with more Satisfaction. The Mother was the first that observ'd her Nose lengthen'd four Foot, after having eaten four Figs: The fifth she threw away half peel'd, and gave a Shriek, which oblig'd *Dogandar* to turn her Head. Oh what a Nose, Madam! cry'd she. Oh my Daughter! said the *Sultaness*, looking on her, we are lost! Upon this they flew both to the Looking-glass, which but too faithfully represented them such as they were. Who can express the different Passions which then agitated their Hearts? The great Noise they made, brought all the Ladies of the Palace thither; likewise the *Sultan*, the *Grand Visir*, the chief of the *Eunuchs*, and several *Emirs*. *Fadhel* was in the utmost Consternation, but because he would not augment the Affliction of his Wife and Daughter, he told them that the Accident which had befall'n them, could be no other than an Illusion; and should it prove even real, it would be easie for him to find out Physicians, to apply a speedy Remedy.

The most skilful Physicians in the Kingdom of *Assen* were immediately assembled to consult on the Disease of the two Princesses. After a long and ineffectual Debate touching the Cause of it, they came to a Conclusion, that those fleshy Substances, a Case they never read of, might, indeed, be cut off without any Danger, but then there would always remain a visible Deformity in the middle of the Face, especially in the Princesses's, because she had been more greedy than the *Sultaness*, and consequently the Base of her Nose amplify'd in proportion to the Length of it. The Result of this Deliberation threw *Dogandar* and her Mother almost into Despair, and made them resolv'd to live conceal'd from View in their Appartments. The Noise of this Misfortune with the

the Decision of the Physicians soon spread itself through the Town, and so undoubtedly reach'd *Tangut*'s Ears, who was waiting impatiently for the News of it.

He address'd the *Sultan* in Quality of a strange Physician, requesting to give his Opinion in so nice a Point, and made him hope every Thing from his long Experience in the Knowledge he had of Simples. *Fadhel* accepted his Offers, and led him into the Lady's Apartment. The pretended Physician felt their Pulses and examined their Noses, then changing the Tone of his Voice, My Queens said he, with a grave and deliberate Air, you resemble Elephants. If there be in Art, any Means to take away the Trunk of an Elephant without cutting it off, the same Recipe would serve to cure you. Such a one I'm convinc'd there is, and believe myself the only Person in the World, Master of the Secret, for I've try'd the Experiment on one of the largest Elephants in the Kingdom of *Pegu*, with Success. But before I undertake so great a Task, I must inform you, that an Elephant is of a quiet, tractable Disposition, which contributes greatly to the Operation of the Remedies we apply; so consequently what I shall prescribe will not have its due Effect on you, without the Humours of your Bodies be in an equal Balance.

After he had made this fine Speech, which he had study'd on purpose to give a Gloss to his Design. *Fadhel* committed the Care of the Princesses intirely to his Management, and assign'd him an Appartment in the Palace, that he might be near them. During eight Days, he made them take only simple Medicines, giving them uncommon Names, to inspire the greater Idea of his Skill. These Remedies having reduc'd, as he said,

said, the Temperament of the *Sultaness* to a juſt Equality, which was abſolutely neceſſary for her Cure, he made her withdraw into her Cloſet, where, having ſhut up all the Windows, he put into her Mouth four good Figs, one after another. She had no ſooner ſwallow'd them, than he ſaid, Madam, you are now cured. Putting her Hand to her Noſe, and finding the Truth of what he ſaid, ſhe was ſo tranſported, that ſhe left the Phyſician, and ran to ſhew her Daughter, who waited with Impatience the Iſſue of the Operation. *Dogandar* beholding the *Sultaneſs* perfectly reſtor'd, imbrac'd her with Tears of Joy; then conjur'd the Phyſician, with lifted Hands, not to delay affording her the ſame Proof of his great Art. *Tangut* coldly reply'd, he wiſh'd her Conſtitution was as good as her Mothers. He examin'd her Pulſe ſeveral Times, then ſhook his Head, and aſſum'd a Look, which ſeem'd to prognoſticate ſo little Succeſs, that *Dogandar* trembled at her very Soul. After theſe Ceremonies, he declar'd plainly, that her Diſeaſe was incurable, and deſir'd Permiſſion to retire, as being incapable of doing her any Service. The *Sultan* and *Sultaneſs*, coming into the Room when this Deciſion was pronounc'd, were extreamly troubled at it. They ſollicited the Phyſician to continue his Preparations for the Patient, but their Perſuaſions being vain, they entreated him however to ſtay ſome time at Court, which he condeſcended to with a ſeeming Reluctance.

Dogandar paſs'd her Nights and Days in Tears: Of what Uſe to me, at preſent, cry'd ſhe, are all the Advantages I have receiv'd from Nature and from Fortune? Alas! theſe regular Features, theſe Eyes ſo full of Life and Fire, the delicate Bloom of this Complexion, this finiſh'd Beauty, for which I have been ſo juſtly celebrated, only ſerve now

now to make my Deformity more infupportable! Was there on Earth a Princefs more happy than myfelf, before this dreadful Misfortune befel me, and which will foon put an End to my Life? But this Reflection only redoubles my Sorrow: The inexhauftible *Purfe*, the formidable *Horn*, and the miraculous *Girdle*, ill become the Poffeffion of a Monfter. One Afternoon, as *Tangut* was going to vifit this Inconfolable, he heard her exclaim much after this fame Manner, which he look'd upon to be the happy Occafion of recovering all he had loft.

Fully bent on making a proper Ufe of it, he enter'd her Chamber, without feeming to have heard any thing, and faluted his Royal Patient as ufual. What! faid fhe, fighing, is it poffible you have condemn'd me to remain all my Life as I am? Have Compaffion on me, I implore you! Make, at leaft, one more Tryal. Doubt you of being fufficiently recompenfed? If the Treafures of my Father feem too little, the unfortunate Princefs, who fpeaks to you, can herfelf make you Prefents, which will oblige you to confefs, never Phyfician was better fatisfied.

Intereft, Madam, reply'd *Tangut*, has never been the Motive of my Actions; my only Aim is Glory. As Conquerors and Kings render themfelves famous, not only for their great Exploits, but alfo for their Magnificence and good Offices, fo in my Profeffion, were it poffible for me to pafs in a Moment from one Extremity of the World to another, I fhould foon make my Name the univerfal Theme, in reftoring Health to the illuftrious Difeas'd of all Nations.

Reftore me the Beauty I have loft, refumed *Dogandar*, I will put you in a Condition to obtain greater Conquefts, and beftow more Liberali-
ties,

ties, than King or Conqueror ever did. Nor shall that be all; I will give you the Means to transport yourself to any Part you wish to be at, with so much Swiftness, that the Flight of Birds shall be slow in Comparison with it. *Tangut*, whose Misfortunes had made him wise, affected a great Astonishment at these Proposals. Madam, said he, smiling, we readily promise every thing, and even Impossibilities, in Hopes of compassing what we strongly wish for. My Promises are not of that Nature, interrupted *Dogandar*, as you shall be immediately convinced. Upon which, she took out of her Cabinet, the *Purse*, the *Horn* and *Girdle*, shew'd them to the Physician, and explain'd their several Virtues. Though he knew more of this Matter than she, yet he appear'd incredulous to all she said, and even pretended to go away, as tired with listening to such trifling Discourse; insomuch that the Princess was obliged to entreat him to carry the three Rarities Home with him, to make the Experiment. He put them in his Pocket, as in Compliance to her Request; but having once more recover'd what he despair'd to see again, he resolv'd not to defer the Conclusion of the Scene. Nothing depending on my Skill can retrieve your Misfortune, said he to the Princess; but since your Gratitude extends so far, you compel me to make Tryal even of Impossibilities: What can be done, you shall know within an Hour. Then he went and girt himself in order for his Departure.

Being return'd to the Princess with a certain Number of Medicinal Figs, and one of the ordinary Kind, which he laid apart, he conducted her to the Cabinet where her Mother was cured. She swallow'd as many of the Figs, as reduc'd her Nose to the Measure of a Foot, and that being

ing done, he felt her Pulse: Ah Madam! cry'd he, how fatal a Change is here, my Remedy operates no more! Continue applying it, reply'd the Princess. I shall, resum'd the Physician, but I wish my Art may deceive me: With these Words, he put into her Mouth the common Fig, which she swallow'd, without finding any Benefit by it. Grief inexpressible! horrible Addition to my Despair! Must I continue then, said she, with a Sigh, as if her Heart were bursting, must I continue then with the Nose of a Foot long? Yes, Madam, answer'd the Physician, 'tis *Tangut* who assures you of it: At the same time, he open'd the Windows, pluck'd off his false Beard, shew'd himself, and nam'd the City of *Hiarkan*, whither the Virtue of the Girdle transported him in a Moment. *Dogandar* wou'd have met Death with Pleasure at the Sight of that cruel Discovery, but she lived in spight of herself, even to an extream old Age, never being able to reconcile herself to the Deformity of her Nose. This Adventure of hers gave Rise to a Proverb, which to this Day is made use of throughout the East. As for Prince *Tangut*, after having restor'd his Brothers the *Horn* and *Girdle*, he settled himself in a fertile Countrey, and founded a very extensive and flourishing Kingdom [a].

Koufchen express'd, in Terms full of Energy, the Pleasure this Story afforded her, and told me, I had now fully discharged my Obligation. As I was about to reply, *Almoraddin* prevented me, saying; Madam, this History is full of Wonders, but I ought to partake with *Abdalla*, the Applause you give it. I know not how the *Persian* inter-

[a] *The Kingdom of* Tangut *is bounded on the North and East, by* Kara-Katai; *on the South, by the Kingdom of* Debor *and* China; *and on the West, by the Kingdom of* Zamor.

preted thefe Words, but they very much aftonifh'd me; and as foon as we had taken Leave, I defired, with fome Impatience, the Explanation of *Almoraddin*, who wore an Air of Difcontent. He oblig'd me to repeat my Requeft feveral times before he anfwer'd: Cruel Friend! faid he at laft, am I not already fufficiently acquainted how miferable my Situation is? Muft you call back the Hiftory of my paft Misfortunes, make me fee *Zulikhah*, in the Character of a perfidious Princefs, and reprefent me three times unfuccefsful in my Aim, that all the little Hope I had left might be totally extinguifh'd? Do you imagine then, reply'd I, that the Hiftory I have been relating, was of my own Compofition? No, dear *Almoraddin!* it is not; I fwear to you by the black Stone [b] at *Mecca*, by the Wells of *Zem-Zem* [c], and by the Tomb of the Prophet. Read the Annals of the Kingdom of *Kachemire*, and you will there find this Hiftory, for 'twas from thence I took it. To conclude, I hope you will not long refemble *Tangut*, for you muft not flatter yourfelf with finding fo eafy a Refource as that of the Fig-Trees. After this, I embrac'd him tenderly, for though want of Learning made him liable to little Miftakes, yet he was foon convinc'd of his Error.

When our Veffel was ready to put to Sea, we took our Leaves of *Roufchen*. Little *Loulou*, tho' very much taken up in running after a Monkey, came quite out of Breath to receive likewife our Compliments, which fhe return'd with one of her Stories. Perceiving fhe had over-heated herfelf

[b] *A Stone very much refpected in the Temple of* Mecca, *built by* Abraham, *according to* Mahomet.

[c] *Wells at* Mecca, *whofe Waters come from the Source that God rais'd in Favour of* Hagar *and* Ifhmael, *as the* Mahometans *fay.*

with her Diversion, and telling her, I thought a Monkey did not deserve she should incur the Danger of an Indisposition; she made answer, You advise me then to be less sprightly, I suppose: Certainly, cry'd I. And for my Part, resum'd she gaily, I would persuade you never to give your Advice, unless it was requir'd; especially when it relates to Monkeys, otherwise it will happen to you, as it did to a little Bird. And pray what befel that little Bird? said I. You will be instantly satisfied, reply'd *Loulou*.

The Third Story of LOULOU.

CERTAIN Monkeys, dwelling in a Wood, assembled together under a Tree to pass the Night there, it being the Begining of the rainy Season, and very cold. Perceiving at a little Distance from them, the glittering of a Glowworm, and believing it a Spark, or a live Coal, they cover'd it with dry Leaves and Wood, and began to blow it one after another. There happening to be a Flock of Birds upon the Tree, who beheld all that pass'd, and laugh'd at their Simplicity; one of them more officious than the rest, charitably flew down to the Monkeys, designing to undeceive them, saying, The Pains I see you take in lighting the Fire in vain, gave me so much Uneasiness, that I could not forbear quitting the Branch I was sat upon, to acquaint you, that you only lose your Labour. But the kind Advice the little Bird gave the Monkeys was ill receiv'd, for one of them answer'd him with a great deal of Pride and Disdain: Prithee, Friend, who desiredst thee to meddle with our Affairs?

Affairs? It's a sign thou hast little else to do: Know, none but Fools advise, where Counsel is not ask'd: About thy Business and sleep therefore, and don't trouble thy Head with what regards us. The little Bird held his Peace for some time, then he began again to speak, and said, What you see shine is not Fire; it's Nature that gives the Reflexion which deceives you. If the Weakness of thy disorder'd Brain, reply'd the Monkey, hinders thee from sleeping, stop at least, thy impertinent Beak. The Simplicity of the little Bird was still so great, that instead of flying away, he added farther; Nothing's more certain than what I tell you concerning the Worm: Sure I ought to know him, since I make so many Meals of his Kindred. He was in Hopes, by this way of Argument, to reduce the Monkeys, at last, to Reason, but he, who had already resented his Endeavours to convince them, not being able any longer to retain his Passion, flew upon the little Pratler and snapp'd him up. *Loulou* laugh'd heartily at the Conclusion of her Fable. You have made me a very apropos Answer, said I to her, and be assur'd, if ever I become a little Bird, I'll never speak, but when it tends to your Praise.

The Continuation of the History of ALMORADDIN.

AFTER our leaving *Calicut*, we sail'd with a favourable Gale, 'till we arriv'd off of *Ceilan*, where we met with such a strong North-East Wind in our Teeth, that we could not pursue our Voyage. This blowing Weather was succeeded

ceeded by a terrible Tempeſt, and continu'd ſo long, that all we could do, was to lay by, and abandon ourſelves to the Mercy of the Waves. We were immediately toſs'd into a Sea, where we ſpy'd out ſeveral Iſlands, without being able to make any one of them. After that, the Ocean ſtill became more raging, inſomuch that we ſaw nothing but Heaven and Water, during thirty Days. At the Expiration of which Time we perceiv'd a high Mountain, ſeeming, by the Diſtance we were from it, to come out of the Sea, and aſked the Pilot if he knew it. I know it too well, anſwered he, not to adviſe you to avoid approaching ſuch eminent Danger. It is an Iſland belonging to the *Div Feridoun*, one of the moſt capricious, blood-thirſty *Genii* ever was heard of. Pray relate to us, ſaid I, what you know of this *Genius*.

The Adventure of the PILOT's Father.

THE Pilot gave a great Sigh, and ſaid: My Father, who was a Pilot as well as I, coming one Day to Anchor, in a Creek of that Iſland, where the Wind blows now full in, went on Shoar with part of the Ship's Crew, to take in Wood and Water. *Feridoun* ſeeing them land, ſet up a Cry, like the Roaring of twenty Lyons in a Foreſt, and approaching them, ſaid; you muſt expect nothing but Death, if all the Men of your Ship do not immediately preſent themſelves before me: Let one of you therefore take the Boat, and ſignify to the reſt my Pleaſure. In Obedience to this Command, one of the Sailors was diſpatched, while my Father and his

Companions, half stupified with Fear, remained Prisoners. Those on Board, hesitated for some Time, what they should best do; but as they had now no Pilot, and the Men who accompanied my Father, were the only Persons, capable of succeeding him in that Office; they resolved at last to share the same Fortune with their Ship-Mates. When they came in Presence of this *Genius*, he said to them; Is there any among you desirous to ask me some Questions? But no Body presuming to answer; look towards Heaven, continued he, and extend your Arms. Then he lifted up his Hands to Heaven like an *Iman* in a Mosque; and they imitated him. After some Moments Silence, the Mariners remaining in the same Posture, he pronounced, in Appearance these Words with great Devotion: *Praise be to God, Creator of Heaven and Earth, Light and Darkness. Those who believe not in their Lord, go astray. It is he that created me of the Flame of the Fire, and you of the Mudd of the Earth.* As he was finishing this Act of Religion, he stretched forth his Hand, seizing my Father's Throat, and strangled him. Ten Men of the Company, the first he came at, expired the same Way, between his Fingers; then, he said to the rest, Praise God, and make use of all my Island affords. After that, he retired to the Summet of the Mountain, where they heard him make most lamentable Howlings.

We asked the Pilot if the Island was inhabited, and if all those who went on shoar there, met with the same fatal Treatment. The rest of the Ship's Company that escaped when my Father was killed, answered he, give an Account of some *Santons* they had seen there at a Distance from them. For my Part, I must own I have met

People

People in the Courſe of my Voyages, that have ſpoken much in the Praiſe of *Feridoun*, and ſaid, that he had not only ſupplied them with Wood, Water, Wild-Fowl and Fruits; but likewiſe anſwered the Queſtions they propoſed, and revealed to them divers Secrets.

 The Wind being now much fallen, and the Sea no longer terrible by its Agitation, *Almoraddin* and I beheld each other, poſſeſſed, as it were, with an equal Deſire of conſulting *Feridoun*. We ordered the Lead-Line to be thrown, and finding good Anchorage, we animated the Pilot with the reſt of the Sailors, got into our Boat with a Pair of Oars, and landed behind a little Rock. We found the Iſland quite covered with Trees, and after having travelled ſome Time, without meeting any living Soul, except a few *Antilopes* and a prodigious Number of *Mice*, who were not at all frightened at our Approach, we came, at laſt to a Hut, in the Middle of a little Garden, incloſed with Bamboos. The great Noiſe we made, cauſed the Inhabitant of it to appear, who was a *Santon*. He made towards us with an affable Countenance, and invited us to viſit his Habitation, ſaying; Praiſe be to God; you are welcome to the Iſland of the beſt of *Genii*. Reverend Father, ſaid I to him, I find then you are acquainted with the Perfections of *Feridoun*. For our Parts, we are very apprehenſive of him; may we therefore, entreat you to ſuccour us by your Advice. We then, recounted to him what the Pilot had juſt been telling us; but added we, it is not very probable, that *Feridoun*, who acknowledges God, would ſtain his Hands in Blood, without a juſtifiable Cauſe. Are ye *Muſſulmen*, ſaid the *Santon*? Yes, Reverend Father, anſwered we, though great Sinners. And are the

People aboard your Ship *Muſſulmen* likewiſe, reſumed he? We believe ſo, replied we. Fear nothing then, ſaid the *Santon*. Remain with me to Night; I will introduce you to this *Genius* Tomorrow, who is at preſent on the other Side of the Mountain. The frugal Entertainment this good *Santon* treated us with, was more ſatisfactory than the ſumptuous Banquets of the moſt voluptuous *Omerahs*. Seated on *Antilopes* Skins, we feaſted on delicious Fruit, preſerved in Cotten, ſome other dry Fruit, and freſh *Coco* Nuts, whoſe Liquor quenched Thirſt, and enlivened us.

During Supper, our Hoſt entertained us with a Deſcription of the Character and Manners of this *Genius*. He told us, he was one of the moſt zealous and rigid *Muſſulmen* of his Nation; that he bore ſuch an irreconcilable Averſion to the Adorers of Fire, and other Idolators, that he directly put them to Death, the Moment they came in his Way; that he diſcerned them by ſome infectious Smell, or otherwiſe; and that our Pilot's Father, with thoſe who ſuffered with him, muſt undoubtedly have been *Magicians*, though they pretended to be the Reverſe. He aſſerted therefore, that *Feridoun* was neither madly Cruel, nor vainly Capricious, but poſſeſſed of an inſpired Zeal. Pray do you know, interrupted I, what kind of *Genius* he is, and why he grieves ſo exceſſively? There cannot be a more dangerous Queſtion propoſed here, replied the *Santon*, than your firſt; God preſerve us from enlarging on it. As for the ſecond, I will anſwer it with Pleaſure, in all its Branches. *Feridoun* likes I ſhould examine that Subject extenſively; ſo what I have to ſay on it, will ſerve as an Amuſement for you, till Bed-time.

The History of the Gyant HARDOUN, and the beautiful NOUR: As also, that of the GENIUS FERIDOUN, and the Princess CHEROUDAH.

THIS Island, pursued he, is pretty large, and was formerly very well inhabited. I shall omit entering upon the Original of its Inhabitants, and only observe that they lived without Ambition, or Distinction of Ranks. Those Families allied to each other, formed a kind of City, in the Middle, without Walls. Every one followed what most suited his Inclination: Some cultivated Rice and large Millet in the Fields; others employed themselves in drawing what was useful from the Coco-Trees, whose Product you are not unacquainted with. The Diversion young People usually took, was in hunting *Antilopes* in the Woods; an Animal so fearful, that even young Maids did not dread going in Pursuit of it.

Nour, the most beautiful Huntress of all the Island, had, as it were, appropriated to herself, one Side of a high Mountain, pretty near the City. She was seen every Morning, repairing to her Sport, armed with her Bow and Quiver; and as she greatly affected Solitude, went commonly alone. Reposing herself one Day, after the Fatigue of her Diversion, under the Shade of some Trees, which the Wind wafted with a delightful Breeze; she heard on one Side of her a sudden Noise, and presently saw a Man approach, of an immeasurable Size. As he came near, he had nothing in him disagreeable; he was young, his Air rather polite than savage, his Hair of a Chesnut Colour, naturally curling, and of

such

such a Length, that it flowed in careless Ringlets o'er his Shoulders. Under his Arm, he held a Cedar, stript of its Branches, which serv'd him either for Support or Defence, as Occasion required. This prodigious Man stood for some Minutes, contemplating the Beauties of *Nour*; then without speaking, came and placed himself near her, who was almost dead with Apprehension. What unkind Destiny, said she, recovering her Spirits as well as she was able, has condemned me to find a Grave in thy rapacious Entrails? Blame not the Destiny which conducted you hither, replied the Giant, nor suspect me guilty of Cruelty. If one of us must be accused, you will certainly find the most difficult Task, in justifying yourself; I have done nothing but languish since I first beheld you, yet durst not till this Moment, appear before you, lest I should terrify what I wish only to please: My humble Love contented itself with contemplating you unseen. How was I Yesterday enchanted! How much did I envy the Happiness of that River, whose murmuring Streams are heard from hence! *Nour* blush'd at these last Words, because the Day before she had been bathing there, without any Precaution, believing herself unobserved. I say nothing which ought to give you Trouble, continued the Giant; banish therefore the ill-grounded Fear, with which you are seized. If the Largeness of my Body surprises you, you will find a Justness of Proportion, in which true Beauty consists; besides I may flatter myself to boast a Birth, not unworthy your Regard.

My Name is *Hardoun*, Son of the Great *Genius Feridoun*, and the Princess *Cheroudah*, Daughter of Sultan *Raz-Andaz*, King of the Hundred Islands, and Chief of all the *Eastern* Sages. All these

these Islands were at first, no more than barren Rocks, but by his Enchantments were rendered fertile, and made so many little Kingdoms. In each Island there is a City, large and well-peopled; in each City a magnificent Palace, in each Palace, a Throne of Gold; and on each Throne, a Statue of *Raz-Andaz*, majestically seated, who spoke, before whom Causes were tryed, and who rendered an exact Justice to every one. The wife *Raz-Andaz*, instigated by a Caprice unworthy of him, made all these Enchantments depend on the Virginity of *Cheroudah*, his only Daughter, whom he guarded, for that Reason, with an inexpressible Care and Diligence, having shut himself up with her, in a Place inaccessible to Mankind.

Feridoun, falling in Love with this Princess, surprized her in Spight of her Father's Precaution, and found her condescending to his Desires of conveying her thence. The Enchantments of *Raz-Andaz* were no sooner broke, than they were immediately supplied by others of a superior Force, and *Cheroudah* enjoyed all the Charms of Love and Liberty with her faithful *Genius*. In me, you behold the only Fruit of their mutual Tenderness. I was about ten Years old, when one Day, *Feridoun* appearing very melancholy, my Grand-father pressed him to declare the Cause of his Trouble; it is yourself, without knowing it, answered he; you have pardoned my Temerity, but your Protectors are more inflexible. *Turasch*, King of the *Genii*, has condemned this Child to be a Wanderer, and forbid us to communicate any Part of our Sciences to him. This is the last Time you will perhaps ever see him. With these Words, he took me in his Arms, and disappearing, bore me to the Island *Subu*, where being arrived, my Son said he, with Tears in his Eyes,

let

let not hard Labour difmay you; nor regret the Pleafures of Enchantments; follow Virtue, that your Glory may derive from yourfelf. By my Aid you will be enabled to go every where; but expect no more, till the Indignation of *Turafch* be over. He fighed, as he vanifhed from my Sight, and I remained a Companion for Tigers and wild Elephants, of whom I foon became the Terror. I ranged many Lands and Seas by my Father's Affiftance, and reftored the Tranquillity of divers Countries, laid wafte by Monfters. The fame generous Defign brought me to thefe Parts, had there been any need of my Succour; but alas! I have loft that Repofe, which I pretended to procure for others: And inftead of acquiring a laudable Fame, I live concealed, left I fhould be deprived of your Sight.

Here *Hardoun* ended his Recital, looking at *Nour* with a ftedfaft and melancholy Air; then entertain'd her with a Song, which he had compos'd in her Praife. His Voice was fo ftrong and melodious at the fame Time, and interrupted now and then with the fhrill Note of a large Pipe, that the piercing Sound filenc'd all the Birds in the adjacent Vallies. When he difcontinu'd that Amufement, *Nour* acquainted him with her Name, and the Affairs of her Family; after which, pretending to be charm'd with the Conqueft fhe had made, fhe promis'd to repair there frequently, and gave him, as a Pledge of Friendfhip, one of her Arrows, which the Giant immediately fix'd in his Hair, juft above his Forehead. *Nour* then took her Leave, refolving within herfelf, never to be expos'd to the like Adventure again. From that Day fhe kept at home, and *Hardoun* fearch'd her, but in vain, thro' all the Places fhe was accuftom'd to delight in. He

He suffer'd, during this Absence, all the Ills disappointed Love can inflict. Sometimes he imagin'd her Parents were the Cause of her Breach of Promise, and sometimes, that a fatal Indisposition, or other unhappy Accident had prevented her coming. Tir'd with a tedious Expectation, he resolv'd at last to go in Person to the City: So quitted the Mountain with the Cedar in his Hand, and his Breast cover'd with the Skin of a Lion. He was no sooner perceiv'd by the People, than all the Houses were close shut; and those who happen'd to be abroad, left off what they were about, to fly from him. *Hardoun* seeing them thus terrify'd, mended his Pace after the last, and seizing one, lifted him from the Ground, and threatned to throw him over the Mountain, if he did not shew him the House of *Nour*. The poor Man, already half crush'd to Death with the formidable Gripe, immediately comply'd. *Nour* was at that time embroidering a *Ser-apha*[a], for *Scimdy*, a young Man, to whom her Parents had promis'd her in Marriage. As soon as she cast her Eyes on *Hardoun*, who had unhing'd the Doors, and enter'd the House, finding no way to escape him, she hid her Face with her Hands, and remain'd immoveable, expecting no other than immediate Death. But the Giant accosted her with so much Softness, that she was presently re-assur'd, and composing her Countenance as when she first saw him, again deceiv'd him into an Opinion of her Love, by alledging, that nothing but a long Indisposition had prevented her coming to the Mountain, and that she would be more punctual for the Future. The Giant now quite appeas'd, desir'd a Pledge

[a] *A Kind of Vest.*

of the Sincerity of what ſhe promis'd. *Nour,* who thought only how to get rid of him, preſented him with the *Ser-apha* ſhe had been working. *Hardoun* fix'd it directly on his Shoulder, and pleas'd with the Shew it made, and the good Succeſs of his little Journey, he betook himſelf joyfully to the Mountain.

The Inhabitants had ſcarce loſt ſight of him, when they flock'd to *Nour*'s, to know the Motive of ſo extraordinary a Gueſt. The Particulars of this Adventure being laid open before the Aſſembly, one of them argu'd, that they could not, without being guilty of a Crime, ſuffer her to fulfil her Appointment at the Mountain, becauſe the Giant would not fail to raviſh, and by Conſequence to kill her. But the others were of a different Sentiment, and reply'd, that the Safety of *Nour* this Way, would be the Deſtruction of the City, when the Giant ſhould return and overthrow all. It was therefore determin'd that *Nour* ſhould continue to keep his Hopes alive, and promiſe to eſpouſe him in a certain limited Time, during which they might perhaps contrive means to deſtroy ſo terrible an Enemy.

This Reſolution being taken, *Nour* was ſent to the Son of *Feridoun,* whom ſhe found ſitting on a Stone, whence he roſe to meet her, with a Tranſport worthy of his Paſſion and Fidelity. *Nour* made her Compliments to him with a diſſembled Pleaſure, and utter'd a thouſand obliging Lies in a graceful Manner. *Hardoun* invited her to honour with her Preſence, a neighbouring Grotto, which ſerv'd him as a Palace. Tho' ſuch a Propoſal could not but occaſion ſome Diſquiet in the Mind of a young Maid, yet as ſhe knew herſelf in the Power of the Giant, and on the other Hand, this Lover appear'd to have for her the

moſt

most respectful Sentiments, she did not offer to oppose his Request. They descended together into a winding Valley, which is nourish'd with the gentle Course of a Rivulet of clear Water. 'Twas here, *Hardoun* led *Nour* into a vast Cavern, where he seated her on a soft mossy Bed. While she was reflecting on the savage Wildness of the Place, the enamour'd Giant collected all the precious Things he was possess'd of, and having laid them at her Feet, he explain'd her each Particular, saying: During the Time my Passion has attach'd me to this Mountain, I discover'd in it a Vein of pure Gold, whence I dug these Pieces, which I now present you with. The Jar, that you see, is one entire *Topaz*; 'twas a Present made me two Years ago by the King of *Queronde*, after having destroy'd a Dragon, which desolated his Countrey. The black Powder, contain'd in the said Jar, is the Sovereign of all Medicines; mingled with Incense, it heals all Sorts of Wounds. Here you see a vast Number of precious Stones, which I brought from divers Countries. This gives Light to Darkness, and that repels the Force of *Tary*[a]; this other is found in the Head of the crown'd Fish, and is dim or clear, according to the Change of Weather at Sea. There's another, continu'd he, which represents a human Tongue, and causes success to those who interfere in the Amours of others. The Foot of this fine *Egret* is all cover'd with Diamonds; *Sobaschid*, Sultan of the Mountaineers, of the Island *Borneo*, made me a Present of it, in Remembrance of my Grandfather. Refuse not, most charming *Nour*, to accept this Necklace of large Pearls, which I took from the false God *Mehahdeu*, when I broke his

[a] *Wine that's drawn from Palm trees.*

Statue

Statue to Pieces, and deſtroy'd his Temple in the Iſland of *Aru*. In a Word, *Hardoun* offer'd his Miſtreſs Gifts of an ineſtimable Value, and ſhe ſcrupled not to make Choice of what pleas'd her moſt. She eat alſo of ſome Fruit, which he prepared for her, and could not help being touch'd with the Generoſity and Magnificence of her Lover; but ſtill the ungrateful Maid ſuppreſs'd what her Soul acknowledg'd to be juſt. To proſecute the Deception ſhe had ſo artfully begun, ſhe promis'd him on her Departure, to conſult the Inclinations of her Parents, touching the Alliance he deſir'd to make with them, and then flatter'd him with a ſpeedy and favourable Anſwer. On which, the Son of *Feridoun* contentedly conducted her to the Foot of the Mountain.

Nour was receiv'd by the Town with ſo much the more Satisfaction and Pleaſure, as ſhe was thought deſtroy'd by *Hardoun*. The very Day of her Arrival, the Inhabitants reaſſembled, and concluded, after a ſecond Conſultation, to cauſe a prodigious deep Pit to be dug, and cover'd over with Branches and Earth, in order to delude the Giant into it. *Nour*'s Parents, at the ſame Time, put the finiſhing Stroke to their Daughter's Marriage; *Scimdy* repair'd to his Father-in-Law's, attended with a numerous Train of Friends; and now, nothing was thought on, but celebrating the Nuptials with the utmoſt Joy and Grandeur. *Mordrek* alone was unhappy; he had for many Years aſpir'd to the Poſſeſſion of *Nour*, and could not behold the approaching Happineſs of his Rival, without teſtifying the moſt terrible Deſpair. He broke his Stick on his Knee, and threw the Pieces of it publickly into the Air, according to the Cuſtom of the Countrey, and then

left

left the Town, fully bent to make away with himself.

Being come to the Top of the Rock, where many other despairing Lovers had put an End to their Lives; Oh Rock! cry'd he, hear the last Words of a miserable Man: Hard as thou art, *Nour*, the perfidious *Nour*, is yet more hard than thee. Ah *Nour!* I am the Object of thy Scorn, and thou prefer'st *Scimdy* to the unfortunate *Mordrek*. This Day thou hast accepted *Scimdy* for thy Husband. *Scimdy*, great God! *Scimdy*, the Shame of Nature! What Prize did he ever gain by his Dexterity? What Dances was he ever applauded for? When did he ever distinguish himself in our Forests with his Bow? What Verses has he ever made? Or, in what Songs has he ever celebrated the Beauties of thy Mouth and Eyes? His Possessions are indeed larger than mine. He has made a Purchase then of thy mercenary Heart? Ah! let the Slave remain with him, and may'st thou, fair Barbarian, be crush'd beneath the Weight of thy Chain, and follow me soon after. As he had finish'd these Exclamations, he was about to cast himself down the Precipice, when a powerful Hand, seizing him suddenly behind, grasp'd his Shoulder and Breast with so much Force, that this despairing Lover, who a Moment before desir'd nothing but Death, became now apprehensive it would arrive too soon. 'Twas *Hardoun*, to overhear what he said, had advanc'd towards him without making any Noise. Just as he laid hold on *Mordrek*, there issu'd from the Bottom of his vast Breast such a Sigh, as made the neighbouring Hills tremble, and frighted Echo into Silence.

Mordrek perceiving who it was, his late Terror gave Place to a secret Satisfaction. He recounted

counted to him at large all that had happen'd, and assur'd him, that the approaching Night would compleat the Triumph of *Scimdy*. He was immediately commanded by the Giant to conduct him where the Assembly met, who vow'd the most horrible Revenge on the City, for the base Design they had contriv'd against him. *Mordrek* inwardly thank'd Fortune, and walking before *Hardoun*, serv'd him as a Guide; and the more to animate his Indignation, shew'd him, as they pass'd along, the Pit had been prepar'd for his Destruction. The *Epithalamiums*, with the joyful Sound of silver Horns and Cymbals, might have distinguish'd the House of *Nour*, had they not already known it. Had the Giant given way to the first Suggestions of his Rage, he had shaken the House about their Ears, but the Thought that his Mistress might possibly have been forc'd to act as she did, suspended it. He enter'd on his Knees by a great Gate into the Court-yard, where, according to Custom, all the nuptial Guests were at Supper, on a large Carpet. Vile and abominable Wretches! cry'd he, Traitors, who contemn God and Truth, and have the Audacity to impose on the Son of a *Genius!* tremble at the Approach of your last Hour. These dreadful Words, with the Sight of him that utter'd them, threw all the Company into an inconceivable Consternation. Some crept under the Carpet, others climb'd up the Trees, but the greatest Number prostrated themselves on the Ground, imploring Mercy in the most humble Manner. The nearest Kindred of *Nour* and *Scimdy* took her in their Arms, and oppos'd her to the Giant as a Buckler, hoping so beautiful an Object might abate his Fury. Their Expectations deceiv'd them not, for he was soon disarm'd of

all

p. 130.

all his Anger, and repented he had caus'd so great a Terror in the Person he passionately ador'd. All chang'd in a Moment, he approach'd her, saying to those who held her, they had nothing to fear, provided he might that Night be happy in his Love. In the present Situation of their Hearts, they would have sacrific'd to him all the Virgins of the City, so were easily prevail'd on to acquiesce with his Demand, protesting at the same time, to him, that durst they have presum'd to hope the Addresses of a Person of so extraordinary a Character, had tended to Marriage, they would never have provided another Husband for her. The Son of *Feridoun* was wholly won by this Discourse, and put his Finger on their Heads in Sign of Reconciliation; then he plac'd himself near the timorous *Nour*, who was persuaded by all there present, to entertain him in the most obliging Manner.

While she amus'd him with a fictitious Shew of Tenderness, the principal of the Assembly went apart, and consulted what was to be done in this Exigence. *Nour*, said one of them, shall make him drink a sufficient Quantity of *Tary*; his Drunkenness will be infallibly follow'd by a profound Sleep; and then, it will be easy for us to hinder the Monster from ever waking more. This Advice being agreed to by the rest, the Master of the House fill'd a large China Bowl with the strongest *Tary* he could procure, and presented it to *Hardoun* by his Daughter. The Giant, equally charm'd with the Liquor and Hand that gave it, drank off the Bowl at one Draught. They took due Care to replenish it, and he was no less diligent in emptying it. This Proceeding continued so long, that all the Company perceiv'd the Giant was no longer Master of his Head. He utter'd nothing but confus'd and incoherent Words; his Eyes rowl'd wildly; and Sleep overpowering all his Faculties, he began to snore. This was the Signal of Victory to the perfidious Conspirators, who surrounded him. They bound his Hands and Feet with thick Cords, and arming themselves with what came in their Way, mounted like so many Pigmies on his vast Body, and at the same Time stabb'd him in every Part of it. This execrable Murther restored *Nour* to *Scimdy*, and Tranquillity to the whole Assembly; at the breaking up of which, *Nour* conducted her Husband and Kindred to the Cavern of the injured Giant, where they found immense Riches.

Feridoun was not long ignorant of what had befallen his Son, and resolv'd to revenge his Death, in a Manner becoming his Grief, the Love he bore him, and the Justice of the Cause. The Inhabitants of the Island repairing to the Town from all Parts, to celebrate a Festival, and to contend for the Prizes which were to be distributed by the beautiful *Nour*, the offended Genius appeared in the middle of them, and declaring whom he was, with a Voice the most terrible that could be, he touched *Nour* with the End of his Finger. On which, all the Limbs of this young Bride visibly extended themselves, till she became of a Size and Stature almost equal to that of *Hardoun*; continuing nevertheless perfectly beautiful, and her Features losing nothing of their Charms, by being enlarg'd. If my Son were yet living, said *Feridoun*, would you still think his Caresses fatal to this Creature? Was not my Power as great in his Life-time, as it is after his Death? Was it not then possible for me to render *Nour* such as you now see her? Ah miserable

ble People! Had my Son conceal'd his Extraction from this ungrateful Woman; had you been ignorant of my Power; had the Tenderness I felt for him been unknown to you, then might you have alledg'd some tolerable Excuse. But, since nothing can justify your Cruelty, be ye all involv'd in the Punishment of a Crime which no Contrition can erace. Inhumane *Nour!* from Giant that thou art, become a Mountain; and ye barbarous Parents, guilty Kindred, and unhappy Fellow-Citizens of that savage Creature, be all shut up within her Entrails, and gnaw them till my future Pleasure. Immediately *Nour* took the Form of a Mountain, which engross'd the whole Land the City stood on, and all the Island was depopulated. Nine Months after this Transformation, the Mountain trembled, groan'd and made such dreadful Roarings, as astonished all the adjacent Isles, whose Inhabitants resorted hither in great Multitudes, to behold a Spectacle which seem'd to promise so much Wonder. After having waited some time, they saw issue from a thousand Openings, prodigious Droves of Mice, who betook themselves to the Woods. Thus it was, the miserable *Nour* deliver'd up, with the most piercing Pains, and under a shameful Form, the Accomplices of her Cruelty; and such was the Conclusion of *Feridoun*'s Revenge, tho' his Affliction did not find a Remedy in taking it. He loves this Island, and hates it at the same time; he protects and detests it, and lets fall more Tears here than his Son shed Drops of Blood. It is the most rigid Theatre of Sorrow, neither are any Body suffered to live here, but such as are overwhelm'd in Grief and Trouble. Is it then inhabited, said I to the *Santon?* Yes, answer'd he, with five *Santons*, reckoning myself,

The other four I expect here to morrow, to say the Break of Day Prayer. With this, the *Santon* rose, and after having set the Place in order we were in, he shew'd us two little Beds, and then retir'd to his Closet, where he pass'd almost the remaining Part of the Night in great Lamentations.

Next Morning the four *Santons* accordingly came, who saluted us, observing a profound Silence: Three of them were young Men, and the fourth more advanc'd in Age. We accompany'd them to the Place of Prayer, purifying ourselves first, in a Fountain near the Hut. Our Host discharg'd the Function of *Iman*; and when the Prayer was ended, he made us sit down round a Chest, rather long than broad, which stood in the Middle of the Closet. Then he took the *Alcoran* out of a Nich, and read a Chapter in it, which we hearken'd to, with the utmost Attention and Humility. After that, he laid the divine Book in its Place again, approach'd the Chest, and extended himself thereon, be-sprinkling it with Tears. The rest of the *Santons* appear'd exceeding melancholy, and we were no less in Complaisance to them. After he was risen from his former Position, he look'd upon us both, saying: *Mussulmen*, I will now shew you the Subject of my Complaints. With that he open'd the Chest, where we beheld the Body of a young Woman, perfectly fresh, and so well preserv'd, that she look'd as if she slept, or, as tho' she was but just departed. The *Santon* left us a considerable Time to reflect on the Corpse, whose Sight caus'd fresh Torrents to flow from his Eyes; after which he clos'd the Chest, and led us into the Chamber, where we repos'd ourselves. Their Visages somewhat chang'd, and if they did not immediately

mediately put on an Air of Joy, at least they seem'd less sorrowful. The old *Santon* began the Conversation, saying, *Feridoun* would not come till the third Prayer. If that be true, said our Host, we shall have time enough to inform these Strangers, who are desirous to consult him of the different Adventures which brought us to this Island: And as they are undoubtedly surpris'd with what they have just now seen, I shall begin with a Recital of mine, if the Company thinks proper. All the *Santons* express'd their Satisfaction with it; and for our Parts, we humbly thank'd him for his Goodness, in preventing our Entreaties.

The Adventure of the SANTON, *Husband of the young Woman.*

I Am, said he, Son of a rich Merchant of *Masulipatan*, my Father brought me up in his Way (and consequently involv'd me in Cares) and when I was at an Age to enter into an Hymenæal State, he made me marry the unfortunate *Kakoule*, whom I bewail. Her natural Parts were cultivated with an Application to reading; her Behaviour soft and engaging; and her Affection for me very tender. As for her Beauty I leave you to judge by the Features, which Death and the Grave have not yet impair'd. Two Years after our Marriage, my Father receiv'd Advice, that one of his Clerks, whom he entrusted with one of his chief Warehouses at *Macassar*, had dissipated, by his extravagant Follies, a great Part of the Merchandise, committed to his Care and Management.

Management. To rectify the Disorder this Breach of Trust might have occasion'd, I propos'd going thither by the first Ship that sail'd. This Offer prov'd very agreeable to my Father, but not so pleasing to my dear *Kakoule*: On the contrary, it flung her into a deep Melancholy, which would have certainly dwindled into a Madness, had I not suffer'd her to accompany me in the Voyage. With all the Resolution and Generosity in the World did she then renounce the Sweets of Life, she had always been accustom'd to. We embark'd with a great Number of Persons of all Sorts of Nations and Conditions; but soon did the Motion of the Ship, the Air of the Sea, the Want of Sleep, the Change of Diet, and a thousand other Inconveniencies incident to a seafaring Life, cause a fatal Revolution in my dear Spouse's tender Constitution. She fell sick, and in a few Days sunk beneath the Violence of her Indisposition. I die satisfy'd, said she, since my last Breath is spent in thy Presence. The only Request I have to make thee, is, that one Grave may contain us, when Heaven shall think meet to call thee hence. As soon as she departed, and the first Shocks of my Sorrow were somewhat mitigated, I put her Body into the very Chest you have seen, and entreated the Officers of the Ship to permit me to preserve it. While Wind and Weather prov'd favourable, no Body oppos'd my Request, but at the least Appearance of a Storm, the superstitious Merchants would cry, it is no wonder if we are lost, since against the Laws of the Sea, there's a dead Corpse in the Vessel. These Murmurings would have been of no Consequence had fair Weather succeeded, but as the Tempest augmented, they likewise encreas'd, till at last the whole Ship condemn'd my Design.

Design. My Entreaties, my Tears, and my Presents were all rejected. I conjure you, said I then, to defer, at least for some Minutes, committing so precious a Treasure to the Insults of the Waves, and the Prey of Fishes: Let the inflexible *Monkir* hear your Invocations, as you shall be propitious to mine. Still all I could say or do was fruitless; so foreseeing nothing but an absolute Submission to their Obstinacy, I went, unknown to every Body, and shut myself up in the Chest. Now, dearest *Kakoule!* said I to her, as tho' she were yet living, thy last Words are fulfill'd: Accept therefore this last Proof of my Tenderness. Then I fasten'd it with a little Lock, which I had fix'd formerly on the Inside for a different Use, and lay as motionless by the inanimate Corpse, as tho' I had been also depriv'd of Life. I suppose the Fury of the Winds augmented, for a little while after they took up the Chest, with an Infinity of Imprecations, and cast it over Board. I lost for a Time all the Faculties of Life, tho' I were still living; neither can I tell how long we were the Sport of the Waves, which drove us at length on this Island. *Feridoun* perceiving the Chest, took it out of the Water, open'd it, and distinguishing some small Remains of Life in me, he restor'd me by his Cares.

Feridoun is happy, cry'd I, to have in his Island such a Prodigy of Love and Fidelity? I know a Monarch who would prefer you to the richest Jewels of the East. Tho' our own Misfortunes, said the oldest of the *Santons,* leave such an Idea in our Minds, as will scarce suffer us to be affected with those of another, yet the Relation of them moves us for the present. You, pursu'd he, looking on the three young *Santons,* whose

vigorous

vigorous Years render you more impatient than me, impart your Adventures to these. *Muſſulmen.* They all readily teſtify'd their Obedience, and he that ſat next me began in this Manner:

We are all three, ſaid he, Natives of the great Iſland of *Schore-Pulou*, and a Law, which Time out of Mind has been rigorouſly obſerv'd there, has render'd us all unhappy. By this Law, the third Male Child of every Family is depriv'd of that, which ought to deſcend to him from his Parents. I ſay depriv'd, becauſe, though the Law expreſſes he ſhall inherit it, provided he executes a Command given him by the *Cadi*, when he attains the Age of fifteen, yet the Injunction is always ſo difficult, that ſcarce ever young Man could accompliſh it. Thus, the Order of our Births ſubjects us all three to this inhumane Law.

The Adventure *of the firſt of the young ſorrowful* Santons.

AT the Age of fifteen, I was preſented to the *Cadi* with all the uſual Solemnities, which are perform'd in a publick Manner. The Command he laid on me, was to procure him three Dates with golden Kernels. After having received this Injunction, my Mother privately ſlipped into my Hands a large Sum of Money, and then I embarqu'd myſelf. I found on Board the Ship ſeveral Fellow-Travellers, who were relating, as an Amuſement, each others Adventures. When it came to my Turn to recount ſome remarkable Paſſage of my Life, I made no Scruple to let them know the Situation of my Fortune, by declaring

claring in a jocose Way, the Command our *Cadi* had impos'd on me, which I look'd upon to be altogether fictitious. Your *Cadi*, interrupted one of the Company, has not so imaginary an Idea as you think him possess'd of; for the Dates with golden Kernels, you mention, actually grow in *Africa*, on a blue Palm-Tree. I have heard my Grandfather several times speak of it, whose Author was King of *Souffel* [a], with whom he had a very great Intimacy, and who assur'd him with his own Mouth, that that Palm-Tree grew in one of his Provinces. How agreeably was I surpris'd at so unexpected a Discovery! I directly intreated the Person, so saying, to let me know the Difficulties I had to surmount, in Order to come at it; but he vow'd, he knew no more of the Matter than what he had just told me. We came to an Anchor, at the Mouth of a small River of the great Island of *Scherne* [b], where I met with the favourable Opportunity of a Ship, just going to pass the Canal, which separates that Island from the main Land. Being arriv'd in *Souffel*, I ask'd divers Persons concerning what I was in search of, but none of them knew in what Part of the Kingdom this blue Palm-Tree grew, though they all agreed, that such a one there was. By what Means were you inform'd of it then, said I? The Inhabitants of *Souffel* answer'd me, they heard it from their Ancestors, who were honest People, and had no Interest in deceiving them. Upon this, I bought a Horse, took Provision with me, and resolv'd to range the whole Kingdom, which was not very extensive. After having examin'd two Thirds of it in vain, I laid myself down, one Night, in a Valley, where I fell fast asleep. Du-

[a] *Or* Sofala.   [b] Madagascar.

ring my Slumber, methoughts I saw a Lady, dress'd in the Mode of that Countrey, who ask'd me, with a great deal of Sweetness, what it was I sought: The blue Palm-Tree, answer'd I; if I could find out where it grows, perhaps I should not be disinherited. I then made her acquainted with the Law of my Countrey, the Injunction with which I was charg'd, and intreated her Assistance. Since you have Recourse to me, resum'd she, it will be your own Fault, if you are disinherited. As you go out of this Valley, you will find a beautiful Fountain, whence runs a Stream, which discharges itself in a large River not far distant from its Source. At the Bottom of the Fountain you'll find a little blue Pebble, which you must not fail to take up; then follow the Stream, till it brings you to the said River, which you will pursue, till you come to a Place, where it divides itself into two Branches to form an Island, or rather a Garden, in the Middle of which the blue Palm-Tree grows. Over an Arm of the River next to us, there is a fine Marble Bridge, whose Passage is defended by Seven and twenty Leopards. Before you come in sight of them, put the little blue Pebble in your Mouth, let your Horse graze on the Margin of the River, then walk on Foot over the Bridge, and pass boldly, for the Pebble will render you invisible. When you approach the Palm-Tree, gather three Dates and no more; but above all avoid eating any. The Lady, having said these Words, disappear'd, and as soon as I awoke, I took the Path she directed. The Fountain, the Pebble, the River, the Bridge and the Leopards presented themselves successively to my View. As I enter'd the Garden, I was saluted with an Odour, inexpressibly ravishing, proceeding from the Flowers and Fruits, which it produc'd in

great

great abundance; but still none of them were comparable to the blue Palm-Tree and its Dates. The Trunck of it resembled the most precious Stones of *Samarkande* [c], with large Veins of Gold: Its broad Leaves had the Brightness of the finest Saphirs: But how shall I describe its Fruit? Imagination can paint nothing so glorious! I swear by *Mahomet*, and by *Ali* his Son-in-Law, Son of *Abutalib*, it's more to testify the Truth, that I speak thus, than to exaggerate the Force of the Temptation, by which I was unhappily overcome. In beholding these marvellous Dates, I was inflam'd with such a Desire to taste them, that I believe to this Day, I should have dy'd on the Place, had I not gratify'd my Longing. I then took the blue Pebble out of my Mouth, extended my Hand, reach'd a Bough, and began to eat of them. The Relish was delicious and enchanting, but alas! the Pleasure was short. The Leopards now cast their furious Eyes upon me, made towards me with incredible Swiftness, and were just on the Point of tearing me to pieces, when the Lady, whom I had seen in my Dream, suddenly appear'd. At her Presence, these fierce Creatures immediately took Flight; and I prostrated myself at her Feet, endeavouring to express my Repentance and Gratitude. You are now lost to all Hopes of your Design, said she, acknowledge your Fault therefore, and go weep in the Island of the *Genius Feridoun*, my Father, who is still more afflicted than yourself. With this, she took me by the Hand, and having conducted me beyond the Bridge, charg'd me to pursue my Journy with all possible Speed, and to put the Pebble in its Place again, as I pass'd by the Fountain,

---

[c] *The finest Stones come from* Samarkande *and* Bokara.

which vanish'd from my Sight, the Moment I had obey'd her Commands. Then I look'd back, but saw neither River nor Bridge. Greatly astonish'd at this Adventure, but much less surpris'd than I had been at the Account the Inhabitants of *Scuffel* gave me, I directed my Way to that City, whence I embarqu'd to come hither.

The ADVENTURE *of the second of the young, sorrowful* SANTONS.

THE Command enjoined me by our *Cadi*, said the second of the young, sorrowful *Santons*, was not less difficult, than that you have heard related, only I add this Advantage, that the Judge himself directed me the Road I was to follow. The beautiful *Amberboi*, Daughter of the *Genius Arrout*, will not, said he, refuse you her Affection, could you find out the Means to merit it. Go! then, and prove yourself worthy of her: Her Palace is in the Isle of *Hao*. I agreed with the Master of a *Portuguese* Vessel from *Macao*, to put me on Shoar at *Hao*, being to touch there, in his Return to *China*. This Island is in the Form of a Sugar-Loaf: On which side soever you land, you discover the Palace of the Daughter of *Arrout*, which is built on the Height. There is no other Way to ascend to it, than by a Pair of Stairs, cut in the Rock, divided by six magnificent Gates, at an equal Distance from each other. Having knock'd at the first, six *Dervises* [a] open'd it, and

---

[a] *Religious* Mahometans. *They commonly wear Skins of Beasts dry'd in the Sun, go bare Head and bare Foot; shave all the Hair that grows on their Bodies; burn their Temples; and wear great* Jasper *Ear rings of divers Colours.*

one

one of them almoſt double with Age, demanded whom I was, and whither I was going? To which, I gave him to underſtand my Name and Buſineſs. If I could depend on thy Wiſdom, reſum'd he, I would, perhaps, adviſe thee for thy good. Oh! aſſure yourſelf, reply'd I, I'll make an excellent Uſe of it, believe me I will. The *Derviſe*, at this ſhook his Head, ſaying, Go on, young Man, go on; thou haſt too good an Opinion of thyſelf to regard any thing I could ſay to thee ; ſo farewell till we ſee one another again. He, and his Companions turn'd from me, and I went up ſoftly to the ſecond Gate, accuſing myſelf, that I had, in Reality, too little Diffidence of myſelf. Five *Calenders* [b] open'd it, and one of them ſaid to me, Who art thou? Whither art thou going? And what are thy Deſigns? I am, anſwer'd I, a poor, unfortunate young Man, oblig'd, by various Motives, to devote my moſt humble Service to the Queen *Amberboi*; I am neither acute, nor learn'd, but I know well how to prefer her Will before my own. Ah bleſſed Knowledge, cry'd the five *Calenders!* Young Man, purſue thy Way. At the third Gate, four *Santons* [c] ſtopp'd me, and he, who ſeem'd to be their Chief, ſaid, Thou com'ſt hither, in all Appearance, to ſerve the Queen: What Wages doſt thou expect to have? And how long doſt thou propoſe to live in her Service? The Pleaſure I ſhall take, anſwer'd I, in executing

---

[b] *Religious* Mahometans *more reſpected than the* Derviſes. *They wear a little ſhort Robe without Sleeves, edg'd with Horſe-hair, or Camel's mix'd with Wooll; ſhave themſelves, wear Hats adorn'd with Fringes of Horſe-hair; a great iron Ring about their Necks, and others of the ſame Matter at their Ears; ſome again of them have another, of two Pound Weight, fix'd to that Part of the Body, which ſerves for Generation.*

[c] Mahometan *Prieſts.*

the Commands of so charming a Princess, will more than recompense my weak Services; and as for the Continuation of them, they shall last as long as I love her, and I shall love her as long as I live. Generously spoken, said the *Santons*, letting me pass. I saluted them, and much pleas'd with myself, arriv'd at the fourth Gate, where I met three *Mullah's* [d]. Is it by *Force*, or *Love*, said they, thou comest hither to serve the Queen? If she commands thee to do impossible Things, wilt thou obey her? The Queen is too just, and has too much good Sense, answer'd I, to impose Laws, whose Execution is impossible. I must own, the Motive that first kindled Inclination, and prompted me to offer her my Assiduities, had a Tincture of Interest in it; but now that's no more; my whole self languishes to be hers. Go up, reply'd the *Mullahs*. The fifth Gate was open'd me by two *Imans* [e], whose Question was this: If thou hadst the Liberty to chuse, which of these two Things would'st thou like best; to live here with the Queen, or for her to go and live with thee? If the Choice was lodg'd in my Power, I would not chuse, said I to them, I would leave it to the Queen's better Judgment. Very well! reply'd the *Imans*, continue thy Steps. At the sixth Gate, I found a most beautiful *Nymph* [f]. If my Mistress, said she, thinks you unworthy of her Favours, what will you do then? Charming *Nymph*, answer'd I, I'll beseech her to render me worthy of them, and I'll defy her to hinder me from adoring her. If she returns your Affection, resum'd the young *Nymph*, be satisfy'd with her Person, and desire no other Blessing.

[d] Mahometan *Doctors*.   [e] Mahometan *Curates*.
[f] *Verbally translated, it would be* Ginne of the second Order.

After

"After giving me this Advice, she introduced me into the Apartment of the Divine *Amberboi*, to whom I devoted myself, and kneeling, kifs'd the Entrance of the Alcove where her Throne was erected. Rife, faid she, I will accept your Offers, be but truly submissive. This faid, two Nymphs took me by the Hands and led me away. For the Space of a Month, I observed all the Queen's Commands with the utmost Exactitude, and perceived, that her lovely Eyes, which at firft looked like Indifference itself, became now daily more favourable. She loved me, at laft, with an Infinity of Warmth, and her Heart being in this happy Difpofition, difcourfed me, one Day in this Manner; Thy great Submission has won my Soul, but this Place is no Ways proper for our Pleafures. The curious and jealous *Ginnes*, who pretend to be my Friends, are too well acquainted with it, and our Actions would be too much infpected into. I know a delightful Retreat, where we shall be much lefs expofed: Let us go thither. I expreffed my Readinefs to follow her. Let us prepare then for our Departure, continued she, leading me into a large Cabinet, which contained her Treafure. At our Entrance, I faw what greatly aftonifhed me, fix golden Tables, on each of which there was a great Turkifh Jar of an old Rock, full of ineftimable Riches. The firft was filled with Topazes; the fecond, with Emeralds; the third, with Rubies; the fourth, with Saphirs; the fifth, with Diamonds and Pearls perfectly round, and as big as Nut-galls;. and the laft, which was larger than the reft, contained all Sorts of Jewels, fo delicately wrought, that Art here furpaffed even Nature, tho' the Matter was nothing but Gold

and precious Stones of a finished Perfection. My Charmer, said *Amberboi*, take whatever you think fit of this immense Treasure, and carry it away with you. I was dazled, but perfectly calling to Mind the Nymph's Advice, My Queen, answered I, my Eyes are only sacred to you; why do you then thus injure them? In saying so, I pretended to leave the Cabinet, but *Amberboi* retained me, throwing her tender Arms about my Neck; and with an irresistible Smile, said, you will not sure refuse this Ring, which she took from the Jar, containing the Jewels, and put on my Finger. I was some Moments admiring the Beauty of it, when I perceived that instead of a Diamond, my Picture was chac'd in it. I was so surprised and ravished at the Sight of such an unexpected Novelty, that made me say to the beautiful *Ginne*, I should think myself guilty of the greatest Breach of Civility, were I to remove that Ring from the Place, where she had vouchsafed to put it. *Amberboi*, at these Words immediately changed her Countenance, for an Air, all proud and full of disdain: Impostor, said she, deceitful, perjured and ungrateful Villain, dost thou then love another Object besides me? Fly, Wretch fly; go and adore thy self. How much astonished was I at these Words! And how little able am I to express the Terror I was in! The Daughter of *Arrout* went out, and fifty Nymphs of her Attendance, furious as so many Lyons, came in; and though I made no Resistance, dragged me down to the second Gate, which was open, as were all the others quite to the Bottom, and the Guards waited in the Passage to precipitate my Departure. The two *Imans* seized me under each Arm, and launched
me,

me, with Impetuofity to the *Mullaks*; thofe hurled me, with all their Force, towards the *Santons*; the *Santons* threw me, with greater Roughnefs ftill, to the *Calenders*; and the *Calenders* made me fly with fuch rapidity, the Space between them and the *Dervifes*, that I know not if I touched the Ground. I fell breathlefs and half dead, in the Midft of thefe laft, who fuffered me to recover my felf a little, on Purpofe to divert themfelves with my Misfortune, which they did fo loudly, that the whole Mountain echoed with their Huzza's. When I came to myfelf; I forefaw well enough, my Son, faid the old *Dervife* to me, that you would have no great Succefs. Prefumption is the Source of too many Vices; and Self-love is too imperious, where Vanity reigns. Be gone, added he, and fit on that Rock pointing to it, until fome Veffel fhall happily pafs by. With thefe Words he clapped too the Gate, and I repaired thither to bewail my Folly. I remained on that craggy Habitation more than three Weeks; during which Time, the old *Dervife* brought me every Day a little Rice, mixed with a bitter Herb, called *Rue*. A Ship, at laft, happening to fail within ken of my Cries and the Signs I made, the Long-Boat was fent to carry me on Board. Juft as I was about to embark, the old *Dervife* advifed me to take Refuge in this Ifland as foon as poffible; and I am not at all diffatisfied with having follow'd his Directions.

The ADVENTURE *of the third of the young, sorrowful* SANTONS.

THE Order enjoined me by the *Cadi* of our Town, said the third of the young sorrowful *Santons*, provoked every Body that heard it; because they looked upon its Accomplishment more impossible than all the Commands he had given on such Occasions, for the Space of ten Years. Go, said he, and fetch me the Ass of *Daggial*[a], whom you will find in the Mountain of *Caf*. I returned Home exceeding Melancholy at my Obligation; and my Grief was such, that even my Brothers melted into Compassion at it, and consented, that my Father and Mother should furnish me with a very large Sum of Money, plainly foreseeing the Improbability of my Return, evermore to be chargeable to them. The first Opportunity that offered, I passed from the Island of *Schore-Pulou* to the Main Land, where I bought a Slave, two good Horses for us, and a Mule to carry our Provision. I armed myself and Slave, promising him his Liberty and large Presents on our Return, provided he proved faithful; and then made the best of our Way to the Mountains. As that of *Caf* surpasses, by much all the rest in Height, it was not very difficult for us to discover the Ridge of it. When we were come to the Entrance of the Mountains, we followed the Tract, making easy Days Journeys, living very well, and taking particular Care to inform ourselves, in all the inhabited

[a] *The Anti-Christ of the* Mahometans.

Places

Places we met with, concerning *Daggial* and his Afs. We travelled during three tedious Months, without being able to procure the leaſt Infight till one Morning, after having paſſed through a ſmall Wood, pretty thick, we heard moſt terrible Cries behind us: Some ſeemed to be menacing, and others utter'd to move Compaſſion. Brother, ſaid I to my Slave, let us turn our Mule a little from the high Road, and go back to ſee what mean thoſe Cries. If any in Diſtreſs have need of our Succour, let us hazard our Lives for them: The Danger they are expoſed to To-Day, may perhaps threaten us To-Morrow. The Slave, who was a Man of Courage, led the Mule into a Thicket, and after having tied him up, rejoined me. We then put our Bows in order, and made towards the Noiſe; which being approached, we ſaw three Men with their Backs towards a large Tree, bravely defending themſelves againſt ſeven Rogues. We did not ſtand long to heſitate, but ſhot directly at the Aſſaultants, and two of them drop'd. The like Succeſs attended our ſecond Diſcharge, and the three remaining, ran to us, with the Fury of Men in Deſpair, to revenge their Companions Fall; but whilſt we were diſpoſing ourſelves to give them a vigorous Reception, the three Men, whom we delivered, had purſued, taken and wounded them.

I embraced theſe Travellers, (who were very acknowledging,) with the utmoſt Satisfaction; ſaying, Gentlemen, I ſuppoſe you are as little deſirous as I am, to hear the laſt Words of theſe unhappy Wretches; therefore I hope you will employ yourſelves much better, by favouring me with your Companies a little Diſtance from hence.

L 3   I con-

I conducted them strait to the Mule, where I entertained them on the Grass, with what Fare I was Master of, and they eat very heartily of it. During the Collation, I recounted the Motive of my Travels, and entreated them to tell me impartially their Opinions on it. A good Action is never lost, replied one of the three Travellers; no Body can give you a more precinct Account of what you are in Search of, than we; for we live at the Foot of the Mountain, that *Daggial*'s Ass grazes on; neither are we ignorant of the Measures you must take, to become Master of this Animal. Praise be to God! Dear Friends, cried I, you put an end to my Fatigues. Be certain of nothing yet, resumed the Traveller: An Undertaking does not always succeed, even though the nicest Precaution be used. Let us pursue therefore our Journey, you will have Time enough when we get thither, to consult your Heart. Moreover, your Equipage will be rather an Hindrance than Service to you now; for we have still a vast Number of Mountains to pass over, and all by Paths in a Manner inpracticable. This News made me very pensive for some Moments; but resuming a fresh Courage and Resolution, I emptied the Panniers the Mule carried, and divided the Provision into five Parts. The three Travellers and I, took each our Share; after which, I said to my Slave, the Fifth will suffice thee, until thou canst reach the first inhabited Place: Besides, I give thee, with thy Liberty, these Animals, and this Purse, which contains about five and twenty *Chequins*; so God bless thee, and pray for thy Master. The poor Slave received my Gifts with Tears in his Eyes; and I left him, thus bewailing his Loss, to follow,

on

on Foot, my Conductors. For six Days successively walking, we saw nothing but numberless Precipices. At last we descended into a Valley that was very fresh and green, and in which was a great Multitude of useless Animals feeding, and a considerable Number of large, but ill-built Houses. He, that for the most Part talk'd to me, let me into one of them, where he entertained me with all the Magnificence a rural Life affords. When the People of his Family were retired, he spoke to me thus: My Lord, on the Top of the Mountain my Habitation touches, you will find a Wood, entirely planted with odoriferous Trees. It is in this very Wood *Daggial*'s Ass dwells, because he lives on nothing else but sweet Flavours. He is as black as Jet, and his Wings are of the same Colour. He can neither suffer the least Infection, the least superfluous Weight, nor the least Fear in the Person that rides him. Due Precautions may be easily taken, as to the two first Articles; but, my Lord, weigh well the third; for if *Daggial*'s Ass finds you in the least timerous, when he flies with you, like an Eagle, into the Air, your Life is infallibly lost; he throws you headlong down, from Heaven to the Earth. Dear Fellow Traveller, replied I, my Courage, I am certain, will not fail me; therefore let us think of repairing the Fatigues of our Journey. Two Days after, I entreated him to set me Part of the Way, who readily complied with my Request. After having mounted a long Time, we reposed ourselves near a very beautiful Fountain, where I wash'd my self from Head to Foot, as also my *Sar-A-pat*, and the little Remains of Clothes I had preserved. It was here my Host took Leave of me, wished all Manner of Prosperity to my Enterprize,

and

and excused himself for not guiding me any farther, for fear of incurring *Daggial*'s Indignation.

I ascended until I came to the sweet scented Wood, where I found the Ass just as he had been described to me. He was not difficult in being approached, and even suffered me to caress him, which I did the longer, to bring him the better acquainted with me. At last, I jumped upon him, and in a Moment he spread his large Wings, began to cut the Air, with an unconceivable Swiftness, and in less than an Hour, we were in a direct Line above the Ocean. I had now felt no Sign of Fear; and was even flattering myself that my Heart was not susceptible to it; when I beheld before me amidst the Clouds, a huge, black Giant, armed with a fiery Javelin, and waiting to pierce me with it. Though his Complexion was black, his Beard, and all the other Hairs of his Body were white. He had but one Eye, and one Eye-lid, but it sparkled like a Comet, and gave a most horrible Look. This Object proved to be *Daggial* himself. I must own, I could not behold so dreadful a Monster, without giving Way to Confusion and Terror. I might perhaps have recovered my Courage, had the Ass allowed me more Time; but he immediately stood on his Hind legs, and shook his Mane and Neck; so being obliged to quit my Hold, I fell headlong down into the Sea. I was fortunate enough, not to be directly suffocated with the great Plunge I made; but coming up again to the Surface of the Water, and being very lightly dress'd, I supported myself by swimming, until I was taken up by some Fishermen; who hearing me fall, came without Delay to my Assistance. Having asked them, when I was pretty well come to myself,

what

what Part of the World I was in, they told me, they lived in an Island adjacent to that, where the *Genius Feridoun* received with so much Humanity, all those, who were truly overwhelmed in Affliction. After having refreshed myself some Days with them, what they had told me concerning this generous *Genius*, induced me to intreat them in his Name, to conduct me to his Island; which they very willingly complied with.

The ADVENTURE *of the Old* SANTON *at the Queen of the Mountains.*

THE third of the young, sorrowful *Santons*, having finished his Adventure, I shall now begin mine.

The great Reputation of Charity, that the powerful *Genius Feridoun* has so justly acquired in the World, said the old *Santon*, made me likewise repair to this Island. Having passed my Youth in the Exercise of Arms, and on all Occasions given Proofs of my Valour to the invincible *Jehan-Guir*; this Sultan of the Moguls, as a Reward of my Services, put me at the Head of a thousand Horse. So glorious a Mark of his Esteem, still more animating my Zeal, I continued to serve him, with the utmost Fidelity, and to be Prodigal of my Blood, in all the Wars he undertook. The last Expedition I assisted at, was the Siege of *Candahar*, which was the only Frontier Garrison of *Persia*, the Sophi believed

impreg-

impregnable. The taking this important Place, having concluded the Campaign, all the Officers had Orders to march their Troops into the several Parts of the Kingdom, nominated for their Quarters. It fell to my Lot to conduct mine to the Frontiers of the Country of *Anberan*. Before I could arrive there, I was obliged to travel over very high Mountains, which separate the Kingdom of *Thibet* from the Province of *Cabul*. These Mountains, or rather the Vallies, which they form, are inhabited. We found there, not only Hamlets, but likewise Villages well-peopled.

Though I always took a particular Care to regulate the March of my Troops, so as to Quarter them every Night in the best Places, yet the Badness of the Roads happening one Day to prevent the Performance of our Stage, we were obliged to halt in a Hamlet, that was only composed of seven or eight very ordinary Cottages. Seeing the Necessity there was to encamp, contrary to our Custom, I ordered the Tents to be put in Readiness, whilst the Officers went to find out a convenient Place for pitching them. As they were marking out the Camp, they perceived at the Extremity of a little, but very delightful Valley, a spacious Edifice, neither wholly in Repair, nor entirely demolished. They immediately asked the Country People, what it was they saw? You see, replied an old Mountaineer, the Queen of the Mountains Fortress. The lawful Possessors, having been compelled to abandon it, through the Incursions of the *Persians*, this Lady rendered herself Mistress of it. She, and her Court, have dwelled there these fifteen Years, and suffer no Stranger whatever to come nigh them. What sort of a Person is this Queen,

Queen, replied the Officers, and what Family is she of? What are her Attendants? Is she at great Expence? I do not know, resumed the Mountaineer, what Extraction she is of; and in Regard of her Appearance, no Body ever had more the Air of a Princess; yet notwithstanding that, I cannot believe her a Woman composed of Flesh and Bones, for I have seen her, several Times, fly like a Bird. The People about her do also very surprising Things, and are so numerous, that they might form a little Army. They never come hither, and very seldom speak to us, so that we are entire Strangers to what they subsist on. We dare not so much as approach the Fortress, since this Queen's Residence there; for several of us have narrowly escaped our Lives, for only feeding our Flocks a little too near it. By the Half-Moon, replied one of our Officers on that, here is an Adventure the most worthy our Curiosity we can meet with. We ought not, by any Means, to neglect making due Use of it; since therefore we have still Day-light enough, let us march directly into the Fortress: It is a spacious Piece of Building; and consequently we shall be less exposed there to the Insults of the Weather, than under our Tents. You will see the Queen will be either afraid to shew herself, or if she does, it will be to give us a gracious Reception. Believe me, the Sight of so formidable a Band as ours is, would even render *Asmough* [a] affable. I would not advise you to depend on that, answered the Peasant; but the rest of the Officers, being for the most Part, giddy brain'd young Gen-

---

[a] *An evil* Div, *that* Aherman *employs to sow Discord among* Men.

tlemen,

tlemen, thought it was derogating from their Character, to difapprove the rafh Propofition of their Comrade. They came forthwith to acquaint me with the Refult of their Deliberation, and being at leaft as curious as they were, I commanded the Horfe to march, and the Peafants to furnifh us with Wood, Provifion, and all the Lamps they had in the Hamlet.

When we had enter'd the Edifice, we vifited it, and finding it in good Repair for an abandon'd Place, we diftributed the Companies into as good Order as poffible. Great Fires were made every where; eating, drinking, and merry making went forwards among them, but ftill every one took care to have his Arms in Readinefs. For my part, I fupp'd with all the Officers, in a fine Hall we had referv'd for that Purpofe, and which was illuminated with all the Lamps of the Hamlet, hanging round the Walls of it. After having diverted ourfelves till after Midnight, we began to feel the firft Approaches of Sleep, and were difpofing ourfelves to retire, when an unexpected and dreadful Noife was heard, adjoining to the Place where we were, that foon made us think of fomething elfe than going to Bed. Far from being difmay'd at it, as Men of fignaliz'd Courage, we betook ourfelves to our Arms, and turn'd towards the Palace Gate, waiting with Intrepidity what fhould happen. The Noife ceas'd all on a fudden, which we then concluded was a Signal. A little after, we faw the pretended Queen of the Mountains appear. She was moft magnificently dreft, preceeded by a Dozen of Guards well arm'd, accompany'd with feveral Ladies very richly adorn'd, and follow'd by a great Number of People, who by their Air, and the

Beauty

Beauty of their Arms and Dreſſes, might be taken for ſo many *Rejas*.

I fix'd my Eyes directly on her, who look'd ſo amiable, and ſo worthy of Reſpect, that I remain'd as ſpeechleſs. What, my Lord, ſaid ſhe to me, with a great Deal of Familiarity, do you ſurpriſe me Sword in Hand? Is it thus then you make your Viſits? Madam, anſwer'd I, you'll eaſily pardon, I hope, the Incivility of a Perſon who expected to find an Enemy here. It is probable you may have found one, in Effect, reſum'd the Queen, but you'll need other Arms than thoſe I ſee to vanquiſh him. As I was about to make a ſuitable Reply to this ſeemingly gay Diſcourſe, a brutal Wretch, whom I thought detach'd himſelf from my Company, advanc'd, and taking the Queen inſolently by the Chin, ſaid he was ready to fight her at what Weapons ſhe would pleaſe to Name. The Queen ſtept back, diſcovering a great Confuſion of Mind, and one of her Ladies flew at this preſumptuous Animal to tear his Eyes out. For my part, I gave him a great Blow over the Face likewiſe, and at the ſame time, all in the Hall drew their Sabres. The Officers belonging to the Queen ſeem'd bent on revenging the Inſolence ſhewn their Miſtreſs, and mine cry'd out let the Guilty be puniſh'd. The Soldiers who were diſpers'd thro' the Fortreſs, haſten'd alſo to the Noiſe; ſo that, in a very little Time, the Hall was ſo full, there was ſcarce any ſtirring in it.

The Queen ſuſpended a while the Diſorder to aſk the Perſon who had cauſ'd it, whom he was? But this Wretch making no Anſwer, her Attendants ſaid it was undoubtedly ſome Body belonging to me. My Officers and I who had never

ſeen

seen him, maintain'd, on the contrary, that he was one of her own Domesticks. The Dispute at last growing more warm, the Lie was given on both Sides, Blows ensu'd, each attack'd his Man, the Lamps were thrown down, Blood began to stream in Abundance, the Fury of the Combatants rather redoubled than abated in the Dark, and the Havock lasted till Morning.

Then those who remain'd, saw the Queen at the Door of the Hall, laughing extreamly, and who seem'd to wear an Air of Joy on her Countenance, saying to them: Wretches! open your Eyes, know yourselves, and learn never to take up your Lodging in another Person's House, without asking the Owner's Leave. I was deeply wounded in two Places, and tho' the great Effusion of Blood I had just lost, render'd me almost incapable of Speech, yet I both saw and heard the execrable Phantom. This second Apparition was succeeded by a dreadful Surprise: Our Eyes were releas'd from the fatal Enchantment that had misled them till that Moment; our Rage dissipated, our Enemies vanish'd, and we plainly perceiv'd we had only been fighting with one another. All those who were able to move, urg'd by a just Resentment, made directly towards the perfidious Queen to be reveng'd of her, but she disappear'd continuing to deride us.

Being reduc'd to the fourth Part of our Compliment, we thought of nothing but interring the Dead, and comforting the wounded. Litters were prepar'd in all haste to transport us to the Cottages, were we recover'd our Healths by little and little. As fast as they were cur'd of their

Wounds,

Wounds, I sent them to join the rest at *Anchezan*, who march'd thither the very Day after the Adventure. They all imagin'd I would not fail to rejoin them likewise, but being asham'd of what had happen'd, as equally possess'd of the blackest Despair, to see the Flower of *Jehan-Guir*'s Army cut off, I was depriv'd of all Resolution of ever more appearing before him. As soon therefore as I was in a Condition to march, I took leave of those remaining uncur'd, saying, I should expect to see them shortly at *Ancheran*, but instead of pursuing that Road, I travell'd towards the Sea Coast. You may be assur'd, Gentlemen, I did not fail cursing the abominable *Div*, during my Journey, for having transform'd one half of my Troopers to engage the other, by means of a Spectre, who began the Quarrel.

Time having insensibly slipt away during all these Recitals, our *Santon* went out to look at the Sun, and coming in again, told us the Hour of the second Prayer was nigh at Hand. We rose up, and separated from each other, in order to prepare ourselves for it, by bathing and pious Reflections. After the Prayer was ended, we perform'd our Meditations in common, and the Company desir'd to be satisfy'd with the Relation of our Adventures, which accordingly we did. It is not very difficult, said our *Santon* to us after that, to guess what you would know of our Genius *Feridoun*; but be careful to remember you give him no other Title than that of Genius [a], calling him neither *Div* nor *Peri*.

[a] Feridoun *would not be called* Div, *because he had been one; nor* Peri, *because he was not one. He is a* Div *converted.*

The loud Sighs we heard at some Distance from the Hut, gave us notice the Master of the Isle approach'd. The *Santon* with whom we were, then took the *Alcoran*, and putting himself at the Head of his Brotherhood, order'd us to follow them. We walk'd in this Manner till we came to the Entrance of a great Alley, which Nature had form'd in the middle of the Wood, and stood there in a Line. *Feridoun* appear'd that Moment at the other Extremity, and advanc'd towards us with large solemn Steps. The Trees agitated by his Sighs, made as much Noise as a great Wind raises in a Forest. Tho' the highest Coco-trees reach'd but to his Shoulders, yet all his Limbs were so well proportion'd, that his Stature seem'd not enormous. The Features of his Face were extreamly fine, but of a masculine Beauty, and full of Majesty; his Arms enfolded in each other, embrac'd his Huge Breast; he inclin'd his Head somewhat forward, and kept his Eyes intently fix'd on Earth, as a Man immerg'd in the most profound Melancholy. When he came within twenty Paces of us he stopt, and the *Santons* advancing, *Almoraddin* and I follow'd them. Then after having saluted him three times, with our Faces bow'd down to the Ground, as is customary to the Sultan of the *Indies*, our Chief open'd the *Alcoran* with all Humility, and in a laudable Voice, read these Words.

" In the Name of the most mighty and merciful
" God. I am inform'd by a Revelation to com-
" municate to the People, that certain *Genii* have
" listen'd to me, as I was perusing the *Alcoran*,
" and said, we have heard the miraculous *Alco-*
" *ran* read; it teaches the Way of Truth, and we
" give

"give Faith to all it contains. We don't believe God shares his Omnipotence, and we are fully persuaded that there is but one independent God, who has neither Wife or Family. The ignorant Part of us blaspheme against his divine Majesty, tho' we never held it lawful for them so to do. There are Men who only implore the Assistance of created Spirits, and who augment their own Confusion still the more, by alledging, God will raise none from the Dead. Certain *Genii* have farther affirm'd; we have tow'rd as far as Heaven, and found it starrify'd and guarded. We repose ourselves in a Place somewhat distant from it for to listen. A Star spies out the Curious, and drives them down. We can't tell whether God hates ye Mortals on Earth, or whether he will shew you the right Path; but we are at present of the Number of those that believe in his Unity. They have lastly added: Oh People! we walk'd before in Error, and thought God was ignorant of what was done on Earth; but the Truth is, no Body can Escape his Power. We have heard the Book that teaches the right Way read, and we give Faith to all it contains. He that puts his Confidence in God, need not fear what Misfortune or Injustice can befall him. There are some among us who are good, and who relyi sincerely on God."

Here the *Santon* shut the holy Book. The *Genius*, being now more tranquil, and consol'd at what he had heard, ask'd, as low as he could speak, who those *Musseimen* were he then saw, and what they wanted. The Character he gave us, assuring us of his Vigilance and Favour, I

made

made a Sign to *Almoraddin*, and as we approach'd, Generous *Genius*, said I to *Feridoun*, you are not undoubtedly ignorant who we are, and what has brought us before you; but since you command us to relate the Cause, this young Man, Son of a Merchant, has lost two thirds of his Substance, in disappointing twice the beautiful *Zulikhah*, Queen of *Barrostan*, and must infallibly lose the remaining Part, if he answers not now her Expectations. As for me, I am one of the Slaves of *Chah-Jehan*, induc'd by a laudable Curiosity: I travel to improve my Mind and Manners, and chiefly to discover the Island of *Borico*, where springs a Fountain, whose Water restores past Youth to such as drink of it. Oh *Genius*, gracious and benignant! we doubt the Success of our Enterprizes, enlighten us therefore by thy Counsels. *Feridoun* made Answer: Let him that is *silent* follow punctually the Advice of him that has *spoken*; and let him that has *spoken*, hope every thing from the *good Work* he does. We bow'd with the utmost Reverence, after having receiv'd this short Answer; and the *Santons* bidding us, in a low Voice retire, we return'd to the Hut.

Tho' my Conduct is henceforward to be regulated by you, said *Almoraddin*, embracing me, yet if I may presume to advise, let us repair to the Ship; our People may perhaps be impatient. With all my Heart, reply'd I, but let us return hither again with some Testimonies of our Gratitude. On this we went down to the Sea-side, and having call'd the Boat on Shore, we stept into it, and were row'd on Board. As we ascended into the Ship, we assur'd them all, we did not come to fetch any Body. The Surprize
and

and Joy of the Sailors echo'd throughout the Veſſel, and the Pilot, who had been trembling all this while, overwhelm'd us with Queſtions, which we deferr'd ſatisfying till a more ſeaſonable Opportunity. By my Direction, *Almoraddin* made Choice of three Pieces of Gold Brocade for *Feridoun*, and compos'd a Preſent for the *Santons*, of five Pieces of fine Cloath, five beautiful *China* Bowls, a Sack of *Bocaro* Plumbs, and another of *Kichmiches* Apricocks. Having prepar'd our Gifts we return'd to the Hut, and left them at the Door, the *Santon* not being yet come home. We have now fulfill'd our Duty, ſaid I to *Almoraddin*, ſo let' us embark ourſelves in good Earneſt. A freſh Breeze of Wind riſing in the Night, and promiſing a favourable Navigation, we prepar'd to ſet ſail.

The Sequel of the Hiſtory of Almoraddin, *and Queen* Zulikhah.

IN Effect, we had no ſooner unfurl'd our Sails, than the Ship was gently carry'd between the North and Eaſt Points. After we had ſatisfy'd the Curioſity of the Pilot, and the reſt of the Mariners, *Almoraddin* and I went apart to Diſcourſe privately with each other. The Oracle, which at firſt ſeem'd to give us ſtrong Hopes, now began to puzzle us. If I expect to ſucceed in my Enterpriſe, ſaid *Almoraddin*, I muſt follow punctually your Advice; and if I do not obſerve that Punctuality to a Tittle, (which I may

fail

fail in, though never so well dispos'd to perform it;) all will be knock'd in the Head, and the Oracle can't be blameable. I am no less dubious than you, answer'd I: the good Issue of what I desire, depends on the Assistance I am able to afford you; but if, by Inadvertency, I omit any necessary Observation, my good Work will be found defective, and both our Attempts frustrated. But, continu'd I, don't we strain the Argument a little too far? I cannot think the *Genius* design'd to deceive us; for it would be no other to exact from us what's e'en almost impossible. Let us consider our several Obligations with an Eye less scrutinous; and as I have more Reason than ever to espouse your Interest, let me know what has pass'd between the Queen of *Barrostan* and you, without omitting the least Circumstance. *Almoraddin* readily fulfill'd my Request, and I devour'd, with a singular Attention, all the Particularities of his Adventures, which were the chief Subject of my Reflections, during the rest of the Voyage to *Sumatra*.

When we came within Sight of the Port, we adorn'd the Vessel with a great Number of Streamers of all Colours. Then we sail'd into the Harbour, firing our Guns, as in Triumph, and anchor'd at a certain Distance from the Town, without dispatching any Body to apprise them of our Arrival. Whilst the Officers came to visit us, we form'd a Consort of Musick, compos'd of Kettle-Drums, *Karnas* [a], and several other sorts of Instruments, which drew a vast many People to the

---

[a] *A* Karna *is a kind of* Hautboy, *a Fathom and a half long, and a Foot wide at the Botom.*

Seaside,

Sea-fide. The Queen and all her Court beheld us with equal Admiration and Curiosity, and all the Windows and Terrasses belonging to the Palace, were likewise crowded with Spectators. At last, we perceived an Officer, guarded with ten Soldiers, making towards us in a Boat, to ask us, in the Queen's Name, who we were, and what our Business was: But he no sooner cast his Eyes on *Almoraddin*, than he knew him again, and instead of asking him these Questions, said, God grant you may observe the Laws of our Royal Mistress better than you have hitherto done. Why do you delay coming on Shoar? Are you afraid you will not be received with open Arms? What detains me, answer'd *Almoraddin*, is the Uncertainty of what may happen to the best of Friends, pointing at me, when he said these Words. If I should, continu'd he, be again unhappily stripped and sent away, would he be kept here against his Will? May the Queen vouchsafe to explain that Article. The Officer went immediately and reported it to her, and coming back a little after, the Law, said he to *Almoraddin*, puts you in full Possession both of the Queen's Person and Riches, provided you fulfil the Condition already known to you: This is all she can grant. This Law confiscates to the Use of the Queen, only your own Person and Effects, therefore your Friend is safe. If you should transgress a third Time, he is at Liberty either to stay or follow you, provided he makes Oath to lend you no Assistance whilst you are in her Dominions. Why did not she then detain me before, said *Almoraddin*, since the Law render'd me her Slave? The Officer reply'd: She permits the Freedom of Departure to her Lovers, to the End they may return again, or becauſe ſhe cannot ſuffer them any long time in her Sight. The Guilty, reply'd *Almoraddin*, bluſhing, deſerve her Indignation, they merit alſo to return again.

 The Oath being tender'd me, I took it, and order'd the Ship to fall down to the Key, where we landed, preceeded by our Players on Inſtruments, and follow'd by the reſt of our Men, all very neatly dreſt. When I ſaw the charming *Zulikhah*, I ceas'd to wonder at the Impreſſion ſhe had made on *Almoraddin*, and verily believe the eternal Virgins of Paradice exceed her not in Beauty. The Day you arrive, ſaid ſhe to her Lover, I look on you as a Prodigy of tender Paſſion, why then do you deceive me in the Night? *Almoraddin* was ſtruck dumb for a Moment at this Reproach, and knew how to excuſe his Behaviour no otherwiſe, than by imputing it to that Exceſs of Love, ſhe herſelf had attributed to him. He then preſented me, with a very good Addreſs to *Zulikhah*, and was much more Eloquent on the Subject of our Friendſhip, than he had Power to be on his own Paſſion. After the firſt Compliments were over, I begg'd leave to withdraw for a while, to give ſome neceſſary Orders to our People, ſome of whom I ſent back to the Veſſel, charging them to obſerve the Directions I had before given, and led the reſt to one of the Apartments of the *Bazar*, where having lodg'd the Preſents deſign'd for the Queen, I return'd to the Palace.

 Almoraddin was ſeated next the Queen, and though his Soul was wholly engroſs'd with her Beauties, yet he made a Shew of admiring the
Singing,

Singing, the Dancing and Agility of a Band of dexterous *Kenchenies* [b]. I mingled with them, and became an Actor in their Buffooneries, the better to inspect the Behaviour of the Courtiers. I found *Almoraddin* was a great Favourite among them: Every one deplor'd his Fate, when they consider'd how miserable they should see him the next Day. Some indeed alledg'd the Queen was more to be lamented than him, since she was oblig'd to make wretched a belov'd Lover, and one, who had sacrific'd so much for her. The Diversions were succeeded by a magnificent Supper, at which I observ'd nothing particular, but that the Gaity *Zulikhah* assum'd, was rather constrain'd than natural. She would now and then fix her Eyes on *Almoraddin*, with a serious and melancholy Air, and on a sudden turn them towards the Guests, endeavouring to conceal her Disquiet. I concluded from this, she loved *Almoraddin*, and knew not herself to how great a Degree of Inclination. Being risen from Table, I dis-engaged myself from the Company, and went to the Palace Gate, where I found three of the most compleat of our Men attending with the Presents, I had ordered to be brought in this Manner.

The Kingdom of *Barrostan* produces gold Dust, Pepper, Camphir and Benjamin, from the Knowledge of which I had regulated our Offerings. The Bearers of them were dressed, by my Orders, after that Country Fashion; I put on a Garment of the same Mode, and conducted them into the great Hall. We ranged ourselves in a

---

[b] *Dancers and Singers by Profession, of whom there are a great many in the* Indies.

direct Line, juft oppofite to the Queen; who not being apprifed of any Thing, was extremely furprifed; and the whole Affembly kept Silence for a Time, expecting the Event. The firft Bearer advanced with his Prefent, and laid it at the Feet of *Zulikhah*; then returned to his Place. His Prefent was the fineft Bafket that ever came out of *China*, full of very extraordinary Paftils, with a little Camphir fpread on the Top, for Form Sake. The fecond made an Oblation of his, in the fame Manner, which was a Lump of Amber-Greafe of fix Pounds Weight, covered with little Pieces of Benjamin in a Bafon of Enamel from *Japan*. The third offered a fmall Tree of maffy Gold, planted in a Jar of Rock Cryftal, full of Gold Duft, which ferved as Earth about the Root of it. When my Turn came, I approached alfo; but inftead of laying my Prefent on the Carpet as the others had done, I gave it into the Hands of *Zulikhah*, faying, Queen of Gold and of Perfumes, difdain not the firft Fruits of Pepper, I prefume to entreat you will accept thefe Grains, becaufe I am perfuaded they will change their Nature, and become very precious in Hands, accuftomed to work Miracles. My Prefent was a great Box of Silver gilt, full of beautiful large Pearls. *Zulikhah* opening it, and examining the Contents, faid, with an Air of Gaiety, fhe never knew there was white Pepper of fo charming a Luftre. After that, fhe returned us Thanks, and difmiffed us in the fame Manner fhe would have done, had we been effectually her Subjects.

We accordingly retired, but as I was changing my Habit, two of our Sailors arrived quite out of Breath, faying to me, my Lord, all the Ship

Ship is in Confusion, our People are cutting one another's Throats, the weakest of them, or rather the most desperate, threaten to put Fire to the Powder, and all will be lost, if *Almoraddin* does not instantly appear. I conducted, that Moment, the two Men before the Queen and *Almoraddin*, making them repeat what they had just said. *Almoraddin* entreated Permission to go and appease this Tumult, and having obtained it, on Condition he would return immediately, we ran directly to the Port. We were no sooner entered the Vessel, than the Menaces of the Combatants, the clashing of their Swords, the Groans of the Wounded, and in a Word, all the Noise we had been told of, was at an End. This was no more, in effect, than a Comedy I had caused to be played, on Purpose to have an Opportunity of discoursing *Almoraddin* alone, and giving him my last Counsels how to proceed, which he received with great Docility. I then reconducted him to the Queen, to whom he made an agreeable Recital of the imaginary Slaughter, which had detained him. The Hour for repose being come, the beautiful *Zulikhah* gave Command to her Officers to lodge me in an Apartment of the Palace, and in Presence of all her Court, introduced the amorous *Almoraddin* into her Bed-Chamber.

FINIS.

PLAYS Sold by T. WORRALL.

Albion Queens,
All for Love,
Ambitious Stepmother,
Amboyna,
Antiochus,
Apparition,
Artful Husband,
Artful Wife,
Assignation,
Athaliah,
Basset Table,
Beaux Stratagem,
—— Duel,
Bold Stroke for a Wife,
Briton,
Busiris,
Cæsar Borgia,
Caius Marius,
Careless Husband,
Cato,
Chymera,
City Ramble,
Clouds,
Conscious Lovers,
Cleomenes,
Committee,
Conquest of Granada,
Constantine the Great,
Contrivances,
Countrey-House,
Don Sebastian,
Double Gallant,
Duke of Guise,
Earl of Essex,
Edwin,
Æsop,
Evening Love,
Fair Captive,
Fall of Saguntum,

False Friend,
Fate of Capua,
Fatal Extravagance,
Friendship in Fashion,
Gentleman Dancing-Master,
Gloriana,
Half-pay Officers,
Hamlet,
Henry V.
Henry IV. of France,
Heroick Friendship,
Humorous Lieutenant,
Jane Gray,
Imperial Captives,
Indian Emperor,
Indian Queen,
Injur'd Virtue,
Island Princess,
Judgment of Paris,
Kensington Gardens,
Kind Keeper,
King Arthur,
King Lear,
London Cuckolds,
Love for Money,
Love in a Sack,
—— in a Tub,
—— Triumphant,
Loyal Subject,
Lying Lovers,
L. Junius Brutus,
Maid's Tragedy,
Maid's last Prayer,
Maiden Queen,
Mar-Plot,
Marriage Alamode,
Massacre of Paris,
Mithridates,
Mock Astrologer,

Nero,

Nero,
Noah's Flood,
Northern Lafs,
——— Heirefs,
Œdipus,
Orphan,
Othello,
Perfidious Brother,
Perplex'd Couple,
Perfian Princefs,
Petticoat Plotter,
Pilgrim,
Princefs of Cleve,
Provok'd Wife,
Refufal,
Revenge,
Revolution of Sweden,
Richard III.
Richmond Wells,
——— Heirefs,
Rival Queens,
——— Ladies,
Rule and have a Wife,
Sauney the Scot,
School Boy,
Scipio Africanus,
Scornful Lady,
She wou'd and wou'd'nt,
She Gallants,
Siege of Damafcus,

Sir Anthony Love,
Sir Walter Raleigh,
Sir Harry Wild-air,
Slip,
Soldier's Fortune,
Sophonifba,
Spanifh Curate,
Spanifh Friar,
Spartan Dame,
State of Innocence,
Succefsful Pyrate,
Tamerlane,
Tempeft,
Tender Hufband,
Theodofius,
Tottenham Court,
Troilus and Creffida,
Tyrannick Love,
Venice preferv'd,
Victim,
Ulyffes,
Volunteers,
Wife for a Month,
Wild Gallant,
Wit at a Pinch,
Wit without Money,
Woman's Revenge,
Woman's Wit,
Wonder.

With many others; alfo great Variety of Voyages, Novels, Poems, and other entertaining Pieces.

BOOKS

BOOKS Printed for and Sold by T. Worrall, *at the* Judge's-Head *against St.* Dunstan's-Church *in* Fleet-ſtreet.

A Treatise of Testaments and last Wills, compiled out of the Laws Eccleſiaſtical, Civil and Canon, as alſo out of the Common Law, Cuſtoms and Statutes of this Realm. The whole digeſted into ſeven Parts, viz. I. What a Teſtament or laſt Will is, and how many Kinds of Teſtaments there be. II. What Perſon may make a Teſtament, and who may not. III. Deſcribing what Things, and how much may be diſpoſed by Will. IV. Decyphering the Forms, and in what Manner Teſtaments or laſt Wills are to be made. V. What Perſon may be Executor of a Teſtament, or if capable of a Legacy. VI. Of the Office of an Executor, and of the ſeveral Kinds of Executors. VII. Shewing by what means Teſtaments or laſt Wills become void, by Henry Swineburne, ſometime Judge of the Prerogative Court at York. The Fifth Edition, corrected and very much enlarged with all ſuch Statutes, Decrees in Chancery, and Reſolutions of Common Law Caſes relating to this Subject, and which have hitherto been publiſhed, with an exact Table to the whole. Price 1 l. 1 s.

The Practising Attorney: Or, Lawyer's Office: Containing, The Buſineſs of an Attorney in all its Branches, viz. I. The Practice of the Courts of King's-Bench, and Common-Pleas; ſhewing the Nature and Forms of Writs, Entries, Declarations, Pleadings, Judgments, Executions, &c. With Directions in all Caſes relating to Cauſes and Trials. II. Proceedings of the High-Court of Chancery, and Exchequer, from the leading Proceſs, the Subpœna, to the final Order or Decree, interſpers'd with great Variety of Bills, Anſwers, Replications, Rejoinders, &c. III. The Attorney's Practice in Conveyancing, with Precedents of Leaſes, Mortgages, Aſſignments, Releaſes of Lands, Deeds to lead Uſes of Fines and Recoveries, Marriage Settlements and
Wills.

Wills. IV. Of Court-keeping, the Charges of Stewards, and Proceedings of Attorneys therein, and the Forms of Grants, Surrenders, Admittances, Copies of Court-Roll, Presentments, &c. The second Edition, carefully corrected and much improved, with the Rules and Orders of the several Courts, and the Laws and Statutes relating to Practice continued to this Time. By William Bohun of the Middle-Temple, Esq; Octavo. Price 6 s.

A COMPANION FOR THE SINCERE PENITENT, Or a Treatise on the Compunction of the Heart, in two Books, faithfully translated from the Greek of St. Chrysostom. To which are added suitable Devotions, adapted to the several Chapters. With a Preface, containing a brief Account of the Life of that eminent Father of the Church. By John Veneer, Rector of St. Andrew's in Chichester. Price 3 s. in Calf.

A NEW FRENCH GRAMMAR, in two Parts: Consisting of the best, shortest, and yet the most easy and plain Rules for the elegant Attainment of that Language in its true Purity and Delicacy. To which are added, several new and curious critical Remarks; with some select Letters of Eloisa and Abelard, now first printed from the accurate Translation of Monsieur Bussy Rabutin: Together, with an Abridgment of the most material Rules relating to the several Sorts of the French Versification. Written in French by Monsieur Malherbe at Paris, in 1725, and dedicated to King Stanislaus. Translated into English by James Seguin, Teacher of the French Language in Bury St. Edmunds in Suffolk. Price 2 s. and 6 d.

THE YOUNG GENTLEMAN'S NEW-YEAR'S GIFT: Or Advice to a Nephew, under these following Heads, viz. *Religion, Civil Government, Bodily Health, School-Learning, Profession, Husband, Father, Master,* &c. Concluding with some *Maxims* of general Use in the Conduct of his Life. By a Gentleman of the Middle-Temple. Price 1 s. 6 d.

THE

THE BUILDERR's POCKET-COMPANION, Shewing, An eafy and practical Method for laying down of Lines for all Sorts of Arches and Curves ufed in Houfe-Building, Ship-Building, Gardening, &c. alfo to make the Centers or Ribs for Vaults or Cielings, and Brackets for Coves, either regular or irregular. Together, with true and concife Rules to find the Lengths, Bevels and Moulds, for the Back of a Hip, in any Kind of Roofs, whether Square or Bevel, Hexagon or Pantigon, &c. Let their Rafters be ftraight or Curves of different Sorts, extracted from the Works of feveral noted Authors. Illuftrated with Variety of Examples curioufly engraven, and feveral ufeful Problems added, never before printed. By Michael Hoare Carpenter. Price 1 s. 6 d.

A SELECT COLLECTION OF NOVELS. Written by the moft celebrated Authors. In feveral Languages. Many of which never appeared in Englifh before; and all new tranflated from the Originals, by feveral eminent Hands, in 6 Vols, 12ves. Price 15 s.

THE VOYAGES, DANGEROUS ADVENTURES, AND IMMINENT ESCAPES OF CAPTAIN RICHARD FALCONER: Containing the Laws, Cuftoms, and Manners of the Indians in America, his Shipwrecks, his marrying an Indian Wife, his narrow Efcape from the Ifland of Dominico, &c. Intermix'd with the Voyages and Adventures of Thomas Randal of Cork, Pilot; with his Shipwreck in the Baltick, being the only Man that efcaped, his being taken by the Indians of Virginia, &c. And an Account of his Death. The fecond Edition, corrected, 12ves. Price 2 s. Sheep, 2 s 6 d. Calf.

THESAURUS DRAMATICUS: Containing all the celebrated Paffages, Soliloquies, Similies, Defcriptions, and other Poetical Beauties in the Body of Englifh Plays, antient and modern. Digefted under proper Topicks; with the Names of the Plays, and their Authors referr'd to in the Margin, 2 Vols. 12ves. Price 5 s.

HUDIBRAS.

FRIENDSHIP IN DEATH, in twenty Letters from the Dead to the Living, amongst which are the following, viz. To the Earl of R—— from Mr.—— who promised to appear to him after his Death. To the Countess of—— from her only Son, who died when he was two Years. To my Lord—— from a young Lady who was in a Convent in Florence. From Ibrahim, a Turkish Bassa, to Philocles, who had converted him to Christianity. To my Lord from his deceas'd Father, dissuading him from engaging in a Duel, &c. And to these Letters are added, Thoughts on Death, translated from the Moral Essays of the Messieurs du Port Royal,

Curæ non ipsa in Morte relinquunt. Virg.

Price 1 s. 6 d.

REFORM'D DEVOTIONS, in Meditations, Hymns, and Petitions for every Day in the Week, and every Holiday in the Year. By Theophilus Dorrington, Rector of Wittesham in Kent. Divided into Two Parts. The Ninth Edition. To which is added, An Holy Office, before, at, and after receiving the Holy Sacrament. By Dr. Edward Lake, 12ves. Price 2 s. 6 d.

THE HISTORY of the AMOURS of the MARSHAL DE BOUFLERS: Or, a true Account of his Love Intrigues, and gallant Adventures, which have been privately carried on by him ever since he first obtained a Command in the French King's Armies, till his Marriage with Mademoisell de Gramont. The whole Relation being faithfully translated out of the French Original lately publish'd at Paris. The second Edition, 12ves. Price 3 s.

MEMOIRS OF THE LIFE AND TIMES OF THE FAMOUS JONATHAN WILD. Together with the History and Lives of modern Rogues, several of them his Acquaintance, that have been executed before and since his Death, for the Highway, Pad, Shoplifting, Housebreaking, picking of Pockets, and impudent robbing in the Streets, and at Court, never before made publick. Written by Captain Smith, Author of the History of the Highwaymen. In 3 Vols. Royal Concubines and Gamesters, intermix'd with strange Discoveries of several unheard of barbarous Murders. All taken out of the Records of Newgate. Continued down to the present Times, 12ves. Price 3 s.

OCEAN, An Ode (concluding with a Wish) occasion'd by his Majesty's late Royal Encouragement of the Sea Service. To which is prefix'd an Ode to the King, and some Thoughts on Lyrick Poetry, by the Author of the *Universal Passion*.

Let the Sea make a *Noise*, let the Floods clap their Hands. Price 1 s.

THE BASTARD, A Poem, inscribed with all due Reverence to Mrs. Bret, once Countess of Macclesfield, by Richard Savage, Son of the late Earl Rivers.

Mother miscall'd, Farewel —— of Soul severe,
This sad Reflection yet may force one Tear
All I was wretched, by to you I ow'd,
Alone from Strangers every Comfort flow'd.

Decet hæc *dare dona* Novercam. Ov. Met.
Price 6 d.

THE COMPLEAT COMPTING-HOUSE: Or, The young Lad taken from the Writing-School, and fully instructed by way of Dialogue, in all the Mysteries of a Merchant, from his first Understanding of plain Arithmetick, to the highest Pitch of Trade; a Work very necessary for all who are concern'd in keeping Accounts of what Quality soever. The Fifth Edition. By John Vernon, 12ves. Price bound 1 s.

A TREATISE OF THE URINARY PASSAGES, containing their Description, Powers and Uses; together with the principal Distempers that effect them, in particular the Stone of the Kidneys and Bladder, as deliver'd at the Gulstonian Lecture in the Theatre of the Royal College of Physicians, London, on the 17th, 18th, and 19th Days of March, $172\frac{5}{6}$. By William Rutty, M. D. Secretary to the Royal Society, and Reader of Anatomy at Surgeon's-Hall. Illustrated with Copper Plates, curiously engraven by Mr. Vandergucht. Quarto. Price 2 s. 6 d.